The Lincoln Special

Kate Warne Civil War Spy Series

Peg A. Lamphier

Writing Wench Press, LLC
Lytle Creek, California

The Lincoln Special
Kate Warne Civil War Spy Series

Copyright © 2017 by Peg Lamphier

Writing Wench Press, LLC

This is a work of fiction. Names, characters, places and incidents may be based on real events or persons, but they have been fictional- ized and are used as such. Thus they are a product of the author's imagination. Any resemblance to a living person or contemporary business establishments is utterly coincidental.

Cover Art by Daniel Aley, www.flutterspace.com

Author photo by Marvelle Thompson

Writing Wench Press, LLC, publishes this edition.

PO Box 113

Lytle Creek, California 92358

Visit the press online at www.peglamphier.com

ISBN: 978-1-947278-00-4

For Paul Lamphier
My First and Best Reader

Also by Peg A. Lamphier

Kate Chase and William Sprague:
Politics and Gender in a Civil War Marriage

Spur Up Your Pegasus:
Family Letters of Salmon, Kate and Nettie Chase,
1844-73
(with James P. McClure and Erika M. Kreger

Women in American History:
A Social, Political and Cultural Encyclopedia with
Document Collection [4 volumes]
(with Rosanne Welch)

Contents

Prologue

December 15, 1856
Chicago, Illinois

Allan Pinkerton always walked to work, even when the Chicago winter turned mean like today. He took a deep breathe of air that smelled steely cold and heavy with moisture. Dead leaves rushed down the street as if they were late for some important date, pushed by the icy air coming off the lake. Allan lived just five blocks from the office, but today it seemed more like fifty. At least the cold tamped down the dead fish and garbage reek that emanated from the city docks in warmer, more redolent weather. It seemed like just another walk to the office, one of hundreds he'd already made and the hundreds more he planned to make.

Allan tucked his chin into his scarf, a thick, Turkey red bit of wool Joanie knit for him to brighten his morning walks. Even today he was glad he lived near enough to his office to walk. It meant he didn't have to keep a horse, an unnecessary expense for a man growing both a business and a family. Joanie picked out their two-story Chicago house almost eight years ago, not long after Allan discovered a counterfeiting operation on an island in the local river. They'd been living out in Dundee and he'd been scouting for trees to turn into whiskey barrels. Instead he found a nest of men printing one-dollar bills in the woods. The tidy cash bonus for his part in busting that operation hadn't been nearly as valuable as finding out policing was more to his taste than barrel making. Several more successes rounding up ruffians brought him to the notice of the Sheriff in Cook County, who hired him as a full time deputy. When that happened Allan and Joanie sold the cooperage, packed up the children and took the chance on Chicago.

Two years in the Sheriff's office got Allan thinking that it might be possible to make a living from crime. At first he'd gone into the detecting business with a lawyer fellow named Rucker who used to hang around the Chicago Police Station. The two men set up the Northwest Police Agency, but a year later Rucker gave up the business to become a judge for the city courts.

"It's a sure thing," he'd explained, "and it's Chicago, so there's bags of money to be made by a man who knows how to work the system."

He supposed Rucker was right, but Allan wanted to make his money fair and square and face the Lord with a clean conscience. He renamed the business and so the Pinkerton Detective Agency was born. They didn't take divorce cases or investigate cheating spouses. Nothing tacky or immoral for his business. No, his agency took only high profile cases, train robberies, corporate theft, that sort of thing. Before he knew it he had the biggest detective agency in the state. No one looking at him today would think he'd come to this country with nothing.

In his hurry to get to work he almost missed the small stand where he bought his *Tribune* each morning. It was an important habit. A man in the business of crime prevention kept a close eye on the news. Allan stepped up to the news- stand, which blessedly sheltered him from the wind and squinted. The morning light was dim, but he could see the man behind the counter was a stranger.

"Good Morning. Where's that old rascal Fergus?" Allan had been buying papers from the same Scottish immigrant for years and he enjoyed their morning banter. Admittedly, the small man behind the counter looked like he sorely needed a job. Dressed in a ragged, dun colored jacket and a collarless shirt, the poor fellow also sported a worn eye patch on the right side of his face and the left sleeve of his coat was pinned up to the shoulder. *He looks like a ragged pixie.* Still, if life taught Allan anything it was that you didn't measure a man by the cut of his coat, let alone by the number of his arms.

The little fellow's voice creaked like a rope bed when he spoke. "Fergus took sick last night. I'm boarding with him and his Missus now. I told him I'd watch his patch today so he could stay in bed. Too cold out for a sick man. And it's not like I have anything much else to do anyway." The man looked down at the counter and sighed.

"When you see him you tell him Allan says to get better right quick. Hand me a *Trib* would you?"

The man held the newspaper out to Allan. "You Mr. Pink- erton?" he asked, keeping hold of the newspaper. "Of the Pinkerton Detective Agency?"

"That I am. It's nice to meet you." Allan took the newspa- per and tucked it under his arm. He stretched his other arm across the counter and shook the man's hand. The fellow's hand was small, but his grip was firm and dry. He smelled vaguely of stale beer and unwashed body, but he looked presentable enough.

"John Coburn sir. It's right nice to meet you." Coburn paused and then the words just tumbled out of his mouth in a rush, like the leaves blowing along the sidewalk. "I expect you and I have some mutual acquaintances and I'd like to tell you, I think you must be about the very model of a gentleman and meeting you is a right pleasure for me. You knowing who you know and all."

Allan thought the man had a funny way of expressing himself, like maybe he suffered from some sort of nervous complaint. "Well, Sir, what or who makes you admire me so?"

Coburn looked him square in the eye and laid his forefinger upon the length of his nose.

Allan returned the signal with a solemn nod of his head. They were both Underground Railroad men.

The small man leaned on the counter, straining toward Allan. "I was in Kansas these two years past. I was in the Wakarusa War afore the Sack— that's where I got this and this." The man gestured at his missing arm and eye. "Dirty ruffians took their medicine at Wakarusa, but one of them slave lovers got me with a load of shot. Blew my durn arm and face to shreds. Doctor man in Lawrence took the arm off at the elbow, and then took the eye for good measure. That was mid-winter. I was still laid up when them depraved ruffians attacked Lawrence come spring—got me some gangrene, lost the rest of the arm." The man paused and twitched his shoulder, like he was remembering his lost appendage.

Allan kept abreast of the news coming out of Kansas. The territory was in a near permanent state of war, with the Free-Staters squaring off against the slavery men. The Sack of Lawrence, a free state town, by pro-slavery men had been a terrible thing indeed.

"Did you ever meet Mr. Brown?" Allan asked.

"No sir, I did not. If you recall, he was not in Lawrence in May, when the ruffians sacked the town, though as you know, he might have been near by." The man winked at Allan.

Five pro-slavery settlers had been brutally murdered in Pottawatomie Kansas just days after the Sack of Lawrence. People on both sides of the slavery issue thought John Brown and his sons had done it in retaliation for the havoc wreaked on Lawrence.

Coburn put his one good hand in his pocket and rocked back on his heels. "If I might be so forward Mr. Pinkerton, I'm a good man, for all that I've got but one arm and eye. I can still work, but no one wants to hire a fellow like me, not when there's so many strong-backed Germans and Swedes about. But if you could ever use me, I'd do right by you. I can read and write just fine, and cipher a little too. Plus no one ever likes to look to close at a cripple, so people don't rightly see me most times. I figure that might be a boon in your kind of business." In his earnestness the fellow strained forward toward Allan, his chin tucked just enough to look puckishly deferential.

"I tell you what Mr. Coburn, you come to my office tomorrow at noon. I'll tell my assistant to expect you. I like to hire all kinds of men. All I require is that a man be honest and able to use the brains God gave him."

They parted, each assuring the other of their mutual good will.

Allan spent the next few hours working at his desk, catching up with the never-ending paperwork. Just before lunch

Mr. Bangly, who ran the front office, opened Allan's door and stuck his head in.

"Mr. Pinkerton, there's a lady here to see you. She doesn't have an appointment, but . . . " Bangly stepped into Allan's cluttered office and shut the door behind him. Standing against the door, he lowered his voice and said, "You'll want to see this one sir. She's a fine looking piece. And she seems mighty upset about something."

Allan sighed and put his pen down. Bangly looked like a thug, but he had a weakness for ladies in trouble and they seemed to sense it. Allan wasted at least two hours a week on distressed ladies who wheedled their way past his fierce looking, but mild mannered clerk. They almost always wanted help with a husband or son gone astray in one of Chicago's many gambling houses and brothels. Allan tried to be sympathetic to the problems of ladies, but his agency most certainly did not handle sordid domestic cases. A man who laid down with dogs got up with fleas. Still, he could listen to the lady and point her in the direction of men who would be only too glad for the work. "Show her in Mr. Bangly, but leave the door open and give her fifteen minutes before you remind me of an important meeting."

The clerk grinned and returned with an entirely stunning female creature in tow. "Mrs. Parrington to see you sir," he announced, using his most official voice.

"My goodness," Allan said without thinking. He rose to his feet with such alacrity that his chair skittered out behind him. "Mrs. Parrington, please come in and make yourself comfortable." Gesturing to the leather upholstered client chair that sat next to his desk, Allan thought maybe he should change his policy about 'ladies cases.' It would be worth a taint of scandal to spend more time with this woman. Gleaming chestnut hair, threaded through with coppery highlights complemented her pale skin, making her look like a flaming cream candle. Her waist looked no bigger than a child's, but the curves above and below said she was all woman. The soft burnt orange colored fabric of her dress complemented her hair. It had some kind of swirly pattern in a lighter color on it and a soft sheen that quietly suggested it had been made to order at some expense. Joanie would know what the fabric was called, though Allan didn't need his wife to tell him the fabric in this woman's dress cost more than he made in a year.

Mrs. Parrington stepped forward and then stopped uncertainly in the middle of the room. She wore a pert little hat just on the top of her hair, with a veil that covered her eyes. She peered through the veil, taking in the portrait-covered walls—Allan had half dozen pictures of Joan and the children, but his real weakness was dog pictures. The room had twelve-foot ceilings and on several walls Allan managed to arrange framed dog portraits four rows high. There was a particularly large portrait of himself on the wall opposite his desk.

Mrs. Parrington's eyes came to rest on it. "Oh," she said softly, her voice no more than a breathy whisper. She looked over at Allan, a light pink blush coloring her cheeks.

"A gift from my wife, Mrs. Parrington. I find it discomforting to look at myself all day, but the Missus directed its installation herself, so there it is." Allan smiled again and gestured toward the empty chair once more. Her skirt rustled softly as she came toward him, smiling uncertainly. She sat on the edge of the chair, managing to collapse her hoops with the kind of grace that came with long practice. The scent of gardenias made her closeness all the more enticing.

"Thank you for seeing me on such short notice Mr. Pinkerton," she said in a softly husky voice that made even a decent man think of bedroom related improprieties.

Allan fought the urge to ask her to call him by his first name. "Mrs. Parrington, I do not know if I can help you, but if you tell me what brings you here I shall do my best to provide you with appropriate assistance."

"You're too kind Mr. Pinkerton." She fingered the carved ivory cameo pinned at her throat. "I don't know where to start," she said, her voice trailing off.

"Mrs. Parrington, what you tell me will not leave this office unless you give me permission to discuss it with others. Let me assure you I have heard many terrible and shocking stories. Yours will seem less terrible once you share it." He looked right at her, hoping she'd raise her eyes from her lap. When she did he thought he'd never seen such eyes. Even with the veil down Allan could see that her eyes were a startlingly green, speckled with tiny coppery brown flecks. He sighed a little.

"It's my husband," she began.

It always was.

"We married only eight months ago. He has always worked long hours— he's in business with his father you see. But lately he hardly comes home at all. And when he does he smells of liquor and cheap scent." Her softly sloping shoulders drooped even lower. "My mother says I'm not to question him. She says Mr. Parrington is my husband and that if he strays it is my fault, not his. She tells me I should try harder to please him."

"Mrs. Parrington, please excuse me for what I'm about to say, but your mother sounds like a woman with little experience in these kinds of problems." Allan actually thought the girl's mother sounded like a blasted fool and one who didn't deserve a daughter like this, though he couldn't very well say so.

"Does your husband ever hurt you?" he asked gently.

"Oh, no, nothing like that. Sometimes he shakes me, but only when he comes home in his cups. He is always very sorry in the morning." She looked down at her lap again and gently sniffled.

Allan rifled around his pockets and produced his handkerchief. Wordlessly, he offered it to her.

She took it, reached under her veil and delicately dapped at her eyes. When she was done she looked up at him, her eyes shining with as yet unshed tears. Her hands began to twist his handkerchief. "I need to know where he's going. So I can do better for him." She paused and took a deep breath. "I just need to know," she half wailed and burst into tears again.

Allan's heart broke at her distress. He should take this poor young woman home to Joanie. "Let me tell you a few things my dear." She was crying in his office so he thought he could call her "my dear."

"Any husband who leaves a wife such as yourself alone in the evening is a fool. Any man who would lay hands upon a lady deserves to be horsewhipped. If you ask me and I guess you are, you need him followed. The Pinkertons do not take domestic cases, but I know just the man to help you."

She looked steadily at him, her breath coming in little pants as she recovered herself.

"You come back to this office tomorrow afternoon. Shall we say one o'clock? I will have a name for a man who can help you. Does that sound amenable to you?"

She wiped at her eyes and nodded at him.

"Do you have money? Because this man will not work for free. Do you need some place safe to stay in the mean time?" Allan found he couldn't help himself. The words were out before he intended to say them. Lest she think him a scoundrel he hastened to add, "My wife Joan would be glad to make up a room for you."

"Oh, thank you Mr. Pinkerton, but I shall be fine. Mr. Parrington is out of town for several days. And Daddy left me some money for my personal use." She dapped at her moist eyes once more before handing Allan back his now damp handkerchief. She took a deep breath and rose to her feet, gently shaking her skirt. "Thank you for your help," she said quietly. And with a whisper of petticoats she was gone.

Allan sat back in his chair. He felt like he'd been hit on the head with an exceedingly sturdy plank.

Standing in the middle of her bedroom Kate pondered the pile of clothes on her bed. Though it was a forbidding, grey day outside, a cheery yellow light flickered from the room's two gas lamps. It was awfully nice to be out of that dreary tenement apartment and living in her own house. A house she shared with Uncle Juba. Her divorce money bought her freedom, freedom from cold and hunger, but most importantly, the freedom to establish herself as an independent woman.

She pulled a shabby jacket from the pile and gave it the gimlet eye. It's cuffs were worn and ragged and the left pocket torn. A slight stench wafted off it, like the wearer had worn it too long without washing either the jacket or the body in it.

She looked over at her window, pondering. Should she hang the poor ragged thing outside to air out? She was done with it for now and it really didn't smell very nice.

She pushed up the window sash and laid the jacket across the sill, lowering the window to catch the coat by its collar. No use losing the thing. A girl could never tell when she'd next need a disreputable jacket.

Kate sniffed the air. Better. Both dresses were far too fine to even share air space with that jacket. She'd had only two days to put together her new wardrobe, even less really because she'd had to spend part of each day watching her target. She'd already used two of her outfits, one of old clothes and one brand new dress. She smiled to herself. If her plan worked it would be money well spent.

She eyed the clothing pile once more and then plucked a dress the color of walnut shells from the pile. She held it up and stepped in front of the tall mirror that hung on the back of her bedroom door. The dress, though a sedate color, had bright yellow braided trim on the arms and at the neck that lifted it just above school marm status. Also, and importantly, the brown didn't clash with her auburn hair. She shed her dressing gown and began the laborious process of getting into the plethora of undergarments required of modern ladies. She tied her corset laces off after taking a deep breath to ensure she was laced to her last quarter inch. She slipped the brown dress over her head, careful not to muss her simple bun and began buttoning the tiny brown buttons. After a frantic five minutes looking for her buttonhook, which she found under the bed, she buttoned her boots, trying not to rush. Boot buttons and boot hooks did not respond well to haste, at least not in her experience. When the last button was done she stood in front of the mirror again. Fine. She looked respectable, but not overly interesting. Kate pinned a sensible little watch to the waist of the brown dress, squinting at it as she did. Thirty minutes before noon. Perfect. She closed the door on her new bedroom room and set out to change her life. Again.

"Mr. Pinkerton, there's a lady here to see you." George Bangly stood in the doorway shifting from foot to foot. "She insists she is your noon appointment. I told her you had an appointment with a gentleman, but she is quite adamant."

Allan glanced up. Mr. Bangly looked more harassed than usual. "Is Mr. Coburn here?"

"Not yet, sir. Should I show her in and interrupt you when he arrives?"

"Yes, let's do that," Allan sighed. Poor Mr. Bangly and his weakness for distressed ladies. He'd have to get rid of this one more quickly than he did Mrs. Parrington because he'd decided to hire Mr. Coburn. This morning he looked over his files and figured out exactly which cases to start the man on. And the lovely Mrs. Parrington would be back in an hour. Allan smiled in anticipation.

In a repeat of yesterday, Allan's clerk announced the unscheduled lady caller.

"Miss Warne to see you, Mr. Pinkerton"

Allan looked up. He couldn't believe his luck. Another fetching young lady. This one wasn't quite so expensively dressed as the enchanting Mrs. Parrington, but her neat brown and yellow dress identified her as a respectable young lady.

"Miss Warne," Allan stood and held out his hand. "How may I help you?"

"I'd like to ask you for a job Mr. Pinkerton. I think I could be a real asset to your operation."

Allan's eyebrows reached for the sky He looked steadily at the young woman before him. Maybe he'd heard her wrong.

"A job?" He noticed his voice had risen a little higher than usual.

"Yes sir, a job," she replied firmly. She stood in the center of the room, watching his reaction with a kind of calm that seemed at odds with her unusual request.

"Miss Warne," Allan started, then paused, pondering what he should say next. "As I'm sure you know, this is a detective agency. My company investigates crime. It is not the sort of work a lady should do."

"I believe what you mean is that it is not the sort of work a lady *could* do, don't you?"

Still standing, Allan surveyed the young woman before him. He frowned. She seemed familiar. Perhaps he'd met her before. But of course he hadn't. Her name wasn't the littlest bit familiar.

"Miss Warne, I have an appointment scheduled for this hour. I can only give you a few minutes." Allan sat behind his desk and gestured to his client chair, trying to convey an authority he didn't entirely feel. She gave him an odd little smile, then sat, neatly collapsing her hoops as she did. He tried not to stare. She really did seem most familiar.

Kate leaned towards her hoped-for employer. "Mr. Pinkerton, as they said in the gambling tents of my youth, I should lay my cards upon the table. Your mid-day appointments are with me. Both of them."

He shook his head, but glanced at his appointment book nonetheless. "Miss Warne, you are mistaken. My Noon appointment is with a crippled man and the appointment after that is with a high society lady."

She looked him straight in the eye. When she was sure she had his attention she squared her shoulders, puffed out her chest, covered her right eye with her hand and in a rasping voice said, "It's right nice to meet you seeing as how I expect you and I have some mutual acquaintances." Then she dropped her hand and smiled at him.

Allan Pinkerton stared at the woman before him, eyes wide, mouth slightly open.

Giving him no time to think, lowered her shoulders and chin and in a breathier voice said, "I need to know where he's going. I just need to know." She ended her sentence with a familiar breathy wail.

Allan's eyebrows shot up. He leaned in and took a closer look at her. "The eyes," he muttered. "I should have noticed the eyes. He pulled her handkerchief from his pocket and mopped his face with it, then stopped suddenly and stared at her again. "What did you do with Fergus?"

Kate tried not to laugh. "I paid him a considerable sum of money to take the morning off. I've been tailed you for few days and figured out you always come to work at the same time and you always stop and buy a newspaper from Fergus. I also paid him for his silence so he wouldn't say anything this morning." Kate watched Allan Pinkerton gape at her like a fish suddenly pulled from the water. She began to think she had him hooked. *It's just like working a con on the midway. People see what you want them to see.* She just had to reel him in now.

"Mr. Pinkerton, I see I have surprised you." She smiled at him again, her lips held close together to hold in a chuckle that wanted out. "Let me explain."

He nodded his head.

"I require work. Useful work. I possess considerable skills, many of them learned in my fifteen years in the circus, though I am done with the circus. I have my reasons and they're my own. I can only assure you there's nothing disreputable there. I have the education to be a teacher, but that life is not for me either. It's too . . . ." Kate paused and searched for the right word.

Allan leaned forward, elbows on his desk. "Too dull for a woman who can pass herself off as both a working man and a fine lady in one day and then come back to this office and ask me for a job, I'd warrant."

She chuckled. "Exactly."

His eyes twinkled in pleasure. "Your parents were circus people?"

"Yes sir, they were. They're gone now. Before I left circus life I learned stage make-up from one of the greatest clowns in America. I learned to run the con and pick locks from one of my father's best friends and I learned to pretend to be some- one I'm not from a fake gypsy fortuneteller. I'm an accomplished equestrienne and I'm competent on a high wire. I can hold the spotlight or disappear in the crowd as need be."

"That's quite a list of skills," Allan said. "Can I assume you have no interest in being a wife and mother?"

Kate sat back in her chair and nodded. "I wouldn't say that sir, not exactly. But I should tell you, I've been married. I did not enjoy how dependent I was on my husband's whims. I would prefer to be self reliant from now on."

"So, you're a widow? A circus widow?"

"No sir, not a widow and my husband was not a circus man. I am a divorced woman." Kate looked defiantly at the man before her. This was the part of her plan that worried her the most. "It's a shabby story. Suffice it to say, his rich parents objected to the match and he came to see it their way." Kate looked down at her lap. She wasn't particularly ashamed of her divorce, but she knew some people thought divorced women were little better than whores.

All she knew for sure was that if he was the kind of narrow-minded bigot that didn't like divorced ladies he wasn't likely to be the sort of man who hired women. This thought reminded her that she had little to lose. She straightened up and met his eyes. He smiled at her, seemingly relieved.

"Miss Warne," he leaned back in his chair, "And it's Miss, am I correct, not Mrs.?"

"Warne is the name given to me by my parents and Miss goes with it just fine, don't you think?" She smiled at him, finding she liked him a good deal more than this interview warranted.

He smiled back. "Your marital state is no business of mine. I only asked because I was curious. I like to know things, which is why I'm a detective. Miss Warne, I'm planning to open one or two more Pinkerton Agencies in the very near future. Thus, I am in the market for at least one more clerk. "

Kate's eyes widened in surprise. "You misunderstand me Mr. Pinkerton. I'm not here to apply for a clerking job or any kind of office job. I want to be an operative."

"An operative? A lady detective you mean? Unthinkable!" He threw himself back in his chair. "There is no such thing as a lady detective. Miss Warne, we do dangerous work at this agency and quite often the sort of work that requires a man to consort with unsavory types. It is not work for a lady, not even a lady like yourself." He sat forward and clasped his hands on top of his desk, as if he was done with the interview.

"But that's exactly where you're wrong Mr. Pinkerton." Kate leaned toward him and put her hands on his desk as well. "You've seen my talent for disguise. I'd lay odds that I'm better than most of your men. I made a pretty convincing man, you must agree. But the real asset I'd bring to your operation is my womanhood." She paused for a second before continuing her argument. "I think you should hire me precisely because I *am* a woman. I'll be able to accomplish things your male operatives can not."

Allan looked like he was beginning to see the shape of her point. "Hmmm."

"Yesterday I came in here as a lady in distress and in spite of the fact that you began our interview wanting to get rid of me as quickly as possible, you changed your mind. Half way through the interview you were ready to adopt me, save me, whatever I needed. You offered to take me into your home. You completely fell for the act. Most men would."

Allan bit his lower lip and leaned back in his chair.

Kate watched him.

Finally he sat forward again and scrubbed at his face with his hands. "I really couldn't help myself. I so badly wanted to help you, to impress you. I feel like a fool now."

She shook her head. "You're not a fool. You're a man, trained since childhood to protect girls and women. I played damsel in distress and you wanted to save me." Kate paused and bit her lower lip. "There's more. Forgive me but I must speak indelicately for a moment. I was once a married woman and I know realities of the male creature that a . . . ," Kate hesitated and then hardened her resolve. "That a less experienced woman would not know. A man may be induced to tell a woman quite a bit if the woman's approach is calculated for greatest effect. Some men respond to the helpless featherhead, others to a more sophisticated and knowing woman. When you spoke of your wife's placement of your portrait I knew you would not be susceptible to a seduction. You're too fond of her. So I went with the lady in need of a savior approach. And lest you think I'm offering to prostitute myself, let me reassure you that I'm smart enough to know that men are the most eager to brag and tell tales when they are held at arm's length by a lady they desire."

"Egad," Allan exclaimed. "You are a most forthright woman."

Kate stood up and shook out her skirt. "Take a good look at me Mr. Pinkerton."

She turned a slow full circle in front of him.

"Miss Warne, I assure you there's no need for this," Allan said, shock and embarrassment painted his face and filled his voice.

"Again, Mr. Pinkerton, I do not mean to be indelicate, but if you are going to hire me as a female operative, then we must be able to speak frankly about the uses to which you might put me."

Having turned a full circle, she stood in front of him, hands on her hips.

"Moreover, my life in the circus has given me skills most people don't have, regardless of their sex. My post-circus education at a Gramercy Park boarding school means I can also pass myself off as a society lady." She stopped, twinkled a grin at Allan, and added, "Suffice it to say, I can move in circles of society most of your male operatives can not. And in those circles my sex creates opportunities a male operative will never have. Ever."

Allan leaned back in his chair again. "You make quite a case for yourself Miss Warne."

"Mr. Pinkerton, I've done my research on you. You're a risk taker. You opened the first American detective agency and you've made it a success with little more than hard work and an open mind. You were willing to hire a one armed, one eyed man, weren't you?"

"Well, yes, but I thought your one-eyed, one armed man made a good point about how people don't look to close at cripples."

"Exactly," Kate said with a jerk of her chin. "It's the same with women. Men see us and don't see us. Men see *women*," she said, "not human beings."

Allan took a deep breath, heaved it out and sternly eyed Kate. "How about this? I'll give you a six-month trial. I'll start you on some small cases and see how you do."

Kate extended her hand across Allan's desk. "You have a deal," she said. "I promise you Mr. Pinkerton, you won't regret your decision."

Once on the street Kate resisted the impulse to twirl circles down the sidewalk. The wind caught at her skirts, as if urging her to defy decorous behavior and twirl to her heart's content. Kate paused and looked up at the grey sky, which looked much grimmer than she felt. It had been a rough year, but maybe the hard times were over. Maybe. As the first snow-flakes began to swirl through the day's murky light, Kate thought about the mistakes she'd made the past year, mistakes that brought her to this day.

Chapter 1

June-October 1856
Rhode Island & Chicago

Her first job after leaving school was as a governess. After five and a half years at Miss Haines School for Girls it was a post for which she was terribly well suited. Miss Haines ran an ever-so-proper school in the Grammercy Park neighborhood of New York City, where she taught girls French and Algebra and deportment and a hundred other things young ladies were supposed to know. It was an entirely different world from the circus, but its safe regimentation had been a welcome respite from the freedom and hardship of the circus. When she graduated from school Miss Haines helped get Kate her first job. Her six-year-old charge, Nora Southam, was only a little bit spoiled even though her family was disgustingly rich. Their estate lie just outside Providence and was quite a bit fancier than even the houses in Gramercy Park. Kate shared a suite of third floor rooms with Nora and a ginger cat that had six toes on each of his front feet. Neither Mr. nor Mrs. Southam seemed overly interested in the details of their daughter's life, though Nora's mother Esther did join them most afternoons for a joint French lesson.

Nora's half-brother Henry more than made up for her dis-
interested parents. Henry was three years older than Kate and
ever so dashing and amenable. He was a glorious creature, all
golden hair and skin, as if the sun shone only for and on him.
Recently graduated from Harvard, where he studied classics,
Henry's parents thought that he would outgrow his poetical
phase and settle down the business of making money before
he married one of the daughters of his father's business associates. In the mean time he idled about the house and took an
interest in the new governess. Within a month of Kate's arrival in Providence Henry was spending most mornings with
Kate and Nora. To Kate's delight, he seemed charming and
well read. What she didn't know was that he was also spoiled
and churlish, particularly when he didn't get his way.

"Come away with me Katie" Henry purred as he rolled
over on the plaid blanket they'd laid on the far south lawn.
Nearby Nora rolled a hoop across the grass, her chubby legs
pumping to keep up with the spinning circle. The light smell
of fresh soil and grass filled the air.

Kate thought the sun shone on Henry's hair like light on a
pond, all sparkly and bright. She wanted little more than to lie
down next to him and let him seduce her, though her years at
Miss Haines had taught her that young ladies did not give in
to such urges. Still, the warm spring sunshine on her skin inclined Kate to think otherwise. "You're entirely too beautiful
for a man, you know," she said, gazing into his ridiculously
cerulean eyes. She knew it was a foolish word for a man, beautiful, but she'd thought it the first time saw him. He was

beautiful. And cerulean. "You'll tire of me and cast me aside."
She put the back of her hand to her forehead in mock melodrama. "I'll be ruined, good sir knight, utterly ruined."

His laugh bubbled out of him, like a fresh water spring. He
pushed himself up onto his elbows and pinned her with a
glowing look. "Then marry me Kate."

"Marry you?" She hauled herself abruptly to her feet and
stared down at him. "Don't tease me like that Henry. It's not
nice." Kate stepped away from the blanket and turned her
back on their picnic.

He followed her to his feet and wrapped his arms around
her, pressing himself against her back. "I'm not teasing. Marry
me. You know I love you. You love me, don't you?" He
grabbed her shoulders and turned her around to press a kiss
against her mouth. A raven flew overhead, screeching at a
flock of tiny songbirds. It startled Kate out of the moment.

She turned in his arms and leaned her head against his
chest. "Henry, you know I love you. How could I not? But
your parents would never consent to our match. I'm the governess for goodness sake. I see the kind of girls your mother
has to tea."

Henry looked down into Kate's eyes. "I don't care. I love
you and you love me. They want me to marry some dreadful
textile heiress or another and expand the Southam empire. I
don't want to be in the textile business anyway, it's awful.
Once we're married they'll have to agree to it. They won't
have any choice." He gave her his most winsome look, eyes
wide, mouth pursed.

She shook her head. "They're just as likely to cut you off
without a penny. Then what will we do?" Kate's protests grew
weaker with each sentence.

Sensing his argument was gaining momentum he pulled her more closely and dropped a kiss on her forehead. "Grandfather left me a trust fund. We can live on that. We can live anywhere. I'll take care of you so you don't have to be a governess anymore. Imagine Kate! Why, I could take you to the opera. It's fantastic and you'd love it."

Kate thought maybe she would. It sounded like heaven, to be taken care of, to not have any more worries about what to do with her life. And she could look for Uncle Juba. She could take Henry to a circus—maybe even introduce him to people she knew. "But I have six more weeks with Nora, you know, before your sister and her family leaves for France."

Kate watched Henry's face turn triumphant. He had her and he knew it. "Leave her. She'll be fine. They'll just hire someone else. Leave her and run away with me."

To her everlasting shame, she did just that.

Of course it turned out badly.

They married in Warwick, on Narragansett Bay just south of Providence. Predictably, Henry's father cut him off from his trust fund. They went to Chicago because Henry heard it was a town where a young man might make his own fortune. After they arrived in the wind-swept, prairie city, Kate thought it might be a likely town for some young men, but not for Henry. Chicago demanded hard work and ingenuity. It's streets were ill-defined thoughts, rife with mud and possibility in equal measures. Rough canals and noisy rail lines contributed to the city's sense of continuous bustle. Pigs roamed through the streets eating the garbage and shitting it out, changing one stink into another. The city did not need a Harvard educated, east coast aristocrat who could read Plato in the original or quote long passages from *Julius Caesar*.

When they ran out of money Kate took a job at a small, not entirely respectable theater that specialized in minstrel shows. She performed sometimes as a man, in blackface, singing racy songs and telling raucous jokes, and other times as a sweet young thing, singing romantic songs. She preferred the former, though audiences most definitely preferred the latter. Her first fifteen years as a circus girl came in handier than anything she'd ever learned at Mrs. Haines' school, though the theater manager said he'd hired her because she classed up the show.

Henry didn't like being alone in their tiny rented room while Kate worked, nor did he like the poverty her meager wages bought them. Eventually he took his frustration out on Kate. It began with loud and bitter recriminations about the things he imagined she did while she was away from him, but progressed to violence. He liked to grab Kate by the arms and shake her so hard her neck hurt the next day. Sometimes he punched her, generally in the abdomen. Once he choked her until she passed out.

Afterwards he would be terribly sorry. He'd cry and tell her he'd never do it again, though paradoxically he always claimed his behavior was her fault. He'd point out how she said the wrong thing, looked the wrong way—he always had an excuse to go along with the apology. At first Kate accepted his regret, charmed by his beautiful blue eyes and tender kisses. It didn't take her long to figure out there would always be a next time.

One of the chorus girls taught Kate how to cover her bruises with stage make-up, though she also learned that she

had to thoroughly remove the grease paint before she returned to their rooms. One night she'd been tired and left the
theater without washing her face.

"Look at yourself," he'd shouted at her, holding her before
their tiny mirror and shaking her. "You look like a damned
whore. Maybe I should just treat you like a whore." What followed had been brutal. When Henry finished he rolled off her,
pulled up his pants and left the room. He returned two days
later, reeking of cheap beer and even cheaper perfume. It got
worse after that.

Afterwards Kate didn't much like to think about her life as
a married woman. Mostly she wallowed in shame and self-
loathing, thanking all that was holy that her parents were dead
and that Juba and Miss Haines didn't know what a mess she'd
made of her life.

Eventually a letter came. Henry tore it opened and read it,
pacing across the floor of their tiny room. "Father writes that
he'll give me access to my trust fund." He looked up from the
letter, his eyes glittering in the yellow lamplight. "There's one
condition though."

Kate waited for the blow to fall. *This is going to hurt. It
shouldn't, but will.* She sat very still.

Henry's eyes betrayed his excitement. "I must give you up
and go into the family business." He shook the letter at her,
smiling a wide, triumphant smile.

Kate could see him thinking about all the things he could
have back.

"Father says he knows a judge who will grant me a divorce.
He also says he'll give you a handsome settlement if you admit
the marriage was your fault and sign the divorce papers." He
shook the letter at Kate. "Don't you see? It's the answer to all

our problems. I can go home and be like I was before. When Father isn't so angry I'll get access to my trust fund again. Then I'll come get you and we'll be happy."

"Oh, Henry," she said. That was all she said. Really, what else was there to say?

Henry packed and left the next morning. Kate pretended to be asleep. He left a note on the table promising to get in touch with her. In the following weeks Kate acquiesced to all of Mr. Southam's demands. She allowed Henry to divorce her for "gross misbehavior and wickedness," a lovely turn of phrase Rhode Island used for adultery. The Southams also asked that she not use their name, nor to have any further contact with Henry. Kate needed no encouragement to leave Henry's name behind. Kate Southam was a stupid woman. In return for her cooperation Henry's father deposited $2500 in Chicago's Marine Bank. He promised another $2500 once she signed the divorce papers. She didn't tell him she would have done it for nothing.

Late at night, when she was home from the theater and too keyed up to sleep, she lay in bed and thought about her mistakes. She'd let down so many people. Mamma, who had been so strong and clear about what she wanted, would have been appalled at her daughter's weakness. So would Mrs. Haines. She'd declared Kate one of the smartest young ladies to ever attend her school. *Maybe a person can be smart and dumb at the same time?* It would be better if she were dumb. Dumb was preferable to weak.

She thought about the days after her parents' death, when all she'd wanted was for Uncle Juba to take her away from the circus. She worried about that part of her that wanted to be rescued. She needed another new life and she needed to be smart about it. No one was going to save her this time, especially not from herself. She made up her mind. She would save herself from now on. That's when she started looking for a new career.

Chapter 2

November 1856
Chicago

She started the next morning with a trip to the Marine Bank. Kate paused a moment on the sidewalk after she left the bank, shivering a little against the cold. Chicago's beneficent fall weather had taken a turn into cruel winter. The *Tribune* said maybe snow by the weekend. The air had that wet, steely smell of an approaching storm. She opened her reticule, extracted the tiny bankbook and looked at the last line of writing. A lady could do a lot with $5,000.

She could buy herself a shiny new wardrobe and go husband hunting. But she'd tried being a wife and was in no hurry to repeat the experiment. She could establish herself in some kind of business, though she had no experience with the kinds of businesses women were allowed to run. She was no dress or hat maker. Maybe a school? She knew how to do that.

Kate stood on the sidewalk, oblivious to the people who brushed past her. The thought of a school did not make her heart leap in excitement. Maybe being respectable was not her cup of tea. She'd been a circus girl for fifteen years and a boarding school girl for only five. What she needed was a really good plan. Something audacious. Kate snorted under her breath, squared her shoulders and walked back to her tiny rented room, the cold November wind hurrying her along.

Two days later Kate was sitting at the window, still thinking about what to do next. The thinking was getting her nowhere. A knock sounded at the door. Startled, she froze for a second, then shook herself. It was probably just her landlady.

Kate pushed herself off her windowsill.

"Yes, Mrs. Kincaid?" she called as she opened the door. The person before her was as far from a large, blowzy, pink skinned landlady as a person could get.

"Uncle Juba!" She stepped toward him and then stopped.

"My little Katie." He grinned, his teeth bright against his dark skin and then he bowed, managing to make the gesture seem both ironic and courtly.

Kate froze, her initial delight turned first to bewilderment and then anger.

He rocked back on his heels, all five foot four inches of him. "Well girly, what do you say to your Uncle Juba?"

"Where have you been? All these years? You're dead, then you're not dead." Kate found her outrage quite satisfying. "You left. I don't need your help. I'm doing just fine all on my own." If he was here to rescue her she'd box his ears, even if he was her elder and almost-uncle. Without thinking about it she slammed the door in his face.

He knocked again, a light double tap.

She glared at the door. Then she opened it again. "How dare you just show up like this?" Her voice echoed down the hall.

Juba leaned against the doorframe, letting her yell at him.

"How did you know where to find me?"

"Miss Haines," he said simply. "I arrived here three weeks ago. Miss Haines told me about your job at the theater. I paid my nickel and saw you, all grown up and singing like a lark." He smiled fondly, almost to himself, pushing back his hat like he used to do when he was thinking.

Kate waited.

"Anyway, I was going to surprise you after your performance, but I saw this young, blond fellow meet you after, so I stayed back. I asked around, found out you were married. I wasn't sure he'd be the kind of man who would like a wife with a . . . ." Juba paused. "A colored gentleman friend."

Kate felt her anger begin to crumble. She really looked at him. His skin was the same rich copper brown it had always been, but he had himself a modest pot belly and his face wasn't nearly so drawn as she remembered. He was wearing a solid brown suit, cut to fit him and a shiny pair of half boots. His hair had a little gray in it, but not much for all that he was at least 15 years older than her.

"How did Mrs. Haines know?"

He shook his head. "No idea. That lady keeps her secrets."

Kate thought Mrs. Haines probably knew a lot more than most people thought. She wasn't sure if she found that idea comforting or terrifying. "You look pretty good for a dead man," she admitted with a shrug. She had too much history with Juba to stay mad at him for long and not so many friends she could afford to throw one away.

"Well thank you kindly." He doffed his brown hat at her. "I waited until I was sure you were alone and it was safe to come see you." Holding his hat in front of him he asked, "You done yelling at me now?"

She nodded again and opened the door a little wider. "OK. Come in."

"Well . . . " Juba peered into the room and then at his feet. He couldn't believe his little girl was living in such a dreary place. No wonder she looked so depressed. "Having met your landlady, I think she'd be only too happy to tell people you'd been entertaining gentlemen of color in your room. Though I suspect her phraseology would be a tad less circumspect, if you take my meaning."

Kate nodded. Of course he was right. Uncle Juba generally was, much as she hated to admit it. He had a lifetime of being careful with this sort of thing.

Kate gestured out the window. "There's a park just down the street, right on the lake."

He grinned again and swept his arm out toward the hall. "Shall we?"

As they walked Kate remembered the last time she'd seen Juba. After her parents' death he'd taken her to Miss Haines School for Girls. Every other Sunday afternoon he would visit her. One afternoon he explained how he could afford such a fancy school. Or more accurately, how she could afford it.

"A few years back I made a lot of money with my dancing." Juba sat at the school's kitchen table, making circles on its surface with his thin fingers. Two mugs of tea sat between them. He was dressed in his black suit, hat in his lap. Cook once yelled at him for putting his hat on the table and he made sure to never do it again. "No one had ever seen that kind of dancing, you see, and people went crazy for it—called it 'juba dancing and though I was challenged many times, I never lost a contest."

"Daddy said you danced for the queen." Kate fidgeted with her teacup. Cook was out shopping, but her presence hung in the room like a cranky phantom. Changing the subject, she asked, "Couldn't we go for a walk?"

"No baby, we can't. Miss Haines says I must never take you out in public." Juba grimaced and continued speaking. "Anyway, I was plum wore out from dancing day and night for everyone, from hundreds of smelly sailors to the Queen of England. And then there was the dancing contests, all of which I won," here he winked at Kate, "and I hardly had time to eat. When I get to dancing I can't hardly stop. I got thinner and thinner, took to eating only oysters and beer. Course I got real sick. I was in England then, so I put myself on a ship and sailed for New York. You remember picking me up at the docks, you and your Dad?"

She hunched her shoulders and nodded. "You scared me. You looked like a black skeleton."

He snorted and slapped his knee. "That I did baby girl. That I did. Your Daddy took me to a boarding house run by an old circus woman and she nursed me back to health."

"Mrs. Fox, right?" Two winters before, when her parents were still alive, the Warnes had boarded with Mrs. Fox. She was nice, Kate thought and smiled to herself. Her son George was a clown and he was nice too, at least when he wasn't drinking.

"Yep, that be her. I had all this money I kept in a little carpetbag under my bed. And everyday I lay in bed and read the newspapers and I got to thinking about stocks."

Kate knew about stocks. One of Kate's schoolmates was a cousin to William Henry Vanderbilt and he'd come to school one day and explained the stock market to the young ladies.

He had the biggest pair of mutton chops she had ever seen and she'd had trouble listening to him because his voluminous whiskers had been wiggle-waggling up and down like he had some kind of small wild animal scrambling around on his face.

"Your Daddy and I worked out a deal where I'd pick the stocks and he would do the buying and selling, at first with my money. I did pretty good, so your Daddy put in some of his money too. He wanted to buy Excelsior for you."

Kate's eyebrows wrinkled again. She'd been trying not to think about her parents being dead and that meant not thinking about the circus and not thinking about the circus meant not thinking about her favorite horse. She wondered how Excelsior was doing.

Juba went on as if he hadn't seen Kate slump in her chair. "When your daddy died I took the money we'd made and split it down the middle. That's what pays your school and your dress making bills."

"Is it a lot?" Kate asked, her voice rising. The thought of being responsible for money made her head throb.

"Sadly, Miss Kate, it's about enough to pay for your education in this place and no more."

Kate knew she ought to be unhappy that she wasn't rich, but she wasn't. She saw the mothers who came to pick up their daughters at holiday breaks. Rich ladies lived in a kind of prison, tied down by big houses, fine carriages and fancy dresses. They danced, gossiped and waited for something exciting to happen. Only as far as Kate could tell, nothing ever did.

Juba never visited Kate at school again. One day a letter came.

Dear Kate:

I hope this reaches you before news of my death appears in the New York newspapers. I have to disappear for a time, for reasons that are my own. I have written to Mr. Mabie, who will pass the word among the folk that I am fine. Mr. Mabie shall also arrange for you to have Sunday visits from old friends. One day you shall look up and see me again. Until then, know that your Uncle Juba loves you,

J

Kate showed the letter to no one, guessing that its contents were meant to be secret. Two days later Mrs. Haines called Kate into her office and handed her a newspaper.

Kate saw that Mrs. Haines had drawn a neat box around the small article.

From the Illustrated London News

The copper colored votary of Terpsichore, Master Juba has jumped away, having danced his last dance at City Tavern in Dublin, Ireland. Irish medical men, if such can be said to exist, say the famed negro dancer died from exhaustion and poor diet. Londoners who saw Master Juba on his last tour with the Ethiopian Serenaders can testify to his virtuosity in song, sketches and conundrum contests, though without a doubt his greatest fame lie in his unique dance form, of such a type as could only be mastered by a denizen of the dark continent. Mr. Gilbert Pell, who performed with Master Juba, has said that his like shall never be seen again on either side of the Atlantic Ocean.

Over the next few years Kate re-read Juba's letter from time to time, until the paper was as soft as velvet and the folds threatened to tear. Some Sundays someone would come to the school's back door, ask for Kate and take her way for the day. Sometimes it was a heavily veiled lady, sometimes an old man in a pork pie hat who smelled like lemons and once a tiny man, no taller than a six-year-old child. Kate always came back from those days out with a glow of excitement about her, though she never talked about how she spent her day or with whom.

Juba bought them both a cup of coffee from a small stand at the park's edge and they sat down on a nearby bench. The day was a dreary grey, so they had the park pretty much to themselves. Down by the water a couple of older boys were throwing stones at the white-capped waves. The early winter sunshine felt good on Kate's face. She took a sip from her cup. "You should see this place in summer," she said awkwardly.

Juba patted Kate on the knee and looked out over the lake, scouting the progress of sailboat scudding across the grey water. "Seems like we each owe the other a story."

Kate snorted a small laugh. "I guess so, but I suspect your story is the less predictable."

"Well, that may be so my dear, but I want to hear about you. Would you start?"

Kate took a deep breath, folded her hands into her lap and launched into her story about Henry. She blushed a little when she admitted how thoroughly she'd believed in him, at least in the beginning. Her voice turned leaden when she got to the last few weeks of their marriage.

"He did that to you?" Juba asked gently. "I know something about brutal husbands, but I never thought it would happen to my little Katie. It just goes to show you." He shook his head slowly and eyed Kate. "The society folks would have us believe that only poor, drunken immigrants beat women, not captains of industry. You're well rid of the scoundrel." His voice turned angry as he spoke.

She smiled a thin-lipped smile. "I want to forget him and the whole sordid mess. Plus his father gave me this to ensure I stayed out of his son's life." Kate took her bankbook out of her reticule and open it for Juba to see.

"Lordy, Miss Kate!" Juba exclaimed, "and here I was about to tell you that I could give you some money and help you find a better place to live."

"I haven't moved because I don't know what to do. I'm waiting for an idea."

Juba nodded. "Far as I can see, money isn't good for buying but one thing: freedom. But I 'spect you know all that now." Juba looked knowingly at Kate.

Kate sipped her coffee. "True. But before we talk about my future, you need to explain yourself." Kate looked steadily at him. "You faked your death. Why?"

"It's a long and sorry tale." Juba leaned back against the bench. "It began four years ago, just two days after the last time we met."

Sitting at his little kitchen table, Juba turned over the letter in his hand. The return address said Gilbert Pelham, Liverpool. He sighed and opened the letter.

Old Friend,

I have been offered a good deal of money for a reprisal of Pell's Serenaders as part of a minstrel tour of southern England, culminating in another performance before the Queen of England. The promoter is most emphatic that the show include Master Juba, performing his plantation dances. I have enclosed a fair hand copy of your contract. You will see that

37

the terms are quite generous. As you know from your previous English engagement, there is also here a number of dancers who would most certainly accept a challenge match from you. As your victory in these endeavors is assured, the economic benefit to yourself would be considerable.

I find myself in financially straightened circumstances, having struggled recently with my own health. Anticipating your eagerness to help an old friend I include a third class ticket on a steamer bound for Liverpool one week after the expected arrival of this letter.

Most Cordially,
Gilbert Pelham.

The ticket was for that very afternoon, leaving Juba with no time to visit Kate, nor send a message.

The touring and performing schedule in both England and Ireland proved unrelenting. Juba performed three times a day, day after day, week after week. The good news was that the English couldn't get enough of his dance style, one he'd invented himself from a mixture of Irish clog dancing and African *gioba* dancing. His rapid heel-toe syncopations turned his feet into percussive instruments that could tap out a melody line as surely as a piano. Plus, the English were endlessly fascinated with the faux-slave culture featured in American minstrel shows. Juba didn't much care for that part of performing, the making fun of slaves' part, but a man made his money where he could.

Whenever he was tired, he skipped meals. When he did eat he ate only oysters, which would slide down his throat without chewing. One morning, in a run down hotel in Dublin, he could not get out of bed. On his second day in bed Mr. Pelham brought a doctor to see him.

The dour Irishman shook his head after his examination. "Sir, you suffering from exhaustion and starvation and if you don't change your ways, and exceedingly quickly, you will most certainly die."

"Die? He's my star performer," Mr. Pelham asked, anxiety permeating his voice. "Can't you give him something? He's already missed two days and we're engaged to perform at Newbridge tomorrow."

The doctor reared back his head. "This man needs bed rest and nutritious food, and plenty of both. And even then he may yet die."

Pelham grabbed Juba's hand. "You can't quit. I need you." Pelham corrected himself. "The show needs you."

Juba looked despairingly at Pelham. This man, who was one of his best friends, would be the death of him. The last time Pelham quit touring he'd suffered a bout of madness and spent six months in a sanatorium. After that he thought work kept him sane. "I'll be ready to perform tomorrow," Juba said gently. "Go tell the others."

Pelham clapped his hands together in delight and hurried out of the room, slamming the door behind him.

Juba turned his face towards the doctor. "You've got to get me out of here before he comes back and kills me. I can't die in Ireland."

Juba, who'd been looking out at some unseen horizon while he talked, turned to face Kate.

"So I faked my death and betrayed one of the best friends I ever had. But I could see my death on that doctor's face and that scared me."

"What happened next?" Kate asked softly. Her coffee, cold now, sat forgotten on the bench next to her. Sea gulls cried in the distance.

"Dr. Brennan had a sister who lived in a small town outside of Dublin, a place called Lullymore. He wrapped me in a sheet and then called two men in off the street. They thought they were moving a corpse. The doc wrote out a death certificate and left it for Mr. Pelham. Dr. Brennan took me to his sister's house." Juba smiled wryly. The American Irish hated negroes or at least a lot of them did, but not the Brennans.

"What happened to Mr. Pelham?"

"Not long after the show closed his family put him in an asylum. Dr. Brennan sends me updates from time to time. Poor Pelham thinks he's the Duke of Devonshire and refuses to wear clothing." Juba sighed deeply. "The doctors think his madness stems from debauchery, if you take my meaning."

Kate bit her lower lip and looked out over the lake. "You mean syphilis like Mr. Rainey, the old horse master. Momma explained all that to me back when I was no more than ten."

"Exactly," he replied. "But to tell you the truth, I'm not sure that's really Mr. Pelham's problem. I think he was born with his problem. Like I was, only I got a different problem. Having everyone look at you, laughing, clapping and the like, I can't get enough of it. It's a sickness. There was either dancing me or living me. I chose to live. I just had to die first."

"So is that what happened to you when I was little? When you stayed with the Foxes?"

He nodded. "Same thing. I vowed then to quit, but then the letter from Mr. Pelham came and I went back to it." He shook his head. "No more though."

"Do you miss dancing?"

"Every day. But it's also a relief, being done with it."

Kate stood up. "Enough. I'm tired of being sad. Let's take a walk along the shore. We can watch those funny little birds with their stick legs run back and forth in front of the waves."

Without knowing it Kate and Juba took the first steps to their new, more dangerous lives.

For the next two weeks Kate's life was too busy to spend much time worrying about the future. Disguised as a respectable widow and her loyal manservant she and Juba inspected a house, spoke to the man selling it and met with his lawyers. For a time the son and his lawyers labored under the delusion that they were dealing with a foolish woman who could be tricked into overpaying for the house, but Kate disabused them of that notion soon enough.

On the first day of December the house became theirs, paid for half with her money, half with his. Juba moved Kate's things from the rooming house and helped her settle into the largest second floor bedroom. He took the basement rooms, on the principle that no one would think it odd that a woman had a black man living with her if that man appeared to be her servant.

On her first evening in the new house Juba brought home a couple of meat pies he'd purchased from a street urchin. He also handed her a folded newspaper.

"Take a close look at the advertisements on this page," he said with an enigmatic smile, and thumped his way down the basement steps to his room. She pulled out a chair at the kitchen table, pushed the beef and kidney pie aside and examined the newspaper, wondering what Juba was up to.

41

She'd been reading the job postings, but there simply weren't any good jobs for women. Everyone pretended ladies were only good for being wives and mothers, while ignoring the poor and immigrant women who worked sixty hours a week in dangerous textile factories or the maids who worked night and day in society houses. Or worse, the female slaves who worked right along men in the fields, giving birth to the next generation of slaves while they did.

It was immensely frustrating. A woman who wanted more out of life than domestic drudgery was labeled crazy, impertinent or wanton. Or all three.

Those woman's rights ladies like Mrs. Stanton were right, though as far as she could see the reformers weren't making much headway. Women were trapped in small lives. Small in opportunity, small in generosity, small in imagination, so small that a woman's dreams died before being born. Kate knew her Momma escaped the trap society set for women and she'd done it over twenty years ago. If Momma had done it, so could she.

Turning the flimsy page of the newspaper with one hand, Kate absent-mindedly reached for her meat pie. Then she saw it. An advertisement for the Pinkerton's National Detective Agency, the words in a circle with an eye in the middle. Underneath the eye was the tag line, "We Never Sleep."

"A detective agency. With offices in Chicago, no less," she muttered to herself. "I bet they never hire female detectives." She paused, looked out the window for a few moments. She smiled and set to work on a plan.

The next afternoon Kate came thru the door of her new house laden with packages and boxes. They were from a fancy store on Chicago's Gold Coast, one that had ready-made

The Lincoln Special

dresses and was willing to do a quick tailoring job for an additional fee. Tomorrow she'd venture into one of Chicago's
poorer neighborhoods for a second hand store. A place like
that would have the sort of clothing she needed. She'd finish
her shopping tomorrow and implement her plan the day after.
It would all be worth it if it worked. Plus, it would be fun.

"Don't take your shoes off just yet, missy," Juba hollered at
her as he came back up the stairs. He was wiping his hands on
a piece of toweling and looking mighty pleased with himself.
"I have something else for you."

She looked up at him from her seat. She had indeed been
thinking about taking her boots off. "Can it wait? I need a stiff
drink and a bath."

"No, it can not wait." He held his hand out and pulled her
to her feet. "You'll want to see this," he said encouragingly.
"In the yard."

Kate followed Juba through the kitchen and out the back
door, irresistibly drawn by his excitement.

"Tadaa!" Juba yelled, raising his arms above his shoulders
and throwing in a little dance step.

And there he was. Big as life. Standing in her back yard.

"Excelsior!" She shrieked and threw herself off the back
steps. The big white horse raised his head when she called his
name. Blowing out a whinny, he shambled over to her.

She wrapped her arms around the horse's neck, nuzzling
his substantial and silky cheek. She breathed in that particular
smell found only on horses.

Kate stepped around to the front of the horse and looked
him right in the eyes. "You remember me, don't you? You
really are the smartest horse ever. And by far the prettiest."

43

Juba watched the pair for a few seconds and then stepped into the kitchen and closed the door.

Some time later Kate stepped into the kitchen. Juba sat at the kitchen table, a cup of coffee before him.

"How did you do that?" she asked, gesturing toward the back yard. "Where did you find him?"

"Well, Mr. Rice finally got himself an elephant, if you can believe that, so he didn't' need the horse. Apparently the elephant can walk a tight rope. And you know Mr. Rice."

"Always the most astounding acts," Kate finished for Juba. "I remember the act before Excelsior. Mr. Rice's 'Learned Pig, Lord Byron.' People thought the pig could do math."

"People think a lot of things around Mr. Rice, most of them foolish."

"Poor old horse. He's lucky he lived that night. The blow down could have killed him," Kate said flatly. She didn't particularly like to think about the night her parents died, but it didn't bother her like it once did.

Juba blew out the breath he'd been holding. "The day we signed the papers on the house I telegraphed Mr. Rice."

Kate knew why Juba did it. For better or worse, they were family and he'd just expanded their little family to include an elderly circus horse. She kissed him on the cheek and went back to the back yard. Juba followed her outside. She grabbed a handful of Excelsior's mane and leapt up, onto his wide back. They moved off, trotting in a tight circle around the yard.

Juba sat on the back steps and watched his girl and her horse until the stars came out.

Chapter 3

November 8, 1860
Marshall Texas

Senator Louis Trevant Wigfall was mad enough to shoot a tame hog. He paced the little office they kept for him at the Marshall County courthouse, for when he was home from Washington City. The newspaper on his desk announced the election of one Abraham Lincoln to the United States Presidency.

He'd taken refuge in his office, door closed, gas lights turned down low just to recover from the shock of it all. At least he wasn't alone. Every right thinking Texan was furious. *And what do they plan to do about it? Nothing!* Still, he saved his greatest rage for the damn stupid pro-slavery men. Sometimes he couldn't believe he was one. Why, they'd practically handed the election to that lugubrious Lincoln, sure as if they'd voted for him. The man was a clown. A woefully inadequate clown to boot. Damned slavery men, splitting up the ticket three ways like a party of fools. You'd think men smart enough to base an economy on cotton and slaves would be smart enough to run one blasted candidate for president instead of three.

One thing was for sure. They should put Stephen Douglas's head on a pike— his foolish talk about letting voters decide slavery had gone and divided the party. God made it clear. Some people were slaves and some people were betters and a whole lot of white folks were no better than slaves. The damn people were too stupid to be asked their opinion on such matters, particularly the ones that had never met a damn nigrah.

Wigfall settled in his cracked leather desk chair and poured himself a drink from a bottle he kept in his desk drawer. He sipped his whiskey, rolling the peat smoke flavored elixir around his mouth. His forehead puckered as he looked out the window at the evening sky. *The People, bah! Look at the mess they made in Kansas.* The Kansas-Nebraska Act let people vote to decide whether they wanted slavery or not and what did they do? Started a war, by God, right there in Kansas. And when right-minded men sacked Lawrence, why all the cowardly northerners protested like the abolitionist radicals hadn't had it coming. It's not fair, they whined. No wonder there were no real men in the North.

If there was one thing Louis Trevant Wigfall knew, it was that the strongest men took what they wanted and took it by violence if need be. He finished his drink and poured himself another—he might just drink the whole damn bottle. He'd heard that the north was so far gone down the road of lunacy that there were ladies going around saying they should vote. Voting women! Might as well put tits and bonnet on a hog and send it to the polling booth for all the sense that made.

The senator curled his lip into a sneer and rotated his chair to look out the window again. It was getting dark. How fitting. It was getting dark all over the country. He snorted a short,

46

brutal laugh. And if that damned Stephen Douglass would have just shut up about "popular sovereignty" and that weak sister Mr. Bell had never popped his damn fool head into national politics at all, why Mr. Breckinridge would be the next president right now.

That's what this country needed. A statesman and man of experience. Mr. Breckinridge had been in politics for decades and he was the damned Vice President. How the country picked that raw-boned clown from Illinois when they could have had Mr. Breckinridge was an everlasting mystery. Lincoln hadn't carried so much as one southern state. Sure he won the popular vote and the electoral vote, but he hadn't won all the states. And who cared about the popular vote anyway? This is what happened when you let the beasts vote. Damned fools. You didn't see Texas making that mistake, by God. No sir.

The second session of the 36th congress wasn't due to open for almost another month, but he figured he ought to get himself to Washington City. Marshall Texas might be the gateway to the Lone Star State, but it sure enough wasn't the gateway to Mr. Lincoln's destruction. Yep, that's what he'd do. Get himself to Washington City. Breckinridge would be there, and others. They'd start planning.

Clapping his hat upon his head, Louis left his office. He wobbled only a little bit as he walked, more than satisfied in his ability to hold his liquor. The dark crept up on the senator as he walked home. Somewhere off to his left a pack of coyotes yipped in the failing light. As his shadow grew fainter and fainter he thought about his course of action. Charlotte could stay home. He wouldn't even take his valet— last time he took Prince to Washington, when the first session of congress was sitting, he'd caught the damned nigrah trying to run off. The wily bastard was even less loyal to him than Charlotte.

Leaving Charlotte here ought to make her happy. Not much he did made Charlotte happy these days. Damned if he knew why. She wasn't like his Momma. Poor Momma died when he was thirteen years old and by then his father had been gone for years— dead when Louis was only a baby. But Momma knew how to be a woman, how take care of her family. All of her family.

His brother Hamden put Louis in a military school in South Carolina after Momma died. He'd wake up in the night amidst all the sleeping boys, half of whom had cried themselves to sleep, and think, how did this happen to me? Remembering that first year at school, with Momma gone, still made him shiver.

He'd tried though, he really had tried to get through the awful loneliness. He would imagine his own home, filled with strapping sons given to him by an adoring wife, someone soft and warm like Momma. Instead he had a cold hearted, daughter-bearing harridan that would hardly touch him. He didn't care. He knew what she thought of him. She'd been raised on a South Carolina plantation, in a fancy house, her every need tended to by dozens of slaves and two doting parents. She didn't understand why he had to work so hard to be a man, why he had to drink more, fight more, duel more than anyone else. It wasn't his fault he'd had to leave South Carolina. The move to Texas had killed any love she'd had left for him after the death of their only son. Poor little mite. He'd been sickly when he was born and no doctor, no medicine could make him well. Louis spent every dollar he had on the boy, but it hadn't done a lick of good. And she never forgave him.

Louis turned over a new leaf in Texas, traded in gambling and fighting for lawyering and politics. But did Charlotte notice? The state legislature made him a United States Senator almost two years ago, but did that impress Charlotte? Nope. *I could die, and be raised from the dead three days later and she'd still turn up her bony nose at me.*

He'd leave the girls here with their mother and hope Charlotte didn't poison them against him. His country needed him to save it from foolishness and disaster. He'd stop this damn Mr. Lincoln and everyone would know the greatness of Louis Trevant Wigfall. Then Charlotte and the girls would be proud of him.

He stopped walking and looked at the house his wife and daughters lived in. It was a good, solid house, new just last year. A yellow glow came from the windows, as did the faint tinkling sound of a waltz being played on the piano. One of the girls laughed. The scent of cornbread wafted out of the house. Louis stood outside in the dark, looking at the house that wasn't his home. He knew what would happen. He'd step inside and the place would go quiet. No one would be happy to see him. Maybe once he was a hero they'd be happy to see him. Smiling at this thought he went inside.

Chapter 4

November 19-20, 1860
Chicago

Kate came in through the door and threw her hat on Mr. Bangly's desk. "It's cold enough to freeze a witch out there," she wheezed. She pulled off her gloves and approached the office's coal stove, grateful for it's glowing heat.

Mr. Bangly picked her winter bonnet off his desk, pinching it between two fingers as if it were a rat and not a perfectly respectable wool lined hat. "Remove this abomination from my desk at once." His voice was full of teasing disdain and he glowered at her, his balding head, bushy black beard and thick eyebrows suggested a fierceness he didn't actually possess.

She turned from the stove, laughing and plopped the offending piece of headwear back on her head. Mr. Bangly looked like a stevedore but had the sensibilities of a French modiste. She liked to tease him with her selection of particularly sensible bonnets. The bonnets were, in and of themselves, a big enough concession to womanhood. She'd be damned if she'd wear a frilled confection of silliness. If she had her druthers she'd wear a wool cap that pulled down firmly over her ears.

He handed her a file, one ominously thick with paper. Kate took it from him with her thumb and forefinger, mocking the way he picked up her bonnet. She hadn't become a Pinkerton operative to sit at a desk and write reports. Still, clients needed to be billed and that meant someone needed to write up a case report. Once she wrote the report she could hand it back to Mr. Bangly and he'd write up invoices and send the bills. He absolutely loved paperwork.

"Miss Warne I've got a telegraph here from Mr. Pinkerton," Mr. Bangly said in his gravelly voice. He gestured down at the scrap of pale yellow paper he held in his left hand. "He's due back from Springfield late tonight and he wants a meeting tomorrow morning, eight o'clock sharp."

"Geoff Bangly, I do wish you'd call me Kate. We've been working together for over four years."

"Miss Warne, you have enough trouble around here, what with some of the men not liking women in the office in the first place. The last thing you need is me calling you Kate like you're a common barmaid."

Kate tried not to laugh. As if it mattered what he called her. The men who disapproved of female operatives didn't much care what Geoff Bangly thought. They didn't even care what Mr. Pinkerton thought. Too damn stubborn and too afraid of a world where women might be as good as men at all kinds of jobs. Not that she cared all that much what they thought. She mostly worked alone, which suited her just fine. No entanglements or attachments, just how she liked it. And when she did work with someone she generally worked with Juba or Hattie, neither of who gave her any grief.

"Fine." They'd had this argument before and she'd never won it. "What were you saying about the telegram?"

"Meeting, his office, tomorrow, eight sharp. He's been down to Springfield. Can you imagine meeting a president?" Mr. Bangly asked, tipping forward onto the balls of his feet.

"Well, he's not president quite yet. Mr. Buchanan has that honor until March the fourth if memory serves me right."

"Old fuss budget Buchanan," he sneered. "I'll take Mr. Lincoln any day. That man's got gumption, you can tell from just looking at him. He'll throw those fire-eating, slavery radicals right out of Washington soon as he gets there. You wait and see. And they'll go home and raise a ruckus. Mr. Lincoln's going to need the Pinkertons to help him with the mess."

Kate tucked her hands into her skirt pockets. "I hope you're wrong and suspect you're not. If the country is counting on the Pinkerton Detective Agency to solve our problems, well then," Kate paused and thought a moment, "that spells trouble. I'm good at investigating bank robberies and train hold-ups. Saving the country . . . That's too big a job."

"Well, we'll see won't we? Eight O'clock don't forget."

Kate took her file of paperwork and opened the door to her office with a sigh. She loved being a Pinkerton detective more than she would have predicted when she first got the job four years ago. She sat at her desk, dropping the file unopened in front of her. She was still amazed that she'd convinced Allan Pinkerton to hire her as detective. A smile crept onto her face as she remembered the way she'd set him up, first pretending to be a one armed man and then a high society damsel. It had been pretty darn audacious. Though admittedly, perhaps not her first or most audacious interview with an authority figure. No, that distinction went to her first interview with the redoubtable Miss Henrietta Haines, proprietress of the Henrietta Haines School for Girls.

After her parents were killed in a circus tent blow down Juba accompanied her on the train and taken her as far as Miss Haines front door. He'd rung the bell and left her with the maid that answered the door. The maid took her to the school office where Kate waited for the head mistress by herself, but for the loud ticking of a mantel clock. Heavy velvet drapes kept Miss Haines' office dim and grey and more than a little scary.

She tried sitting on the small sofa, but it was stiff and upholstered in some shiny stuff that wanted to slide her onto the floor. Instead she paced the room until an older woman appeared.

Dressed in a severely tailored black dress, with tiny pince-nez glasses perched on the end of a narrow nose, Miss Haines positioned herself behind her desk and gave Kate a thorough visual inspection. "Well, at least you have impeccable posture. I am Miss Haines, head mistress of this school." Her voice rustled like a pile of old leaves. She picked up some papers, looked at Kate and then the paperwork again. "I think there's been a mistake my dear."

The "my dear" was couched in such dry tones that Kate didn't think Miss Haines meant it as an endearment.

"Your guardian did not write anything for previous schooling."

Kate planted her feet in front of the old woman's desk and tucked her hands behind her back. "I took lessons from my mother and sometimes my father, in between learning to ride, walk the wire, tell fortunes and call the bally. And my mother says," Kate shifted her feet and corrected herself. "My mother used to say that impeccable posture is the key to standing on the back of a cantering horse."

"Bally?" Miss Haines asked, her eyebrows arching ever so minutely.

"Like a talking man," Kate explained. "They stand outside the ticket booth at a circus and call the bally, or the pitch and grind, to persuade rubes to buy a ticket. Or maybe see a side-show. Mr. Mabie, who owns a circus my parents work for," Kate paused and scrunched her forehead, as if remembering a particularly difficult math problem. *I will not cry.* "Worked for before they died, well he thought a bally girl would attract a better crowd than a bally man so he taught me the pitch and grind." Just talking about the circus made Kate yearn for its sights and smells. Horse manure and stale popped corn smelled way better than the dry, chalky air of this school.

"The pitch and grind?" Miss Haines asked in an extra po-lite tone, clearly hoping she didn't understand all too well what it meant.

"You know, like this." Kate hopped up on a small, tufted stool that sat in front of the visitors chair, took in a deep breath and her loudest voice hollered, "That's right, come on in, it's all inside. See the bearded lady and her dog-faced boy. Wire walkers, ladies on horses and a snake charmer. It's all inside, come on in and see wonders of the Mabie Brothers Circus."

Kate paused for a breath. "Like that. Sometimes I'd bally for the cooch show too." She hoped this would shock the old lady, maybe bad enough that she'd toss her out of this awful place.

One of Miss Haines eyebrows edged a wee bit higher. "Heavens," she said after a pause. "Cooch show?" she inquired with the delicacy that came with teaching deportment to unruly girls for decades.

"Oh, where the girls take their clothes off for gentlemen. Mama always said we ought to be nice to the cooch girls because they weren't bad women, only ones who had suffered misfortune. Miss Adele was an actress before she became a cooch dancer. She and I used to read Shakespeare together."

Kate saw a gleam come into the old woman's eyes and knew she'd failed. Her tutorial on circus life appeared to have only presented the lady with a challenge.

And so, in the intractable and obdurate hands of Miss Henrietta Haines, Kate's training as a Young Lady began. It worked too. A few years with Miss Haines and the other girls, most of them daughters of the east coast elite, and Kate could tell a oyster fork from a fruit fork, speak passable French and write a polite letter. She'd also learned some astronomy, chemistry, mathematics, poetry and ancient history. Chemistry was, for a time, her favorite. Oddly, her time at Miss Haines had been a perfect training ground for a detective, or at last for a lady detective. Her detecting job required her to mix with all sorts of people, but the sort of people who could afford to hire a detective were generally more Miss Haines than circus.

Her first case for example, required just such a lady's touch. She looked back over her shoulder at the framed bearer bond that took pride of place on the wall behind her desk. Old Alvin Adams, who'd one day found over $50,000 in stock certificates and bonds missing from the company safe in New York City, hired the Pinkertons to save his company. Allan put his best men on the case. They came to the conclusion that culprit was Mr. Adams' chief clerk, an oily man named Maroney, but they couldn't prove it. So Allan sent Kate to New York. One month later Mr. Maroney was taken to prison and Mrs. Maroney acquired a nice nest egg for the post-cheating-husband phase of her life.

Mr. Adams, pleased to have the bulk of the missing funds recovered, thanked Kate by presenting her with a recovered bond, across which he'd written "Never send a man to do a woman's job." She framed it and hung it on her office wall.

Not long after her success with the Adams job Allan Pinkerton visited Kate in her office.

He sat in her client chair, tipping it back so it balanced on two lets. His ever-present cigar made a cheerful wreath of smoke around his head. "Miss Warne, I'm not ashamed to say that hiring you was about the smartest thing I've ever done. I'm of a mind to expand the experiment. I'm going to make you the head of the new Pinkerton Women's Bureau."

"Really? Me?" Kate squeaked. A sobering thought occurred to Kate. "Would we be investigating women's matters, sir? Cheating husbands, wastrel sons, that sort of thing?"

"Oh, goodness no," Allan exclaimed, thumping his chair forward. "The Pinkerton Detective Agency will never stoop so low. I want your new department to do just what you're doing right now, using womanly talents to investigate matters that stump my male detectives. How's that sound?"

"Marvelous sir." Kate couldn't believe her luck. "When do we begin?"

"How about right now? Have anyone in mind?"

Kate thought for a couple of seconds. "I might. Give me a few days."

It was a long shot, but if she could find Hattie and get her to agree, they'd make a devastating team. Just as they had once before, long ago.

Kate met Hattie Lawton when she was thirteen years old. The Warne family had just signed on with the Spalding Circus, which traveled the Mississippi River on a boat so big there was no room for engines. Tugboats pushed the *Floating Palace* from one river town to the next. And fancy? The ring was two stories high and had velvet covered armchairs and carpeting in the aisles.

Hattie and Kate struck up an almost instant bond of friendship, in spite of the fact that Hattie was a good five years older than Kate. With her dark hair and eyes Hattie played a gypsy fortune-teller on one of the boat's upper decks. When *The Floating Palace* filled with paying customers she let Kate help her. Hattie taught Kate to read people by looking carefully at their faces, their clothes, their shoes, and then paying extra close attention not only to what they said when they answered the gypsy's initial questions, but how they said it.

Kate once told Hattie she thought she was pretty enough to marry a rich man and leave the circus. That's when Hattie told Kate her two biggest secrets. First, she was really a runaway slave. Her mother was one of New Orleans famous octoroons and she'd helped Hattie run away when they found out Hattie was about to become some white man's mistress just like her mother.

"They call it placage," Hattie explained. "Rich white men keep two families, one white and one colored. Some men free their colored families, but some don't." At this Hattie looked crestfallen.

"Did your daddy have two families?" Kate asked in horror. Circus morality was fairly loose, but they sure as heck didn't condone polygamy.

"He did," Hattie said, firmly nodding her head. "Which it turns out he couldn't afford. Just before my sixteenth birthday he told my Momma he was going to put me in the next season's balls."

"Why?"

"Cause those dances are really just trumped up slave auctions and Father needed the money."

Northerners couldn't fathom slaves that looked white like she did. Plus, she'd changed her name. Hattie never told Kate her birth name and Kate didn't' figure it mattered much. She was Hattie Lawson, circus fortune-teller and best friend. Hattie's other secret was less shocking. She didn't like men, or at least not to marry. She liked ladies. Kate knew women like that in the circus, several of them the cooch show ladies who had sex with men for money, but lived with women for pleasure. Kate couldn't imagine feeling that way about other women, but she didn't figure she had any right to judge.

Kate sent letters to every circus owner she could think of, directing some to northern towns known for being safe havens for circuses in winter and others to southern towns that were popular stops on the winter circuit. Each letter asked the circus owner or manager to find Hattie and send her to Kate in Chicago.

Four weeks later Kate heard a knock at her door and looked up to find her friend standing in her office doorway.

Hattie twirled her sky blue parasol, making sure Kate noticed it matched her impeccably tailored walking dress. "Tell me about this job you have for me," she said with a wicked grin.

For the next three years the two of them had the time of their lives, wreaking havoc on embezzlers, counterfeiters and bank robbers alike. They both broke some hearts, though Kate thought Hattie broke more than she did. Hattie was a bigger flirt. What they were really doing, though neither of them knew it, was preparing for Abraham Lincoln's election to the presidency of the United States.

The next morning Kate stood in her chemise, drawers, corset, under-petticoats and stockings in the middle of the up-stairs bedroom she used for clothing and disguises. She frowned at her choices. A gathering of the Pinkerton opera-tives required an outfit that balanced feminine appeal with a no-nonsense approach to fashions. Too "miss-ish" and the men wouldn't take her seriously, too severe and she made them nervous, as if they expected her to rap their knuckles with a ruler like a cranky school marm.

She pulled on her maroon Garibaldi shirt, struggling a lit-tle with buttons hidden behind a braid-trimmed placket. It had white stitching and white cuffs, complemented by navy blue braided cording around the wrists, collar and down the front. The shirt tucked into a dark blue skirt the same color as the braided trim, with a four-inch border of red at the bottom. Kate stood in front of her looking glass and appraised the final product. She'd worried the red color would clash with her auburn hair, but her modiste had been right— she looked daring and stylish, but without the frou-frou frippery of ruffles. And the maroon really did set off her green eyes. She didn't have Hattie's knack for fashion, but when she made an effort she did all right.

Kate stepped into a kitchen toasty warm with the smell of baking bread. "Morning Mrs. Barrow. This nasty weather hasn't set off your lumbago, has it?" Kate draped her wool cloak over a kitchen chair and stepped over to her housekeeper to peck her on the cheek.

"Don't you look lovely dear." Mrs. Barrow took a step back and surveyed Kate from head to toe. "And thank you for asking after my poor bones. I feel just fine today. A warm kitchen helps, doesn't it?" Mrs. Barrow beamed at her and held out a plate of fresh muffins. "Eat before you go dear. A good woman can't catch bad men on coffee alone."

Kate took a muffin and a cup of coffee from her housekeeper. Hiring Pansy Barrow was one of the best things she'd ever done. Years ago Pansy taught Kate's mother the tricks of equestrienne circus performance. She'd been standing next to Momma the first time Kate ever stood on the back of a horse. When Kate was about eight years old a broken hip ended Pansy Barrow's career, but not her association with the Warne family. A considerable number of Kate's Sunday afternoon visits at Mrs. Haines' school had been orchestrated or carried out by Mrs. Barrow.

After Mrs. Barrow signed on with Kate and Juba, Madame Clofullia came to stay in the house, along with her son. The bearded lady and her furry son lived in a second floor suite of rooms during the winter months, when the Madame wasn't doing sideshow work. She recognized that her hair covered son would cease to be an attraction once he attained adulthood— hairy men were no rarity and certainly no one would pay cash money to see one. Madame wanted her boy to be a lawyer. His opinions on career choices were hard to discern, he being only eight years old.

Mrs. Barrow shoved Kate towards the kitchen's back door. "Now you take your coffee and muffin outside and say hello to your horse. He's been standing at the backdoor for half an hour waiting for you. I keep catching him staring in the window like he's trying to make me feel bad." Mrs. Barrow herded Kate toward the back door. Kate smiled to herself. Being bossed around by her motherly housekeeper was oddly comforting.

Kate grabbed an apple and stepped outside. Excelsior ambled over to meet her.

"Hey there, you bad old boy. Letting yourself out of your stall again?" Kate didn't know all Excelsior's tricks, but one thing was for sure, the big white horse could open just about any latched door he wanted. She held the wrinkled apple out to him and he gently lipped it off her palm and eyed her muffin.

"No, the muffin is mine you old beggar. I don't know how long this meeting will last today, and it's cold, so I'm leaving you here. If I'm done early I'll come home and we'll go for a ride—sound good?" Excelsior nickered softly in response. *If only all the male creatures I deal with were half so accommodating.*

Back in the kitchen Kate called down the basement stairs, "Uncle Juba, you ready to go?"

"Up in a tick," she heard him holler. When they first moved into the house Kate had tried to get him to move upstairs, but he'd refused.

"Girl, I have to look like your servant or a lynch mob is like to show up at this house. Servants live in the bottom or top floors of houses like this and I'm a sight warmer in the winter and cooler in the summer downstairs than I would be up on the third floor. Plus, I have a pretty cozy nest down there."

Kate had to admit he was right. He'd been a collector on his travels and his basement apartment was filled with oddities that somehow made a coherent whole. It was all she could do to buy bedding that matched the curtains. He liked to take her shopping and make her buy towels and furniture and stuff like that. Kate pretended to hate their shopping outings.

She waited a few seconds and then hollered down, "If I'm late Mr. Scully will frown at me."

Juba came up the stairs, already buttoned into his black greatcoat and holding his cap and scarf. "Girl, Mr. Scully gonna frown at you no matter what you do. He jus' don' like de uppity ladies."

Kate snorted in disbelief. "Your slave act isn't going to make me less nervous about being in the same room with him. You're more of a gentleman than most of the men we work with," Kate said, stepping towards the door.

"Baby, I'm more of a gentleman than most of the men who live in this fair city." He bowed, then doffed his hat. "Dat be fo sho."

Chortling at each other, they set off for the meeting that would change their lives.

Chapter 5

I t looked to Kate as if Mr. Bangly had been wrestling two chairs into Mr. P's office and one had wrestled back a little bit. She considered suggesting he should move them one at a time, but she held her tongue, having learned from experience that gentlemen rarely enjoyed advice from ladies. Instead she took her coat and bonnet to her office and left chair moving to the men.

When Kate returned to Allan's office she found Juba and Mr. Bangly positioning the last chairs. Mr. Scully was already seated, ensconced in a large and well-tufted chair near Mr. Pinkerton's desk. She nodded to him and he nodded back, his thick black beard somehow suggesting dissatisfaction. The coal fire did little to mute the chill between her and Mr. Scully.

Timothy Webster stood from his seat so rapidly he dislodged a dog picture hanging on the wall behind him, his lanky limbs unfolding like an accordion. He hastily rehung the picture, leaving it more than a little askew and wrapped Kate in a hug so tight her corset creaked.

"Timothy! Are you back? Well of course you are, for there you are right before me. It's so good to see you." Kate looked up at her friend. At over six feet tall, to her just over five foot, that took some looking up. He was old enough to be her father, and indeed had a son only a little younger than Kate. His brown bushy hair and wooly beard made him look a little bit like a bear in a suit, though he was in fact an ex-New York City policeman with a mind as sharp as any Kate had ever encountered.

"Katie my dear, it's good to see you. The California job took longer than expected. Thought I'd never get home to my two best girls."

Kate knew he meant her and his wife Charlotte. The Websters had two living sons, but both their daughters died years ago. She was over to the Webster's apartment enough to count as an adopted daughter. She sometimes wondered if they were all friends because they genuinely liked each other or because the Websters wanted a daughter as badly as she wanted parents.

"I missed you too. We both did. Charlotte had me for dinner twice, but it's not the same if you're not there."

Kate gave Webster a final squeeze and turned towards her boss, who was sitting at his desk. She put her hands on her hips and with faux seriousness asked, "You're not too important for mere mortals are you? Now that you've met with a president-to-be?"

Allan Pinkerton stood and bowed towards Kate, tucking a hand inside his blue jacket. "Mr. Allan Pinkerton, detective to presidents, at your service Madame," he announced in a deep, booming voice. "And I would do anything for a lady looking as beautiful as you are today. And Mr. Lane," Allan added, turning towards Juba, "I'm so glad you're here. I think the case we are about to undertake will benefit from your particular talents."

"Then I am at your service," Juba said, mimicking Pinkerton's tone. "And the service of the new president if he needs me."

Kate watched the two men carefully. They'd been out on several cases together, though she didn't know exactly what they'd been up to. Kate suspected their work had something to do with the Underground Railroad, but she never asked and they never said.

Allan clapped Juba on the back and motioned to the chair next to his.

For all of his success, Kate thought Allan Pinkerton might be about the kindest man she'd ever met. He had a gift for seeing into the heart of people, regardless of what they looked like. He'd seen how she'd make a good detective almost right away, and later hired Juba as well. Allan always said he didn't care about a person's sex, color or station; only a person's character mattered to him.

Kate leaned over, kissed her boss on the cheek. "Mr. Lincoln is lucky to have you Sir."

"I fear that remains to be seen," Allan said gravely. "But Mr. Lincoln does need us, whether he knows it or not. Better not get ahead of myself." Allan paused a moment. "Are we all here?"

"Hattie's in my office talking to Mr. Davies. I expect they'll be here momentarily."

Just Hattie stepped through the door, resplendent in a dark green dress with brass buttons. "Here I am, sorry to be late." She headed for Kate, holding both hands out. "Kate, you look ravishing. Red agrees with you." She grasped Kate's hands and added, "I just left the case notes from the Western Union job on your desk."

"Just what I need—more paperwork."

"So, we're all assembled now?" Pinkerton asked. "I see Mr. Davies slipped in after Miss Lawton." Allan nodded at the man who had just taken a chair next to Mr. Scully. If Kate was the head of the Women's Bureau, then it could be said that Harry Davies was the head of the male Pinkertons, or at least second-in-command after Mr. Pinkerton. A quiet man who never spoke unless he had something essential to say, Davies often took the lead on the firm's most difficult cases, though he'd recently announced his intention to retire from field work. He nodded at Mr. Pinkerton and twitched his mustaches infinitesimally. Pinkerton operatives knew that was as close to a rousing greeting as one was likely to get from Davies.

Kate took a deep breath and looked around the room. Most of them were present. Mr. Lewis was in Tennessee investigating a murder. His absence suited Kate just fine because while Lewis was a fine detective, his absolute belief in his own excellence could be wearing.

Allan Pinkerton surveyed his operatives. "Yes. Well, as you know I've been down to Springfield the past few days. Norman Judd, who's a lawyer here in Chicago and one of Mr. Lincoln's closest advisors, came to see me last week. He had a telegram from Major Hunter asking for advice and help. The Major is the head of Mr. Lincoln's security detail."

"Mr. Lincoln needs a security detail?" Webster asked. "He's only just been elected."

"Well, most presidents haven't needed any protection ever, but the slavery radicals have convinced themselves that Mr. Lincoln's going to personally steal their slaves away. Of course he'll do no such thing, but right now they can't be reasoned with."

Juba spoke up. "They're poor losers if you ask me."

Allan nodded at Juba. "This is worse than being disappointed about losing the election. Mr. Lincoln's been getting some pretty nasty mail. Stuff like this." Allan held up a tattered piece of paper and read from it.

To Abraham Lincoln Esq.

Sir

You will be shot on the 4th of March 1861 by a Louisiana Creole. We are decided and our Aim is true.

Beware.

Allan looked at around the room. "There's quite a few like that."

"That's terrible," Kate said. "When did Americans start shooting the winner of an election? I mean, if the majority of American voted for Mr. Lincoln, then Mr. Lincoln is the rightful president. What happened to democracy?"

"These lunatics don't care about democracy," Timothy Webster spat out. "They care about getting their way."

Allan shook his head. "I think they understand democracy just fine, it's that they have a much narrower view of who the real Americans are." He picked another piece of paper off his desk. "This one is even worse."

Dear Sir I have heard several persons in this place say that if you ever did take the President Chair that they would go to Washington City expressly to kill you and your wife and children. Don't take the chair if you do you will be murdered by some cowardly scoundrel. Have you had any application for this post, if not I wish you would let me have it— if you take the Chair as president of the United States but don't you take it. Resign. If you don't you'll be murdered. I write this as a friend please answer this letter so I can know whether I must go to Washington city and raise a body of men to guard you.

Yours truly &c

R. A. Hunt

"He's insane!" Hattie declared. "He wants a job but he threatens Mr. Lincoln and his entire family? A madman, plain and simple."

"Yes, Hattie, I fear you're correct in your assessment, but that's exactly the problem. Every week Mr. Lincoln gets a basket full of mail, some of it job seekers, but a lot of it is murder threats, and much of that seems to be written by lunatics. Just before I arrived in Springfield, Mr. Lincoln hauled a stack of threatening letters out of his office, took them downstairs to the cabinetmaker's shop and threw them in the stove. Lincoln refuses to take the threats seriously and has his clerk put the hate letters in what they're calling the "hot-stove" file. It's driving Captain Hazzard, the army intelligence man in Springfield, plum crazy. Hazzard and Hunter both want the letters cataloged and investigated. More importantly, their commanding officer Colonel Sumner agrees with them and has freed Army funding to pay the Pinkertons to look into it."

Mr. Scully shifted in his seat and spoke. "It seems to me that Mr. Lincoln thinks he can make the threats against him go away by ignoring them, which seems foolish."

A few of the people in the room nodded their assent, but Kate could understand Mr. Lincoln's position. She saw Allan looking at her.

"Kate, would you explain?" Allan asked.

Oh for goodness sake. Why can that man read every thought I have? He makes me want to write my own crazy letter. "It's like this, I think." She sat forward in her chair. "He's been elected by *some* of the people, but he has to be the president to *all* of the people. I bet he's thinking he has every intention of being fair with the slavery folks, and they'll see that once he takes office. So right now he thinks these letters are not unlike what Macbeth called, 'much sound and fury, signifying nothing.'"

Scully snorted, signaling his disgust. "That's just crackbrained thinking."

"Oh, I quite agree with you Mr. Scully," Kate assured him. "Mr. Lincoln is entirely incorrect in his reading of the situation. I'm just telling you what I think he's thinking."

"Quite right Miss Warne," Allan said. "Mr. Scully, I think we all agree with you in this instance. Mr. Lincoln needs saving from himself."

Everyone in the room began talking amongst themselves until Allan called them back to order.

"Let me finish," Allan said, "Myself, Mr. Judd, Major Hunter, Colonel Sumner, Captain Hazzard and Mr. Lemon met for the better part of two days, going through what letters Captain Hazzard has saved from the stove and adding our own thinking. Here's what we came up with."

Allan paused dramatically. He wanted everyone looking at him for what he was about to say.

"We're absolutely convinced that Mr. Lincoln is in danger. Mr. Judd had us lay out the facts like they were a law case, finding motive, means and opportunity. Unfortunately, it was all too easy to find. For example, there's motive aplenty for interfering with a Lincoln presidency. Far too many men want to nullify the election to preserve their right to own slaves."

71

Juba sat forward in his seat. "Did any of you ever notice that the very same fellows who go on and on about their right to own slaves also blather endlessly about the importance of freedom and liberty? It's like they see their own hypocrisy and it makes them all the more fervent in defense of their peculiar institution."

Hattie chimed in. "I think it's worse than that Juba. They can go on and on about liberty while defending slavery because they don't think negroes *are* people. And in seeing daily what slavery does to people, they value liberty all the more."

Kate thought they were both right, but fundamentally it didn't matter. Keeping Mr. Lincoln alive didn't require an understanding of anyone's motives.

Allan agreed. "Mr. Lincoln needs us *now*, not four weeks from now when we're done talking about ideology and hypocrisy. It's clear there's more than a few men who'd be glad to pull the trigger for the glory and honor of murdering Mr. Lincoln, whether they themselves were killed in the act or not. Southerners place a powerful premium on honor and they're not afraid to use violence to enforce their code. Any man who did so would be a hero to the entire slave-holding south and quite a few Northerners to boot. Not unlike how they glorified Mr. Brooks for beating Senator Sumner half to death on the floor of the United States senate a few years ago."

Allan let them think about that for a second and then went on. "And sadly, there are motives beyond lunacy and honor. There's two camps of thinking about secession. One camp is all for seceding from the union and forming a Slaveocracy. Evidence suggests they think killing Lincoln would whip up enthusiasm for their cause. The other camp wants to keep slavery, but not break the union. They hope killing Lincoln will demonstrate how serious they are about their rights."

"But isn't Mr. Lincoln's vice president even more anti-slavery than he is? How do you suppose the slavery folks imagine President Hannibal Hamlin would help them?" Scully asked.

"I can't rightly figure, Mr. Scully. I'm not sure logic and reason has any place in politics these days." Allan stood and walked to the middle of the room. "So we have motive, but do we have means? General Hunter and his superior officer, General Sumner, think we do. The generals point out that most of the officers in the United States Army are southerners, and many of them are also secessionists. Southern officers have control of most of the federal arsenals and forts. Moreover, on his way to his inauguration Mr. Lincoln has to travel through Baltimore, a town famous for its violent mobs. And that city's chief of police, a man named George Kane, is both corrupt and secesh. We have means aplenty." Allan put his hands in his pocket and surveyed his operatives.

Kate finally spoke up. "So is the problem getting the president-elect in and out of Baltimore alive? How do we know there won't be trouble before and after?"

"Simply put, we don't. Washington City is a southern city, full of southern sympathizers. Worse, President Buchanan has never had much control over his party."

Allan returned to his desk. He fiddled with a new cigar, but didn't light it. "Thus far we have motive and means. Do we have opportunity?" He waited for a moment until it was clear he hadn't asked a rhetorical question.

"Ye gads, we do," Timothy Webster said loudly. "Every darn newspaper in the country has published the Lincoln Special's route. We know where he's stopping to speak and where he's stopping for the night—we even know what train changes he'll have to make. Anyone who wanted to do him dirty need only read the newspaper to know where he'll be any given day." Webster sat forward, rubbing his hands upon his woolen trousers. "He's a dammed sitting duck."

"Exactly," Allan said, "That's the bad news. But it might be the good news too."

"If we can get him to change his route, you mean" Kate said. "We could disguise him as a very large, very ugly woman, sneak him into the capitol and lock him in a closet until inauguration."

Juba threw his head back and guffawed.

Allan rubbed his hand through his hair, making it stand up on end. "Well, that's one approach. But he says he'll not change his plans. He wants his trip to Washington to be a kind of triumphal tour, thanking people for trusting him and speechifying along the way to allay people's fears."

"So, you actually met him?" Juba asked, his voice brightening. "You didn't tell us about that."

"Well, I didn't so much as meet with him as he poked his head into our meeting on the second day. Told us we could plan and scheme all we wanted, but he wasn't going to run scared."

"Is he as tall as everyone says?" Hattie asked. "And as funny?"

"Well, I don't know about funny. He didn't talk to the four of us for more than a minute or two, but he is awful tall. And it's not just that he's tall. He's long, if you take my meaning. He's also stubborn. And smart."

"Did you like him?" Kate asked. If Allan liked Mr. Lincoln, then maybe Mr. Lincoln was worth protecting, in spite of himself.

"Yes, I did. Which brings us to the crux of the problem. While we know there is means, motive and opportunity to interfere with the new president, we don't have anything specific. Or we have too many specifics. Too many threats. If there is a real threat against Mr. Lincoln, no one but the conspirators know what it is right now. Our job is to do what we do: investigate and find out who's serious."

At this point Allan decided he would light his cigar, making the room wait while he clipped, lit and puffed. "Miss Lawton and Mr. Webster, I want you two to travel to Baltimore. You're looking for two things: plots to kill Mr. Lincoln and plots to join the secession movement. Even Mr. Lincoln conceded that Maryland cannot secede. Baltimore would be the center of that movement if it exists. Miss Lawton, I'm particularly relying on you."

Hattie nodded. "Men do seem to like to tell me things. Can't imagine why," she said with a wink.

Mr. Scully snorted and rolled his eyes, but Mr. Pinkerton just continued with his plan.

"Mr. Webster, I'd like you to get a handle on the Baltimore police force there, and any militant groups associated with them. You've genuine New York City Police force credentials, and that's not going to hurt you with the Baltimore men."

"It's just that there are so many anti-Black, Irishmen in the force sir," Timothy said with a rueful smile.

Allan nodded. "And you're not like that. I know. But you can pretend you are. We're interested in who's loyal and who's not and if the Baltimore Chief of Police there is as bad as Captain Hazzard says he is. Mr. Bangly has your train tickets, hotel arrangements and identity papers. The Captain says the Barnum Hotel is a hotbed of secessionist sentiment, so keep that in mind. The two of you will arrive separately of course, and pretend not to know each other, at least until you get the lay of the land and decide otherwise."

"Do we have a part in this investigation," Kate asked, nodding over at Juba.

"Absolutely. That's the second part of my plan. You and Mr. Lane will be taking the train to Washington City. Obviously it's crucial the capitol be held should Maryland or Virginia make good on their promise to secede from the union and surround the city with hostile territory. We also need to assess the threats to Mr. Lincoln from within the city. Miss Warne, I want you to follow the same course as Miss Lawton— see what information you can get from the city's power brokers. From what I hear congress is still in session."

"It is sir," Mr. Bangly contributed, leaning forward eagerly. "The 36th congress sits until Mr. Lincoln is inaugurated. They'll have to certify his election with a count of the electoral votes to make his election official. They'll probably wait until the last moment before they do so. Mr. Breckinridge isn't going to want to do it at all, and-- "

Allan interrupted him. "Thank you Mr. Bangly. I'm sure you have a firm grip on the politics and if we need to know more we shall certainly consult you. Miss Warne, you need to find out which men are merely disgruntled and which are set on taking violent and treasonous measures. Mr. Lane, you'll also be in Washington. I think it might be helpful to have a man on the scene who can infiltrate the darker side of the city, if you'll pardon the metaphor."

"Yassuh, Massa," Juba intoned. "We darkies do likes to help."

"I know, I know, but honestly Mr. Lane, only a man of your complexion is going to get inside Washington's black community. They'll be an invaluable resource for what's really going on in the city." Allan puffed at his cigar, creating a cloud of smoke above his head.

"Plus, I can keep an eye on this one here," Juba said, gesturing toward Kate. "You know how she likes to make trouble."

"The plan does have that advantage as well," Pinkerton said with a foxy smile.

Kate sent Hattie the smallest of winks. They'd see who needed watching over and who didn't soon enough.

"Mr. Scully and Mr. Davies, I'm sending you to Richmond to take a sounding of the place and then on to Charleston, if it's convenient. If secession comes it will most certainly start in South Carolina. The question is, are they really serious or is it all talk by radical blow hards? And if they are serious, how much has secessionist talk has taken hold in Virginia. Mr. Lincoln wants to know if Virginia will stand with the union. Be prepared to be recalled though, should the Baltimore or Washington City operations have need of you."

The two men nodded.

"I'll stay here in Chicago, where I'm only a short ride away from Springfield. Mr. Lincoln won't be leaving until early February. Until then either I or Mr. Bangly will go down to Springfield every couple of days to exchange information with the colonel. Mr. Bangly has included the cipher we'll be using for telegrams in each of your files. I don't need to tell you to keep it safe."

Allan looked around the room. "So, you have your assignments. Keep in mind that the Pinkerton's have been entrusted with ensuring safety of the next president of the United States. Are we in agreement that nothing untoward will happen to him on our watch?"

They were. Failure would spell disaster and not just for Mr. Lincoln and the Pinkerton Detective Agency.

Chapter 6

November 21-26, 1860
Chicago & Washington City

Two days later Juba and Kate shivered on the platform of Chicago's Great Central Depot. Rain slanted under the roof, driven there by the wind, which smelled of northern ice. The massive depot was only four years old and every week hundreds of trains passed through the station, moving grain and other agricultural goods from the west to eastern cities. This morning Kate thought it could have used a larger covered platform.

While waiting for the train, Juba looked through the file Mr. Bangly put together for them, being careful to hold the folder close to his chest so it didn't blow away. "Says here you've got a room reserved at the Kirkwood Hotel when we get to the capitol," Juba said. "Mr. Bangly didn't rightly know what to do about me, but I told him to no never mind--I have friends in every city I ever performed and I know just the man to put me up in Washington City."

"Who?" Kate asked. Large parts of Juba's life remained a mystery to her.

"Columbus, that's who," Juba said proudly.

"Columbus? Like the man who claimed the Americas for Spain?"

"Yeah, just like that, only black as the ace of spades. He was a slave once, but Columbus bought himself free about fifteen years ago. We met at a dancing contest, where I soundly defeated him. He's a big man and never could keep up with Master Juba's moves."

Kate asked Juba a question that she'd been wanting to ask for ages. "Juba?"

"Yea honey?"

"Why'd you fake your death to get away from dancing, but then keep your name. It doesn't seem like a very good disguise."

"Well girly, my mother named me William Henry and my last name is Lane, just like my Momma, who was a free black woman in New York. Juba just be my dancing name, but people knew me as William Lane too, so I can't go back to that. But, everybody know Juba, so I can keep using that."

"That doesn't make any sense."

He laughed.

Kate loved it when he laughed, even if he was laughing at her a little bit. This deep, rolling sound of pure joy rumbled out of him.

"Well, it's like this. Back twenty years ago, I got famous. *Real* famous. The white fellows I first danced with called me Master Juba, on account of "juba" being slang for a challenge dance or a circle dance."

"I know what a challenge is, but what's a circle dance?"

"Well, it's a type of challenge dance you see, but instead of being on a stage with judges, all official like, a circle dance is informal like. Two fellows dance, each trying to copy the other, circled by a crowd that claps and stamps out the rhythm. There's lots of calling out, back and forth in a juba circle. It was a street dancing kind of thing, but the minstrel shows picked it up, turned the circle into a half circle and put it on stage. That's a "Juba" too. And sometimes all the clapping and leg slapping is called "patting Juba," though you can also pat Juba on a fiddle or a drum."

"So, it's named after you?"

"No baby, I'm named after the dance, not the other way 'round. I was "Master Juba" which means "master dancer." He said the last two words extra deep for emphasis. "Why, you go down to the wharves in New York or any other port city, there'll be men there dancing juba for their supper. Sailors and the like throw them eels and holler 'Dance, Juba dance.'"

Kate pondered his story. "It's like I don't know anything about you."

"Oh, you know plenty, but no one ever knows everything about anyone. There's things I don't know about you, right?"

Kate nodded gravely, shifting her feet a little bit as she did so. She didn't like to think about those days with Henry.

"Well then. The point is I can go by Juba because it's a common name for black men. It's a shuffling name, if you know what I mean. Not like a real name. Makes some white folk feel mighty superior to call a black man by a not-name. That makes Juba a kind of disguise name. It says, "don't look at me. I'm nothin' but a no account Juba Man.""

Kate grimaced. "People are stupid."

He shrugged. "Maybe, maybe not. It just be that way. That our train coming down the track?" Juba leaned out over the platform for a closer look. "Yep, that's us. "Nuff talking.

81

Let's get ourselves gone." He hoisted his ragged carpet bag onto his shoulder.

Kate looked at the porter who had command of the small cart with her traveling trunk on it. She'd probably packed too much, not knowing what she was going to do or who she was going to have to pretend to be. She looked at Juba's single bag and sighed. It took her one entire bag just to pack her unmentionables.

They arrived in Baltimore early Monday morning. Rain and snow followed their train the entire trip, so that the train cars never really warmed up. And as was always the case with rail travel, cinders and soot from the engine's fire boxes got into everything and everyone on the train. In Maryland they had to wait while their train cars were ferried across the Susquehanna River from Perryville to Havre De Grace. Dark skinned railway men loaded iron railway coaches onto ferries in the dawn's grey light and floated them across the river. The thought of how quickly a coach would sink in the frigid water if a ferry overturned gave Kate the willies.

Once across the river they re-boarded for the short ride to Baltimore. In Baltimore they got off the train at one depot and took an omnibus to a station on the other end of the city's waterfront.

Juba saw Kate examining the route to the Camden station. "It's a mess, isn't it? I mean, if I wanted to create mayhem, this would be a good place to do it."

Kate shivered against the cold wind. "Here or on the river. But this is near impossible to defend."

"Yup."

Kate looked around again and rubbed her eyes. "It's too big a job. No one can keep him safe in these conditions. No one." She clenched her fist. *Dammit anyway.*

Juba patted her on the shoulder. "Remember, like as not the southern states are leaving the union. When they do they leave the country to the rest of us. Why, with the northern abolitionist in charge it'll be no time at all before women can vote and the president is a black man."

Kate gave Juba a dead panned look. "Juba, I fear you've lost your ever lovin' mind."

Kate and Juba stepped out of the train in Washington City into the weak early morning sunlight to find they were only two blocks away from the Capitol grounds. Just down New Jersey Avenue the unfinished dome of the Capitol rose in front of them, like a half-seen ghost. Kate found it oddly beautiful.

"How do they keep out the rain and snow?"

Juba chuckled. "Maybe they don't. From the way those politicians been acting I'd say they don't have the sense to come in out of the rain, let alone the snow."

Kate smiled wanly at him. "You might be right. But still, I'm going over there to see it up close. *After* I've had a bath, that is." Kate looked wryly down at her grubby traveling clothes. "Is this where you and I part ways?" She knew it was, but dreaded it.

"Yep. Columbus's store is just up the street here a couple of blocks. I'll call a carriage and get you that much closer to your bath. I'll figure out where and when we can meet and let you know." Juba looked up the street for a hack carriage. He gestured to one and turned back to Kate. "Now, if I remember the city aright, your hotel is just up Pennsylvania Avenue, in-between the Capitol and the President's House. You'll find it mighty convenient. "

"Convenient for what?" Kate asked pertly. "Do you think I'm meeting with Congress or something? Senator Warne?"

"Katie my dear, I got a feeling you and this town are going to get along just fine."

Kate wished she were half so sure.

Chapter 7

Juba shouldered a 25 pound sack of flour. The work felt good after days of sitting on the train and the winter sun of Washington provided considerably more warmth than back in Chicago this time of year.

"Last one," Columbus called. He was a big, heavily muscled fellow, providing stark contrast to Juba's compact, wiry frame. Where Juba's skin was a light coppery brown, Columbus was so black his skin seemed tinted with midnight blue.

"Reatha has lemonade and something to eat in the kitchen. How 'dat sound to you?" the big man called to Juba.

"Sounds mighty fine." Juba dropped his last sack of flour on a pyramid of flour bags and wiped his hands on a piece of toweling that hung on a nail by the door. "I thought this was a feed store. Why all the flour? Don't tell me they're baking bread for the fancy people's horses now."

"Ha, don't say 'dat too loud. Mayhap some of them southern gentlemen what treat their horses better than their slaves hear you and think it's a fine idea. No, I bought me a little warehouse over in Georgetown, right by Rock Creek. Put a little grist mill in there. Grain comes off the train at the depot, then we cart it over Georgetown, mill it and then get back to the store for sale. It's a pretty good business, but a man gotta move a lot of heavy bags." Columbus wiped his hands as well and gestured toward the back of the house that was his feed store. "Hold on. Gotta close these gates so the durned horses don't disappear.

Juba looked around the feed yard. The house and shed were old and none too sturdily built, but the white wash was fresh and everything had a place. "You've done pretty well for a man that can't hardly dance a lick," Juba teased.

Columbus threw back his head and laughed. "That be true."

They went in the back door and up the stairs. Columbus and Reatha lived above the feed store, under the sloping roof. "Baby! Come see who I found wandering the street." Columbus's voice boomed through the small space as he kicked off his boots.

Reatha stepped into the kitchen, her face wreathed with a wide smile. "Master Juba, the dancing fool. Been a long time, you old fox," she said just before she folded him into a wiry armed hug. Where Columbus was big and loud, Reatha was a wisp of a woman with a quietly controlled voice. The tiny upstairs was warm from Reatha's cook stove and smelled like home. "Sit down you fool," she said to her husband, "befoe' you hit your dang head again." She smiled fondly at him, and then turned to Juba. "You take a load off as well. I see by the flour dust on your shirt that Columbus done put you to work already."

They had but two chairs and Columbus was already sitting in one of them. Juba looked doubtfully, first at the chair, then at the tiny woman.

She saw him looking. "No, you go ahead. Someone's got to mind the store and I 'spect you and my man have some palaver ahead of you." She thunked a heavy pitcher of lemonade on the table and another of buttermilk. Along side that she placed a pan of cornbread, two bowls, a ceramic pot of what looked like strawberry jam and two spoons. "A little something to hold you."

As she clumped down the stairs Columbus called after her. "Don't you even think about lifting anything down there baby. You call me, you hear?" A muffled sound of assent came from the stairs. Columbus looked at Juba. "She a good woman, 'dat for sure, but she tends to forget how little she be compared to some of the sacks of grain we got. And some of the white men don't mind standing there while she lifts their wares for them."

Juba just nodded. He knew white men who wouldn't let their wives or daughters lift anything more substantial than a down filled pillow and yet wouldn't blink an eye at a Negro woman carrying a forty pound sack of oats.

Columbus changed the subject. "Its sho nice to see you, but I 'spect you're not here jus for a visit. What you got on your mind?"

"I'm going to tell you just enough that you can decide if you want to help me. That sound all right to you?"

Columbus nodded and reached for a slab of cornbread. "If I can help you, you know I will."

Juba watched him crumble it in a bowl, spoon jam onto it and pour buttermilk over the whole thing. "Thank you," Juba said gravely, and poured himself a glass of lemonade. He'd eat once he told his tale. "You remember, about fifteen years ago, when the Robinson Circus came to town and performed at

the National Theater, back when it was brand spanking new?
I was traveling with a white family?"

Columbus did remember.

Juba explained about how Kate became his ward after her
parents died and how she came to be hired by Allan Pinkerton.

"A lady detective," Columbus exclaimed. He ran his hand
up along his close cut, dark hair. "Don't that jus beat all?"

"Yes it does, my friend. Mr. Pinkerton hired me too if you
can believe that." Juba paused and took a long drink of lemonade.

"What you investigating'? Someone rob the President's
house?" Columbus threw back his head and laughed again.

"Well, that's a mighty close guess. It's Mr. Lincoln. We're
helping him."

Columbus tipped his chair back. The poor over-worked
chair groaned in protest. "Wooeee. You run in some high fa-
lutin' company. If Mr. Lincoln needs me all he gotta do is
ask."

"He's not going to ask you, but I am. There's men who'd
like to stop him from becoming president. My job, and Miss
Warne's too, is to find those people and see how serious they
are. Might be only talk, might not be."

"The white folks can pretend otherwise but you and I
know it's not just talk. Those slavery men, it's like they've got
brain fever. They're terrible afraid. And a scared man is the
most dangerous kinda man there is."

"Oh, I quite agree. You know this city. I don't know how
to get inside, but you do."

"That I do." Columbus leaned back in his chair, a thoughtful look on his face. "I got a friend, name of John Howard,

keeps a livery stable just a few blocks from here. Lotta white men in and out of there. They use Mr. Howard's back room for meetin's and such. Crackers, most of 'em. Nobody as hateful about negroes as poor whites."

The two men shared a look. Each knew all too well the fear and hate generated by slavery.

"And they talk in the stables? In front of your friend?"

Columbus nodded his head. "He's a white man. But they talk right in front of me too. You know how these kinds of fellers be. They think a black man cain't understand, like we're dogs or something."

Juba thought for a moment. "Can you get me a job there? At the stable? Tell your friend he need never pay me-- just give me a place."

"I 'spect he'd do that. Hold on." Columbus got up, his chair screeching on the floor as he pushed it back. "Reatha!" he hollered down the stairs, "Close up the store baby. We got to go see a man about a horse."

Juba looked ruefully at the cornbread and jam. He should have kept his darn mouth shut until after he ate.

She looked at the city from a hotel room window, fresh from a hip bath full of warm water. There was nothing like clean hair and a soft dressing gown to make a woman feel better. Admittedly, the view from her second story window at Kirkwood House wasn't as striking as her first view of the Capitol building, half finished though it was, but the hotel did look out on bustling Pennsylvania Avenue.

The Kirkwood was one of a half dozen hotels that routinely housed politicians. Few men came to the city with their wives and families, preferring to stay in a hotel or in boarding houses they called "messes." Both boarding houses and hotels tended to be either on Pennsylvania Avenue or on a side street not far off.

The same hotel maid who brought the hot water and the copper bath promised to bring Kate a breakfast tray at nine o'clock. Maybe she could tip the girl to help her unpack her trunks. Kate found maids to be an invaluable source of information and they would talk if you were nice. She needed to know where the political gentlemen spent their evenings in Washington, particularly those with southern sympathies. Spying was like untangling a ball of yarn. The hardest part was finding the beginning. Once she did she could pull the string and begin to make order of the tangle.

A knock came at her hotel room door. Eager for breakfast, Kate turned away from the window. The sooner she ate the sooner she could start pulling strings.

After breakfast Kate stepped into her navy blue polonaise day dress. She had planned to wear one of her less respectable, more dubiously tailored dresses and make the rounds of theater back doors, but after talking to Biddy, a plump Irish woman who worked as a hotel maid, she changed her mind.

"Oh, miss, all the fine ladies go up to the Willard Hotel, to the Ladies Parlor for tea," Biddy enthused. "My cousin Mary works there, she's a maid too don't you know, and she says the Ladies Parlor is always full of women in the most lovely dresses you ever did see."

"Ladies?" Kate inquired. Taking a shot in the dark, based on the fact that most Irish immigrants had little love for abolitionists, many of whom were also anti-Irish Catholic, Kate decided to play southern sympathizer. "I heard the Willard

90

was a liberal stronghold. I'm not sure I want to make the acquaintance of any of those rabid abolitionist or women's rights people. My Papa, he says northern women aren't ladies."

"Oh, yes Mam. I know what you mean. There are all sorts of people who stay at the Willard. Seems they don't all get along, so Mr. Willard made separate entrances-- the Southerners use the Fourteenth Street door and the women folk use the Ladies Parlor on that side of the building. The Yankee women, well they come and go from the Pennsylvania Street door and use one of the front parlors. Least ways, that's what Mary says."

The Willard was only three blocks up Pennsylvania from the Kirkwood House, making it an easy walk, particularly since the day had warmed up. Carriages clattered up and down the street in a mosaic of bright colors and sounds. Kate's eyes widened as one of the city's omnibuses went by pulled by six matched horses. It was a big, open carriage filled with people, but most astoundingly the side panels featured a mural of Greek gods at the Parthenon, some of them barely clothed. Kate couldn't help but stare at the conveyance as it rolled by, part gaudy, part gloriously ebullient.

As she approached the Willard Kate took a moment to appreciate its splendor. It really was quite a bit grander than the poor little Kirkwood. For one thing, it was huge, taking up most of the block upon which it sat. Clad in pale grey stone it loomed above the street like an architectural colossus. She walked the length of the facade and turned the corner at Fourteenth Street, looking for the entrance. Ah, yes, there it was. The trick would be walking in without anyone noticing she was an unaccompanied lady. She approached the door.

"May I help you Madame?" The dark skinned doorman managed to look obsequious and forbidding at the same time.

She paused before the door, appearing to be indecisive and in need of help. It was her experience that gentlemen of all colors were generally eager to help a confused woman. "Oh, I don't know. This is the Willard Hotel, isn't it?" Kate rushed on before the doorman could tell her what she already knew. "Mr. Barley and I are staying here. We're from Kentucky, you see? I wanted to go for a walk and I didn't take my maid. She's unpacking, you see? And I thought, just a walk around the block wouldn't hurt. But the blocks here are just so big!" Kate wailed a little at this last. "I think I'm lost."

"No Ma'am you're not," he reassured her. "If you're staying at the Willard you've found your way just fine." He opened the door for her and gestured her inside.

Kate smiled to herself. *Works every time.*

On the wall inside were small, discretely lettered bronze plaques directing guests to Grand Ballroom, Ladies and Gentlemen's parlors and dining rooms and the two front halls. The Willard's Ladies Parlor exceeded all of Kate's expectations. Gas lamps gently illuminated the rose colored upholstery on chairs and settees. Thick flowered carpets anchored the seating arrangements, while discreetly placed flower arrangements both matched the decor and lent the room a gentle scent. Kate looked around the room. Ah, there. A lady all alone. An older one.

Kate glided over and quietly sat down. "Excuse me," she said with her best upper-crust southern accent, "Is it all right if I sit here with you? I don't want to sit alone and my feet are just so tired. At home I don't walk so much as here."

"I'd be happy to have you join me. Where is home, dear?" the lady asked solicitously.

Kate thought she ought to be careful. If she said Kentucky and this lady was from Kentucky as well they'd have to play 'do you know so and so" and Kate's fake identity would fall apart.

"Ever so far away it seems. And you? Where are you from?"

"I call the great state of Georgia my home," the lady proudly replied. "Allow me to introduce myself. I'm Miss Matilda Stephens, sister to congressman Alexander Stephens. I always accompany my brother to Washington. My dear brother's body has never been as strong as his mind. I am the shoal upon which he rests."

Kate thought Mr. Stephens must not take after his sister. She had a robust look about her and inquisitive black eyes that appeared to miss very little. She reminded Kate a little bit of Miss Haines. "Miss Stephens, it is so very nice to meet you. Oh, how foolish of me. I haven't introduced myself. I am Mrs. Katherine Barley. My husband and I are from Kentucky."

"What county does your husband represent Mrs. Barley? I don't think he's a senator is he? I know Mr. Crittenden is from Kentucky."

"Oh, no, nothing that grand I'm afraid. My dear husband is advising Mr. Buchanan on South America." Almost the entirety of American politics was taken up by the slavery question these days, so much so that no one of any consequence worked in foreign policy.

Kate signaled a waiter and, after asking Miss Stephens to join her, requested a tea tray. The two ladies spoke for another half hour while they drank their tea. Kate listened to Miss

Stephens expound upon the religious and moral foundations for slavery. All Kate had to do was make small noises of agreement from time to time, which tested her patience quite enough. Finally Miss Stephens announced she had leave to meet her brother.

"I've enjoyed our little talk, my dear," the older lady said to Kate as she stood. "Perhaps you would like to walk with me tomorrow afternoon? I could show you around the city."

"That would be lovely," Kate enthused. "My dear husband is busy day and night and I do get so lonely. Maybe tomorrow you could tell me about the people here in Washington." Kate paused to indicate delicacy. "Who I should talk to and who I should not. My dear Poppa always says a lady can not be too careful."

"I'd be glad to fill you in on the good people and the scalawags Mrs. Barley. Shall we say 2 o'clock?"

Kate agreed and Miss Stephens sailed away, her hooped skirts swaying as if trying to keep up with her.

Kate watched her go and then walked back to the Kirkwood, entirely pleased with her first foray into the deadly swamp that was lady's tea.

Chapter 8

November 28-30, 1860
Washington City

As he hoisted another shovel of manure filled straw Juba thought about how much he hated manual labor. Shoveling metaphorical shit was one thing, he'd done plenty of that in minstrel shows, but real shit?

"Now, I don't want any trouble you see? None at all." Mr. Howard put his hands in his pockets and rocked back on his heels.

Juba looked at the stable owner, who was speaking loudly enough to be heard throughout the building. Juba thought he'd never seen a man whose ears made up such a prominent part of his physiognomy. Of middling size, with short black hair neatly combed back from his forehead over a slightly lumpy nose, Mr. Howard had ears of both prodigious size and magnificent protuberance. Trying not to stare, Juba asked in as mild a tone as he could muster, "There a problem Mistah Howard?"

Mr. Howard looked around and yelled, "In my office, right now." He turned on his heal and marched away, clearly expecting Juba to follow him.

Juba followed Howard to an open door at the far end of the big brick building that was the livery stable. He entered an office not much larger than a storage room. A desk stood against the wall, it's top as neat as the rest of the stable. Columbus was there, standing in the middle of the room. The two black men nodded at each other.

Shutting the door, Mr. Howard turned and looked at them. "We couldn't talk when Columbus brought you by yesterday, not with the place was crawling with those Virginia boys. Columbus can tell you, I like their business, but I don't like their politics." The small man grinned ruefully, rubbing his head as he did. "Oh, and sorry about yelling at you out there. I want them to think you're getting your ass chewed."

Juba assured the stable owner he understood the rules of the game.

Howard gestured at the two black men. "Don't know how you're going to get them to tell you anything."

"Oh," Juba said with a sly little grin, "I 'spect they'll tell me plenty. They just won't know it when they do."

Mr. Howard looked Juba over, head to toe. "I don't cotton much to slavery. I figger a man should be free, no matter what his complexion. Ladies too, for that matter. My wife's smarter than most of the fellows I know. But that's a secret I got to keep in this town." Howard stopped and gave Juba a hard stare. "You a man that can keep secrets?"

"Sir, most of the world thinks I'm dead."

Howard stared at Juba and then laughed. "Dead huh? That's a hell of a secret."

Juba nodded his head once and stuck out his hand.

Howard took it. "Welcome aboard. Now back to shoveling shit."

That afternoon Juba cleaned tack. The tack room was next to a back room where group of weasel faced men had a rat baiting ring. The room had a ten foot circle made of hay bales, two high. The men would throw a bunch of rats and a dog in the ring and bet on how long it would take the dog to kill the rats. Juba didn't have any special fondness for rats, but he thought rat-baiting was revolting for it's cruelty to both rats and dogs. How men who engaged in such a past-time could imagine they were members of a superior race was a source of everlasting mystery.

Air, redolent with the scents of blood, sweat and spilled beer roiled out of the room and into the tack room. Juba was rubbing saddle soap into a harness when one of the men from the back room appeared in the doorway. He leaned unsteadily on the doorframe and held out a silver coin. "Nigger, run git us some more beer. Here's six bits-- oughta get two buckets of beer. Step lightly now!"

"Yassah. Ole Jupiter be right quick," Juba said. He leaped up and took the coins from the man's grubby hand.

"And you better not drink any on the way back. Onliest thing worse than a nigger is a drunk nigger."

"No sah," Juba nodded his head, scooted past the man and out the door, wondering why unwashed, drunken, rat baiting hillbillies thought they were so great.

When Juba returned he pushed open the door to the rat-ting room with his foot and carried in two buckets of beer, being careful not to spill any. The men were hollering at a small brown terrier in the ring surrounded by dead rats. He had only one more to go when Juba sat the beer on a table. Juba watched as the last rat climbed the hay bales, trying to get away from his canine nemesis. The little dog seized the rat in his teeth and briskly shook it. The rat's neck broke with a loud crack.

"Seven minutes, thirteen seconds," the man holding a watch cried. The men hollered while money changed hands. Juba stood quietly against the wall, hoping they'd fail to notice he was in the room, when the man who'd given him the beer money turned to him.

"Here's your change Massah," Juba said, holding out a two-cent piece.

"Why, an honest nigger! Lookee here boys!" the man cried in mock glee. "You like rattin' boy?"

"Well suh, never seen much. That dog look plenty lively," Juba said, gesturing to the terrier just out of the ring.

The young man holding the squirming little dog said, "You're a good judge of dog flesh, boy. My dad breeds ratters on his farm. I bring the best into town."

Juba thought the young man looked a little bit like a rat himself, with his thin nose, high forehead and wispy chin whiskers. "Well, sir, I can surely see dat." Juba started to edge around the crowd, making towards the door now that he'd been noticed.

"Stay and watch, boy," the young man half-yelled from across the room. "Little Titus goin' to see how many rats he can kill in twelve minutes. I heard tell there's a dog in New York that can kill a hunnerd in that time."

The men yelled their disbelief, but seemed inclined to let Juba stay and watch the small dog's feats of rat murdering prowess. Juba ended up hanging around the rat ring until after dark. He learned a few things in the process. At the end of the day he left, entirely disgusted with rat-baiting. Still, he hoped his combination of joyful cries of admiration and shuffling humility had impressed upon the men his complete and utter harmlessness. They'd be less likely to guard their tongues around him if they thought he was a fool. One of the men had already talked about "the meetin' tonight," before he'd had the sense to shut his damn fool mouth. Juba figured they'd keep making mistakes like that one.

The same evening, while Juba matriculated in rat-baiting, Kate baited a trap of her own. The day before she'd gone on an exceptionally fruitful walk with the voluble Miss Stephens. Kate wasn't sure whether the lady always talked so much, or if taking care of her brother in a city full of political men left her starved for female companionship. Probably both. While the two ladies strolled Pennsylvania Avenue to the President's house Kate had only to make agreeable sounds and ask the occasional leading question. Kate wore only a shawl over her brown walking dress to keep her warm. In Chicago she would most certainly have required her wool coat.

"You're lucky it's a mild November. As you see," Miss Stephens swept her arm before her, "the President's house has a lovely garden. It's beautiful in summer, though few people walk here."

"Oh?" Kate asked, endeavoring to appear as wide-eyed and dewy as possible.

Miss Stephens stopped walking and pointed south. "You see that area over there? That's the Potomac Flats. And next to it is the city canal. It's a more fetid, mosquito infested area than any national capitol should rightly tolerate."

Kate sniffed, picking up the faint scent of rotting vegetation and sewage on the breeze. She'd heard the city dumped its sewage right into a canal that ran through town. She didn't realize the canal ran right past the president's house.

"And what's that down there?" There was a blocky red brick building sitting smack dab in the middle of Pennsylvania Avenue.

"Oh, that! Mr. Buchanan had that built to house his horses, on account of the fact the President's House doesn't have a stable and he didn't want to use the one at the Willard Hotel. He thinks the Willard is a hotbed of abolitionist radicals, though my own dear brother, a veritable epitome of southern gentlemanliness, makes his home there." Miss Stephens tugged sharply at her shawl, clearly vexed with the topic. "Let me tell you Mrs. Barley, there are plenty of rapscallions you should stay away from. And keep in mind, not all the scoundrels look like scoundrels. A good many of them are congressmen and senators, but men no better than they ought to be."

"Oh, my," Kate said, "Would you mind telling me who? I ask only so I can guard myself against them and of course, to tell my husband to be careful as well."

"Well . . ." Miss Stephens said, "I don't like to gossip."

Kate thought Miss Stephens liked little more than gossip and bless her loquacious heart for it.

"Well, there's Mr. Breckenridge and his cronies."

Kate reared her head back in faux dismay. "The vice president?"

A most unladylike snort emanated from Miss Stevens. "Well, the way he carries on, I don't like to say."

"Carries on?" Kate prompted.

"Well . . . Mr. Breckinridge has never brought Mrs. Breckinridge to town with him. Ever. They say she lives on their farm in Kentucky with all six of their children, while he's here, cavorting with hussies. Do I shock you Mrs. Barley?" Miss Stephens eagerly leaned in to see Kate's face around her bonnet.

Kate tried to looked shocked so as to not let down the eager Miss Stephens. "Well, yes and no. Mr. Barley is good man, but my father was a trial to my dear departed mother."

"Then you know how men can be. And of course you're a married woman, so we may speak frankly. I hope you won't think badly of me Mrs. Barley. I've seen a bit of the world as my brother's care-taker."

Kate nodded and smiled encouragingly. "Who else?"

"Well, I hear Senator Wigfall is the worst of Mr. Breckinridge's set. There's a group of them that carouse in the bar at the National Theater in the evenings. Mr. Wigfall is a Texan you see." Miss Stephens winked conspiratorially at Kate. "You know how they are."

"I'm afraid I don't Miss Stephens. What are Texans like?" Kate needed details, not generalizations about the immorality of Texans.

"They say he shot a man once."

"No! Do tell."

"He's a dueling man. He killed a man, though a jury found him not-guilty, or so I heard." Miss Stephens glanced around guiltily, then continued her gossip. "He once dueled Mr. Brooks. You know, the man who caned Senator Sumner a few years ago. Word is that Mr. Brooks was the better shot and left two bullet holes in Mr. Wigfall. It was after that duel that Mr. Wigfall moved to Texas. And his poor wife. You have no idea.

101

She was his cousin. They say he neglects her terribly, leaving her in Texas while he besports himself with trollops here in Washington City."

Ah, ha! Trollops. Kate smiled to herself. Time to shake out the shiny dresses. Here's hoping Washington's smell wasn't the only rotten thing in the city.

The next afternoon Kate walked up Pennsylvania Avenue to the National Theater. She didn't remember the large light-colored stone building from her childhood. Mama used to like to tell the story about how Kate made her stage debut at the National, standing on a horse at the age of four as it trotted around the theater stage. That theater burned down three years ago, so this building was the theater's second iteration. Kate circled the block to the back of the building and found the stage door propped open.

She stepped into a dim passage-way and took a deep breath. In her experience theaters all smelled pretty much the same, of sweat, grease paint and fractured dreams. "Excuse me," she said to a harried looking man carrying stage lanterns. "I wonder if you could tell me if the manager is in and if so, where he might be found?"

"You looking for a job, girl?" The man didn't wait for her reply. "Mr. Grover is in his office, down the hall, green door at the end." The man pointed down the badly lit hallway.

What luck. Daddy used to talk about Mr. Grover. Maybe he'd remember her. He'd most certainly remember her father. Poppa said the two of them would stay up late talking about politics. It used to drive Momma crazy.

It turned out Mr. Grover did remember Kate.

"You were a sight to see up on that big horse and you so small. Coulda had you onstage every day of the year and filled the house" he'd enthused, while pumping her hand most vigorously. "Audiences love an infantile performer. Your dad with you?"

She had to tell him. She wasn't sure who was more miserable, her for having to tell the story of her parent's death or Mr. Grover for having to hear it. After they'd commiserated Kate changed the topic. "I need your help."

"Anything for the girl on the horse." Mr. Grover stuck his thumbs in his brightly embroidered waist coat, before remembering his manners and gesturing for her to take a seat in front of his cluttered desk.

When they were both settled Kate asked the first of her questions. "Does your bar still serve a dual purpose?"

"I guess you could say it does. The Gentlemen's Lounge, as we call it, is considerably grander than the one in the old building, but it operates on the same principles. Respectable ladies and gentlemen visit before performances drinking tea and Madeira, then after the show we break out the hard liquor and the disreputable crowd takes over."

"And ladies of dubious reputation?" Kate arched her right eyebrow at Mr. Grover.

He grinned at her. "Always. Some actresses, some fallen ladies looking for benefactors. You know how it is."

Kate did. She told him her plan.

Later that evening she re-appeared at Mr. Grover's office door, this time wearing her tightest, shiniest dress. Emerald green satin, trimmed in ivory, set off her pale skin and auburn hair. Bands of ruching crisscrossed the bodice, drawing attention to her bosom, while her arms were bared to her

103

shoulders. The sort of gentlemen who hung around theaters after performances would recognize the message in the dress.

"You look just right," Mr. Grover said, giving her mock up and down leer. "Though I'm sure your parents would strangle me for cooperating with your scheme."

"My dear departed Momma taught me a few tricks for fending off amorous gentlemen." She grinned wickedly.

"Fine," he said, holding his hands in the air in mock surrender. "Let's get you introduced to impolite society. Remember, you're Joseph Jefferson's niece. He's a good friend and he'll cover for you if asked, which he won't be. He's sailing for Australia after the holidays. Says he's going to take his Rip Van Winkle act around the world."

"I'm impressed," Kate said, turning to leave Grover's office. "They say Jefferson's a comic genius."

"He is. He made a real splash here this past summer. And if we say you're his niece people will believe you're an actress."

Kate followed Mr. Grover through the theater. Gleaming gaslight chandeliers dripped with gaily colored crystals, competing with softly shining gold wall paper and richly appointed theater chairs. She tried to keep her mouth shut as she took it all in.

"The Lounge is on your right," Mr. Grover gestured in that direction once they'd passed through the main theater and out into the lobby. He tucked his hand into the crook of her elbow and walked her to the darkened side room. The smell of cigar smoke greeted her. Gas lamps, turned low, illuminated the dark paneled walls and arched ceilings. Provocatively dressed ladies seated at small, candle lit tables, dotted the room, some alone and others in the company of men. The smell of cheap perfume almost overwhelmed the reek of cigars.

Mr. Grover approached a large, darkly bearded man standing at the bar. In one hand he held a glass of something amber, while in the other hand he clutched a brass knobbed walking stick. A gleaming beaver top hat and leather gloves stood on the bar near his elbow.

"Senator Wigfall, how are you this evening?" Mr. Grover asked with a deferential bow.

"I'm in fine fettle Mr. Grover." Wigfall's voice boomed out over the bar. Several men glanced over and hurriedly looked away. "Who's the pretty lady?" he asked, looking Kate up and down.

Kate felt like a calf at auction. She reminded herself it was just the effect she'd intended.

"Senator, I'm pleased to introduce you to Miss Fanny Jefferson, niece to the great Joseph Jefferson and fine little actress in her own right. She'll be on stage here at the National next week."

Kate dipped a curtsy and then looked boldly into the senator's eyes. "I've been just dyin' to meet you Sir," she said, using her most honeyed accent.

"You were, huh?" he asked, allowing time for his eyes to make another circuit of Kate's body.

Oh, he's a smooth one. "Why yes sir. My Daddy admires you so. For your firmness on the slavery question. I can't wait to tell him I met you." At this Kate snapped open her fan and fluttered it at chest level, just in case he'd somehow missed that area. The senator looked down, caught in the fascination of her bosoms, which were gently heaving.

He shook himself back to awareness. "Where you from little lady? Do I detect a little Louisiana in your inflection?"

"Why aren't you a clever one?" She smiled brightly and tapped him with her fan. Years ago Hattie taught Kate the particulars of a New Orleans accent. "I'm from just outside Baton Rouge," she drawled and took a particularly deep breath, which caused yet more bosom heaving.

"I just knew it. Pretty woman like you had to be Southern." Wigfall gestured to an open chair. "Could I buy you a drink Miss Jefferson?"

Mr. Grover discreetly withdrew from the bar, leaving Kate alone with her prey. She ignored the chair the senator pulled out for her and leaned in closer to him. "I'd love to have a drink with such a handsome gentleman," she said, brushing her bosom along his coat sleeve as she did. The bosom thing generally made gentleman take notice. It most certainly did this time.

Chapter 9

December 1-4, 1860
Washington City

Saturday morning Kate made her way to Franklin Square. The five block walk from the Kirkwood House gave her time to clear her head, which was a little foggy after yet another late night with Senator Wigfall.

As she walked she made her way around at least a dozen pigs. Most cities had some pigs around to clean up the garbage and the dead things that ended up on city streets, but Washington City seemed to excel in porcine excess. They came in an impressive array of colors and sizes, from spotted to striped, smallish piglets to massive, bristling boars. Kate wondered what kept the city's poor from turning them into dinner. *Maybe they do. How else would the city keep the pig population under control?*

Kate found herself surprised at Washington's size, or lack thereof. The capitol had streets laid out for thousands of houses and businesses and that didn't come close to filling the space. Miss Stephens told Kate the city, which lie in a low lying swamp, was nigh unto unbearable in the summer months. Between the stench coming from city's swamps and canals, and the mosquitos and flies that sprang from such places, everyone who could afford to leave the city did each June and returned in the fall.

Kate suspected the bugs couldn't be more annoying than the politicians. The Senator and his cronies seemed to have an inexhaustible desire to talk about themselves and the perils of abolition and Lincoln. Wigfall lubricated his monologues with endless glasses of brandy, needing only the occasional noise from Kate to reassure him she was paying rapt attention. She poured most of her own drinks into a bedraggled potted palm near the bar, a task made easier by the fact that his eye often strayed across the room, as if he were making sure no one more interesting than himself had come in. As midnight tolled on the bar clock, Kate fanaticized about pulling her little pepper box derringer out from under her dress and shooting the old boy in the eye. Twice. Or Three times. Whatever it took to shut the self-important bastard up.

The good news was that the big Texan was so inflated with his own self-importance that he'd never stopped to wonder what Fanny Jefferson wanted from him. Or maybe Senators were used to being approached by ladies of dubious reputation, eager to make a powerful man's acquaintance. Kate wondered if those ladies also yearned for the derringer remedy or if Washington women became inoculated against puffery and bombast.

Still musing on shooting senators, she arrived at the park and waved discreetly at Juba, who was sitting on a bench. Franklin Square was not one of the city's better known parks, nor one its better tended. Unlike Lafayette Square, with its carefully manicured grounds, circular walkways and imposing statuary, poor Franklin Park appeared to be little better than an empty lot.

Kate approached Juba's bench in the middle of the park. "I can see why you picked this place for our meetings. There's not much chance any one of importance will stop by. Or anyone at all."

"Exactly. I like the veil. Nice touch." He patted the bench.

Kate took a seat at the far end of the bench. "I thought if I was heavily veiled and gloved no one would know if I was a white lady or a colored lady and there wouldn't be any trouble. You look tired." Kate didn't add that he was also grubby and smelled of manure.

"Been mucking out stalls already this morning." Juba smiled wryly at Kate.

"Sounds like we've both been doing things that make us feel awful. I've met the most horrid man and I think he's going to tell me exactly what we need to know."

Juba pressed his lips together and nodded. "I've met some good men and some bad men—hows about you tell your story first, then I'll tell you mine." He scanned the park, keeping an eye out for anyone taking an interest in their bench.

Kate launched into her story of how she'd met Miss Stephens. Juba whistled at the Stephens name.

"That's a mighty big fish Missy, mighty big." In the middle of Kate's story a man walked into the park and sat on a nearby bench. "Better keep our voices down," he said, jerking his head toward their neighbor.

"I see him," she said in a low tone. "I think he's just feeding squirrels." Kate kept watch on the man while she explained how Miss Stephens tipped her to some of the radical's predilection for morally dubious company. After that she told him about her meeting with Mr. Grover.

The man at the nearby bench crumpled his bag of peanuts and stood.

Kate watched him until he turned and walked away. "The senator's a bully. Also, he thinks he's smarter than he is. And he's arrogant about it. At one point he told me how nice it was to spend time with a woman who knew her place." Kate clenched her jaw and huffed out a breath of dissatisfied air.

Juba raised his eyebrows at this. "Did you slip a knife between his ribs?"

"I wanted to shoot him. He reminds me of a circus bear, all lumbering and hairy, though without a bear's charm."

"Keep in mind he's probably a lot like a circus bear. What I remember about them is that they seemed kinda funny and harmless doin' their tricks, but if you don't watch them they'd just as soon take a swipe at you and eat your innards for lunch."

Kate heaved a sigh. "Probably. But this morning I'm just so disgusted with myself. I get tired of *acting* stupid for men who *are* stupid." A lady pushing a baby carriage entered the park.

Juba told Kate his story about the rat baiting ring. "Just last night they talked again about this meeting they've got coming up— called themselves the Knights— said they were meeting at a boarding house owned by one of the fellow's mother. Mrs. Surratt, if she has the same name as her son."

"Knights," Kate repeated in a low, urgent voice. "They must be Knights of the Golden Circle."

Juba nodded.

Kate knew enough to know the Knights of the Golden Circle were pro-slavery fanatics who wanted the annexation of Mexico, Central American and even the Caribbean, making a so-called 'golden circle,' of slave territory for the United States. Lately the Knights seemed to have changed their focus from the expansion of slavery to secession.

Juba rubbed his hands together in an effort to warm up. "I've got to be getting back to work, but I'm thinking we need someone in that boarding house and it's got to be you." He handed her a folded newspaper and pointed to a small circled item. "I found this. Mrs. Surratt's looking for a boarder."

Kate took the paper from him and tapped it with a finger. "This makes sense. Fanny wouldn't be able to afford the Kirkwood, not seeing as how her family has fallen on hard times and forced her before the lime lights. I'll ask Wigfall if he's heard anything about the Surratt boarding house. I can show him this." Kate gave the newspaper a little shake.

"Sounds good."

Juba and Kate walked east, down North I street to 7th, where they turned south for a block to H Street. Little birds rustled around in the leafless trees, calling out to each other in anxious little birdy voices. Juba nodded at a passing horse drawn omnibus. "You seen those down on Pennsylvania?"

Kate nodded. "They're hard to miss. I was going to pay my 12 pennies this morning, but I thought the walk would do me some good."

Juba smiled and waved his hand down the street. "Well, this here is the Seventh Street extension, and Mrs. Surratt's boarding house is just one street over, on Sixth." Juba pointed east.

Kate checked the traffic and stepped out into the street. "It occurs to me that if I had a reason to go to the stable we could meet there. Instead of out in the open like this." They crossed the street and walked on.

Juba snorted. "Sure it would be safer than a park, even an empty park, but what reason would an actress to have to frequent a stable?"

Kate cocked an eyebrow at Juba.

"No." He said, raising his voice and shaking his head. Remembering they were on a public street he said again, this time more quietly and more firmly, "Absolutely not. There's something like fourteen reasons why it's a bad idea. And don't give me that look."

Her eyebrows were up, eyes wide, in a parody of innocence. "What look?" she asked innocently. "The way I figure it—if Fanny's family has fallen on hard times, then they used to have good times, right? She'd have a horse."

"A horse maybe. But Excelsior's a damn wonder horse."

Kate laughed. "But no one knows that about him. I promise I won't ask him to solve math problems for anyone."

Juba stopped on the corner and turned toward Kate. "What kind of man would give his daughter a big Kentucky stallion? The senator will never believe you." He shook his head again.

A little vertical furrow appeared between Kate's eyes. "For goodness sake Juba. I'm a pretty woman. If I tell a man that big horse is mine, a gift from my imaginary indulgent Papa, they'll just be intrigued. No one is going to see him and think 'wow, that horse obviously belongs to a spy.'"

Juba's mouth turned down in a frown while he thought about it for a moment. "Fine."

"Oh, goody," Kate said, clapping her hands together. "I'll send Mrs. Barrow a telegram."

Juba scrubbed his face before looking at Kate with only the slightest of eye rolls. "Might as well send Mr. Pinkerton a telegram too. Maybe you can get the blasted horse on the pay roll."

That night Kate broached the subject of Mrs. Surratt's rooming house with the Senator. He was only too eager to get her out of the respectable Kirkwood House and into a boarding house.

"Mrs. Surratt goes to bed early I hear," he said, running his forefinger down her arm with an accompanying expression that could only be described as lascivious.

It was all Kate could do not to reach for her little pistol and shoot him.

The next morning after breakfast Kate knocked on the door of a narrow, three story house. The narrow front stairs, tiny front stoop and shuttered windows gave the place the look of a sly, slumbering animal. A girl in an apron stained with what looked like furnisher polish opened the door.

"I'm here about the room. Senator Wigfall sent me," Kate told the girl, careful to keep her voice soft and undemanding. "Is the proprietress home?"

The house maid led Kate thru a narrow and dark hall into a surprisingly roomy front parlor. Maroon draperies on the two front windows complimented the maroon and green carpet, while ivory striped wallpaper kept the space from being overly dark. A fireplace on the far wall crackled and popped merrily.

"Can I help you miss?" asked a soft female voice.

Kate jumped a little and hurriedly turned around. A middle-aged lady stood in the parlor doorway. She wore a dark grey dress, belted in black, with plain white collar and cuffs.

Kate had seen Quaker women dressed similarly. The lady had a serene look on her face, like the Madonna paintings she'd seen in Catholic churches.

"Oh, yes," Kate said, using her breathless, wide-eyed manner. "I'm hoping you are Mrs. Surratt and that you have a room to let."

Kate made a quick decision. This didn't look like the sort of lady who would tolerate a lady of dubious reputation under her roof. "I'm having ever such a terrible time finding a respectable boarding house I can afford. I'm an actress you see, but I'm a good girl Ma'am, I assure you. My family fell on hard times and I have to support myself you see. Our slaves ran away, the ungrateful wretches, and those Yankees don't seem to think my poor Papa deserved to get them back. And he couldn't afford any more, and with only old John to help him with the harvest." Kate trailed off and wrung her handkerchief. She brightened, as if remembering something. "Senator Wigfall recommended you to me. He's such a gentleman. Don't you agree?"

"I do, dear," Mrs. Surratt said dryly, as if she believed no such thing. The lady paused and motioned Kate to take a seat. "I am Mrs. Surratt dear. I had a note from the senator this morning. May I assume you are Miss Fanny Jefferson?"

"Yes I am Ma'am. It's nice to meet you Mrs. Surratt," Kate said, bobbing her head. Mrs. Surratt cast a keen eye over Kate, making her glad she'd worn her sturdy grey wool walking dress. "My uncle is an actor, which is how I got the idea to take up acting. I'm staying at the Kirkwood right now, but I plan on sending some of my wages home to Papa, so I have to be careful with my money. The senator said your rooming house would cost me less than a hotel."

Mrs. Surratt nodded in approval. "I'm in charge here and I run a respectable house. No gentlemen callers, leastways not outside this room. Not even the Senator. I mean it young lady. I hear actresses get up to all sorts of shenanigans."

"Oh, goodness me," Kate gasped. "You wouldn't believe what I've seen since I started at the theater. But I'm not like that Ma'am." Kate figured the lady couldn't be all that proper if she accepted the idea of a married senator making calls on an actress in her front parlor, but it was best to play along with her facade of gentility.

"You'll want to see the room." Mrs. Surratt stood abruptly and walked out of the parlor. Kate scurried after her. Mrs. Surratt turned left, into hallway, which seemed to swallow light and spit back darkness. Lifting her skirts she started up a narrow set of stairs. Kate followed her, feeling like she was walking into a great beast's mouth. The lady of the house opened a door at the head of the stairs and stepped inside. Kate stood in the doorway, oddly reluctant to go further.

"This used to be my son John's room, but he's moved back to the farm. As you can see," she said sweeping her arm toward the far wall, "it has a coal fireplace. I charge $1.25 a week for the room and board. You get breakfast and supper."

Kate looked into the room. Two windows looked out on the side street. The low winter sunshine streamed in, making the room a refuge from the hall. "This will do just fine Ma'am."

The lady nodded. "My son Isaac lives on the third floor. He's in and out at all hours. Two other young men live upstairs as well. Several gentlemen have the rooms in the attic. I try to keep a quiet house, but sometimes the men are noisy."

Kate assured her new landlady that she could tolerate a little noise and the two made their way back to the parlor.

"My room is through there," Mrs. Surratt gestured toward the door at the back of the parlor, "so I hear everything." She half-glared at Kate under lowered brows. "You understand?"

Kate nodded, though privately she thought she understood very little about what was going on in this house. But soon enough she would.

Kate won a small role in the theater's current production, *The Seven Sisters*.

Mr. Grove looked shame faced when he told her about it. "This play is filling Laura Keene's Metropolitan Theater every night. New York critics think it's rubbish and they're quite right, but people want to see it and these days I'll produce anything that sells tickets."

As they rehearsed Kate discovered why critics hated the play and audiences loved it. She was one of seven actresses on stage in dresses cut shockingly low in the bosom and high on the calf. They were supposed to be Satan's seven daughters, which apparently gave them license to sing naughty songs and besport themselves in a variety of suggestive poses. What the play lacked in premise and plot, it made up for in song and dance numbers.

Kate's entrance to the Gentlemen's lounge that evening after the performance caused several masculine heads to turn, including Senator Wigfall's.

"There you are my dear. Bring your lovely self over here. I'll introduce you to some of your admirers," he hollered across the room.

Classy. Kate's hand unconsciously moving toward the gun strapped to her thigh. *What lady doesn't want to be hollered at across a bar room?*

She pasted a smile on her face and approached her target. "Senator Wigfall, I do declare, you get more handsome every day. Thank you for the flowers. They are divine," she trilled at him, laying her hand on his arm as she did.

"Fanny, my girl, the blooms are not nearly as beautiful as you. May I introduce you to Mr. John Floyd." Wigfall gestured to a tall gentleman with a high forehead and sharp cheekbones. With a little flourish with his wrist he added, "And John Breckinridge, Vice President of these United States."

The latter gentleman's silvery eyes gravely appraised Kate. He was tall, tall enough that she had to crane her head up to look at him and pale, like he never went outside. He looked a little like a disappointed ghost.

"Goodness me. Two," Kate corrected herself, smiling brightly at Wigfall, "Three eminently distinguished gentlemen. And all of you so handsome. It's simply too much for a lady's constitution." She snapped her fan open and waved air around her bosoms again. Just for fun she threw in some eye batting so her breasts wouldn't have to do all the work. The three men grinned at her like demented children. Apparently the more powerful the man, the more susceptible he was to base flattery and cleavage.

"A Vice President," she said, nodding to Breckinridge, "and the Secretary of War, no less. Senator, you do keep august company." She fluttered her fan all the harder, allowing her bosoms to express her girlish awe.

After further drinks were disbursed, talk turned to business.

117

Wigfall opened the conversation. "Gentlemen, we can speak in front of Miss Jefferson. She's one of us. Right little lady?"

"Oh, my goodness me, I surely am. My darling Papa, well he just about killed himself working the farm after our ungrateful slaves ran off. Those Yankee abolitionists! They put ideas in our poor nigrahs heads. It makes me so mad." Just for fun she stamped one of her feet.

The three men chuckled indulgently. "Poor darling," Mr. Breckinridge consoled her. "Louis here told us your sad story. That such a thing would happen to the very flower of southern womanhood," he shook his head regretfully, "well it helps a man to know he's doing the right thing."

The senator patted Kate on the shoulder. "Fanny, you just wait and see. I'm going to put a scare in that rascal who thinks he's going to be the next president." Wigfall's eyes narrowed as looked at the two men, who lifted their glasses to him.

For the rest of the evening Kate sipped Madeira and took it all in.

Three days later Kate again walked over to Franklin Square. She sat on a the same bench and waited for Juba, turning her face up to the sunshine as she did. Between the theater and Wigfall and the boarding house and the Surratt crowd, Kate felt like she hadn't had a moment to breathe since she arrived in Washington. The city had more discontent and tension in it than it had pigs.

"You look relaxed," Juba said, startling Kate from her reverie.

She smiled up at him. "I'm practicing holding my temper." She shook the newspaper she was holding at Juba. "Did you see this?" She shook the paper again for emphasis.

"No I didn't. Hardly seemed like a good idea for the stable boy to be seen reading. Hows about you take a deep breath and tell me what's got you so worked up." Juba sat down at the far end of the bench from Kate.

"Oh, I'm sorry. It's just that I thought President Buchanan was a more moderate and fair man than Senator Wigfall and the Vice President. Then last night they came straight from the Senate Chamber, where a clerk read Mr. Buchanan's last State of the Union address. They were all terribly excited. It seems Mr. Buchanan's taken a stand in sympathy with secession. Here, look at what I've circled," Kate thrust the newspaper beneath Juba's nose.

He took the paper and read aloud from it. "The long-continued and intemperate interference of the Northern people with the question of slavery in the Southern States has at length produced its natural effects. The different Sections of the Union are now arrayed against each other" Juba lowered the paper and squinted at Kate. "Well, that's true isn't it? That we're arrayed against each other?"

"Intemperate interference? By us? Most northerners don't care about slaves one way or another, but they sure don't want to have to compete with slave labor. Regular people are just protecting themselves. But that's not the worst of it. President Buchanan essentially gave southern states permission to secede and go to war." Kate snatched the paper from Juba's hands and read from it. "The Slave States, having first used all peaceful and constitutional means to obtain redress, would be justified in revolutionary resistance to the Government of the Union."

"Well," Juba drawled, "that's one way of looking at it."

Kate whacked the bench with the newspaper. "Oh, don't pretend you don't care. Something awful is brewing."

"I agree. The fellows running the rat-baiting ring at the stable seem mighty pleased with themselves. And they're over-confident. They say too much in front of me. We need to fig-ure out if the ratter types are connected to your fancy gents. Is there some kind of conspiracy afoot or just a whole lot of upset secessionists?"

Kate took a deep breath. "I don't know if I'm over-reacting or not, but two things. First, Mrs. Surratt seems to have a more than passing acquaintance with Senator Wigfall, so there might be a connection. And second, last night Wigfall said something odd. Breckinridge was there, so was Floyd and a couple of others, and they all seemed to know what he was talking about. And after he said it the Vice President changed the subject right fast."

"What?" Juba sat forward.

"Well, Wigfall was bragging like he does, saying how he liked Mr. Buchanan all the more for his speech and that he regretted what was going to happen to him. And then he said somebody would be president, but it wouldn't be Mr. Lin-coln." Kate worried her lower lip with her teeth. "I think Misters Wigfall, Breckinridge and Floyd have hatched some kind of plan to replace Mr. Lincoln with one of the slavery men."

Juba reared back his head and scrubbed at his face with his hands. "How do they figure to do that with Mr. Lincoln law-fully elected and all? And don't forget, Mr. Lincoln's vice president, Mr. Hamlin—if they get rid of Mr. Lincoln they end up with him and he's no friend to slavery either. It makes no sense." Juba rubbed his hands over his face.

"I know. That's what we need to figure out. And quick," Kate said. "Before something happens to Mr. Lincoln. Or worse, before there's war."

Chapter 10

December 5-11, 1860
Washington City

Aknock came at Kate's bedroom door. "Miss Fanny," Mary Surratt called through the door, "the Western Union boy brought a telegram for you."

"Oh, my, how exciting," Kate twittered through the door. Kate had to take particular care to 'be' Fanny at the boarding house. She didn't think Mrs. Surratt would overlook a gaffe.

She also suspected that Mrs. Surratt was the brains behind the Knights of the Golden Circle meetings. What little Kate managed to over-hear so far confirmed her suspicions. Mrs. Surratt had been careful to close the parlor's sliding doors when the Knights met. Unfortunately the boarding house was solidly built and had thick wooden doors that muffled voices. One afternoon Mrs. Surratt opened the parlor door and almost caught Kate, who escaped suspicion only because she was dressed to leave the house. Kate pretended she'd been about to knock on the door to tell her landlady she would be back later than usual. Mrs. Surratt seemed to believe her, but she kept a close eye on Kate after that nonetheless.

Mrs. Surratt handed Kate a slip of paper. Kate looked at it, and then up at Mrs. Surratt. "Oh, Mrs. Surratt, isn't it exciting? My Papa is sending my horse on the train so I don't have to ride those awful omnibuses anymore. And if I pay to feed and board my own horse then Papa doesn't have to feed him," Kate said in as empty-headed manner as she could manage. "He's coming in on the train today, at noon. The horse I mean. Not Papa of course! That would be silly, wouldn't it? Well, I guess it wouldn't be silly for Papa to ride the train. What I meant was . . .."

Mrs. Surratt interrupted Kate's flow of nonsense. "That's fine dear. Do you have a livery stable in mind?"

"Oh, yes. Isaac has been most helpful. He told me you keep your horses at a stable just two blocks from here." After Mrs. Surratt left the room Kate felt only a little bit ashamed of herself.

Noon found Kate on the B&O Railroad Station platform just as a prodigiously large steam locomotive chugged into the station, its engines belching dirty cinders into the air. Standing on her tiptoes and leaning forward, she peered down the track. She wondered . . . how did one go about collecting a horse from a train?

"Excuse me," she said, raising her voice against the roar of the steam engine and grabbing the arm of a friendly looking porter just stepping off the train. "Could you tell me how I find my horse? He should be on this train."

"That big white charger is yours? Miss, we all been visiting with him every time the train stops. Never seen such a pretty piece of horse flesh in my life. Gentle as a puppy too."

Kate beamed from ear to ear and nodded her head. "That sounds like Excelsior." She'd thought about giving him a secret identity, seeing as how he'd once been a pretty famous circus horse, but people might notice if he didn't answer to his

124

name. If anyone asked she'd just say she'd named him after the famous horse.

The porter gestured down the track. "Go down about six cars, see that first freight car? The one with the slatted sides?"

Kate nodded.

"Your high stepper be in there—they'll bring him off soon as they get a ramp set." The man hurried off before Kate could thank him. She walked down to the first freight car. "That you Celly?" she called out. A high pitched neigh rang through the air. "Just hold on now boy." Excelsior stamped his feet in impatience. She felt like joining him.

Once her horse was off the train Kate gave him a thorough going over, taking particular care with his legs. Excelsior hadn't changed much in the years since her parents died. Like most true white horses he had blue eyes. At 17 hands, he was a tall horse, really too big for someone Kate's size, but he was such an easy goer that his size didn't matter all that much. Mr. Rice bought Excalibur thirteen years ago as a three-year old and taught him to jump rope, walk up and down steps, shoot a gun and stand still on a platform while ten strong men lifted it and carried it around the ring. Kate thought that Mr. Rice was pretty foolish to retire Excelsior in favor of Lallah Rookh, but circus elephants were all the rage these days.

Finding his legs cool and his eyes clear, she stood and took his lead. "Come on boy, let's go see Uncle Juba and get you settled." The horse nickered his approval and followed Kate up the street.

When they came to the stable she turned to him. "Now let's make a good impression Celly." He nodded his big head so vigorously his forelock flew into his dark blue eyes. Kate gave his halter an affectionate tug and they stepped inside the low roofed stable building. The comforting smells of fresh hay and horse manure greeted her. A bay horse stuck its head out of his box stall and whinnied. She breathed out a sigh. There was nothing more comforting than a well-tended stable full of contented horses.

Juba was standing outside a box stall when Kate appeared in the wide stable doorway. "You there, boy," she called, using her most supercilious tone. "Where's your master?"

"He in 'da back, Miss. Let me show you," Juba said, scraping a small bow together and gesturing to the back office. Kate followed him down the aisle and stepped into the office just in front of him.

Juba closed the door behind them and introduced her to Mr. Howard.

Before Kate left to go to the theater she had one last talk with Excelsior. "I'll be back soon," she whispered into his neck. "You be ready for whatever comes next."

Monday afternoon Mrs. Surratt knocked on Kate's door to tell her the Senator was waiting in the front parlor. Kate checked her hair in the little oval mirror over her chest of drawers and went down stairs.

"A vision of loveliness, as always," the Senator said in his usual booming voice. He gestured to the other half of the settee where he had been sitting. "Sit down my darling. I need a brief word with you."

Mrs. Surratt followed Kate into the parlor, commandeered a corner chair next to the stove and took up her knitting. Apparently she intended to chaperone them.

Kate appraised the cramped settee and chose a small, armless chair instead. She folded her hands demurely in her lap and fluttered her eyelashes. "It's awfully nice to see you Senator. I mean, outside of the theater. What brings you here?"

"Darling, I won't be able to see you until Friday. I'm making an important speech Wednesday and it'll take some work to get just right. I'd like it if you came to see me give it. Ladies often sit in the senate gallery. But I know you have a performance that evening, so you must look for reports of my speech in the newspapers. I expect it to make quite a splash. I can't see you Thursday either. I have an important meeting scheduled the same time as the play."

At this last Louis's gaze shifted to Mrs. Surratt, whose softly clicking needles briefly stuttered before resuming their work.

Kate leaned over and patted the senator's knee, mostly to disguise the fact that she'd noticed the little exchange. "I *will* miss you but you must do your important work." Kate simpered and batted her eyes a tiny bit. She found that no amount of female foolishness deterred the senator.

Wigfall rubbed his hands together, obviously pleased. "Good, good. Shall I see you in the lounge after the performance on Friday night?"

Kate assured him he would. *Interesting. He wants me out of the way.* Kate started putting two and two together. Any way she did the math it added up to trouble.

Chapter 11

Senator Louis T. Wigfall sprawled in his favorite green leather armchair. His senate office had a number of fancy chairs but most of them were more for show than comfort. He made visitors sit in a particularly stiff and thinly upholstered side chair. It encouraged them to keep their stay short.

Though it wasn't quite noon, the senator had a drink in his hand. Whiskey, made in Texas, drunk neat. He sipped and thought about his speech. He was going to put those Yankee bastards on notice. What they didn't understand was that slavery was part of God's design. The Bible said so, right there in Ephesians 6:5. "Slaves obey your earthly masters with fear and trembling." Negroes were the sons of Ham. That wasn't anyone's fault. It just was. The scientists said slavery was natural too. They'd studied negro brains and negro bodies and everyone agreed they were just naturally inferior. It wasn't their fault, just God's design. Hell, even the United States Supreme Court agreed. How had Chief Justice Taney put it? 'The negro has no rights the white man is bound to respect.'

Why, it sounded a little harsh when you put it like that, but damn it, reality could be hard.

Did these abolitionist rascals want to go against God? And what did they think would happen if all the slaves were freed? Did they expect to invite one for dinner or, God forbid, marry one of their daughters? Not likely. At least slave owners took care of their slaves, fed them, housed them, and called the doctor. Not like all those poor devils working in factories in the North. Louis had seen the slums in New York. Damned awful they were. How did northerners live with that and still act all sanctimonious about slaves? Damned if he knew. Hypocrites, that's what they were, every last one of 'em.

He put his half-empty drink on the side table and leaned back in his chair to think about his speech. He'd tell them they were wrong about the Constitution. It did allow for slavery. Of course it did. Damned fools. We ought to outlaw abolitionists, not slavery. Make their damned newspapers illegal and their foolish speeches. He'd say southerners would stop all talk of secession if, and only if, they support an amendment to the constitution that makes slavery legal throughout the country. Of course the sanctimonious bastards will say no, but then they'd have only themselves to blame for what happened next.

He'd give his speech today and tomorrow night he'd take the Vice President to the Knights meeting and explain the plan to everyone. It was a daring and brilliant stratagem and the Knights would be only too eager to throw in with men who would save the nation rather than see it destroyed by slack-brained, liberal poppycock.

He picked up his drink and refilled it from the decanter that sat on the table. After today people would no longer dismiss him as a crazy man. He knew what people said about him. That he was dangerously violent. That he was a whore-monger. So he liked the company of pretty women. Nothin' wrong with that. Any man with sense knew women were dangerous things to fool with. A woman ruined the first man and a woman would ruin the last one too.

At least Fanny was sweet with him. Like a wife should be. He wondered what it would be like to have a little house with Fanny. Fanny didn't think he was a ne'er-do-well, that much was for sure. Not like Charlotte.

He'd married Charlotte as a kind of business deal. He'd run up some debts, like a young fellow will do when he's sportin' and drinking'. And then no one would hire him for lawyering, not after the damned Brooks family made him a pariah. So he married Charlotte for her inheritance. Things got worse after he spent all that money, some of it on the baby. He'd been forced to leave Carolina, which made Charlotte plenty mad. But Texas turned out pretty good for him, he had to admit. Except for the wife, of course. She hated Texas.

Little Fanny was another matter all together. Louis took a sip of his long-forgotten whiskey and sighed with anticipation. None too bright and fallen to boot. That meant she couldn't get all high and mighty with him. Knew her place, did that girl. That's what he liked about her. That and the way she filled out her bodice. Nothing like young tits, that was for sure. He couldn't wait to get his hands on them. Soon, very soon.

As to the dueling, he'd only ever shot two men . . . well, maybe three. And anyone paying attention could see they all needed shooting. No one ever remembered that he'd taken some bullets himself. His own brother Hamden died on the dueling ground. What could be more honorable? They'd buried him next to dear Momma. Now they were both moldering in their graves, leaving Louis all alone.

Louis's mind drifted back twenty years ago to when he'd met that rascally Preston Brooks on the dueling ground. What kind of man sent his son to do his fightin' for him? Damn Brooks family. They thought they were the kings of Edgefield South Carolina, controlling the land, public offices and then even the church.

A Southern Gentleman did not refuse a duel and expect to be considered a gentleman. Louis met every challenge that had ever been tendered him. And when old man Brooks refused his duel he as good as told everyone that Louis Trevant Wigfall was not his equal. So what had he done? He'd marched himself down the courthouse and right there on the public notice board he'd posted the dueling rules from Wilson's Code of Honor. Next to it he'd pinned a public letter calling old Brooks a scoundrel and a coward. And then he'd stood there, literally standing by his word. Like a gentleman and man of honor by damned. A couple of Brooks' toadies came by and tried to tear his letter. Ha! He'd shot them both and killed the young one. And they'd called him a murderer. Everyone knew it wasn't murder for a man to defend his honor. No court in South Carolina would say otherwise. Nor in Texas. Texans understood the importance of a man's honor, that was for damned sure.

And had any of that smoked out old Whitfield Brooks? No, it had not. The rapscallion sent his son Preston to meet him on the dueling ground. A wet-behind-the ears pup. They'd fired, each missing their first shots. On their second round he'd hit young Brooks in the hip, but Brooks returned fire and hit him in the leg. A little too high on the leg. Wigfall shifted uncomfortably in his chair. One hand drifted towards his lap, protecting his manly region. And when the damned Brooks family tried to say the affair was settled, he'd corrected them right quick and offered the old man yet another chance to settle the matter on the field of honor.

He liked to think he'd taught young Preston a thing or two about honor and gentlemanly behavior. He must have. The son surely hadn't learned it from his father. When Preston Brooks marched into the Senate chamber four years ago and soundly beat that rascally abolitionist Charles Sumner with his walking stick, young Brooks had been acting on the example Louis Trevant Wigfall had set for him. But did anyone give Louis credit for caning the abolitionist bastard? No! Young Brooks became a hero. That damn Brooks family. If they rolled in shit people would say they smelled like perfume.

Louis stood up, grabbed his favorite beaver hat and brass topped walking stick. He stumbled a little and then steadied himself. It was time to take the short walk to the Senate chamber. He studied his image in the mirror he kept by the door. After today people would think differently about Louis Trevant Wigfall. He left his office, looking forward, not back.

Chapter 12

December 13, 1860
Washington City

Tonight was the night. Tonight she'd figure out what was going on in those meetings at the boarding house. Yesterday she walked into Mr. Grover's office and told him she needed the next evening off.

"Seems fair, darlin'. It's not like I'm paying you anyway. Just tomorrow?" He reached for the calendar he kept on his desk. He made a little notation on it.

"Absolutely. The senator will expect me to be here Friday. I'd hate to let him down." Kate made a little moue of disgust. "Though, I think I should tell you, if tomorrow night doesn't pan out, Fanny may suffer a deadly accident."

Mr. Grover set down his pen and focused on Kate. "That senator really is wearing on you, isn't he?"

Kate snorted. "The fact that the man hasn't yet been found dead in an alley, stripped naked and riddled with bullet holes is a testament to my patience."

Mr. Grover stared at Kate's deadpan face for a moment, then threw his head back and roared with laughter. When he caught his breath he wiped his eyes and said, "I'll put that cute little blond chorus girl in your place."

"I've got an idea for your next spectacle," Kate said, twinkling at Mr. Grover. "*Radical Secessionists: The Musical.* You could get old men to expose their calves in a kick-line. Imagine the songs."

Grover threw back his head and dissolved into laughter. Kate took her cue and left the building.

The next afternoon she went to the stable like she did most days.

As usual Juba pretended not to know her. "You want the shay today, Miss, or put the side-saddle on him?" he asked.

Kate generally alternated between riding Excelsior and having him harnessed to a two wheeled shay. The shay had a folding hood over its single seat, so it was better for wet days, but it was easier for Excelsior if he only had to carry her on his back, him being an elderly gentleman and all.

"Well, that's a good question boy," Kate said, looking down her nose at Juba like she smelled something ripe. "The newspaper says a storm is coming, but not till tomorrow. How about I ride him today because I think he's going to have to pull the gig this weekend. Unless it's really bad— then I'll leave him here and take the omnibus."

"Good thinkin' Miss." Knowing the whole conversation was for show Juba threw a little extra bowing and scraping into it.

Kate hated the sidesaddle. It required a lady sit sideways on a horse, while twisting her torso to face front. Kate, who had grown up under the tutelage of the finest equestrians in the country, thought sidesaddles were foolish and uncomfortable for both rider and horse. Still, she couldn't very well ride through the city streets astride.

Once seated atop Excelsior Kate leaned over, pretending to adjust her stirrup. "Like we said," she whispered, "just at dark."

"Right Miss, there you go," Juba said loudly, knowing she'd understand. "You have a good evening now." He patted Excelsior's silvery rump and the horse moved off.

Kate rode out of the stable and down North G Street, like she was going to the theater. As she passed the city jail Kate gave some thought to where she could pass the time before dark. The air had a distinct chill in it, a harbinger of the coming storm no doubt, so she needed somewhere inside. There was a livery stable down by the National Hotel, but she couldn't take the chance she might be recognized when she was supposed to be at the theater.

Then she remembered the Smithsonian. The "Castle," as locals called it, featured a herbarium with thousands of plants and tropical birds. Miss Stephens waxed rapturous when she described it to Kate. It would be an excellent place to wile away a few hours.

The museum didn't have a formal stable, but there was a shed at the back of the building that housed employee's and visitor's horses. A tall man who looked more like a librarian than a groundskeeper was only too glad to house Excelsior for a few hours. She'd unsaddled him and headed for the museum as a pack of raggedy boys gathered around the big white horse, each competing for his attention.

"They won't do him no harm miss," the older man told her, his down east accent vanishing the r's so that 'harm' became 'hahm." "They're street boys. I let 'em play in the shed when it's cold."

137

Kate turned and looked at the pack of semi-feral children. Every city had them—you learned not to see them or risk breaking your heart.

Three hours later she'd seen all the foliage and birds one woman needed to see and left the Castle. The boys were gone and the man had Excelsior saddled and ready to leave.

"Thought you'd be coming out before dark Miss," the groundskeeper librarian called to her. "I had the boys get him ready for you."

Kate walked over to the man, who laid down his newspaper, stood and cocked his head at her. She gave him a handful of two-cent pieces. "Could you please give these to the young gentlemen when you next see them? With my thanks for taking such good care of my horse."

He pocketed the coins and gently waved his newspaper at her. "Did you hear miss, there's Slave Power senators standing up in the Capitol, bold as brass and speechifying about how hard pressed they are by Mr. Lincoln's election. Threatening secession, they are."

"Men have been talking secession since about fifteen minutes after they signed the Constitution," Kate pointed out.

"Yeah, but not on the floor of the U. S. Senate. Time was that kind of treasonous talk was secret talk, for barrooms and such. Not no more. You hurry yourself home, you hear. This city's not safe no more. Ain't fit for a lady after dark, even if the biggest criminals like to be up at the Capitol tonight." The man cupped his hand for Kate's foot and heaved her up into the saddle.

She leaned down. "We Yankee girls are pretty tough," she said in her real voice. "Here's something for you." Kate pressed a silver half dollar into his hand. "Maybe you could forget you ever saw me?"

"Sure Yankee girl. I'm already wondering what you're doing here. Be gone with you now," he grinned as he said it, then picked up his paper and loped back into the shed.

Kate and Excelsior crossed the bridge across the canal, Kate holding her breath against the swampy reek that rose against the cool night air. He was right. The city felt off somehow, like a low slung, lurking beast slouching toward end times. She clucked Excelsior into a trot, suddenly eager to be anyplace else.

Dark found Juba, Kate and Excelsior in the alley behind Mrs. Surratt's boarding house. The moon was a quarter full, creating enough light that it wasn't pitch black. Somewhere in the distance pigs squealed, fighting over some street delicacy no doubt.

"Quiet," she whispered to Excelsior. She only had to tell him once.

"This going to work?" Juba whispered.

"How else do we find out what's going on in there?" Kate pointed at the Surratt house and then pulled a button hook out of her pocket. She leaned against her horse and went to work on her boots. She nodded at the saddle, already off the horse and sitting on the ground.

Juba shifted the saddle behind the trash bins, where passers by wouldn't abscond with it, or worse, look for the horse that went with it. Juba threw a large, dark wool blanket over Excelsior's back, causing most of him to disappear.

Kate handed her shoes to Juba. She whispered in Excelsior's ear. He bent his left front leg and made a low bow. Kate grabbed a hank of mane and threw herself onto his back.

She leaned down and grabbed the collar of Juba's coat, pulling him close. "I'm not kidding. Any trouble, you whistle and then hot foot it out of here. A white woman on a horse is far less likely to take a beating from the night watch than a black man on foot. And if the Knights catch me, you can't help me."

"Right, I'll run," he whispered back, looking her square in the eye. She knew he was lying and he knew she knew.

She tapped Excelsior with her heels and they approached the house as silently as possible. Kate had briefly considered muffling Excelsior's hooves with feed bags, but doing so would ruin her ability to play innocent if someone caught her.

Mrs. Surratt's front parlor was on the first floor, while the kitchen and dining room were in the basement, but the basement was only half underground. This meant the first floor windows sat fairly high off the ground. The good news was that they were high enough that they created a sense of privacy, prompting less concern of being over-heard for people inside. At least Kate hoped that was the case.

After days of careful observation Kate noted that while Mrs. Surratt kept the parlor's front windows curtained, the curtains on the side windows were generally open, probably because there was no building next to the house on that side. Even better, most nights the window was cracked open a tiny bit on account of the coal fire, which tended to over-heat the room. Tonight, with the parlor packed full of warm bodies the window would surely be open.

The trick was getting access to the open window. She and Excelsior moved slowly over to the side the house and then along it's outside wall until they reached the parlor window. She squeezed with her knees and he stopped. Leaning forward she breathed into his ear, "Freeze." Excelsior wouldn't move again until Kate told him too. She leaned forward, brought her legs up and slowly stood on her horse's wide rump. She leaned her shoulder against the plastered wall and carefully edged forward a few inches. Yep, the window was open. *OK. Stand still and keep quiet. And don't pee yourself.*

She listened for a few moments, allowing the voices to sort themselves out.

The speaker sounded like an unhappy Isaac Surratt.

" . . . don't care how much everyone admires your precious speech. You've given us away."

"Don't be a fool son. If I *hadn't* spoken up people would be much more suspicious. They expect me to . . .."

She'd recognize the senator's voice anywhere. She shifted an inch closer to the window. Either her position markedly improved the acoustics or Wigfall speaking more loudly.

"My speech made it clear we're thinking secession. We want them thinking secession. Nothing else."

"That's right son," an unfamiliar voice said. "The more publicly pro-slavery we are the less likely we are to be suspected when the president disappears."

Was that Mr. Breckinridge?

Then another strange voice. "I still say it's crazy. The president is a good man. He's *our* man, too."

"But Mr. Vice President is also our man. He should have been elected president. That is the *real* crime here, not what we are about to do."

141

Kate recognized Mrs. Surratt's voice.

"I say we quit talking about it and get it done. We're running out of time."

This last speaker had a strong accent. He stopped talking before Kate could place it.

Then Wigfall again. "I agree. Mrs. Surratt, you'll have a wagon standing by, as we planned?

A shadow passed before the window. Kate flattened herself against the wall. *Why was her head so big?*

"Yes. John will be here for Christmas. He'll bring the big wagon with the false bottom. We'll use that to transport the President back to the farm. John's prepared a room in our old carriage house. It's set back from the road. No one will ever know he's there." She sounded grimly resolute.

Before Kate could figure out what they were talking about she heard someone's boots thumped floor, sounding ominously close. She flattened herself against the side of the house and held her breath, fighting the urge to drop down onto Excelsior's back and gallop away.

The window shifted up with a large cracking sound. Kate's heart exploded up into her throat. A cornered rabbit had more cover than she did. She held her breath and pressed her spine against the bricks as hard as she could. Excelsior stood his ground.

"As we planned, Mr. Luckett will supervise the president's capture, with Mr. F. as second in command."

Whoever pushed up the window walked away, boots thumping softly on Mrs. S's wool carpet. Kate relaxed her shoulder and leaned her head near the window crack again. She had to strain to hear over the pounding of her heart.

"Mr. Luckett, I'll introduce you to the president tomorrow. You'll have to convince him to meet with you alone. If you tell him you have fool proof investments to fund his lifestyle after the presidency he *will* want to talk to you. Here's the drops for his drink."

There was a pause. Then the stranger again.

"These days he's as nervous as a cat in a room full of rocking chairs and he's drinking more than usual. Just be sure he doesn't see you fiddling with his drink."

Someone answered, presumably Mr. Luckett. Kate couldn't hear the words. They must have been over by the hallway door.

"Gentlemen, we need this kidnapping to go off without a hitch. If we do this right, a grateful nation will reward you with accolades and riches."

The voices continued while Kate's brain whirled. *Kidnapping? They were going to kidnap Mr. Lincoln?*

"Mr. Breckinridge, prepare yourself to step into the breach and assume the presidency."

"Yes, yes, shock and disbelief," the voice said hurriedly and half dismissively. "Then blame the abolitionists and declare marshal law."

Why would anyone believe abolitionists kidnapped Mr. Lincoln? And why would Mr. Breckinridge take over? Mr. Hamlin was Mr. Lincoln's vice president.

Wigfall spoke again. "We're in agreement then. The president will disappear right after the new year. Chief Justice Taney will be only too glad to go along with a pre-emptive impeachment of that rascal Lincoln before he ever enters the city."

Finally the pieces snapped into place. Kate resisted the impulse to smack herself on the forehead for her foolish blindness.

"Baltimore will be ready if need be."

It was the man with the heavy accent again. It occurred to Kate that he sounded like the Italian trapeze artist that had traveled with Mr. Rice's show back in the early 50s. What part did this Italian play in all this?

"Good," Wigfall continued. "The country will beg the Vice President to make his presidency official. By March fourth you'll be the next president of the United States Mr. Breckinridge. And once we've accomplished that we can convince Mr. Buchanan to corroborate our version of the events and release him. He'll be a national martyr and only too glad of the fame and the fortune that goes along with it."

Congratulatory cries rose on the air, allowing Kate to drop down onto Excelsior's back unheard. *These people are planning a coup. They're going to kidnap Mr. Buchanan. Their own president. And they're going to blame it on Mr. Lincoln.*

Barely able to get her brain around the enormity of what she just heard, Kate gently thumped Excelsior with her heel, signaling him to back up toward the rear of the house. She dropped down onto his back once they'd cleared the window. At the back of the house she turned him and trotted down the alley to where Juba waited.

Wordlessly she held out her hand. He was about to refuse when he looked at her. Whatever he saw convinced him. He let her pull him up behind her. They rode off into the night, to the comparative safety of Mr. Howard's stables.

Kate's body quivered with emotion, though whether it was fear or anger she did not know.

144

Chapter 13

December 14- 21, 1860
Washington City

"I feel like I'm standing on a train track with the engine bearing down on me and I can't move," Kate said. Words of panic and disbelief bubbled in her throat. *Get ahold of yourself Kate. This is no time to succumb to a lady-like fit of the vapors.* She took a deep breath and looked at Juba.

He stared back, dumbfounded. "You sure? Absolutely sure? It was dark and cold. You were scared, maybe you misheard."

She glared at him.

He shook his head abruptly. "You didn't mishear. I'm wishful thinking and there's no time for that now."

They'd put Excelsior away in his stall without a word between them. Only the yellow glow of their lantern and the whispery sounds of horses shuffling in their sleep disturbed the night. In the privacy of Mr. Howard's office Kate told Juba everything.

Once he'd done with disbelief he pushed a pad of paper toward her. "Write it all down, every word," he said, steering her to Mr. Howard's desk. "You write, I'll think."

For the next half hour, to the muted sound of a scratching quill, Juba considered their options. The more he thought, the fewer they had. Finally Kate put the pen down and looked up at him.

He opened and closed his mouth, like a great slow fish caught on a line. Forcing the words out, he said, "I've got two lists in my head: the Bad List and the Good List."

"I think I've got those lists too," Kate responded. She pulled a clean sheet of paper towards her. "Let's make them official, shall we?" She found written lists reassuring. She drew a line down the middle of the paper and wrote on one side. "What's the first thing on my bad list?" Kate asked, using her best 'teacher' voice.

"You and me, I figure."

"Right." She scribbled that down. "A black man and a white woman just uncovered a plot to kidnap the president of the United States and circumvent the results of a legal election. Who's going to listen to us? Add to that, you and I don't know anyone with any real power we can tell." She scribbled some more. "On the other side of the list we can write, 'Allan Pinkerton.' He'll believe us, and someone should believe him."

"And he knows the men with Mr. Lincoln right now. So that's good. But does he know anyone in Buchanan's orbit? Because that's who we really need to convince." Kate re-applied the pen to her list.

"Is that our real problem then? Finding someone who knows Buchanan?"

Juba looked at her. "The question is can Mr. Pinkerton get someone in Lincoln's camp to believe this story and can that someone get Mr. Buchanan to believe it and put a stop to it?"

"Right," Kate said again. "It's a lot we can't control, which I hate. What we really need is some kind of government police force for these sorts of things." Kate looked up from her list. "You know, so we could just hand this off to someone else."

If she were a man, then maybe somebody would pay attention, but a man couldn't have put this information together. It took her and Juba. That was the conundrum really. They uncovered this plot because no one took them seriously and now their hands were tied for the very same reason.

"Katie, as far as I can see, you and me couldn't go to anyone anyway, not without blowing our cover. So it don't matter much who we are. Because even if we stop this kidnapping . . ." Juba faltered.

Kate finished for him. "These people aren't going to quit. They hate Mr. Lincoln too much for that."

It started to rain at dawn, just as she and Juba left for the train depot. Grey drizzle left the hem of Kate's dress heavy with dirty water and cold against her legs. One of them had to go to Chicago and the senator expected Kate that evening. And she couldn't disappear from the boarding house and not raise suspicions. Juba, on the other hand, could be "fired" by Mr. Howard to explain his absence, so he drew the short straw. As she watched Juba's train pull out of the station she thought maybe she'd made a mistake.

The rain, the train whistle, the sight of her friend leaving her, it all made her feel sadly abandoned. She caught herself hoping this all didn't turn out like the fifth act of one of Shakespeare's tragedies, with everyone dead or wretchedly unhappy. In the cold, grey dawn light Kate walked back to the

147

boarding house, doing her best to avoid the puddles. She crept up the back stairs to her room, stripped off her soggy dress and crawled into bed. Outside the rain turned to sleet and rattled against the windows.

When she woke the house was quiet, though she could still hear the storm. The wind howled around the house and rain slashed at the windows. She checked her pocket watch. Half past noon.

She buttoned herself into a clean dress and pulled her heavy coat from a hook on the wall, the one she hadn't worn since she left Chicago. Downstairs, Kate peered into the front parlor. The room was empty and Mrs. Surratt's bedroom door was closed. *It looks just as it did before.* No change marked the room as a site for the planning of dark deeds.

Kate left the boarding house and slogged towards Pennsylvania Avenue, past slushy leaves and fallen tree branches. Excelsior deserved a quiet day in his stall after last night. Plus she felt too blue to deal with her horse. Her steps as leaden as the sky, she made her way to the telegraph office next to the National Hotel. Her job was to send a telegram to Allan alerting him to Juba's arrival.

Even the city's street noise seemed muffled today. Shivering, she thought about that night's performance, both on and off the stage. She didn't generally stay on a case after she'd found what she was after. She'd also never had a case where she was pretending all the time, at work and at home. There was no respite on this assignment. Had she ever been this tired?

She paused outside the theater stage door, squared her shoulders and thought, "Strap 'em on Kate." It was something one of the clowns used to say and she felt a little more cheerful for repeating it in her head.

That evening's performance also lifted her spirits—there was nothing quite so revivifying to a girl's spirits as playing Satan's immoral daughter. In her dressing room after curtain calls, Kate smiled at herself in the mirror as she wiped stage make-up off her face. She suspected the senator had a seduction planned for the evening and she found a certain relief in facing it. She wasn't an old-maidish woman who abhorred the physical realities of the human body. Circus people lived in too close a company for over-much squeamishness about sexual matters and had little tolerance for the prudery of the respectable classes. Kate supposed you could take the girl out of the circus, but you couldn't take the circus out of the girl. Which didn't mean she wouldn't enjoy thwarting the senator's intentions. It would serve the old dog right.

Nonetheless, in her career as a Pinkerton operative she managed to avoid fully acting the fille de joi. She'd found, just as she'd told Allan four years ago, that most men enjoyed the chase as much as the final deed. But, she'd never had a con go on this long. Louis had a reasonable expectation that she would fulfill her implicit erotic promises one day soon.

A knock sounded at her dressing room door only a moment before it opened.

"Darlin', after being away from you for days, I just couldn't wait to see you." He stepped into her cramped dressing room and rocked back on his heels, hands clasped behind his back, grinning at her like a four year old boy or a rabid raccoon. Honestly it was hard to tell which. He probably thought he was charming. He stepped toward her, arms outstretched.

"Senator, what a surprise," she'd trilled at him.

"I have told you time and again, Darlin', call me Louis. No need to stand on ceremony, don't you agree?" He made to take her in his arms. She stepped back. Though she knew they were trashy, Kate read novels of the type where villains "leered" at the heroines. Seeing Wigfall's face just now she had a new understanding of that facial expression. *Ick.*

"Louis, I really must insist you wait outside while I finish my toilette." She gestured toward her mirror, which reflected back a Kate with shiny clean face and a rose satin dress that ended just below her knees.

"But Darlin . . . " He started, before she held up her hand.

Here goes nothing. "I'd remind you sir, that though I am an actress, I am still the daughter of a gentleman. I know the ways of the world sir and I know you can not marry me." She waggled her hand to keep him silent. "Let us have no false words between us. If ever there were two star-crossed lovers they were you and I." *Is he going to swallow this twaddle?* Kate watched Wigfall carefully. It appeared to be working. "If you have any esteem for me whatsoever you will treat me as a lady."

He puffed up his chest and then said, "You mean to say, you want to be courted?"

Kate stepped toward Louis and placed her hand on his chest. "Just so, my darling. Just so. And don't you think, my dear, that my submission will be all the sweeter for its delay? In knowing you better and being assured of your regard, one day I will be able to give myself more fully to you?" For her big finish she batted her eyelashes at him.

He leered some more.

Ick.

Two days later Kate woke with a sore throat and stuffy nose, undoubtedly the product of being up all night and then getting thoroughly soaked in the rain the next morning. By lunch she felt like someone had whacked her upside the head with a big stick and stuffed her nose with old cotton. She made her way downstairs to the dining room for some tea and toast. Mrs. Surratt took one look at her and sent her straight back to her room.

"You must rest, Miss Fanny," she said once she'd tucked Kate back into bed. "I'll look in on you from time to time and have Isaac make sure you have plenty of coal. It's Monday, so the theater is closed, isn't it dear?"

"Yes, ma'am, it is," Kate snuffled.

"Good. I'll just send Isaac down there tomorrow with a message that you're sick. You should spend the next few days in bed or you'll end up with pneumonia." Her landlady bustled around the room, turning down the gas light and briskly hanging up Kate's cloak and bonnet.

"Thank you Mrs. Surratt and if you're worried, I have some money saved. There's three dollars in my top drawer."

"You never mind that now, dear. It's nice to have a woman about the house. And besides, the senator would be quite put out if anything happened to you."

Kate ended up spending almost a week in bed. After the fourth day she felt considerably better, but there really wasn't much to be done until Juba returned anyway, so she succumbed to her landlady's urgings to fully indulge her illness. Mrs. Surratt loaned her Willkie Collins' new book, *The Woman in White*, a cheap melodrama she ended up enjoying quite a bit. She eagerly followed Walter Hartright's efforts to detect the origins of the mysterious lady. She took heart from the fact that Mr. Hartright also found sleuthing difficult.

In the afternoons Mrs. Surratt sat by her bedside, reading the latest installments of Mr. Dickens new book from *Harper's Weekly* (which Kate enjoyed, but not as much as the ever so trashy Collins book). The two women talked a fair bit as well. One afternoon Kate learned that Mrs. Surratt was not, as she'd assumed, a widow woman.

"No dear, my husband is alive and well. I am sad to say that he is a drunkard and a speculator. Through drink and mismanagement he lost the land I inherited from my family. A few years later a slave he mistreated burned down our second farm, ruining us a second time. After that I was done with him. He owns an inn and a tavern at a crossroads not far from this city, all of which he's named after himself, the arrogant devil."

Kate made sympathetic sounds, hoping to encourage Mrs. Surratt to keep talking.

"The tavern is prosperous, though how I don't know—my sons say he drinks up the profits. My eldest John made his father buy this house and put it in my name so I'd have something he couldn't drink or gamble away. And now Mr. Surratt keeps a slave concubine at the new place. I'm sure he beats her now that he hasn't got me. The poor woman," Mrs. Surratt mused.

After Mrs. Surratt left her for the day Kate wondered if there were any really bad women, or only women whose life circumstances had forced them into base behavior. Or maybe that was true of both men and women? Was anyone naturally bad? Would Mrs. Surratt so willingly toady to Senator Wigfall and the Vice President if her life hadn't been so disappointing? And how many choices did she have anyway? Maybe if women had more choice about their lives they would be less likely to fall under the spell of men who were bad for them. *Like I did with Henry, maybe?* Still, and all, Mrs. Surratt wasn't exactly homeless and desperate. She certainly had a lot more options than the slave woman living with Mr. Surratt.

Kate hadn't seen much slavery up close. Maybe those who did learned to live with it by convincing themselves it wasn't all that bad. She knew she loved Uncle Juba and a world that said he was a second class human being wasn't her sort of world. She'd known a number of negroes in the circus and found them no better and no worse than anyone else. Mostly, she hated the unfairness of slavery. And unfairness was a disease. She knew first hand how unfair life was for women, even white women. Kate thought that the nation's willingness to tolerate slavery lie in the fear that emancipating slaves would lead to emancipating women. Too many men understood who they were by who they controlled. Kate picked up her book, thinking she and Mrs. Surratt were quite the pair, both constrained by their sex and both heading down a dangerous road.

The next morning Mrs. Surratt delivered a tea tray to Kate's room. Lying next to her bowl of oatmeal was a neatly folded newspaper.

Mrs. Surratt sat the tray on Kate's bedside table and handed her the newspaper. "Since we have to wait for the next *Harper's* before we can read more of Mr. Dickens tale, I thought you'd like to see the news." She had a sly look of anticipation on her face. Kate saw it was not so much a newspaper as a one-page broadside.

CHARLESTON
MERCURY
EXTRA:

Passed unanimously at 1.15 o'clock, P.M., December 20th, 1860.

AN ORDINANCE

To dissolve the Union between the State of South Carolina and other States united with her under the compact entitled "The Constitution of the United States of America. "We, the People of the State of South Carolina, in Convention assembled, do declare and ordain, and it is hereby declared and ordained, That the Ordinance adopted by us in Convention, on the twenty-third day of May, in the year of our Lord one thousand seven hundred and eighty-eight, whereby the Constitution of the Untied States of America was ratified, and also, all Acts and parts of Acts of the General Assembly of this State, ratifying amendments of the said Constitution, are hereby repealed; and that the union now subsisting between South Carolina and other States, under the name of "The United States of America," is hereby dissolved.

Kate felt like someone kicked her in the stomach. She took a chance and showed Mrs. Surratt all the disquiet she felt. "So they really did it. I suppose the other slave states will follow."

"I suppose they will. This is the end of the country."

Kate glanced over at Mrs. Surratt. She didn't look as happy about the news as Kate thought she would.

"It's a little scary, isn't it?" Kate said quietly. "For all the arrogant Yankees have only themselves to blame for it," she added, lest she be misunderstood. Or understood all too well. Mary Surratt was no fool.

"It is a great and terrible day." Mrs. Surratt's grim face matched her tone. "It is up to brave patriots to save the country from its own folly. As they say, desperate times require desperate measures." She paused, looked out the window and then turned to Kate.

Kate could see that her landlady had made up her mind about something.

"Do you agree Fanny? That terrible events require terrible steps to be taken. And that patriots who take such steps are guilty of no real wrong doing?"

"I do," Kate spoke as solemnly as the moment seemed to require. Her definition of patriotism differed quite a bit from Mrs. Surratt's, but she understood what motivated the quiet woman all too well.

"Would you agree that any act that saved the union, no matter how bad it seemed on the face of it, would be justified as an act of ultimate service to this great nation?

"I would Mrs. Surratt." Kate carefully held the woman's soft grey eyes with her own.

"Would you like to help your country in its hour of greatest need?"

"Any way I can." Kate all but held her breath after her words, suspecting she stood on the edge of some great precipice.

And so on a quiet and snowy afternoon, while sitting on the edge of Kate's bed, Mary Surratt explained the entirety of the plot to kidnap President Buchanan, overthrow the government and forestall a Lincoln presidency. The more she talked the more horrified Kate became.

Chapter 14

December 14-28, 1860
Chicago, Springfield & Washington City

I t took Juba the better part of six miserable days to travel from Washington to Chicago. He had to ride in the third class cars, which were often little better than cattle cars. The weather didn't help, nor the poorly constructed rail lines over the mountains of western Virginia, where trains could go no faster than ten miles per hour. After he changed trains in Cincinnati the trip improved considerably, both in the speed of travel and the accommodations. Ohio conductors let him buy a second class ticket. Nonetheless, when he disembarked at the Great Central Station he felt like he'd been in a dog fight and lost.

Fortunately the Pinkerton office was only a six block walk from the depot. Unfortunately, it was December in Chicago and the wind blowing in off Lake Michigan bit right through him. He pulled his collar closer to his neck and tugged his hat down firmly on his head. At least the frozen city didn't smell of rotten garbage, offal and human detritus that filled the air in every American city he'd been in in the warm months. Heaving his bag up onto his shoulder, Juba set off down Michigan Avenue. Fifteen minutes later he stood in the Pinkerton headquarters' office. He sighed in happiness as he took off his coat, breathing in the warm air and scent of freshly brewed coffee. After a short meeting with Allan he went home for the first time in weeks. Madame Clofullia squealed excitedly at the sight of him while Petronella Barrow pretended to be vexed at the way he upset her carefully constructed domestic schedule. Juba noticed her irritation didn't stop her from feeding him enough food to sustain a family of four.

The next day he found himself back on a train, this time accompanied by Allan Pinkerton. Because he was with Allan the train company let Juba ride in the first class car, a fact Juba viewed as both good news and bad news. First class had far more comfortable seats and a better carriage stove, but anyone riding with Allan Pinkerton gave up clean air.

Once the train got rolling Allan lit one of his stinky cigars. "I want you to tell them what you've learned. So they get it first hand."

Juba leaned back in his cushioned seat and stretched his feet towards the little coal stove in the aisle. The rocking of the train car, combined with the heat and a belly full of Mrs. Barrow's griddle cakes, made staying awake a chore.

"Never mind," Allan said abruptly, but not unkindly. "I'll wake you when we get there and you'll see for yourself. There's one man who may be of some help. Let's see if you can pick him out."

An hour later Juba woke as the train slowed with a screech of brakes and steam. Juba didn't have any bags and Allan had only a slim case with him. A short walk brought them to a lovely two-story, white frame house with dark green shutters. A plain wooden door in the center of the house opened.

"We've been waiting for you," a large and bluff voiced man called from the door.

As they entered the front hall Juba glanced to his left. There was a tall beaver hat hanging on a coat rack. It hit Juba then. *I'm in Abraham Lincoln's house.* If only the orphan mob he used to run with in Five Points could seem him now.

Seeing Juba stare at the hat the big man apologized. "Abraham is out, I'm afraid. That's his old hat there. Mary, Mrs. Lincoln I mean, made him buy a new one for the fancy doin's coming up. He says he's breaking it in. Mr. Pinkerton, it's good to see you. Please come in." The man shook Allan's hand and then turned toward Juba and held out his hand. "Ward Lamon. I 'spose you're the man with the great and terrible news we must hear."

Juba could only nod. He was still thinking about the hat and where he was standing.

After introductions Ward ushered them into the front parlor. The velvet drapes just matched the maroon in the patterned carpet, making the room seem both formal and warm. Four men stood as they entered.

"Gentlemen, Mr. Pinkerton and Mr. Lane are here." Lamon waved his hand at a heavy set man with a Quaker beard who introduced himself as Judge Davis. The trio of men in military uniforms introduced themselves as Colonel Edwin Sumner, Major David Hunter and Captain George Hazzard. Sumner, with his head full of silver hair, was easily the oldest of the three, while the Captain had the full, dark hair and un-lined skin of a man barely into his thirties.

They all took their seats and Allan said, "This man you see with me, Mr. Lane, is one of my most trusted operatives and you have my word that everything he is about to tell you is

159

true." Allan paused and looked sternly around the room. "Mr. Lane, would you please relate to these gentlemen the account of your activities in Washington City and what you and your partner uncovered?"

Juba took a deep breath and began. As he told his story the men questioned him, so much so that the telling took over an hour. At one point a young maid brought a large tray of tea and sandwiches into the parlor, which the men, but for himself, fell upon like wolves. Juba's anxiety to have the afternoon over and done with was such that he feared he'd regurgitate anything he ate right onto Mrs. Lincoln's fancy carpet. From what he'd heard about the lady he thought he best not sully her carpet.

As he talked it became clear that the military men were taking his tale to heart. Colonel Sumner asked piercingly astute questions and Captain Hazzard kept nodding as Juba spoke, like a man having his suspicions confirmed.

When at last he finished the Captain erupted into speech. "Dammit all, its worse than last summer and just as I suspected. The capitol is rife with treason. The main difference is that before the election the Democrats were scrapping amongst themselves, one camp too busy destroying the other to take much aim at Mr. Lincoln. Remember, I said the Democrats were as profane as the old English monarchs and just as disorganized. Sounds like they've fixed that problem. They've united around their common hatred of Mr. Lincoln."

Colonel Sumner spoke up. "Captain Hazzard refers to his activities of last summer. He infiltrated the Democrats, first in Indianapolis and then in Washington City. He made some exceedingly tight connections in the burgeoning secessionist movement. Mr. Floyd, for example, at the War Department, took a shine to the Captain."

While Colonel Sumner explained, Juba studied the captain. He had glossy dark hair, cut just at his ear lobes. He had cheekbones most women only wished for, yet he managed, in spite of his pretty features, to look decidedly masculine. Juba supposed the man's astute eyes, strong jaw and forceful mustaches helped, as did his immaculate navy wool uniform. Wait till Katie saw this one—she did like a beautiful man.

"That rascal Floyd is the worst of them if you ask me," Hazzard said, reaching for his tea as he did. He took a sip, thought for a second and asked Juba, "You sure his name didn't come up in any of this?"

"Well, Captain, I'm not saying he's not involved. We don't know the full extent of the conspiracy and given their time-table, I didn't want to wait around Washington any longer finding out. Right now you know everything we know."

Hazzard stood, walked over to the window, and then turned to speak. "Well, I'd lay odds Floyd's involved. That man is so crooked he has to screw his pants on in the morning. Happily, he's willful and corrupt. They say President Buchanan made him Secretary of War just because Floyd reminds him of Rufus King."

The room went silent for a moment, though Juba had no idea why. Before he exposed his ignorance, Colonel Sumner spoke. "President Jackson, under whom I had the privilege to advise when he was president, called them 'Miss Nancy' and 'Aunt Fancy.' I don't approve of that sort of thing, but I will say Mr. Buchanan and Mr. King were as devoted to each other as any married couple."

Ohhhh, Juba thought.

Hazzard continued. "Well, there's a lot of folks that think Buchanan got his slavery ideas from Rufus King and that he stays in the pro-slavery camp to honor King's memory, though he's been dead for years."

Mr. Lamon spoke up. "Gentlemen, I fear we tread far afield. We must decide a course of action and launch Mr. Pinkerton and Mr. Lane in the necessary direction."

Colonel Sumner leaned forward in his seat. "As the ranking military officer in the room, would anyone object if I proposed a plan of battle?" He paused just long enough to create the illusion of choice and continued. "I am loath to send too many men after what may be, in the end, a red herring. And Mr. Lincoln has forbid us the military option, for both the special train and cities we'll travel through. On the other hand, should the conspirators be in earnest and the Pinkerton intelligence accurate, we would be remiss if we failed to act. Agreed?"

"Yes sir," Major Hunter and Captain Hazzard barked in unison.

Juba almost said something, but thought better of it.

Sumner looked around the room, daring the others to disagree with him. No one did. "Therefore, I propose that Mr. Lamon and the men under my command stay here to guard Mr. Lincoln. All but Captain Hazzard. I want the captain in Washington. Judge Davis, I assume that meets with your approval."

The judge, who had been sitting quietly in a corner looked up suddenly, as if he'd been caught dozing. "The more people Abraham has around him, the better, in my opinion, but I suspect we could spare more than one man Colonel."

Juba smiled to himself. The judge had not been caught napping after all.

"I think one man is all we'll need in this case, Judge. Mr. Pinkerton and Mr. Lane didn't come here looking for muscle. They came looking for someone who can get them in to see President Buchanan. Am I correct in that assessment gentlemen?" The colonel turned toward Allan and Juba, skewering them with his silvery eyes. The coal fire popped in the small silence.

"Absolutely," Allan agreed, with far more confidence than Juba felt.

And that was how Juba found himself, the very next day, back on the train, this time with both Allan Pinkerton and Captain Hazzard as company. As the train sped east Juba found himself wishing it would go even faster. While he spent days just sitting on a train the conspirators were out there. Conspiring. It felt like the Pinkertons were running out of time.

Chapter 15

K ate had a considerably better Christmas than Juba, Allan and Hazzard, who spent it on the train. After Mrs. Surratt brought Kate into her confidence she began treating Fanny as if she were a daughter. Christmas day Kate joined the Surratt family at church, after which they ate a glorious dinner of cooked goose and roast potatoes. Afterwards they all went up to the parlor where Isaac and John sang hymns and carols while their mother accompanied them on a small, square piano. The senator stopped by for an hour or so after dinner, but happily under Mrs. Surratt's stern eye, he kept his hands to himself and his comments suitable to the day.

In her bed that night Kate reflected on the funny turns life made. She'd been horrified to discover the plot to kidnap the president, but equally surprised to discover the Surratts were nice people. It would be easier if they were monsters. Kate found their insistence on the supremacy of white people repugnant and perplexing, but she was finding that people could hold monstrous ideas, yet not be monstrous themselves.

Mrs. Surratt took care of her family and kept a clean and orderly house. Hadn't the woman spent her life just as the magazines, newspaper articles and novels said women should? Kate snuggled down into her blankets Christmas night. Maybe that was the problem. *Too much blind obedience to men gets women into trouble.* Thank goodness obedience wasn't one of her problems.

Four days after Christmas Kate hired a large carriage from Mr. Howard and took the short ride to the train station to pick up Juba and the others. She first delivered Juba to the feed store before driving Allan and Captain Hazzard to the Willard Hotel, working hard at a studied disinterest that she in no way felt. She'd sent Juba off to Chicago alone and he came back with Allan and the most delicious piece of man flesh she'd ever seen. From his shiny dark hair to his snugly fitted uniform trousers, the Captain was quite simply the most attractive man she'd laid eyes upon in years. She pretended not to notice him. Allan noticed her not noticing Hazzard and laughed at her behind the Captain's back. That night she had a dream full of dark haired, swashbuckling men in form fitting trousers and big swords. Predictably, the pirates all looked like Captain Hazzard.

The next morning she and Juba met Hazzard in the Willard's fourth floor hallway just outside Allan's room. Juba left her to flounder in awkward conversation with the captain while they waited for Allan to open his door. Kate, who couldn't get the sword wielding pirate image out of her head, stammered like a nervous girl when she said good morning. He smiled enigmatically and took her hand. He bowed over it and placed a small kiss on the back of her hand. Her knees went weak. *Crap.*

Finally Allan opened the door. The men stepped back so Kate could enter first. "You might have helped me," Kate hissed at Juba after they stepped into the room. Juba raised both eyebrows at her, the very picture of innocence.

Over coffee Allan announced that he and Captain Hazzard would try to see President Buchanan that very morning. Hazzard seemed to think they could get in to see the president without an appointment because he carried a letter of introduction to the president from Colonel Sumner, who happened to be the second most senior field commander in the U. S. Army, exceeded only by General Scott.

Kate and Juba waited in Allan's rooms while the two men made the short walk from the Willard to the President's house. While they waited she told Juba everything she'd learned from Mrs. Surratt.

"So it's not just a kidnapping," Juba said when she was done.

"Right. They want to prevent Mr. Lincoln from entering Washington at all. They'll stop him in Baltimore, though I don't know the specifics. Either Mrs. Surratt didn't tell me or she doesn't know in the first place."

"And you're just telling me now? You should have told all of us when you picked us up at the train station."

"You think I don't know that," she snapped at him. "I wasn't sure what I could say in front of that Army captain. Discretion seemed the better part of valor; at least until I knew for sure we could trust him. And remember, Hattie and Timothy are up in Baltimore. I'm not saying anything that might put them in more danger."

Juba scrubbed his face and sighed. "You're right. It just gets worse and worse, doesn't it? I was hoping we'd hand this

167

mess to some higher authority today or tomorrow and go home. Away from your lecherous senator."

"Me too," Kate said with a little moue of regret. "But I fear we're in Washington for the long haul." She gestured at the tall windows and the city that lay beyond. "If we don't have to go to Baltimore."

"You should write it all down and hand it to Allan when he gets back. In case he has the Captain with him. I think the Captain's on our side, as it were, but that's for Allan to decide."

"Already done. The writing I mean. I'll give it to him when he gets back. As for Wigfall, I've got a plan and I'm going to need your help."

"Not if you're planning on putting yourself in danger girl. I've had about all the worry for you I can stomach."

Kate contemplated her friend. She hated it when men tried to protect her or tell her what to do, but he was family and so she tried to give him a little leeway. "I think we can make it work with little or no trouble. But what I've got in mind isn't a one woman show. I can be the straight man, but I need you for comic relief."

Juba heaved a great big, mostly fake sigh. "I *never* get to be the straight man."

It was over two hours before Allan and Hazzard returned. They came through the door still brushing snow from their hats.

"He had a cabinet meeting this morning," Allan reported. "We have an appointment for tomorrow, 1 PM."

"Miss Lane was receiving callers in the Blue Room," Hazzard added, "So they made us wait in there. There was tea."

168

Hazzard produced a look of faux horror. "All those ladies in their best dresses. It was hard duty indeed."

Juba laughed, but Kate only looked hard at Hazzard. If her short marriage to Henry taught her anything it was that overly-handsome men should be avoided at all costs. Which was too bad, because in the dying afternoon light, his hair tousled by the weather, Hazzard was more than a little appealing. The realization made her as nervous as a fox at a hound convention.

Agreeing to meet again the next afternoon for dinner, Kate and Juba went on their way, Kate back to the National Theater for that evening's performance and Juba to his room at Columbus's house. Before she left she handed Allan her bundle of papers.

"I had an interesting afternoon with Mrs. Surratt. You're going to want to read that and destroy it."

Eyebrows raised, Allan said quietly, "My dear, you never fail to surprise me." He glanced at Hazzard, then back at Kate, one eyebrow delicately raised. Kate gave her head a tiny shake. Allan was an inveterate matchmaker and she'd never been able to convince him that she found the marital institution not at all to her liking.

Late the next afternoon Kate hitched Excelsior to the little shay, picked up Juba and the three of them made their way to the Willard Hotel. As they turned onto Pennsylvania Avenue Excelsior figured out where they were going and picked up his pace, trotting eagerly past several larger carriages in his eagerness to arrive at the Willard. One of the hotel's stablemen indulged the big white horse's passion for apples and Excelsior never forgot anyone who dispensed his favorite treat.

They found Captain Hazzard and Allan already ensconced in chairs before the fire, drinks in hand, the room redolent with Allan's cigar smoke. Juba poured himself a matching drink, raising his glass to Kate in invitation, who waved him off. She had another performance tonight.

"Well?" she asked, fairly bursting with the need to know.

Allan began. "It went better than I expected, though not as well as it could have. I found Mr. Buchanan to be a reasonable and thoughtful man, for all the unkind words said about him."

"He had some trouble believing us at first," Hazzard added, "but the more Mr. Pinkerton talked the more the president seemed to accept what he was saying."

Kate sat forward in her chair and pinned Allan with a look. "So you told him?" She glanced over at the Captain.

Allan nodded. "Colonel Sumner and Mr. Lincoln trust him, so I think we can."

Hazzard watched their exchange, but wisely kept his mouth shut.

"So? What did you tell him? The president I mean." Kate was having trouble imagining just how that conversation would have gone. How did one tell a president that his Vice President and his cronies were plotting to kidnap him? And cause a riot to prevent the president-elect from entering the nation's capitol.

"I did the only thing I could think of. I told him the truth. He seemed flabbergasted at first, insisting that it couldn't be true, but like I said, he came around to it. He's been keeping an eye on both Wigfall and Breckinridge."

"Also, he agrees with me about Floyd," Hazzard added. "Which I admit surprised me quite a bit. It turns out the bloom is off the Floyd rose, so to speak."

"Right. Wait till you hear this." Allan turned to Hazzard. "You've had dealings with Floyd, so you tell it."

Hazzard flashed his white teeth under his dark mustache. Kate tried not to notice the captain's resemblance to her dream pirates.

"Mr. Buchanan says Floyd's got a nephew who works in the Interior Department at the Indian Agency. This nephew removed a pile of bonds from the agency safe and Mr. Floyd has been redistributing them in return for political favors. They're bonds paid for with Indian money, held by the government as a way to pay for Agency projects, so the bearer can redeem them for cash. Anyway, the nephew took them over a year ago and no one knew until an end-of-the-year audit found them missing. We couldn't get in to see the President yesterday because he was in a meeting about this Interior mess."

"Didn't I read something about that in the newspaper?" Kate asked.

Allan answered. "I expect you did. I found the story in Greeley's *Tribune* on Christmas day. Which is good news for us because Mr. Buchanan came up with a scheme to expose the kidnapping plot and blame it on Floyd."

Kate frowned. "He doesn't want to expose a senator and a vice president as traitors, does he?"

Juba shook his head in disgust. "Did you think he would? The bigger the man, the more likely they are to get away with nefarious behavior. I bet Buchanan would have let the Floyd thing go if it hadn't already become public."

171

"I expect you're right Mr. Lane," Hazzard agreed. "But I think we can all agree the kidnapping plot must be crushed. We want Mr. Lincoln in office in two months, not Breckinridge."

Kate wanted to get back to the explanation of Buchanan's plan. "So how does he think he puts an end to all this by blaming Floyd?"

Allan leaned forward and said, "Well, that's the beauty of it. Floyd has to go, one way or the other. Buchanan will ask for Floyd's resignation based on the bond scandal. Then he'll call a meeting with Senator Wigfall and the Vice President and tell them the real reason he dismissed Floyd is that the Army discovered a kidnapping plot, master-minded by Floyd. Breckinridge and Wigfall will know their plot's been discovered and be forced to abandon it."

"Wiley old fox, isn't' he?" Hazzard said with admiration. "I suppose that's how Mr. Buchanan got to be president in the first place."

"Oh, it gets better," Allan explained, taking an expansive sip from his brandy glass and then waving the glass in Kate's direction. "He's going to appoint a committee made up of his friends and to hold senate hearings. He doesn't figure to catch any big fish, but the hearings should send them swimming for deep waters."

Kate thought about it while the gentlemen in the room congratulated themselves on the neatness of the plot's conclusion.

After a few moments she interrupted them. "Gentleman, I don't share your optimism. I've spent more than my share of time with these people and they're true believers. They're not going to be deterred by one forced resignation by an outgoing president and some toothless hearings."

Hazzard, Allan and Juba all looked at her in astonishment.

"This isn't the end," Kate said regretfully. "It's another beginning. They'll just switch targets."

Hazzard tipped his chair back on its back two legs, as if distancing himself from Kate's pronouncement, then thumped his chair back down and stood to refresh his drink.

Kate tried not to look at him, but couldn't seem to help herself. He'd worn his parade uniform to see the president—a double breasted artillery jacket in Prussian blue with gold buttons down the front and at the wrist. Because he was an mounted officer in an artillery company he wore the short jacket, rather than the longer frock coat. Much to her discomfort, Kate discovered she vastly preferred the short jacket because it allowed her to assess the fit of the captain's sky blue trousers. She caught herself visualizing a trouserless Hazzard. *Dammit. Focus Kate.*

Hazzard gave her an odd look then turned towards Allan. "Mr. Pinkerton whatever the case may be, my hands are tied. It's an impossible job, keeping Mr. Lincoln safe. He's coming to this city, into hostile territory and his itinerary is no secret. Hell, *everyone* has it. Sorry Ma'am," Hazzard said with a nod to Kate.

She nodded back at him.

"It's like we painted a target on the train. A private detecting agency isn't going to keep the president-elect safe. It's going to have to be the army."

"Captain Hazzard, I share your frustration," Kate said, hating to agree with him about anything after he'd just dismissed her argument. "But doesn't Lincoln intend the entire trip as a kind of inaugural procession meant to drum up support for his presidency, support he badly needs? And he won't be able to do that in the midst of an army. He'll look weak."

Hazzard shook his head abruptly. "It won't matter how he looks if he's dead. Only the army can keep him safe."

Kate stood up and stepped towards the captain. She clenched her fists, thinking of all the senator's pawing. And lying to Mrs. Surratt for weeks and weeks. And the general aggravation of pretending to be Fanny. For the first time she understood why men challenged each other to duels. She'd very much like to shoot this varmint right between the eyes. She didn't care how handsome he was, no one suggested the Pinkerton's were incompetent. "Are you suggesting, Sir, that we are less committed to Mr. Lincoln's safety than you? Are you? After all I've done? And Juba? All we've discovered? You military men didn't even know there was a real plot. All you had was nasty letters. And you would have never found it. Not without the Pinkertons. "

Hazzard stood up and stepped back. "I apologize Miss Warne." He accompanied his apology with a short, jerky bow.

Allan and Juba froze in their seats, watching the two of them.

She saw uncertainty in his eyes and stifled a laugh. The poor man, she'd scared him half to death. "You don't spend much time with women, do you?"

"No Ma'am. Been in the Army since I graduated from West Point back in '47."

Kate stepped towards the captain and held out her hand.

He took it.

She held his hand in a firm grip as she spoke. "Captain Hazzard, we don't know each other very well. I am a rare female detective in a country that thinks women are no better than witless children. That man over there," she jerked her head towards Juba. "He's the smartest and kindest man I know and in this country he's considered little better than an animal by too many people."

Kate paused to take a deep breath, hyper-aware of the fact that she still held the captain's hand in her own. "I want very much for Mr. Lincoln to be the next president of this country. Without him Juba and I are going to be second class citizens a lot longer than I care for."

As she spoke Kate realized she meant every word. This job started out just another job, but somewhere along the way it changed. Getting Lincoln to his presidency and keeping him there was now a personal mission. She glanced over at Juba. He gravely nodded at her. Kate realized he'd figured all this out a while ago.

Hazzard looked down at Kate's hand and then up to her eyes. For a second she thought he might kiss her. Instead he let go and took a step back. "You have my sincerest apology ma'am." They stood there, watching each other for a moment. Kate heard Allan and Juba begin to laugh.

During a dinner of oysters, beef roast and glazed parsnips they came to a few conclusions. The first was that they needed to move their base of operations from Washington to Baltimore.

"I've got a small team up there right now," Allan reminded them. "Just give me a couple of days. I'll go up to Philadelphia tomorrow, see if I can get some funding, seeing how Mr. Lincoln can't pay us out of the federal budget just yet. Kate, if all goes well I can be in place by the first of February. Be in Baltimore by then. You'll need to figure out how to extricate yourself from Washington without rousing suspicion."

Kate and Juba grinned at each other.

"Oh, she's got a plan and it's a doozy," Juba said.

Hazzard reminded them he was going back to Springfield. "I'm going to be on that train with Mr. Lincoln, come hell and high water, excusing my language Ma'am."

"You can quit treating me like a lady. Think of me as one of the men."

She dapped at her lips with her napkin and looked over at him. He had that queer look on his face again.

"Ahem." Allan retrieved their attention. "I've got an idea and I think you're going to like it. We'll be infiltrating white secessionists up in Baltimore and that's a task for which Mr. Lane here is ill-suited."

Juba snorted.

Allan waved his fork at Juba. "I want you to go with Captain Hazzard and join Mr. Lincoln's personal guard. I'm thinkin' we pass you off as his valet."

Juba looked down at his plate and then back up again. "That might work."

Hazzard stared hard at Allan.

"Captain, you can't be everywhere. Ellsworth is earnest, but so young he smells of nursery powder. And Mr. Lamon . . .. He's a hot head and too inclined to think he can take care of Mr. Lincoln by himself. We need a man who will have an excuse to be with Mr. Lincoln on the most intimate terms. And wouldn't a man as important as a future president have a of personal servant?"

"He would at that," Juba said with a broad smile.

Hazzard must have seen the sense in Allan's idea because he nodded his agreement.

Allan gestured at Juba. "Juba here can do that. And he has much the same advantages Kate has—people don't see him."

Hazzard turned to Juba. "Are you trained with a gun?"

Juba leveled a fierce look at the captain. "Son, I grew up in Five Points, New York, the meanest slums in this country. I learned to fight before you were born. As for guns, I don't have one. Wouldn't be safe for a black man."

Thus they agreed that Captain Hazzard and Juba would both go to Springfield.

Allan wanted them to leave together the next morning, but Kate objected. "I need Juba at the theater. He's going to help me keep the senator at arm's length he visits my dressing room. And he's crucial to my plan. Mr. Grover is willing to hire him as the back door porter. And the Lincoln Special doesn't leave Springfield until mid-February, right? So there's no hurry."

"How about this," Hazzard suggested, "I'll go back now. Mr. Lane can follow in early February." Hazzard paused, his eyes widening in realization. "Wait a second. The senator visits your dressing room? Alone?"

"Yes Captain. We've come to an understanding, the senator and I. He acts like a gentleman, insofar as he is able, and Miss Fanny promised to deliver the goods at a later date. He was oddly amendable to the deal." Kate smiled an evil little smile.

"Egad," Hazzard said, burying his head in his hands. "It's worse than I thought."

"Oh, it gets a mite worse than that," Juba warned.

By the time Kate finished explaining her plan both Allan and Hazzard had their heads in their hands.

Chapter 16

January 13, 1861
Washington City

Kate opened her dressing room door and stepped into the dimly lit hall, pulling the belt on her velvet dressing gown tight around her waist as she did.

"Juba," she hissed. "Now!"

He stepped out of a dark corner. "I heard a thump."

Kate grinned wickedly. "He's a big old bastard." She opened the door a little wider as Juba approached, allowing him a glance inside.

The last few weeks with Juba backstage had been almost fun. She'd always enjoyed working with Juba, plus he proved invaluable in the care and management of the senator. He specialized in well-timed knocks on Kate's dressing room door.

Juba looked in the door and chuckled.

Inside the dressing room Senator Louis Trevant Wigfall lay splayed out on the floor, the shards of a broken flower vase scattered around his body.

"I can't tell you how much I've been looking forward to whacking this bastard on the head. I'd like to do it again. And then maybe one more time after that. You know, just for fun."

Kate felt weirdly exalted. *Maybe I should conk men on the head everyday. It's refreshing to a lady's spirit.*

She pulled herself back to the matter at hand. "We can't just stand here in the doorway, grinning at each other. Let's get to work."

Juba stepped into the room and quietly shut the door behind him. He grabbed the senator by the boots and pulled him over to the ratty rose colored chaise lounge in the corner of Kate's dressing room. "Here, take his feet. I'll get his shoulders. On three." They heaved him up onto the chaise with a muffled thump. "You want me to loosen his clothes for him," Juba asked, "or have you been yearning to undress him?"

"I insist you have that pleasure," Kate said with mocking politeness. "And splash him with this." She handed Juba a decanter of brandy. "I'll wash out the glass with the laudanum in it. And sweep up this mess." Kate gestured at the broken vase and scattered roses on the floor.

"Why'd you hit him? I thought the idea was to let the laudanum do the job?"

Kate grabbed the broom standing in the corner and went to work. "The old rogue wouldn't go down. He got to swaying and shaking his head, but he stayed on his feet. He was grousing about Texas secession and I think he was so worked up he wouldn't pass out. So I bashed him on the head with a vase. He dropped like a felled ox"

Juba, who'd been unbuttoning the senator's waistcoat and shirt, paused and looked at Kate. She was sweeping with a little more vigor than the mess called for. She made light of the situation, but he could tell she really had just about had it with Senator Wigfall.

"You going to be all right, Katie?" he asked gently.

"I've got to be." She stopped sweeping and leaned on her broom.

"I 'spose you already figured out how to make this little accident work for you," Juba said, straightening up and stretching his lower back. The senator was even heavier than he looked. "You going to pretend he had his way with you?"

"Egad, no! He'll just want more. No, it'll go just like we planned only better," Kate said brightly. "I'll tell him a rascally Yankee broke in here to ravish me and he protected me. The vase was broken in the struggle and he slipped in the mess and bumped his head, but not until after the dastardly attacker ran away. It's ridiculous, but he'll believe it because he can't conceive of himself as anything but heroic and me as anything but harmless."

Juba suppressed a laugh. "You? Harmless? Right there's proof the man's a damn fool."

"And thank goodness for it," Kate said. The two of them glanced at each other. Unable to resist any longer, they broke into laughter.

An hour later the senator snorted, sat up precipitously and just as abruptly slumped back again.

"Dizzy," he mumbled, grabbing his head in his two hands.

Juba leaped into action. "Laws Massa," he exclaimed, "It sho' good to see you up and around. You one powerful brave man, that be for sho'! You saved this poor little gal's life!" He gestured towards Kate, who was slumped in her dressing chair holding a handkerchief to her forehead in as melodramatic fashion as she could manage. Her robe gaped just enough to expose the cleft between her breasts.

"What?" The senator tried to sit up, but didn't quite make it, falling back with a heavy whump.

Kate and Juba rolled their eyes at each other.

"Here," Juba volunteered, "let me help you Massa. Fight like that take it out of any man."

Finally upright, Wigfall looked at Kate, then Juba, and then back at Kate, all the while gingerly rubbing his head. "What is the meaning of this Fanny?" he grumbled.

"Oh my, you don't remember, do you? You did take quite a blow to the head" she trilled, being sure to bat her eyelashes just the tiniest bit as she did. "The doorman," here she gestured at Juba, "and I have been so very worried about you. He wanted to get the police, but I didn't want to be left alone." Kate clutched at the neck of her robe and whimpered a little.

Juba jumped in to help. "Oh, sir, you was a sight to behold. This ruffian pushed right by me at the door. Stop! I yell to him, but he paid me no mind. He'd been hanging around the back door all week, mooning over Miss Jefferson here, saying he loved her and all that. I know my job sir. I keep fellers like him out." Juba hung his head. "Leastways I did till tonight."

"Right," Wigfall said. His voice came out pitched a little high. "Right," he repeated, this time an octave lower.

"Oh, Louis," Kate cried out and leapt across the room and threw herself into the senator's arms. "You were just so brave! I was never so afraid in all my life! You saved me from a fate worse than death!"

"I did, uh?" Wigfall asked, his arms tightening around Kate. "Of course I did." He started to look mighty pleased with himself.

"I'm afraid you'll hate me," Kate wailed. "I tried to help by throwing the beautiful flowers you gave me, but it just fell

182

on the floor and then you slipped in the water and the fiendish coward ran away. You hit your noble head so hard I feared for the worst." Kate broke into fake tears, burying her face in his shirt front to hide her desire to laugh.

He believed it. Every word.

"I am a southern gentleman, my dear. It's what we do. We keep ladies safe." Wigfall sat up a little straighter as he spoke and puffed out his chest.

Juba saw the senator take the bait. "She not safe here Massa. That man done got away, but he'll come back, you mark my words. What if you're not here next time?" Juba rolled his eyes and shuffled his feet in a parody of meekness he'd learned in minstrel shows.

"Miss Fanny, I fear the nigrah is correct. You're not safe in this city. I am about to travel up to Baltimore. You shall go with me."

And that easily, it was done.

Chapter 17

January 13- 14, 1861
Washington City

L ouis closed the door to his hotel room and fell into the closest chair with a dull thump. He gingerly probed the back of his head, grimacing as he did. He had a knot the size of a roast potato back there. What an evening. He'd foiled an attack on poor little Miss Fanny, for all he didn't remember it. He must have drunk too much. He sniffed at his shirt. He did smell like he'd over-indulged a mite.

Fanny had made her sentiments about the damn abolitionists pretty well known. And she was a mighty pretty little thing. No wonder some crazy man attacked her. Louis reached for the whiskey decanter, got a whiff of himself and thought better of it. He poured himself a glass of water instead. What he needed was a bag of ice for his poor head, but the thought of getting up and ringing for a hotel porter made his head throb even more.

Hell, that damn fool theater doorman just about made the case for slavery all by himself. The foolish nigrah let the dastardly assaulter in the building in the first place. If the fellow was his slave he'd whip him soundly for being a fool.

But the problem wasn't the nigrahs. One expected them to be foolish. It was the abolitionist types, the sort of men who should know better. This attack on Fanny was just the sort of thing right-minded men had been warning the country about. Slavery kept the lower sorts in their place, which kept white women safe from the horrors of race mixing. Well, he'd keep Fanny safe, no worries there. His own wife said she didn't need him anymore, but by gad, Fanny did.

The senator heaved himself up from his chair and stripped off his coat. He looked down at his boots. Better get those off too. He sat down again and leaned over to pry off his boots and almost toppled from the chair. No, he'd leave them on. It wasn't like there was a woman around to chastise him for sleeping in his boots.

He hauled himself to his feet again and made his unsteady way toward the bed. He laid his head on the pillow, careful to avoid putting pressure on the soft spot on the back of his noggin. He'd feel better in the morning and then he'd get to work on fixing the mess made by Floyd's dismissal and the hearings. What was Buchanan thinking? The so-called Committee of Five asked foolish questions of every witness they called. It was like they wanted to be lied to.

All wasn't lost yet. He funneled all that money out of the War department before Buchanan forced Floyd to resign. They'd make good use of it in Baltimore. Cursed Buchanan, anyway. Fellow couldn't see the nose in front of his face. No wonder everyone called him Old Public Functionary. And how had the president discovered the plot anyway? Or more accurately, who forced the oblivious old fool to pay attention to what was happening right under his nose. Hell, that's why they'd put him in place to start with. So he'd turn a blind eye to everything they did.

Until now that deal had worked admirably. While Buchanan stood idly by Floyd managed to move thousands guns and artillery pieces from federal arsenals into the control of southern states. State after state seceded, each fully armed for war. Why, Mississippi, Florida and Alabama had already joined South Carolina in secession. He needed time to spread some money around Baltimore, organize the resistance, pay off the police . . . Just thinking about it made him tired.

He'd feel better after a few hours of sleep. He could visit Fanny over at the boarding house, tell her to get ready to travel. Mr. Lincoln would not make it to Washington alive while Louis Trevant Wigfall drew breathe. Minutes later ostentatious snoring filled the room, while outside snow started to fall again, its lightness obscured by the night.

Chapter 18

February 3-4, 1861
Washington & Baltimore

K ate looked around the stable for someone to help harness Excelsior. Two members of the rat baiting crew were loitering around the back of the stable, seeming generally disinclined to look her way, let alone help. Mr. Howard finally came to her rescue, complaining to her in a voice that carried down the stable aisles that his worthless black stable hand had quit and left him short handed.

More quietly, as he settled the harness on Excelsior's back, Mr. Howard said, "You tell your friend if I have any news from those fellows back there," he jerked his head toward the rear of the building, "I'll find a way to get it to him or you."

Kate nodded and then in her own loud voice said, "Thank you so much for your help Sir."

She was about to lift herself into the carriage seat when the world turned upside down. A deafening wave of booming sound slammed her against the carriage wheel, shoving her up against the axel. A flash of blinding light accompanied the cataclysm. Mr. Howard slammed into her back, forcing the air out of her as he did. Her forehead bounced off the top of the wheel.

The smell of char and smoke followed swiftly after, filling Kate's nose with an acrid stench. There was a moment of absolute silence before the stable erupted in yelling. A high ringing in her ears made words difficult to differentiate but she could hear someone yelling about a bomb.

"You all right?" Mr. Howard yelled into her ear. He pushed himself off her but kept his arms around her.

"Yes, I think so." Kate tried to turn to face Mr. Howard, but her reticule was caught in the carriage wheel. Its straps were looped around her wrist and refused to let go. She disentangled herself and then reached up to probe her head. She had two sore spots, one at the front and one at the back. Mr. Howard's forehead must have hit the back of her head, and then knocked her face-first into the wheel. "And you?"

He nodded abruptly and turned to look behind them. "Fire," he blurted, his voice filled with panic. He released Kate and scurried down the stable aisle. The two men who'd been loitering at the back of the stable lie on the ground, unmoving. The stable wall behind them had all but disappeared, turned into shards of smoking wood. Kate could see that one of the men had only bloody stumps where his legs should have been. Mr. Howard kneeled, checked the men and then pushed himself up from his knees. Kate moved toward him, then stopped. The two men were clearly beyond help. Howard grabbed a water bucket with one hand while waving the other at Kate. "You get out of here. Go, now!"

"Do you need help?" Kate yelled back. Or at least she thought she was yelling. It was hard to tell. Her voice sounded swaddled in cotton wool and the pounding in her skull seemed unnecessarily loud. She stared at the two downed men.

They'd been fine just seconds ago— two men, alive one second and a mess of burned and bloody gore the next.

"GO!" Mr. Howard roared at her, "Before the police get here."

Startled out of her daze, Kate clambered up the wheel and into the carriage seat. Excelsior twitched his ears at her. Ashy bits fell out of the air onto his back. Kate thought once again how lucky she was in her choice of horse. A bomb went off not thirty feet from him and he stood there, steady as a preacher in the pulpit. With her mashed up against the carriage wheel and her reticule entwined in the spokes, he'd have killed her if he'd bolted. "Good horse," she called at him and chucked the reigns. Excelsior took off briskly down the street, leaving the smoke and wreckage behind them.

Kate walked into the depot to find Allan and Juba sitting on one of the benches. Relief flooded through her.

The two men took in her appearance with consternation. "What happened to you?" They asked at about the same time and quite a bit louder than Kate would have liked.

"I'm sorry," she said, pulling her bonnet down lower on her forehead. *Ouch.* "A bomb went off at the stable, at least that's what I think it was. I bumped my head. Two men are dead. Maybe more. I'm not sure. It was like the world went topsy turvy for a few seconds and then I got out of there."

"Girl, you've got ash and straw and dirt all over you." Juba brushed at her skirt, but made little real headway. "Are you all right?"

"I'm fine. Celly's fine too. You should have seen him. Bomb went off and he hardly twitched."

Juba bumped her shoulder with his. She knew he wanted to hug her, but didn't dare. Not in public.

Cutting through their wordless exchange, Allan asked, "Do you think the bomb was for you?"

Kate bit her lower lip, then winced. It hurt too. "Noooo. It went off at the back of the stable. Juba can tell you, Excelsior's stall is almost at the front door. The rat baiting crew's usually at the back of the stable and the two dead men were from that crowd. I've seen them both at the Surratt's, so they're Knights of the Golden Circle. Or they were."

Juba nodded at Allan. "You thinkin' what I'm thinkin' boss?"

"I suspect so. Someone had to take the fall for the leak that exposed the kidnapping plot. Those two men were just made an example of and a brutal example at that."

The three of them contemplated that reality for a few seconds.

Kate shrugged her shoulders, suddenly exhausted beyond all measure. "Can we keep this short? I want to go back to my room and call up a bath and the biggest pot of tea Mrs. Surratt can find."

"You think that's wise, going back there?" Juba asked.

"She's fine," Allan said for Kate. "The fact that two men from the Knights were targeted makes it clear they don't suspect Kate."

Juba folded his arms and frowned. "Does it? She was in the building when the thing went off. How do we know Kate wasn't the target? We don't know anything except that she was almost killed."

Kate shoved her bonnet back off her forehead in frustration. "I'm right here you two. Quit talking about me as if I'm a four-year old. I wasn't almost killed. I think Allan's right. First, the bomb was in the back of the stable, not the front. Second, I'm not usually at the stable until closer to 4. I was early today because I wanted to see you two off. Unless you think the bomb thrower showed up four hours early and waited around for me. Unnoticed."

"I just think it's an awful big coincidence that you were there when a bomb went off," Juba insisted.

"But it's not," Kate insisted right back. "It's the stable I use and I use it because the Knights use it, which is why you used to work there. I'm in and out of the place every day. And the Knights are there. All the time." She gave Juba her hardest stare. "I'm fine," she said firmly.

"Enough," Allan said. "Kate's right. We don't have time to argue about this." He turned and looked Kate in the eye. "Watch your back over the next couple of days. I'll find out what I can and let you know."

Allan gestured for the three of them to sit. "Anyway, slight change of plans. Juba's going back the Chicago as we planned, but I'm going to Baltimore instead of Chicago. Someone needs to scope out the leadership up in Mobtown."

"I'll be quick then. The Senator visited me yesterday. He's awful impressed with himself for saving me." Kate tipped Juba a wink. "Anyway, he's eager to get to Baltimore—and as luck would have it, he's taking me along."

Kate glanced at Juba, suppressing a laugh as she did.

He paused, and then twitched his shoulders, like he was shrugging off his concerns about the bomb. "Well, a man gots to protect his lady from de evil doers, dat be fo sho," Juba said in the broad slave dialect he'd been using for the senator's benefit the last few weeks.

Kate's heart lightened. His joke, however weak, meant he'd decided to trust her instincts. "And Mrs. Surratt is closing up the boarding house at the end of the week. She says her husband is ill and needs her, which is a huge load of hooey if you ask me. I don't think she'd offer him a glass of water if he was on fire." Kate rolled her eyes. "More likely she and her boys are worried about being arrested."

Allan nodded in agreement. "Sounds like the rats are leaving the ship. What else did your good senator have to say?"

"Well, he says he's got a contact in Baltimore, a stockbroker named Luckett. Luckett's the leader up there, or one of them."

"How many stockbrokers named Luckett can there be in Baltimore?" Allan rubbed his hands together with satisfaction. "Oh, and I've been in contact with Mr. Samuel Felton. He runs the Philadelphia, Wilmington and Baltimore Railroad. Mr. Lincoln plans to use the P. W. & B. for the final leg of his journey, especially since the president of the B. & O. declared his railroad would be available to anyone who wanted to fight northerners."

"Isn't that treason?" Kate asked.

"It's only treason if someone's willing to prosecute. The federal government, as it stands right now, is too pro-Southern to give a damn. Look at how weak Buchanan's efforts to break the kidnapping plot have been."

"Mr. Felton, he's a pro-Union man?" Juba asked.

"Oh, I should say so." Allan stood and straightened his coat as a steam whistle sounded in the near distance. "That's our train. Felton wants his rail line and the president-elect protected and he's hired us to both." Kate stood and followed Allan and Juba out to the train while Allan raised his voice above the engine's racket. "This means we no longer need to pry money out of the Lincoln camp. Felton's paying the bill now."

At the first class carriage door Allan turned towards Kate. "Kate, don't think I'm taking what happened to you lightly. I'll find out what I can. If I have to pull you off the case and send you back to Chicago, I will." He tipped his hat at Kate and stepped into the train carriage. "Look for a telegraph from your uncle tomorrow."

"Right," she said. *You can try and send me home and see how that works out.* Kate turned towards Juba. "Give Mrs. Barrow my love, would you?"

"I will," he said gravely. "I won't be home long. Mr. Lincoln's train leaves in eight days and I aim to be on it. You take care now. Anything happens to you, I don't know what I'd do."

She nodded, not trusting herself to speak. The two men stepped into the train carriage and the porter closed the door shut with a clang. The train whistled again and a great cloud of steam rose from the engine. In a wink they were gone.

It was well after dark when Allan stepped off the train at Baltimore's Camden Street Station. A inquiry to the station master took him to the Howard House, a hotel only three blocks from the station. Far less opulent then the downtown hotels, the seven story Howard catered to respectable merchants and businessmen.

He surveyed the hotel's lobby. *Perfect.* This was not a hotel for the idle rich. Men who stay here worked for a living. After he checked in he asked the clerk to send a city directory up to his room, along with a sandwich, a bottle of brandy and a box of cigars.

Early the next morning Allan set off walking down Howard Street. At Lombard Street he turned north, just as the hotel clerk directed. The city was quiet, though Allan suspected that the docks and streets would be crowded and noisy before too long. A brisk breeze blew off the basin harbor just to the east, bringing with it the tangy brine scent of the ocean.

According to the City Directory, James H. Luckett, Stockbroker, had his offices at 44 South Street. Allan didn't think Luckett would be in this early. Indeed, Allan hoped he was not.

A few minutes later he stood in front of a four-story building. He'd already walked around the building and couldn't believe his luck. It was a free standing building with doors on all four sides, each opening to a street or a wide alley. A person who had his office in this building could have a myriad of visitors and no one would notice because they could all come and go from different doors.

Best of all, an "Offices to Let" sign sat in one of the building's narrow front windows. Allan knew that after the Panic of '57 a good many of the city's port businesses relocated to New York, leaving quite a few Baltimore office buildings partially empty.

Allan checked his pocket watch. Twenty minutes before eight. Someone probably unlocked the building at eight o'clock, but he didn't want to be standing here staring at the place when that person arrived. His stomach rumbled, reminding him all he'd eaten in the last twelve hours was an anemic hotel sandwich.

An hour later, thoroughly fortified with a breakfast of sausages and eggs, Allan walked up a short flight of stairs and through the front door of 44 Howard. The building directory told him that Luckett's Brokerage lie on the second floor. He headed for Luckett's office. On his way there he noticed several empty offices, including the one next to Mr. Luckett's. Luckett's door was cracked open, so Allan entered without knocking. The office space relied over-much on the weak morning sunshine, leaving it under lit and dingy feeling. The ghosts of cigars long since smoked hung in the air. Oak file cabinets lined one wall and neat stacks of papers lie on the desk.

"Please excuse the interruption, sir." Allan walked toward the man sitting at the desk. The fellow looked to be in his fifties, with wavy light grey hair brushed back to expose a receding hairline. When he looked up Allan saw that he had light grey eyes that matched his hair and bushy eyebrows. "I wonder if you would be so kind as to help me. Do you know who I speak to about renting in this building?"

"James Luckett, at your disposal sir." Luckett stretched his hand across the desk.

"John Hutchinson, at yours sir," Allan said as he shook hands with the stockbroker. "I'd be much obliged if you could help me. I can't stomach New York City any longer—too many pushy northerners with too few manners. I'm looking to relocate to this fine city."

"Can't say I blame you there. The building manager's on the first floor, office nearest the back door. If you came in the front you wouldn't have seen it. What kind of office do you plan on, if you don't mind me asking."

"I'm a stockbroker by trade. Got my start in New Orleans." Allan could tell from Luckett's accent that he was born and raised somewhere in New England, making New Orleans a safe city to pretend to be from and one that would immediately establish his rebel credentials.

Luckett exclaimed as how he was a stockbroker too and together they commiserated on the fluctuating wheat market and the volatility of railroad stocks. After a few minutes of making friendly noises at each other Luckett took Allan downstairs to the building manager's office. An hour later Allan had a signed contract for his new office, right next to Luckett's.

That afternoon Allan was, as his Daddy used to say, as busy as a beaver before it rains. Having been raised in cities Allan had no idea why beavers would be so busy before rain, but he sent about a half dozen coded telegrams and went shopping for office accessories that would add verisimilitude to his operation. Just up Howard Street from his Hotel, Allan found Hustler Brothers dry goods store, where he bought all manner of things, including a gas lamp for each of the office's two desks. By late afternoon all his acquisitions had been delivered and arranged. Feeling exceedingly pleased with himself he poked his head into Luckett's office.

"Say Mr. Luckett, I wonder if you know where a man can get a good steak and a drink?" Allan was careful to project the kind of bonhomie common to businessman.

"I do sir." Luckett stood from his desk and took his hat from its hook on the wall and swung it up onto his balding head. "I'll take you there if you let me buy you dinner. We'll call it a 'Welcome to Baltimore' celebration."

Late that evening the night clerk brought a telegram to Allan's room. He opened it with clumsy fingers, only too aware

that he'd had one or maybe two drinks too many with Luckett. He'd done it to build the man's trust but he already
regretted the sore head he'd have in the morning.

Washington 4 Feb 1861

Uncle

W to Balt. We meet with L tomorrow 4 PM—

Looking forward

Mrs. B.

Allan smiled. Mrs. Barley was Kate's favorite alter ego. He
tore the telegram into small pieces, laid them in the ashtray
and applied his cigar to them. He plotted his next step as it
burned.

Chapter 19

February 5-10, 1861
Baltimore

She adjusted her dark blue velvet hat, cocking it so the bit of veil reached her eyes. The clock on the mantelpiece chimed the half hour. The senator ought to be knocking on her door any minute. They'd traveled up to Baltimore by train that morning and taken a hired hack to Barnum's City Hotel, an establishment that rivaled the Willard for size and elegance. Barnum's took up an entire city block and at one time housed luminaries like inventor Eli Whitney and the English writer Charles Dickens. President Buchanan stayed at the Barnum when he was in Baltimore.

"Wait till you see the menu in the restaurant," Wigfall enthused while they were waiting for their rooms. "Why, they've got everything on it, from roast goose to soused pheasant and every kind of vegetable you could imagine. And the dessert cart! Just you wait. Cakes, jellies, pies, puddings, fancy cheese like you've never tasted. Oh, darling, you're in for a real treat."

Kate had to admit that his excitement was infectious. It helped that the senator agreed she should have her own suite of rooms on an entirely different floor from his. Louis hadn't even tried to share the rooms with her. She was beginning to suspect Louis's designs on her were not so much erotic as they were exhibitory. Squiring a pretty young woman of dubious reputation about town made him feel like a bad boy, but the ease with which she put him off made her think he wasn't a committed seducer. His eagerness for Fanny's company, which had once irritated Kate, seemed more than a little sad now. It was a sentiment she found exasperating.

A knock sounded at the door. She opened it to find the senator. "You look extremely handsome Louis," she told him, lying hardly at all. He looked as gleamingly shiny as a well-groomed cat. Clearly he'd visited the hotel's barber and made use of a variety of the man's services.

He stepped in her room with a small bow. "Not half so nice as you darlin'. Better get your coat. The wind's up and you don't have all my padding," Wigfall spoke loudly, as if under the influence of several brandies, but he jovially clapped his hands to his midsection to emphasize his point.

Why, he's having fun. The thought surprised her. The poor man just needed human contact. Maybe because his family was far away in Texas. In that way the two of them were not entirely unalike, both lonely people searching for somewhere to belong. Kate shook her head. Feeling sorry for Louis didn't make her job one whit easier.

After a leisurely walk through waning light of the day Kate and the senator found themselves at Luckett's office building. She noticed "Mr. John Hutchinson, Stock Broker" stenciled on the frosted glass in the door next door to Luckett's, the letter paint so new it still looked wet. The light was on in that office as well. Kate knew Allan used Hutchinson like she used Barley and here was a Hutchinson right next to Mr. Luckett. *Interesting.*

"Here we are darlin," Wigfall said, opening the door to Mr. Luckett's office. "Luckett, it's good to see you," he called out in his booming voice.

A grey haired man came around the desk. "It's good to see you again Senator." As they shook hands Luckett looked toward Kate. "And the lady?" he inquired with a delicate crook of his eyebrow.

Wigfall puffed out his chest and said, "May I introduce my particular friend Francis Jefferson. She lets *me* call her Fanny, but I don't know about you, you old rascal." The two men chuckled at each other.

Kate thought they looked like jackals sharing a particularly meaty kill. She held out her hand. "Dear Louis tells me you are going to help us. If that's true I shall allow you to call me Fanny." She looked him in the eye and batted her eyelashes the tiniest bit.

"I'd trust this little gal with my life." Wigfall motioned Kate towards one of the office chairs.

Luckett regretfully released Kate's hand. "Please, take a seat. Any friend of the Senator's is a friend of mine." He gave her a time tested up and down gaze, his eyes traveling the length of her body. Then he rocked back on his heels a little bit, clearly pleased with what he saw. He shot Wigfall an approving wink.

To her everlasting disgust, Kate failed to miss any of it. *Wasn't this just the way with men? You got to feeling a little bit sentimental and they did something that reminded you how irritating they could be.*

"Fanny here is one of us. When I return to Washington she will act as my proxy."

Thinking furiously, Kate decided to gamble. "Let me be honest with you James. I know my dear Louis is married, but do not mistake me for a harlot. Our relationship is an honorable one. My Daddy was a gentleman who fell on hard times and I am educated as a gentlewoman. I used to help Daddy keep the books—he taught me double entry bookkeeping. Louis here tells me important men have freed up considerable sums of the federal government's money to help you fight the injustices this country now faces. I volunteer my services to your cause."

James Luckett stared open-mouthed at the woman before him, clearly unable to think of anything to say in return.

"Ain't she something?" Wigfall asked, tipping his seat back in delight. "I have control of a considerable sum of money. I am loath to hand it over in one fell swoop, even to you Mr. Luckett. Too dangerous by half."

Luckett only nodded.

Louis pressed on. "As you no doubt heard, Texas seceded from the union five days ago and by all accounts I ought to be packing my bags for home. But as long as Congress sits, I have reason to stay in the viper's nest that is Washington City."

Luckett kept nodding.

It occurred to Kate that he realized he'd entirely lost control of his own office.

A preemptory knock sounded at the door before it opened.

Allan Pinkerton stepped into the office and did his best to look chagrinned. "I'm sorry for interrupting. I didn't know you were with clients. I'll come back later."

Kate watched as Allan pretended to retreat.

"No, no," Luckett stood and reassured the man he thought was John Hutchinson. "These fine people aren't clients. In fact, they're two folks I'd like you to meet." Luckett turned towards the Senator and Kate. "May I introduce Mr. John Hutchinson, late of New York, which to his credit he entirely despises. We had an exceedingly congenial exchange of views last night at dinner. Mr. Hutchinson, may I introduce Senator Louis Wigfall and his companion Miss Francis Jefferson."

Kate held out her hand for Hutchinson, who bowed and kissed it. Allan's eyes twinkled merrily at her as he did. Kate felt immediately better.

Introductions were made all around. When Mr. Hutchinson was comfortably installed in the last chair, he apologized again for interrupting.

"It's just that I need a clerk quite badly and don't know where to find one. I need someone reliable to cover the office when I'm out inspecting investments and maybe even keep the books as my business grows."

Kate almost gaped at Allan. *The old devil. He was listening at the door.* She saw his plan laid out before her, as if they'd already discussed it. She did so enjoy his utter belief in her.

Luckett frowned and said, "I'm sorry to say I don't have a clerk, let alone one I could share. I've been meaning to hire one, but the events of the last few months have been such that I have not had the time."

Kate leaped into the opening Allan just made for her. "If I may, gentlemen, I have a solution to both your problems." She turned toward Mr. Hutchinson. "Before you knocked I was assuring James that I was capable of acting as an intermediary in his business with the senator." She laid her hand on Wigfall's arm and gave him a little pat. "I also affirmed my

205

facility for keeping accounts. I would like to offer my short-term services to the each of you. The senator can attest that I am utterly trustworthy, an assurance you will not get with a stranger."

"Why Fanny!" Wigfall eyed Kate with delight, "You are full of surprises."

With as much dignity as she could muster Fanny defended her position. "I happen to know that the Treasury department hires lady clerks, as do some of the larger mercantile stores. Why not here? Besides, the senator wants me in Baltimore to help with his special project and no one knows more than myself that what the senator wants, the senator gets." She smiled modestly at Wigfall, who puffed up his chest and beamed back at her.

"Well, I don't know about any special projects, but I think it's a fine idea," Allan enthused. "If you gentlemen say Miss Fanny is reliable that's good enough for me."

The men talked among each other and agreed to Fanny's plan.

Wigfall stood and tugged down his waistcoat. "Gentlemen, I told this little lady I'd take her to dinner at Barnum's tonight. What do you say we make it a party?"

That evening they drank a good many bottles of champagne and claret while eating the largest and most varied dinner Kate had ever seen in her life. Many toasts were made to "Miss Fanny," each more enthusiastic than the last. The beverages encouraged a good bit of loose talk among the gentlemen and ample protestations of brotherhood. After dinner and brandy, which none of the gentlemen appeared to need, the two stock brokers agreed that Fanny could start work after lunch the next day, giving everyone plenty of time to recover from their evening bacchanal.

At the end of the evening Wigfall escorted Fanny to her door and left her for his own bed. A few minutes later a knock sounded at her door. Kate cracked the door open, relieved to find Allan there, grinning like a pleased four year old. She invited him in.

Allan took the seat closest to the glowing coal fire. "I've got news about your bomb."

"My bomb? I thought we agreed it wasn't mine?"

"Well, as it turns out, it has something to *do* with you, but I still agree with you that it wasn't *meant* for you."

"Mmmhmm."

"Mr. Howard telegraphed me. He says the captain of the Metropolitan Police examined the stable and found the remains of a Ketchum grenade."

"Which I assume," Kate said as patiently as she could, "is a type of bomb."

Allan shifted in his seat and lit one of his stubby cigars. "An exceedingly specific type of bomb. Grenades are designed to be thrown, which is the good news. The grenade exploded when it landed, so it was aimed at those two men. You were far enough away from the dead men for us to be certain about that."

"Well, that's good news isn't it? I mean, not for those two men, obviously, but for our operation."

"Well, it's more complicated than that. The Ketchum grenade is new, so new it hasn't been granted a patent yet. Grenades have always been hollow cast iron balls filled with gunpowder. The blasting cap makes the ball unbalanced, so they're hard to throw with accuracy. Worse, the thrower has to light a grenade and then throw it so that it explodes just as it arrives at its target. That requires the thrower to have perfect timing."

"Sounds like a pretty stupid weapon, if you ask me."

"True. But the idea is a good one— grenades contain more potential damage than a bullet and they're more mobile than traditional artillery. The Ketchum is distinctive because it's designed to fly accurately. They're oblong and have guide fins. And they've got a percussion cap in the nose so they only explode on impact."

"And that's what killed those men?"

"Yes, sadly, it is." Allan put his cigar down. "Sadly, because right now Mr. Ketchum is manufacturing them in secret for just one customer."

Kate sat forward. "Really? Who?"

"The United States Army." Allan picked up his cigar and examined the end.

"The U. S. Army is responsible for a bomb at Mr. Howard's stable? That doesn't make any sense."

"No, it doesn't. But Captain Hazzard says that Fort Sumter in South Carolina had a supply of Ketchum's, as did the federal arsenal in Virginia. The commanding officer at Fort Moultrie just moved his troupes to Fort Sumter and he reports that most of the artillery munitions are missing."

"Missing? The federal government has misplaced things that blow up? Does this have anything to do with the late and unlamented Secretary of War John Floyd? And maybe his friend from Texas?" Kate's brain whirled.

"Let's just say we know military supplies, mostly weapons, have disappeared from uncounted arsenals and forts in states that have seceded. It's one of the problems Colonel Sumner brought before Mr. Lincoln last fall. Unfortunately, Mr. Lincoln can't do anything about it before he's president."

"So we can deduce that a stolen military grenade, thrown in a building the Knights of the Golden Circle are known to use, was probably retaliation for an imagined security breech by secessionists? Right?"

"That's about it," Allan conceded. They both stared at the fire for a time. "Here's the thing Kate. You spend a lot of time with the senator and I see how he is with you. And today I saw how you are with him."

"No," Kate interrupted. "You saw how Fanny is with him."

"Maybe I did, maybe I didn't. I've learned a few things chasing criminals the last ten years and one of them is that no one is entirely evil and everyone who ever committed evil acts thought they had a good reason. When you get to know them, the bad guys aren't always all bad. But do not, under any circumstances, confuse the man and his deeds. He's deep in a dangerous game and he'll kill to protect himself and his cause. He might be fond of Fanny, but make no mistake, he'll kill Kate if he catches her."

Kate stood and walked over to the little drinks table. She poured two short brandies and handed one to Allan. Taking a sip, she looked over the edge of her glass at him. "Then I'll just have to make sure Kate and Louis never meet, won't I?"

The next few days went surprisingly smoothly. Fanny worked for Mr. Hutchinson in the mornings and Mr. Luckett in the afternoon. Allan and Kate spent their time deciphering and reading reports from Pinkerton operatives placed around

Baltimore and sending return messages, also in cipher. Sometimes Timothy Webster came to report in person, though he never brought Hattie with him, mostly because they could concoct no reasonable excuse for a woman to visit a stockbroker's office.

On her second day as a broker's clerk Senator Wigfall burst into Hutchinson's office waving the morning edition of the *Baltimore Sun* in the air. "Great and terrible news my girl!" he boomed, excitement overcoming any sense of discretion. Before she could reply he rushed forward and slapped the newspaper on her desk. The banner took up the top half of the newspaper.

NEW CONFEDERATE GOVERNMENT
PROCLAIMED
IN MONTGOMERY, ALABAMA
PROVISIONAL GOVERNMENT FORMED
FROM SEVEN FORMER STATES

The news shook Kate more than she imagined it would. She put both hands on the desk and gaped at Wigfall. "That's astounding news. I mean, I expected it, but still, I'm surprised. Aren't you?"

"Surprised? I'm pleased as punch, girl. What's the point of seven states seceding from the union if they don't form their own government?" He stepped behind her desk and wrapped her in a hug, lifting her out of her chair in his excitement. Still holding her he looked down at her upraised face. "I've got to get back to Washington. And maybe contact the fellows down in Alabama. Or go there." His look turned serious. "I will depend on you Fanny to protect my interests here." He stepped back and grasped both her hands.

After what seemed like an interminable exchange of mutual protestations of affection and trust, all of it excessively melodramatic, Louis marched Fanny next door to the Merchant's Bank. There he introduced her to the bank's president and explained what he needed. The man prepared the essential documents and presented them to Senator Wigfall and Fanny Jefferson.

With one looping signature Fanny Jefferson, alias Kate Warne, Pinkerton operative, became a signatory for a pile of embezzled federal money.

On the short walk from the back, back to the office building Louis gave Kate her orders. "Don't give it to Luckett all at once. I don't know him all that well and he could spend the money on cigars and fast women. Or run off to Cuba. And make sure he's using it like he's supposed to. Go along with him to some of the meetings, that kind of thing."

"He's not going to like that."

"Oh, I'll take care of him before I go." They climbed the stairs to the stock brokers' offices. Wigfall put a hand on the small of her back and pushed her towards Allan's office. "You go see Mr. Hutchinson. Me and Mr. Luckett will have ourselves a little talk. When I'm done with him, he'll know who's in charge."

Her hand on the doorknob, Kate turned, arched her eyebrow and asked, "And that would be me, I assume?"

Louis bellowed his laughter. "You're a caution, that's for sure girl. Go on now." He patted her rear end as he spoke. "I'll see you back at the hotel for dinner. We can try that fancy dining room one more time."

"Oh, Louis, that would be grand," she said as she wriggled her rear end out of his reach. A woman could only be expected to put up with so much. She checked the hall and stairway, and then stood on tip-toe and chastely kissed the senator on the cheek.

He looked mighty pleased with himself as he stepped into Luckett's office. "Wear something special," he called over his shoulder before he shut the door.

She looked appraisingly at the closed office door. *I'll wear my pepperbox pistol and if I don't shoot you during dinner it shall be a testament to my good nature.*

Chapter 20

February 12, 1861
Baltimore

K ate rattled the newspaper. The Baltimore Sun contained a number of articles about the Lincoln
Special, all of them entirely too informative for her
liking. Clearly the Special was no regular train, but a spectacle, not unlike the extravaganza's put on by circuses at the
beginning of a show. She shared Hazzard's frustration with
the public nature of the Lincoln Special. It wasn't as if Mr.
Lincoln could speechify his way out of disunion. Nope. Haters
couldn't be reasoned with. Logic and morality flew out the
window when people were in the grip of hysteria.

In spite of the threat that loomed over Lincoln's train,
there was nothing for Kate to do this morning. She'd dusted
the tops of the filing cabinets and straitened the desk drawer
contents. She sighed. The problem with a fake stock brokerage was that there was no real work to do.

She needed something to do. Now. She folded her newspaper and put her head on the desk. There was nothing to do.
And it was too early for lunch.

Allan was up in Perryville, a small town on the Susquehanna River just north of the Baltimore. He planned to meet with Timothy and Hattie, who'd infiltrated a secessionist group in the area. Kate argued with Allan this morning about her going to Perryville too, but she'd known it was a lost cause. Fanny would be minding the office during work hours, especially when the boss wasn't in. And in his hyper-vigilant state Luckett would notice anything odd, even if it was only a girl clerk not where she was supposed to be.

Kate sighed again, picked up the paper and folded it in half, leaving just the headlines visible. The day before, in Springfield Illinois, amid great fanfare, the train carrying the next president of the United States and an entourage that included a black valet, pulled out of the station. Kate smiled to herself as she thought about Juba on that train.

This thought led Kate to imagine Hazzard in his dress blues, a thought she followed with a moment of self-recrimination. She needed to stay away from the delicious captain. If history taught her anything it was that she made bad choices when it came to men. Worse, she had once let a man derail her life. But still, a girl could *think* about a man, couldn't she? Look, but not touch?

She picked up the folded newspaper, resisting the urge to smacked herself on the head with it. A side-bar said that Mr. Lincoln's wife and two youngest sons weren't on the train when it left Springfield. Apparently they intended to join the entourage in Indianapolis the next day. Today, Kate thought, correcting herself. He's in Indianapolis this morning, probably giving his speech right about now.

The second page had a map of the Special's route. The train would follow a long, looping run east and north that kept Mr. Lincoln in friendly territory as long as possible, before turning south. The day before Mr. Lincoln arrived in Wash-

214

ington he'd be in Baltimore. And here she sat, as the train moved inexorably this way, doing nothing. The tick tock of the office clock seemed more ominous today than it had before. Tick tock.

Kate stood up, grabbed the newspaper and walked next door to Luckett's office. Might as well stir the pot.

"Fanny my dear. What a great day it is. A great day indeed." Luckett was up, pacing the office in obvious high fettle. "I was about to come over and share my news with Mr. Hutchinson."

Kate's detective antennae quivered. "Mr. Hutchinson is out. He'll be back this afternoon. Can I help you James?"

"You'll do for the news as well or better than Mr. Hutchinson, I suppose."

Kate took a seat and nodded encouragingly at Luckett. So far she'd had no luck getting him to divulge helpful information. Day after day Luckett ignored Wigfall's order to keep her in the loop. He was gone half the time, so she knew he was up to something.

Luckett stopped pacing and faced Kate. He picked a piece of paper up from his desk and examined it in the light from the window. "I've got a letter here from Governor Hicks. He's just back from testifying before that wretched Senate committee and he's mad as a kicked dog about it."

"I can't believe those rascally northern senators had the temerity to call the Governor of Maryland to a hearing, like he's a common criminal." Kate enjoyed expressing faux moral outrage immensely. It added spice to an otherwise boring day.

"Exactly! In his letter to me he inquires about recruiting for the National Volunteers. He says he has control of a federal arsenal and he's willing to hand it over to us if our

215

recruiting is suitably strong. He's got an idea. Here, I'll just read it to you." Luckett held the letter up. "Will there be good men to send out to kill Lincoln and his men. If not, I suppose the arms would be better sent south."

"I don't believe it," Kate exclaimed, excited for reasons Luckett could not know of. "Can I see?"

He handed the letter over to her. The first page was on State of Maryland letterhead and the sentences Luckett had read toward the bottom of the second page. "And he's refer-ring to the men we're funding out of this office? He wants to use them to assassinate the president? Do we have men ready for that?"

"Absolutely. Dozens of men sign up every day. But there's more. See here in the governor's letter he writes that the legis-lature will call a Secession Convention and that I'm to be a delegate. He wants me to vote against secession, can you be-lieve that? What can the daft fool be thinking? He want's Lincoln dead, but he wants to stay in the Union?"

"Doesn't matter much what he wants," Kate pointed out. "You must vote your conscience at a secession convention."

"Now is the time for good men to act, even if it puts our lives in peril," Luckett proclaimed, puffing out his chest in self importance. "If the people, or the damned governor call it treason, then let it be so, but the rights of Maryland and the Southern Confederacy must be protected."

Kate clapped prettily at his speech. "Well spoken James!"

"You're so forceful and adamant. It's exciting." *Hook baited. Now cast your line.* "Can you tell me about the volunteers? I would so like to know how you'll be spending the money. It's all just so thrilling, with history being made and all."

"It is pretty exciting," he agreed, mustaches twitching. "With the money from Senator Wigfall our recruiting has doubled. Which reminds me, I need more. Mr. Hillard and Mr. Ferrandini, who you really must meet, he's a most excitable Italian fellow and most entertaining, visit taverns and bars where working men may be found. I go too sometimes. We tell them the dastardly Northern railroads are planning to transport troops to Maryland and Virginia, replace our state governments with martial law and thus prevent secession. This naturally outrages loyal southern men, who are then only too glad to join the National Volunteers as a consequence."

"I had no idea the railroads were planning such a despicable act!"

"Don't be daft girl. There's not a whit of truth in it. But the fiction whips up the men. Our ten-dollar enlistment bonus doesn't hurt either. Fools, everyone of them, but damned useful fools. I tell you what else they like. We tell them we shall stop Mr. Lincoln's passage through Baltimore by instigating a riot the day his train arrives. They love it. People like that like nothing better than a mob."

Kate feigned awe. "My goodness!"

Luckett preened and strutted behind the desk. "We tell them all their sufferings come from Abolitionist Rule. And they believe it, because they want to. It's preferable to admitting they are each the authors of their own misfortune. Plus, the poor devils are desperate. We offer them cash money and tell them there will be the same every month if they'll join up with us. Some men join us only because it puts bread on the table, but mark my words, when the time for action comes they'll follow orders."

Kate went fishing for more. "So you're recruiting is that successful?"

"Successful isn't the word for it Fanny. The senator's money has made all the difference. I've even made contacts in the Plug Uglies and the Rip Raps."

"The gangs? Isn't that dangerous?"

Luckett swaggered and puffed up even more.

I'm afraid he's going to explode. Kate resisted the impulse to push her chair back so as to not be splattered by an eruption of self-important man flesh.

"You've just got to know how to handle fellows like that. A hundred dollars to each gang leader will buy us both gangs. They'll be cheaper than our regular recruits. And they want to be National Volunteers, I'm sure for no better reason than it has a better ring to it than Rip Raps or Plug Uglies. Can you believe there's a gang what calls itself the Plug Uglies? And Rip Raps? They're the dregs of society and looking for someone to blame for their servile condition. God knows they'd never blame themselves, not when they can blame Negros and northern liberals."

"Aren't they dangerous?"

"Exactly. Violent men accustomed to villainous deeds."

"Well, I think you and your friends are shrewd operators." She'd almost said 'operatives.' Thank goodness she hadn't, operative being a word firmly linked to the Pinkerton Detective Agency. "Why do you need all these men James?"

"It's like I already said." His eyes glittered with excitement. "We're going to use them to stop that damned ape from getting to Washington."

"But won't that leave you with Mr. Lincoln's vice president, Mr. Hamlin? The newspapers say he's more anti-slavery than Mr. Lincoln."

"You miss the point entirely my dear. I suppose that's why the ladies don't run governments. They have no long range planning skills."

Kate reminded herself that, if she did this correctly, she could one day skewer this man with his own words. "Then explain it to me for goodness sakes. So I'll understand."

He sat down in his chair and leaned back, hands laced behind his head. "All right Fanny, pay attention. What we're planning is the largest public uprising in the country's history and we'll do it the day Mr. Lincoln's train comes to town."

"I thought Governor Hicks and Marshall Kane promised Mr. Lincoln safe passage through the city. That's what the newspaper said."

"It's easy to *promise* protection and a whole other thing to deliver it."

"But won't Mr. Lincoln just wait for the riot to end and go set up shop in Washington anyway?

Luckett shook his head. "If all goes as planned Baltimore will be the spark that ignites the revolution."

"To what end? I'm still confused." Kate hadn't said a truer thing during this whole conversation. *What could they possibly hope to accomplish, but for senseless violence and destruction?*

Luckett sat forward and prepared to lecture. "Right now only states in the deep south have seceded. We need more states to break the Union and guarantee the survival of the southern confederacy. The provisional Confederate government plans to meet as soon as Baltimore rioting commences. They'll pass a law prohibiting the importation of slaves from

219

any state not in the Confederacy. Slave owners in the states that haven't seceded will panic, particularly when we get one of our men to stand up in the United States congress and propose abolishing slavery in the remaining states as a punishment for all the mob violence. That'll push the rest of the slave states to join the Confederacy, to protect their investment in slaves. We'll get all fifteen slave states, including Maryland and after that we'll have the damned abolitionists over a barrel." Luckett beamed in excited anticipation.

"Baltimore will ensure the downfall of the union?" Kate forced herself to smile. "That's brilliant!"

Luckett smiled and made a small bow. "They'll understand they must legalize slavery to save the nation or bring down the whole country with their own arrogance."

Speechless, Kate could only stare at Luckett. These men were going to cause a riot, which would surely kill dozens if not hundreds of innocent people, prevent the duly elected president from taking office and secede from the union in an attempt to force the legalization of human bondage. Just to protect their ideological and economic supremacy. And they thought Northerners were arrogant.

Kate went back to Hutchinson's office and waited. At dusk Allan came through the door on a wave of damp sea air. He kept his coat on and stepped right up next to her so he could speak softly. "We need to talk and not here. I've got news from Timothy and Hattie up in Perrymansville."

She stood and whispered back. "What I've got to say can't wait. Luckett's next door but if we're quiet we should be fine."

Kate locked the hallway door, turned down the lamps and pulled her chair over to Allan's desk so they were only inches away from each other. In her lowest voice told him about her morning conversation with Luckett.

"Are you serious?" Allan asked when Kate had come to the end of her tale.

"Sadly, I am," Kate said gravely. "If we're going to expose a plan of this magnitude and get anyone to believe us we need more than one source of information." Kate paused and put her hand on Allan's. "Luckett needs to repeat it all to you."

"Kate, I trust you. I'd say so to anyone who doubted you." As soon as he said it Allan pinched his mouth together and then bit his upper lip.

"See? And I'm not feeling sorry for myself. He told *me*, Allan. And I'm going to get him to tell you. Here's what I want you to do."

She waited while Allan made a trip next door to the Merchant's bank. When he got back Kate walked him over to Luckett's office.

"Mr. Luckett, I hope you won't be angry with me," she said, wringing her handkerchief for effect, "but I just knew Mr. Hutchinson would want to help your noble work and I knew," here Kate played her trump card, "the senator would want as many important men involved as possible. So I explained a little of what you told me to him." Kate gestured at Allan, who was standing in Luckett's doorway.

Allan strode forward and held out his hand to Luckett. "Dear Mr. Luckett, I am brimming with admiration for you and your cause." Allan took out his wallet and removed a sheaf of bills. "I have here fifty dollars. I should like you to take it and employ it in any manner you see fit."

Luckett took the money and deliberately fanned through the bills.

Allan spoke again, rushing his words. "I know how irregular this is. I only ask you to be exceedingly cautious about discussing my involvement with outsiders."

Luckett looked up at Allan, indignation evident. "My men are sworn to secrecy. You too must be sworn to secrecy. And the penalties for breaking the code of silence are severe indeed."

It was all Kate could do not to snort in amusement. *The code of silence? I'm afraid if the cleaning lady showed the slightest interest you'd tell her your plan.*

As if to disprove Kate's thought Luckett said, "Last night we had to take a man out past the river and hang him. He drank his ten dollars away and threatened to go to the police if we did not give him more money."

Kate's stomach rolled. Suddenly Luckett didn't seem so ridiculous. They'd murdered some poor devil. However ridiculous she found these conspirators individually, she needed to keep reminding herself that they were nonetheless profoundly dangerous.

That same evening Kate knocked on Allan's hotel room door. She looked up and down the dingy hall while she waited. The smell of cooked cabbage wafted through the air. The Howard House was no Barnum's, which she supposed was the point. None of the senator's friends would see her coming in and out of this dreary place.

Allan opened the door and gestured her inside.

To Kate's dismay there was another man in the room, sitting in a corner chair. "Mr. Scully! I'm surprised to see you. I thought you were down south. Richmond wasn't it?"

"Charleston," he half grunted before remembering his manners and standing. "It didn't take a work of genius to figure out the people running South Carolina are sincere in their desire to rebel. As the city is not on the Special's route, Allan recalled me to Baltimore." He stopped, looked her up and down and barked out, "That going to be a problem?"

"Now Mr. Scully, you hold on a mite. Miss Warne's done some capitol work on this Baltimore mess and you're going to want to watch your tone." To take the sting out of his words Allan gestured towards the round table in the middle of the room. "I've had tea and coffee sent up, and bought these little cakes from a bakery down the street. We've got a lot of talking to do, so help yourself."

Kate made for the table with the baked goods. She'd missed dinner, what with putting in an appearance at Barnum's, changing clothes and walking across downtown to the Howard. Besides, dessert was always best if it preceded dinner. Cake was just so much more delicious than vegetables.

"John arrived here just moments before you did Kate, so I haven't had a chance to explain your work with Wigfall and Luckett. Why don't you fill him in?" Allan sat and lit one of his cigars.

Kate took a small preserved cherry tart before she sat down next to Allan. While Allan smoked Kate recapped her Baltimore findings between bites of pastry.

Scully was singularly unimpressed. "Harrumph. Sounds like you've been busy. Makes me wonder about your tactics."

"What were you wondering Mr. Scully?" Kate used her sweetest voice.

"Weeell," he drawled. "How's a gal that looks like you get so much information?"

"John," Allan slammed his cigar down, sending a shower of sparks out over the carpet. "I'll ask you to apologize right now."

Kate smiled coldly and leaned forward in her chair. She drew her pepper pot pistol from her skirt pocket. "Mr. Scully, I often say I am no lady, but neither am I a whore. Call me one again and I'll put a bullet in you."

Scully shifted uncomfortably in his chair while Allan and Kate waited for his response. "Miss Warne, I owe you an apology. Guess I was a little envious is all. You've made a lot more headway than me." He stood and bowed stiffly in her direction.

Kate inclined her head at Mr. Scully, trying not to laugh. She didn't really care if he was sincerely sorry or just worried about being shot, so long as he shut his damned mouth. She decided to change the subject. "Mr. Scully, I would be most interested to hear what you've been up to. I'm sure you've learned more than you credit."

Allan looked gratefully at Kate and relit his cigar.

"Weeell, there upon hangs an interesting tail," Scully drawled. "I been hanging around the Pagoda Saloon and Hemlings Billiard Room— sayin' the right kinda things to get me noticed. From what you say Miss Warne," he paused and nodded at Kate, "I think I got myself in on the lower levels of the organization. I've never seen Luckett, but I have met Mr. Hillard. If I was a guessing man I'd say Hillard is the fellow right below Luckett."

Kate interrupted. "Luckett says pretty much the same."

Scully nodded laconically. "Mr. Hillard seems to have taken a shine to me— he takes me around in the evenings and introduces me to people. I mighta given him the idea I was good with explosives and he might a figured, all on his own like, that I'd come in handy should he need things to go boom." Scully grinned wickedly at Kate and Allan.

"Mr. Scully," Kate exclaimed, in pretend shock. "You have unplumbed depths."

"Anyone in particular we need to keep an eye on?" Allan asked.

"Oh, I should think so," Scully said. "Hold on." He poured himself a cup of coffee and continued. "Hillard took me to Miss Travis's house one evening. Seems to be a regular meeting place for these Volunteer fellows. Mrs. Travis, she's a . . . ." Scully paused, searching for the right word.

"A prostitute?" Kate filled in helpfully. "A courtesan? Fille de joi? Strumpet, harlot, whore?"

Scully and Allan both looked at Kate in surprise.

"Gentlemen, Travis is a well known Baltimore madame and her house is visited by the upper echelons of society. I'd like to see it."

"It's no place for a lady, Miss Warne," Scully interjected, "not even a detective lady. I was right disgusted when I was there. Hillard's got a favorite at the house and he's not above kissing her right in front of people. Turned my stomach, I can tell you that."

"Mr. Scully, you're a moralist!" She smiled at him to show she was teasing.

"Well, I don't know about that," he huffed. "It's just that Hilliard's got a wife. And children. A family man ought to be at home in the evenings, not drinking whiskey and consortin' with low women."

Allan raised his glass. "Here here."

Kate snorted. "Houses of prostitution *are* disgusting. Men prey on women who have no other way to make their living. And taking whatever disease they pick up home to their poor wives. It's morally offensive. If more women could be detectives, and doctors and the like, there'd be fewer prostitutes."

Scully slurped his coffee and said, "I'm not sure Mrs. Travis would agree with you— she makes a good living. Anyway, I've also been to some midnight drills, where companies of Volunteers march up and down in an empty field like they were real soldiers. And Mr. Hillard meant to introduce me to the barber at the Barnum Hotel, a fellow named Ferrandini, but he wasn't there. I get the impression the Italian fellow is a highly placed member of these Volunteers. "

"The Barnum's barber? You're kidding me? The senator met with him the day we got here, I'd be willing to bet." Kate remembered Wigfall's tonsorial splendor a few days ago.

"How dangerous do they seem to you," Allan asked.

Scully thought about it for a moment. "What's scary about them isn't their marching, nor their talk. It's the shear numbers of them and their fervor. Miss Warne's explanation about the funding explains the numbers, but there's a zealousness in the movement that no amount of money can buy."

Allan stood and poured himself a cup of coffee. "That jibes with what Timothy and Hattie have to say. They're up in Perryville. They say the Volunteers up there are well funded too, so we have to guess that's more of the money Wigfall liberated from Washington—money Kate's been helping disburse." Allan looked over at Kate.

"It's not like I could *not* do it," she protested.

"No, I didn't think you could stop the flow of money. I was just thinking how much damage your senator's caused and what he'd do to you if he found out you weren't Fanny."

Kate decided to ignore this line of discussion. "Perryville?"

"Oh, yes. Timothy and Hattie are posing as disaffected southerners. Hattie's having the time of her life, or so she says, putting one over on people who think they're superior to Negros."

Kate sighed. "Hattie has a weird sense of humor."

"They both do," Scully added. "Webster's a bit of a trickster."

"That's probably why they work so well together," Allan said. "They say the Perryville Volunteers are set to block the Lincoln Special at the Susquehanna. One plan is to blow the track outside of Perryville so the train doesn't get to the river, and failing that, sink the ferries that carry the train cars across the river.

Scully sat forward in his chair. "But they could just put the President on another boat or in a carriage. It makes no sense!"

"Remember, the Volunteers don't think they're stopping the president so much as they think they're stopping forced occupation by thousands of troops," Kate reminded him. "Plus, this is all just part of a long range plan to force all of the slave states to secede so that they can ultimately force the federal government to legalize slavery in all the states."

Scully could only stare from Kate to Allan and back again.

Kate had to ask. "*Are* there plans to bring in the army and occupy Maryland?"

"What do you think?" Allan asked her.

Kate considered the question. "Well, the sitting president would have to order it and I can't see why Buchanan would to that.'"

"Exactly," Allan said.

"One more dumb question," Kate leaned forward towards Allan. "Reason and logic aside, why wouldn't they be planning to kill Mr. Lincoln? As a means to stopping him and causing chaos?"

Allan rubbed his chin, pondering the question. "That's the key question isn't it? So far we haven't found any real evidence of an assassination plot."

"Doesn't the absence of information make you suspicious though? Isn't the *absence* of talk worrisome?"

Standing, Scully said, "I wouldn't put anything past these scoundrels. I say we kill 'em all and let God sort 'em out."

Kate nearly spit out the tea she'd been drinking.

"I'm not sure we're empowered to do that," Allan said dryly. "And in answer to your question Kate, I'm as worried as you are, but without any evidence there's nothing we can do. So we keep digging. In the mean time, I'm going to wake up a telegraph operator and send a message to Hazzard on the Special. Where are they tonight?"

Kate's heart did an uncomfortable little flutter thing at the mention of Hazzard, but she tamped it down firmly. She glanced at Allan to make assure herself she hadn't given herself away with a visible display of girlish vapors. "Hmmm. Cincinnati. We've got ten days before they get to Baltimore." She wearily pushed herself to her feet and made for the door.

She put her hand on the door knob, then turned back. "Five Pinkertons and ten days. Seems about right."

Chapter 21

February 13, 1861
Baltimore

K ate stared at her morning newspaper, her eyebrows
climbing toward her hair line. It just couldn't be.
But there it was. A quarter page advertisement,
bold as brass.

The Front Street Theater Presents
DAN RICE'S GREAT SHOW
For Two Weeks Only!
FEATURING
CHEVALIER BLONDIN, HERO OF NIAGRA FALLS
Buffo and Shakespearean Clowns
Mrs. Rice's Famous Dancing Horses
Wednesday and Saturday Matinees Featuring
CHINESE SPECTACLE,
Astounding
LALLAH ROOKH
& Never Before Seen
TAME RHINO
Dress Circle, 50c, Family Circle 25c, Colored Circle, 15c
Shows 2 PM and 7 PM

Forehead knotted with concentration she perused the advertisement. She made some "if, then" calculations based on what she knew about the situation in Baltimore. An idea so outlandish it was either insane or brilliant bloomed in her brain.

She went to work and shared her idea with Allan. He laughed, but didn't tell her it was a bad idea. After lunch Kate threw on her coat and bonnet, made her excuses to both of her employers and hurried down the stairs of the South Street office building. Walking up Baltimore Street Kate felt oddly exhilarated, as if she were playing hooky from school to indulge some secret and wicked habit.

Her parents played Baltimore's Front Street theater years ago, though Kate was so young that she barely remembered it. Circuses played the really large theaters when they could so they didn't have to set up tents and stands, nor suffer the cold or heat of whatever season they were in. Philadelphia had the Walnut Street Theater, Washington the National Theater, where Kate had so recently performed and Baltimore had the imposing Front Street Theater.

As she approached the theater she began to feel less sure of her plan. She hadn't seen Mr. Rice since the day she left the circus. Still and all, he had given her Excelsior. That probably meant he wasn't angry with her for running away from the circus.

"One ticket for the matinee please," Kate said, smiling at the ticket agent in a not entirely successful effort to keep the anxiety and excitement out of her voice. She pushed a half dollar coin at him, adding, "Dress circle seats."

"You're in for a good one today miss," he said, pushing the ticket across the counter at her. "You get the Steeple Chase and the Spectacle both."

She grinned back at him and took her ticket and made her way across the theater's gaudy lobby. A boy no older than twelve stood at the double doors. Kate knew his job was to check tickets and point customers toward their seats, but she was early and he was just standing there kicking his heels against the wall and looking bored.

"Good afternoon young man." Kate leaned over a tiny bit, so she wouldn't loom over the boy. "Do you work for the theater or the circus?"

"The circus, Ma'am. My pa's a tumbler."

"Does he do any leaping?"

"He does! He can jump over three horses. At one time! How'd you know?"

She leaned in and whispered, "My parents were circus equestriennes and I've known my share of gymnasts and tumblers. And clowns. Why, long ago, I even trained on the wire with Mr. Blondin."

"Ya did not!"

"Why sure I did. He used to do this act where he'd dress like an ape and walk the wire, pretending to eat nits off it." Kate thought there was a good chance Blondin still did some version of that act in his show and if so it ought to establish her bona fides.

"Nah! You never!" The boy looked at her and scratched his head. "Whatcher doin' out here, dressed like a lady then?"

"My young friend, thereby hangs a lion's tale." She took a sealed letter out of her reticule and held it toward the boy. "I wonder if you could give this to Mr. Rice for me? I know how

231

busy backstage is before a show and I wouldn't want to interrupt. But I would like Misters Rice and Blondin to know I'm in the house." Kate looked encouragingly at the lad. "Could you do that for me? And take this for your trouble?" Kate held out a coin.

The boy snatched the coin out of her hand, clearly impressed with her largesse. "Sure miss. I'll run it right back, afore I get too busy." He scampered off, through a side door, leaving Kate to find her own seat.

Three hours later Kate stood to make her way backstage. The show left her feeling visually and emotionally overwhelmed. After months of tight control it had been heavenly to gasp in delight and laugh until her belly hurt. In the first act the clowns performed the Hamlet travesty, with Mr. Rice playing a dimwitted Hamlet, to the great merriment of the audience. Half way through it a Pete Jenkins act interrupted them. Kate had to admit, though she'd seen versions of the Pete Jenkins dozens of times before, she'd almost been taken in. One of the performers pretended to be a drunken rube who crawled up on stage and disrupted the act. After bumbling around stage, exchanging rude repartee with the clowns to the audience's delight, the man crawled on a horse, conveniently on stage and took several comic prat falls before throwing off his rustic pants and shirt to expose glittering equestrienne tights. Soon after Maggie Rice joined him with three horses. Kate particularly delighted in Maggie's performance because she remembered her Poppa teaching Mrs. Rice how to train horses.

Tumblers came out after the horses, and then more clowns, one of whom broke into song several times. The crowd sang along, using Dan Rice Song Books they'd brought with them. The Chinese Spectacle proved to be a pageant of oriental fantasy, capped by the appearance Mr. Rice's elephant Lallah Rookh, who performed her famous headstand. The rhino also appeared with Mr. Rice, and performed a few simple tricks while bedecked in red tassels that matched Lallah's adornments.

Just as the rhino left the stage a baby spotlight shown from the stage to the back of the theater, forcing the audience to turn around and look up. There, Mr. Blondin stood at the end of a wire so thin that Kate hadn't even noticed it before. He tripped out on the wire, twirled and somersaulted, then walked the length of the wire, before offering to carry an audience member on his back. A boy volunteered. Kate recognized the theater page, which made sense. Blondin could undoubtedly walk the wire carrying anyone, but the task would be most safely done with someone trained to be still. The performance came to a close with a modified steeple chase, in which horses and riders rode around the stage, before jumping off and galloping up the aisles and out the theater doors.

Feeling as light as a helium filled balloon, Kate made her way forward, against the flow of the crowd, toward a door at the side of the stage. Just as she was about to reach for the knob the door flew open. A tall, lean man with a graying Quaker beard threw himself at her and enveloped her in an enthusiastic embrace.

"Katie! You've gone and growed up." Dan Rice held her at arm's length and looked her over. "But I'd know you anywhere. You're the spitting image of your mother, aren't you?"

"Where is she? Dammit Rice, get out of the way." Monsieur Blondin pushed past Mr. Rice, grasped Kate's shoulders

233

and kissed her on both cheeks. "Why, you are beee-you-ti-ful," he said. Kate remembered that Mr. Blondin's accent increased in direct relation to his excitement level. Since she'd last seen Blondin he'd become quite famous for crossing Niagara Falls on a tight rope, first with a pole, then without. He'd crossed the falls blindfolded once and another time sat down on the wire midway to cook and eat an omelet.

"Oh, Mr. Rice and Mr. Blondin." Kate's eyes threatened to overflow. That she could have put away this part of her life or worried that they'd still accept her, filled her with hot shame.

"Now, none of that girly," Mr. Rice pronounced, his voice gruffer than it had been seconds before. "Come backstage and meet everyone."

Mr. Blondin spoke up. "I have a leettle boy and a leettle girl you must meet, and a wife to go with them. You will come see." He gestured her to follow him down the hall that stood behind the door. Mr. Rice held the door and stepped behind Kate.

Maggie Rice stood in the hall giving instructions to a young man who had to be one of the horse hostlers. She didn't see Kate, so Kate stood next to her and nudged her with her shoulder.

Maggie's look of annoyance cleared when she realized who'd bumped her. "Oh, my stars. The prodigal daughter is returned!" After more hugging and more tears the four of them retired to Maggie's dressing room.

"It's so very good to see you Mr. And Mrs. Rice," Kate began. Before she could go on the two Rice's burse into laughter.

Mr. Rice slapped his knee and said, "Maggie divorced me last summer."

"Divorced?" Kate could only stare.

"Don't look so flummoxed, Kate," Maggie said, laughing merrily as if they were announcing a wedding, not a divorce. "Me and Dan, we had three girls together and we've always liked each other just fine, but we were more like brother and sister than man and wife. I figured we both deserved better, so I divorced him. This way I get to work with the old rascal when I want, but he and I are both free to work with other people too." Maggie winked roguishly at Kate at the word 'work.'

Kate gaped at the two of them. Most couple's didn't have marriages as amicable as this couple's divorce. Nor had she ever heard anyone speak of divorce with anything but shame and recrimination. The Rice's attitude about it bore thinking upon.

The next hour passed swiftly by. Mr. Blondin retrieved his wife and two small children and several circus people stopped by to meet Kate, most of whom remembered her parents. Kate filled them in on Excelsior's life after the circus. Finally, Mr. Rice stood up, reminding everyone in the room they had an evening show fast approaching. After much more hugging and promises to write, the room emptied.

Mr. Rice took Kate's note out of his pocket, opened it, looked at it as if to remind himself of its contents and then asked, "Now, what's this about needing a favor?"

Kate looked steadily at the man before her. He'd been one of her father's best friends. The two men had stayed up late many a night drinking in the Warne's wagon, arguing politics and the nature of morality, while Kate listened intently from her bunk. She knew him to be as steadfast a foe of slavery as any man alive. At least he had been years ago. She needed to know if he was still.

"If my father and Juba were here, would you all still be friends? Would you agree with the two of them about the current state of the nation and which side to stand on?"

Sensing the seriousness of her question, Mr. Rice took his hands out of his pockets and stepped toward Kate. "I would Kate. I say and do a lot of foolish things as a circus clown, but I swear upon my honor and your departed father's head, I hate slavery and am a Union man."

Kate nodded her head and stood up to shake Mr. Rice's hand. "I thought as much. I have a proposal for you. That is, if you'd like to help Mr. Lincoln." She swallowed a great lump of nerves and explained what she needed.

Chapter 22

L ouis dipped his pen into the inkwell and signed the paper before him with a flourish worthy of John Hancock. He looked up from the paper, leaned back in his chair and put his feet on the desk. He looked at his boots and frowned. *Hell, there was a smear right there on the left one.*

That was the problem with free nigrahs. They didn't understand work, none of the coloreds did really, but a free nigrah man couldn't be compelled to do a job like a slave could. No wonder the damn country was falling apart. Irritated by the smudge on his boot, Louis dropped his feet to the floor and looked at the piece of paper again. A self-satisfied smile spread across his face.

My dear Mr. Luckett,

I would like you to introduce my beloved Fanny to Mr. F so that she might give him a large packet from the building next door. It is of utmost important that F be adequately compensated and encouraged in his work. Show this note to dear Fanny, particularly the postscript below.

Yours in Brotherhood,

W

PS Dear girl, I regret I must place duty to my country before personal pleasure. Know that I think of you daily and have the utmost confidence in your ability to assist the men of Baltimore in the accomplishment of our great work.

Perfect. The trick with managing subalterns was to give them just enough information to make them think they were central to the mission, but not enough for them to ruin an operation. Luckett and the Baltimore crowd certainly didn't need to know he had a back-up plan should the barber fail.

Best they think all the players in this little drama were independent actors and not puppets on sets of strings. *Speaking of back-up plans and actors . . . .* Louis grinned to himself and pulled a clean sheet of paper from his desk drawer. He dipped his pen in the ink bottle.

My Dear Mr. B.

Meet me the evening before the train, at my hotel. I'll have with me materials you shall require to accomplish your task. I shall pay you half the agreed upon amount at that time. The other half will come upon completion of your task. I and your country thank you for your service.

Most Sincerely,

W

Louis held his note out at arm's length. He really did have a gift for this sort of thing. He sealed his letter with an extra big gob of hot wax and sat it on the table near the door. He'd get it in the mail first thing tomorrow morning.

Chapter 23

Allan poked his head into Luckett's office and looked pointedly at Kate.

Kate gestured him in. "He's out. I'm not sure for how long, but he took his coat. I'd be gone too, but I thought I'd get his books in order first. Verisimilitude, you know." Kate paused while Allan took a seat. "By the way, any word from our man?"

After their late-night meeting earlier in the week, Allan sent a ciphered telegraph to the Chicago office, outlining what they'd learned. Mr. Bangly was supposed to catch up with the Lincoln Special and meet with Colonel Sumner and Captain Hazzard.

Allan looked chagrined. "Apparently the Colonel and Captain took our Baltimore intelligence seriously. They suggest meeting in New York in a few days. " Allan pulled out Luckett's client chair and sprawled across it. "Oh, and I think I know where Luckett's taken himself off to— he's gone to the barber. We're going out tonight."

Kate delicately raised one eyebrow. "And he wants to look his best for you? Because you're such a catch?"

Allan struck a pose, tucking one of his hands inside his waistcoat. "Joan *does* say I'm a fine figure of a man."

"Ha! You're no Louis Trevant Wigfall."

Allan reared back his head in faux affront. "I cry foul! You've set the bar too high." They chuckled at each other. "This morning I told him how having you around all the time has about driven me mad with manly need."

Kate squealed at him, "Gross Allan!"

"I know," he said gravely. "And yet it worked. He thinks it's high time I see the inside of Mrs. Travis's house of ill repute. I think he's killing three birds with one stone. The senator's note commands him to introduce you to this mysterious F, he wants me to meet with the men on the ground of this Baltimore plot and he wants to visit this brothel. Interestingly, that Italian barber Mr. Scully warned us about is named Ferrandini."

Kate crooked an eyebrow at Allan. "The mysterious F. The plot thickens," she said in her best spooky voice. "And I'm supposed to be going along? When were you two going to mention it to me. A lady does need a little warning."

"I just told you."

Kate scoffed. *Men.* "I did say I wanted to see the inside of a brothel."

"I've seen a few in the course of my detecting career and trust me, you're not missing anything. Though I am glad you're coming along. We'll be able to count on an excess of loquaciousness in the gentlemen, spurred on by drink and men's natural desire to show off for beautiful women. They'll all want to impress you, both because you're a fine looking woman and because you hold purse strings."

"Mostly the purse strings I suspect and thanks for reminding me. I need to visit the bank," Kate grumbled.

"My dear, don't underestimate yourself. Remember, I've seen you at your feminine full power. Your more than a little scary."

"I am, am I?" she asked, unable to help herself. Goading Allan was just so much fun.

"You have no idea my dear. No idea."

When the knock came at Kate's door she stationed herself in the middle of the room and called, "Come in."

Allan opened the door, took one step inside and stopped, mid-step. Luckett, who'd been right behind Allan, ran into him. Both men gaped at Kate.

"In the name of all that is holy . . . " Allan paused and closed his mouth. He opened it to say, "You look magnificent Miss Fanny."

"Uh, huh," Luckett grunted, clearly straining the boundaries of his current vocabulary abilities.

Kate hoped her dress would have this effect. The key to it's allure was not an obvious appeal to sexuality or a shiny cheapness that advertised the wearers availability to the highest bidder. This dress depended on impeccable tailoring and French corsetry. Made from a light silk moiré in a gold-toned ivory, the dress had no frou frou embellishments but for a metallic gold appliqued border shaped like a leafy vine that circled the bottom of the skirt. The maid laced Kate into an especially cut corset that thrust her bosoms up and out in a most alarming manner. The ivory silk of the dress fit the corset like a second skin and was cut for maximum exposure of

241

her gravity defying bust. Tiny puffed sleeves exposed most of her arms, leaving Kate's upper-torso more naked than not. What made the dress so devastatingly sexy, the dress maker explained to Kate when they'd had the final fitting, was its combination of exposed skin and restrained elegance.

Kate thought the possibility that her breasts might pop out of the dress at any minute figured in it's attractions as well, particularly for the gentlemen, but who was she to argue with a professional dress maker? The point of the dress was to get men to tell her things. "Shall we go Gentlemen?"

"After you my lady," Allan said with a gallant bow.

She grabbed up her bag, made heavy by her derringer. As they left it occurred to Kate that poor Mr. Luckett still hadn't managed a complete sentence.

Anna Travis's house looked like any other prosperous home on the block. Three stories high, a pinkish granite encased the lower portion of the house, while the upper two stories were mauve painted wood siding. In deference to Kate the gentlemen called a hack to take them there, though the house was only blocks from the Barnum Hotel. An entirely respectably dressed, dark skinned maid greeted them at the door. She couldn't have been more than twelve years old.

"May I help you Sirs? And Madame?" She performed a small curtsy as she spoke.

"We'd like to make a call upon Mrs. Travis, if she's receiving tonight," Mr. Luckett offered.

The little maid let them all in. Kate wondered how a girl that age ended up answering the door at a fancy house and what would happen to her when her body matured.

They stepped into a small front foyer, with drawing rooms to the left and right. On the left, next to a short bar, a three piece ensemble played something familiar. Kate paused and listened. Mozart.

Men stood around the room, talking to surprisingly well-dressed women, some white, some light skinned colored women. More women reclined on chaise lounges. A dark skinned black woman in a restrained navy blue dress moved among the crowd, delivering drinks and picking up dirty glasses.

"Mr. Luckett! You have arrived. I am so happy!" A small, lithe, dark haired man approached them, beaming from ear to ear. "I am so bored. You bring me a new lady I see." It was hard to miss the small man's heavy accent.

"Captain Ferrandini," Luckett enthused. "I'd like to introduce you to Mr. John Hutchinson and his companion, Miss Fanny Jefferson, who also lately came to this city in the company of the esteemed Senator Wigfall. She is, shall we say, his proxy?" Luckett winked at Ferrandini.

Ferrandini laughed. "We all should have such a proxy, no? And where is the illustrious senator this evening? What kind of man would abandon a creature as exquisite as this vision before me?" He made to slip his arm around Kate's waist.

She eluded his grasp by stepping back to lift a glass of champagne off a tray carried by a passing maid. "Senator Wigfall is in Washington. The Senate must certify the electoral vote. My dear senator must be present for that distasteful task."

"Distasteful indeed." Ferrandini's voice rose, before he caught himself. "But no matter. We shall bravely carry on. Come meet our hostess. She is an utterly delightful woman. We shall ask her for a private room where we may discuss

matters without prying ears. And then some time with the ladies, no? We shall take our enjoyment as men do." He
gestured around the parlor. "So many beautiful women."

Kate thought the barber sounded like an Italian and acted
like an ass.

An epiphany struck her. *Sounds like an Italian? Wait a second.
I've heard that voice before. I was standing on Excelsior's back listening
at Mrs. Surratt's window. The rat bastard!*

Fighting the impulse to scurry out of the bordello and find
a telegraph office, Kate smiled at the small man instead. He
winked at her.

Rat bastard.

Ferrandini walked them over to a small table next to the
bar where a middle-aged, but nicely formed woman sat, a pair
of tiny spectacles perched upon her nose and a book before
her. She looked less like a bordello proprietress than she did a
school teacher.

"Madame Travis," the Italian announced.

She sighed and looked up, putting her finger in her book to
mark her place as she did. "What is it Mr. Ferrandini? I've
told you, I have no girls under fifteen. I am not in that trade."

"I must correct you fair lady. I am *Captain* Ferrandini," he
said, clicking his heels together and straitening to his full
height, which didn't take long considering his diminished stat-
ure.

"You're a barber," the lady said dryly.

Kate thought Mrs. Travis looked tired, not so much physi-
cally as spiritually. *An opportunity.* Before the so-called Captain
could argue his title, she stepped forward.

"I see you are reading Mr. Dickens' new book. Is it as
wonderful as I've heard?"

Anna Travis looked startled, as if she were seeing the woman in ivory silk for the first time. "It's astounding. From the very first line, a work of genius." She slipped a bookmark into the middle of the book and held it out to Kate.

Kate opened to the first page of text and read aloud. "It was the best of times, it was the worst of times, it was the age of wisdom, it was the age of foolishness, it was the epoch of belief, it was the epoch of incredulity, it was the season of Light, it was the season of Darkness." Kate closed the book and looked at Mrs. Travis with new respect.

"Impressive prose, is it not?" the older woman asked, holding her hand out for the book.

"Sounds like he lives in the United States, not England," Kate offered.

"That's exactly what I thought. But then again, he has been here. About fifteen years ago." Mrs. Travis carefully appraised Kate, taking in the dress and it's effect on the men in the room. "Tell me my dear, what is your favorite Dickens novel?"

"Oh, that's easy. I adore *Bleak House*. It's a masterpiece of drollery. Dickens at his covert comic best, if you ask me."

Apparently Kate passed the test Anna Travis set for her because before she walked away, the lady laid her hand upon Kate's arm. "If these men begin to tire you, as men of this sort can do, come find me." The lady smiled, turning the fine lines around her eyes into lovely crinkles. Mrs. Travis was quite beautiful when she smiled.

"The nerve of that woman," Ferrandini half-screeched, waving his glass of brandy about and sloshing a small wave of it on the table.

They were in a small private room on the bordello's second floor. Ferrandini took his seat with an abrupt thump. Kate detected that the glass in his hand was not his first libation this evening.

"I am Captain Ferrandini, Captain of the Volunteers, who shall one day be celebrated throughout the land as a hero. Why, I myself I shall deliver this nation from a great evil. And she treats me as if I am scum. She shall rue the day."

Kate stilled, trying not to react to the man's melodrama. *Rue the day? Was this little man for real?* She was afraid if she made even the tiniest move Ferrandini would remember she was at the table and turn his conversation to heavy-handed flirting. Then she really would have to laugh at him.

Allan leaped into the breach. "I take it, Captain Ferrandini, that you are a man of southern sympathies."

"Oh, very much so sir. I came here twenty years ago from Corsica. A poor and violent place indeed. My ship docked at Charleston. Such a wonderful city. Warm and seagoing like my homeland. I came to understand that southern men are the real heart of this nation. Northerners are money-grubbing vermin with no sense of honor or decency. This last election was a tragedy for the nation."

Luckett waved his glass in the air. "If those northerners have their way this country will be all industrial endeavor and good men will become wage slaves in soulless cities and factories."

"It's the arrogance I object to," Allan said in his capacity as Stockbroker Hutchinson.

246

"It is all those things and many more that make our cause honorable and good," Ferrandini proclaimed, sloshing more brandy into his glass for emphasis.

"Which reminds me, Mr. Ferrandini," Kate said, digging a bulging envelope out of her evening bag.

"Captain Ferrandini, my beautiful lady."

"Captain," she amended, resisting the impulse to cuff the irritating man upside the head. "I've a packet here for you from the Senator. In support of your work. Five hundred dollars." She slid the envelope across the table to the barber.

He grabbed the envelope, peeked inside and then smiled broadly at Kate. "Your senator is a great man."

The conversation turned to Wigfall, who'd met him, who had not. Every man in the room seemed anxious to assert their admiration for the senator.

The sycophancy and over-warm room made Kate sleepy. *I wish I could go downstairs and talk about books with the lady of this house.* When the conversation turned to Mr. Lincoln she was glad she'd stayed.

"The election of that ape was an outrage," Ferrandini half yelled, emboldened by the envelope full of money and a belly full of brandy. "An outrage I tell you. Loyal citizens would be entirely justified in resorting to any means to prevent that cur Lincoln from taking his seat." The Italian glared around the table, his outrage coming off him in palpable waves.

"What did you have in mind Captain?" Kate knew she shouldn't push, but she couldn't help herself.

"Murder of any kind is justifiable to save the Southern People. Any kind I tell you."

"Here, here," Allan murmured, raising his glass.

247

"That man shall never be president, not as long as I, Cipriano Ferrandini, draw breath. My life is of little consequence and I would willingly give it up to save my country, as the great Orsini did for Italy." By now Ferrandini was standing and gesticulating wildly.

"Orsini?" Luckett asked.

Kate resisted the impulse to explain. Her Dickens expertise was worrisome enough in hindsight. Luckett and the others might believe an actress would read novels, but she ought not know Italian history.

"An Italian liberal who was executed after an assassination attempt on Napoleon the Third," Allan supplied.

"Exactemente!"

Kate resisted the impulse to point out that Orsini's failure made him a less than stellar role model.

Ferrandini, though, was just warming up. "This Lincoln shall never, never be president. If I die, I shall die, but the Captain will prove himself a hero on the day the presidential imposter comes to this city. A shot will be fired and the traitor will be dead and all of Maryland will be with us and the South shall be free. Lincoln will die in this city and I alone will do it!"

Luckett, Allan and Kate openly stared at the Corsican. He was fairly quivering in his enthusiasm. Allan broke the spell by standing, lifting his drink and proposing a toast. "To the Captain! May he succeed and live to tell the tale."

They stood and saluted Ferrandini's bravery.

Kate had never been quite so horrified in all her life.

Chapter 24

"The damn lunatic Italian intends to assassinate Mr. Lincoln. Am I in Bohemia now? I thought we didn't do that in America. And is anyone prepared to fix this? Of course not. Why do we not have a branch of government that polices and protects presidents? What would be the point? Dammit!" Kate kicked the settee with her ivory slipper.

Ouch! She knew she was having an ill-advised temper tantrum, but it felt good to rant and rave for once. Or twice. OK, maybe one more time. "Why do these crazy people keep telling us these things? It's like they *want* to get caught. Morons! Imbeciles! No, no. Cretinous fanatics. Jug headed, doltish."

Mr. Scully made one of his throat clearing noises.

Kate turned and glared at him.

He stretched out his legs. "You wouldn't' listen to my advice so it's your own durn fault," he drawled.

"Your advice?" She glowered at him as forbiddingly as she could manage. It was hard to look scary in a sexy white dress.

" I *said*, kill 'em all and let God sort it out. But nooo, you had to go do your job. See what comes of that?"

Kate stopped pacing around the room and stared open-mouthed at her Pinkerton nemesis. Was he really making a joke right now? She caught herself. *I am being a little bit ridiculous.* She tried to quell a rising smile. She clamped her lips together, but it did no good. "Fine," she said, and sat down with a chuckle. "But admit it—I'm not wrong."

Allan finally dared open his mouth. One of the things Kate liked about Allan was that he knew enough not to interrupt a woman in the full flow of outrage. No good ever came of it. "No, my dear, you are not wrong. A matter of this sort ought not be left in the hands of a private agency. Once Mr. Lincoln takes office I'll talk to him about some kind of federal agency for presidential protection. Perhaps offer the services of the Pinkertons. But right now, we badly need a plan."

After Ferrandini's revelation the evening pretty much came to a close. One of the maid's knocked at the door of their second floor private room and asked if the gentlemen would like some "company" sent up. Ferrandini and Luckett embraced the idea, but a panicked look from Allan brought Kate to her feet, professing a headache.

Thus the ever-helpful Mr. Hutchinson volunteered to take Miss Fanny back to her room. Kate and Allan all but scuttled out of the brothel and into a waiting hackney carriage. Back at the Barnum Hotel they found Mr. Scully in the hotel bar, where he'd been nursing a drink and waiting for their return. The three of them discreetly removed themselves to Kate's suite, where Kate had her tantrum.

"Can we get word to Hazzard on the Special?" Kate asked, taking a seat and discreetly rubbing her foot. She shouldn't have kicked the chair so hard.

"We can and I will, but I'm not sure how much that's going to help us." Allan scrubbed at his face. He looked up from his hands. "Mr. Lincoln has made it abundantly clear that he will not change his plans for what he calls idle threats. We're not going to get much help from that quarter. We have to neutralize the threat here at the source, before the Lincoln Special gets to Baltimore."

Scully stood up, walked to the fireplace and turned, facing Allan and Kate. He put his hands behind his back, as if to warm them, and asked, "Am I correct in understanding that, at least according to your assassin, he's is acting alone?"

"It did seem that way, didn't it Kate?" Allan turned towards her.

She thought about it for a few seconds, reviewing the evening. "He did say "I" several times. Also, there was martyr talk."

Allan looked at Scully. "What did you have in mind John?"

"I suggest we make sure Ferrandini really is a one-man assassination team and if so neutralize him."

"Neutralize?" Allan asked.

It suddenly occurred to Kate that Mr. Scully hadn't been entirely kidding about God and sorting.

The gruff man rocked on his heels, then caught himself and stood still. "We assassinate the assassin. It's our only choice and you know it Allan. The police in this town certainly won't arrest him, not as long as the police chief's a secessionist. We either act or we let the Special roll through Baltimore and hope the men aboard can keep Mr. Lincoln safe while they're changing trains. Anyone here want to gamble on that?" Scully pinned both Kate and Allan with his stern glare.

Unable to sit still, Kate took to pacing the room again. "Everyone knows Mr. Lincoln speaks at every stop. One well-aimed bullet, fired by someone who doesn't care whether they live or die, will be hard to stop." She sighed. "I'm not wrong, am I?"

Allan heaved a matching sigh. "No Kate, I'm afraid you are not."

"It gets worse. Mr. Lincoln arrives in Baltimore on the 23rd. We need to act before the Special gets to Philadelphia on the 21st or Harrisburg on the 22nd. Any later and we won't be able to reroute the train."

Allan nodded. "And that's assuming Mr. Lincoln will even approve an alternate route. You know how he is about this."

"That leaves us with four days," Kate said. "And gentlemen, if we're going to do this we need to be clear. We're planning a murder, plain and simple."

"Oh, it's a murder all right," Scully drawled. "But there ain't nothing simple about it."

Over the next three days the three of them scoured the city. Mr. Scully submerged himself in Baltimore's unsavory underbelly trying to get a line on possible Ferrandini associates. Allan spent what began to feel like entirely too much time with Mr. James Luckett, a hardship that included a return trip to Mrs. Travis's house of fallen ladies.

Louis Wigfall made a brief trip back to Baltimore, arriving one day and leaving the other, but he gave up no information of worth during his visit. He mostly talked about the joint session of congress and its electoral vote count. Circumstances forced Vice President Breckinridge to declare Abraham Lincoln's election official. Predictably, Louis was incensed and felt the need to share all his feelings with Kate. Happily, she saw him for one dinner and one breakfast before he was gone again, back to whatever dark deeds he was up to in Washington. Not so happily, his obsession with the electoral college left her no wiser about the assassination plot.

Allan showed up at Kate's hotel room early one morning. "Mr. Scully is not at his boarding house and his land lady hasn't seen him since yesterday morning." Deep worry lines furrowed Allan's' face.

"Well, he's probably deep under cover," Kate told him in as reassuring a tone as she could manage, though the news did worry her. "Should we get Timothy to come down from Perryville and have him search Baltimore's under-belly? See if he can shake Mr. Scully loose?"

"Good idea. I'll send a telegram." Allan collapsed in one of Kate's chairs. "Oh, and Luckett told me that Ferrandini is their lone assassin."

"And Luckett would know for sure?"

"I think so."

"Could he be lying?"

"He could be, but I don't think he is. He came by my hotel room last night. He was drunk and angry. The convention didn't declare for secession."

"Is it time to plan our own assassination then?"

"That's my other piece of news. We can't. The barber's in the wind."

"You're kidding me?"

"Sadly, no. Luckett says he's gone into hiding and will be incommunicado until it's time to kill Lincoln. No one in the organization knows where or when. No one but Ferrandini, that is."

Kate was horror struck. "You're kidding me? What do we do with that?" She paused. "Maybe Mr. Scully has him. Do you think?"

"It's impossible to know. If Scully doesn't surface today we're in a bind. We'll have to convince Mr. Lincoln he'll likely be killed if he continues on his present course." Allan took a deep breath and pinned Kate with his eyes. "What I really mean is *you* need to convince Mr. Lincoln. I dare not go. Luckett would be right to suspect me if I disappear right now. You have to go to New York and convince the President-elect that he's in danger."

She shook her head so hard she felt it in her neck. "Me? No, not me. You have to go." She knew she sounded half-hysterical, but she couldn't help herself. "They'll believe you."

Allan sighed. "I'm not kidding Kate. I can not disappear right now, not after Luckett's taken me into his confidence. You, on the other hand, can. I'll tell Luckett and the others you had to go home. No one will question that. *Because* you're a woman. This is exactly the sort of thing I hired you for."

"Yes, and my great weakness. I'm no good in a situation where I need multiple strange men to take me seriously."

"I think Captain Hazzard will believe you. And maybe Juba can help, though I'd just as soon he didn't break character. Not yet." Allan paused and sat forward in his chair. "Hazzard's a non-traditional thinker. He must be or he wouldn't have taken a leave from the Army to protect Lincoln when no one else would. And, if you'll pardon me for saying so, it won't hurt your cause that he's half in love with you."

"He is not! Don't be ridiculous Allan." To Kate's dismay, her protestation came out of her mouth in a high pitched squeal. And in spite of herself, her heart sped up a little bit.

"You were all he could talk about one evening— after we'd all met and you'd left. Oh, he tried to be casual about it, but both Juba and I could see what he was up to."

"He's paid me no attention whatsoever. Allan, you're making a huge mistake. You're pinning the success of this mission on a delusion. You think everyone is half in love with me."

"Not everyone my dear. Only the men between fifteen and ninety years of age." Allan smiled at Kate.

"It's not funny. I won't do it." Kate's heart raced and her palms felt itchy. He was asking her to do the very thing she'd avoided her entire life—step out from the shadows and onto the public stage. "I'll stay here—we'll come up with a story Luckett will believe about why you're gone. I'll make him believe it. According to your theory, he's half in love with me too."

"He is," Allan said, as if it were an obvious statement of fact. "Why do you think he wanted you to go to that fancy house with him? Why does he keep telling you secrets? Why, Kate, did Ferrandini spout off that night like he did? For God's sake woman, wake up! Men show off for you. They can't help themselves." He made his way to the door. "I'm not arguing anymore. I'll be back in the morning with your train tickets and a letter."

Kate could only gape at her boss. *He's done with this discussion and he's leaving?* She couldn't be more affronted. "I'm a perfectly competent detecting operative, not a siren luring men to their deaths upon the rocks."

"Oh, you're both my dear," Allan said, opening the door. "Which is exactly what makes you so devastatingly effective." And with a soft snick of the door he was gone.

Chapter 25

February 18-19
Baltimore

Night trains were invented by sadists to inflict misery upon unsuspecting travelers. Not even the seats in first class were comfortable and train cars were always either too hot, if the stove was going full bore, or too cold, if the train had recently stopped and the doors opened. Kate tried to read, but the jangle and clatter of the car made the words on the page bounce in a manner calculated to induce nausea. Instead she spent most of the trip staring out the window into the night. Finally, at four in the morning, the train pulled into the Manhattan station. Kate wearily lugged her small carpet bag out onto the platform and into the station. From there she found a hackney carriage that would take her to Astor House.

"The Astor's a pretty fancy place, miss. You sure you wouldn't prefer someplace more modest?" He looked her over with a critical eye.

After sitting up part of the night, her dove grey dress was a little worse for wear, but she figured it was the fact that she wasn't traveling with the kind of immense trunks ladies of quality lugged around with them.

"Well, I should hope not." Kate replied haughtily. "My Papa wouldn't want me anyplace but the Astor." She looked down her nose at the man, a considerable feat seeing as he was about six inches taller than she. "I told the porters to send my trunks along once they unloaded the baggage car. I didn't want to wait at the station alone."

"Oh, yes ma'am." With her credentials as a snob established he took her carpet bag from her hand and opened the carriage door. As they rattled along they passed under a banner strung across the street that read, "Fear not, Abraham, I am thy shield, and thy exceeding great reward." Flags decorated every pole and bunting adorned the shop windows they passed. It was nice to be someplace where everyone didn't hate the new president.

The Astor looked smaller than Willard's, but bigger than Barnum's. The front desk clerk did not want to check in an unescorted lady with no trunks, particularly one who didn't have the grace to show up in the afternoon, like most guests. Kate discreetly offered him a silver half dollar, after which the clerk's attitude became markedly more friendly.

Her fourth floor room was nothing like her suite at the Barnum. At Barnum's she had a two rooms, a dressing room and a bathroom, while her single room here contented itself with a small water closet and a changing screen. The difference between Wigfall's and Allan's standards she guessed. Allan clearly didn't have a stash of embezzled federal funds at his disposal.

By 6:30 in the morning, when the rest of the hotel's guests were just waking up, Kate had enjoyed breakfast and a bath. A good humored, middle-aged Irish maid helped her undress and get into a small hip bath she'd filled, keeping up a stream of meaningless chatter while she did that Kate found immensely soothing.

After her bath Kate slipped on her cozy blue velveteen wrapper and gave her grey dress to the Irish woman to be sponged and pressed, after which she plunked herself down into one of the room's two chairs and picked up the newspaper with a contented sigh. Apparently the Lincoln Special was scheduled to pull out of Albany this very morning. They'd stop in Poughkeepsie for lunch and a mid-day speech, before rolling on towards New York City, arriving at the Thirtieth Street Station at 3 in the afternoon. That gave Kate most of the day to catch up on her sleep.

She'd slept badly the night before her trip, too worried about the trip to New York to succumb to sleep. She'd tried counting circus performers she knew, and when that proved too interesting, resorted to a mental inventory of the Pinkerton's office supply closet. Towards dawn she slept for a couple of hours before Allan knocked on her door and woke her up.

Standing in the doorway, he held a slim packet out to her. "I've got tickets for you on the 5:16 to New York and reservations for you at the Astor House. The President is scheduled to be there tomorrow night— it's a night train so you'll beat the Special to New York. Allan also handed over a letter from himself to Colonel Sumner explaining all they'd learned."

Kate had that letter in her bag now. Its existence should have eased her mind but it didn't. She crawled into bed and opened her worn copy of *Bleak House*. Snooty Lady Dedlock and villainous lawyer Tulkinghorn's schemes sent Kate off to a dreamless sleep.

She awoke to the room clock chiming four o'clock and the sound of a crowd outside. She pushed back the coverlet and went to the window. She peered down at a street full of people pushing and shouting. New York policemen, truncheons out, held them back while a line of black carriages pulled up in front of the hotel. In the middle of the line of carriages an ornate open barouche pulled by a team of six black horses caught Kate's eye. She'd read that the mayor of New York arranged for Lincoln to ride in the same august equipage that carried the Prince of Wales when he visited New York several weeks before. It looked as if the mayor had made good on his promise. She watched the carriage closely. From her fourth floor vantage she could see little more than the tops of hats and coats. *No, there he is. That has to be him.* A man taller than the men around him stepped out of the barouche and looked straight up at the hotel. Kate saw his face. *How tired he looks.* He stretched, turned towards the crowd and waved. Their cries, half approval, half boos, rose to her window.

Time to spring into action. While she slept a maid had quietly returned her grey dress. Kate hurriedly pulled off her wrapper and donned her newly sponged and pressed gray dress. She smoothed her hair and eyebrows, suddenly nervous. Captain Hazzard was down there somewhere. *Get a grip. Allan would have said anything to get you to do this job.*

Hurriedly she rang her service bell and then scribbled a hasty note. The maid was not the same one as this morning. Instead the hotel sent a slim young black girl. *The nation seems to have an unending supply of young black women.* It occurred to her that she ought to hire a black woman for the Pinkerton's Women's Bureau. A black woman could be more invisible to men of power than even a white woman. But what if she got caught? Kate caught herself. *Really? You're going to worry about this now?*

She handed her note to the maid and asked her to deliver it to Captain Hazzard's room.

"He's a member of Mr. Lincoln's party, so he's just arriving," Kate explained, "but it's crucial he get the note right away. Please."

The young woman bobbed her head. "Yes Ma'am. Maybe I'll get to see Mr. Lincoln. Wouldn't that just be something." She grinned and scurried out of the room. Kate grinned at the girl's back. She couldn't agree more.

Ten minutes later Kate opened her door to a man she'd never seen before.

"Yes?" the two of them said at the same time.

"I'm sorry, I was expecting Captain Hazzard," Kate explained to the portly gentleman at her door.

"Mr. Lincoln is about to give a speech from the second floor of this hotel. Afterwards he has a reception to attend. Both the Colonel and the Captain are with him, as is proper."

"And you are?" Kate asked. The man before her was older, balding and built like a man who missed very few meals. His suit was of good quality and his shirt linen snowy white. Someone important, no doubt.

The man puffed out his chest and announced, "I am Mr. Edward Sandford, President of the American Telegraph Company and traveling companion for Mr. Abraham Lincoln. Who are you, young lady? And what do you want with Captain Hazzard?"

Kate wanted to ask the man when he'd become Hazzard's keeper, but rudeness would not get her what she needed. Instead she smiled prettily at Mr. Sandford. "I am Mrs. Barley, sir. I need to see the Captain. More than that I cannot say."

261

"I think not young lady. You are an attention seeker. Even an old man like myself can see that. I came as a courtesy. To tell you that your sort should stay away." Mr. Sanford turned and marched himself down the hall.

Kate blew out a long breath. She'd warned Allan and he hadn't listened. Mr. Sanford was not even a quarter in love with her. Quite the opposite.

Well, if the Hazzard won't come to me, I must go to the Hazzard. Kate left her room. A hotel maid would know the president's schedule.

Five minutes later she was stationed outside Mr. Lincoln's suite. A crowd of men walked down the hall toward her. She could see Lincoln's signature top hat in the middle of all the dark suits. She peered around the men and found Hazzard. She'd forgotten just how delightful he was to look at.

Hazzard stepped out of the flow of men as they worked their way into the soon-to-be president's room and grabbed her elbow. "What are you doing here?" he whispered at her.

She looked at him, feeling utterly at sea.

He had the good manners to look embarrassed. "It's bad, isn't it?"

She nodded.

"You need to talk to me. And maybe some of the others?"

"Yes," she whispered. *Pull it together.* She straitened her shoulders and gathered her resolve. This was no time to drop her basket. "I've got a letter for Mr. Lincoln's advisors. It can't wait."

Hazzard nodded slowly. "Your timing isn't great. It's been a trying day, a trying week truth to tell, he'll be ready for dinner and bed soon. And his Missus will want him after she's put the boys to bed. Give me an hour. I'll bring reinforcements."

His steady gaze reassured her. "Room 477," she said and hurried away before she could make an even bigger fool of herself.

It was closer to two hours before they had their meeting. The tea Kate ordered turned bitter and luke warm while she waited. She had just taken a bite from a drying tea sandwich when a knock came at the door. Calmly, she sat the sandwich down on a saucer and opened the door. Before her stood Hazzard, Mr. Sandford and another fellow she didn't know.

Hazzard stepped forward into the room. For a second Kate thought he was going to embrace her. She became hyper conscious of the bed behind her.

Instead he bowed and swept his arm toward the other two men. "You've met Mr. Sandford?"

Mr. Sandford bowed. "I apologize Ma'am. I was unforgivably rude. The Captain here assures me you are above reproach and entirely trustworthy."

"Well, I don't know about that," Kate replied, smiling at the older man, "but please consider yourself forgiven. Where Mr. Lincoln is concerned one can't be too careful. I admire your dedication to his protection."

Sandford blushed and thanked Kate.

Kate glanced back at Hazzard, who looked distinctly cranky. Feeling awkward she smiled at him. To her relief his face cleared.

Hazzard gestured to the second man. "May I present Mr. Norman Judd. He and Mr. Sandford have been of great assistance on this trying journey." Mr. Judd bowed at Kate. "It's a pleasure to meet you miss. The Captain has vigorously sung your praises, though he was most mysterious about your name or your place in the great scheme of things."

"For the purposes of this discussion you may call me Mrs. Barley. Mr. Pinkerton, with whom you have all met, sent me to you. I bear a message from him. "

"Ah, I see," Judd said expansively. "A lady of mystery. How intriguing." Judd had a lovely thick white beard and mustaches that reminded Kate of drawings she'd seen of Father Christmas.

Once everyone settled themselves, each of the gentlemen with a plate of dry sandwiches, Kate unfurled Allan's letter. It was five pages long. "As I said, this is from Allan Pinkerton. I would like Captain Hazzard to read it. If he deems it appropriate, you two gentlemen," here Kate nodded at Sandford and Judd, "may also read it. After that we shall see."

A half hour later Sandford finished the letter, the last of the three men to do so. Hazzard and Kate spent the time pretending not to notice each other.

Sanford shook the sheaf of pages at Kate. "This can't be true! It's preposterous. Utterly preposterous."

Judd shifted in his seat. "Oh, I don't think so. I've been sitting here thinking. My first impulse was deny the whole thing too. But the more I think on it, the more this plot Mr. Pinkerton describes sounds feasible."

Hazzard spoke. "I know two things absolutely. The first is that Mr. Lincoln signed off on this investigation because Allan Pinkerton runs the finest detective agency in the country. The second thing I know is that this woman is one of his most trusted lieutenants. You've never heard of her and if she does her job correctly, you never will, but I've seen her with Mr. Pinkerton and she has his absolute trust."

Kate turned and looked at Hazzard, a tiny ray of hope blooming in her heart. "I am also here, gentlemen, because Mr. Pinkerton is in position in Baltimore as we speak, continuing to gather intelligence. He lives under the glare of the enemy and he dare not blink."

"Really, miss, how foolish do you think we are?" Sanford's disbelief was evident in both his tone and posture. "You want us to believe there is a plot to attack the rail lines in Baltimore, engage the city in a riot and assassinate the president in the ensuing mayhem. And that this plot has the explicit approval of both the Maryland governor and the head of the Baltimore police force? It's preposterous!"

She mentally took her gloves off. "Mr. Sanford, there are words to describe men who willfully ignore facts and evidence. These words particularly apply to men who will not take the word of an loyal military officer. Should I apply these words to you now?"

"Harrumph! Of all the temerity!" Sanford rose, as if to leave.

Judd waved his hand at Sanford. "There's a very real danger here Mr. Sanford. Mr. Pinkerton says so. Mr. Felton says so. They both can't be wrong. And don't forget all those threatening letters."

Once Sanford regained his seat Kate spoke again. "Thank you Mr. Judd. Consider, for a moment only, that the letter might be correct. The stakes are enormous. I'll add here that we know for a fact the enemy uses military grenades, which if deployed against the president could cause untold damage to innocent people. Because we're not talking about just Mr. Lincoln's life and presidency here. We talking about protecting the people who will be injured or killed if Baltimore erupts into violence. And what will happen to the union should mob violence precipitate the secession of the border states? We'll lose the nation's capitol if this plot succeeds because, mark my words gentlemen, if Maryland secedes, Virginia will follow and Washington City will be surrounded by hostile territory. We'll have to hand over the city to the secessionists. And what then? With half or more of the states gone and the capitol lost, will the United States survive?"

She paused and looked at the three of them. "And what of us gentlemen? What will become of us if we do not act? What will you tell your children and grandchildren?"

Kate looked around the room, more sure of her words than she'd ever been of anything before in her life. "If you fail to act, no one will know but the men in this room and a few Pinkerton operatives in Baltimore. Will that make your failure any less enormous? Benedict Arnold will look up from Hell and thank God he is not us. Our crime will be greater than his. Far greater." She sat down and stared defiantly at Sanford.

Silence reigned in the room for several long seconds. Finally Hazzard rose. "Mrs. Barley, I wonder if you would excuse us. I think we need to talk in private." Kate nodded. The three made their excuses and were gone. She didn't know whether to weep in frustration or do a little dance of triumph. While she was deciding she picked up her abandoned sandwich and took a hearty bite.

Well after midnight another knock came at her door. Kate pushed her blankets back and sat up. *What fresh hell is this?* She pulled on her wrapper and went to the door, wishing she'd made room in her bag for a pair of slippers. "Who is it?"

"Captain Hazzard, Ma'am. I need just a moment."

She opened the door and gestured him inside.

"No," he said softly. He looked down at his boots and then up into her eyes. "I dare not," he said with a wistful tone.

Kate stood there in the doorway. "Oh," she breathed out. She bit her lower lip and searched frantically for words. For months afterwards she'd be mortified every time she remembered what she said next.

"I was married once, did you know that?"

He raised his right eyebrow at her. His devastatingly beautiful eyebrow. Kate thought that if a woman ever nearly fainted from pleasure from the crook of one eyebrow, it would be her, now.

"Miss Warne," he began.

"Kate," she rushed to interrupt him. "When it's just us, I wish you would call me Kate."

He smiled at her. "If you'll call me George."

"Do you mind, very much, if I call you Hazzard? Not Captain Hazzard, just Hazzard." She grinned at him. "It fits you as George never will."

"Hazzard it is then, Kate." They stood in the doorway staring at each other like a pair of simpletons.

"I came to tell you that you're going to get some help. I'll be by in the morning. I'll bring some people with me."

"Oh," she said again. She couldn't think what else to say.

"I should go. You look tired." As soon as he said it distress showed on his face. "I mean, you look fine. More than fine. Beautiful."

"Hazzard," she said quietly.

He stopped babbling.

She went up on her tip-toes and kissed him softly on the mouth. His lips softened and then parted slightly. Kate put

267

her hands on the back of his neck and pulled him to her. She felt his hand on her waist, but only just barely. Mostly she felt his lips. His soft lips and his bristly mustache providing a delicious contrast against her own mouth. After a moment he lifted his head from hers. She stepped away, put a hand on his chest and pushed him gently back. Then she closed her door, leaving him standing out in the hall.

She leaned against her hotel door, unaccountably happy. Some time passed before she heard his boot heels thump on the wooden hallway floor as he walked away.

Chapter 26

February 20-21
Philadelphia

Kate held the yellow telegram paper up to catch the morning light streaming through her hotel room's window.

Baltimore, 20 Feb.

Mrs. B.

Tell Judd yesterday bookmakers offer Ten to one. Also, F still missing.

The Boss

Interesting. And a little anxiety provoking, though not nearly enough to ruin her morning. For the first time in days she'd had a decent night's sleep. She had faith that Hazzard would talk sense into Lincoln's men.

Hazzard. She didn't know what to think about kissing him. She couldn't say she regretted it, but she wasn't sure it had been a good idea. Mostly she thought that she ought not think about it at all. Until Lincoln was safely ensconced in the President's mansion she didn't have time to indulge romantic thoughts about the handsome Hazzard. Still, she felt oddly light hearted this morning.

An hour later the same bell boy who delivered Allan's telegram came to her door with a sealed note.

"I've been asked to wait for a reply," the boy said.

Kate smiled at him. He looked to be in his young teens, with spotty skin and gangly elbows.

"Come in." She gestured at the little table that held the remnants of her breakfast. "The kitchen sent up scones. I wonder if you could help me eat them?"

He goggled wide-eyed at her, before he eagerly stepped over to the table.

She opened the note while the boy gobbled her scones.

Mrs. B.

We are busy today with the Mr. L—could meet with you at 2 PM. I apologize for any inconvenience. Judd asks you to go on to Philadelphia. If that's amenable to you I shall make the arrangements.

Yours,

Hazzard

Kate's heart skipped a little at the "yours," before she reminded herself it was more letter writing convention than statement of fact. He had signed it with just his last name though. No Captain. No George. Just Hazzard.

She scribbled a hasty assent and handed it to the boy. Her scones were miraculously gone, but an intact orange still sat on the tray. She saw him eyeing it. She held her note out to him.

"You'll take this to the man who gave you the letter?"

He nodded at her.

"And take that orange with you, would you?"

Their business concluded he disappeared, along with her breakfast.

An hour later Kate found herself standing in front of Barnum's American Museum. She was reminded of Mr. Barnum's emporium of oddities by the New York newspapers, all of which mentioned Lincoln's plans to visit that afternoon. Apparently Mr. Lincoln was a great admirer of Mr. Barnum's. Kate smiled up at the huge building. Mr. Lincoln was not alone.

Located on Broadway, Barnum's was easily as large as the Astor House. The museum was New York's most popular attraction, entertaining upwards of 15,000 people per day. She paid her twenty-five cent admission fee and asked the man taking tickets, "Is Mr. Barnum here today? I ask because we are old friends and I would like to say hello to him."

Clearly dubious, the ticket clerk issued a thin smile. "Who should I say is asking for him, miss?"

"Tell him it's the baby bally broad from Turner's Circus."

"The what?" The man practically barked at her.

Clearly not a circus person. "Just tell him. He'll know what it means."

Minutes later a stocky man in a black suit and a flashy blue and yellow striped waistcoat stepped into the museum lobby from a door set discretely in the back wall. "Katie!" His voice boomed across the marble clad space. "You've turned into a lady." He strode toward her and threw his arms around her and murmured into her hair, "It's awful good to see you."

"Oh, Mr. Barnum, it's beyond lovely to see you." She held him out at arm's length. "Why you don't look one bit older than the last time I saw you."

"Oh, you really are a circus girl, with your bally nonsense." Long ago, when Kate had been no more than six or seven years old her parents spent a summer traveling with the Aaron

Turner Circus. Phineas Barnum worked the circus as a ticket collector, famed for both his speed and his patter. Once the ticket rush passed he'd sometimes take Kate to the midway, stand her on a box and teach her to call out descriptions of the acts in the most colorful way possible. Most of the girls who did the job were affectionately called 'bally broads,' but because Kate was, as Mr. Barnum said, 'an infant prodigy' he'd taken to calling her his 'bally baby.'

"I was awful sorry to hear about your parents Miss Kate. Your father had a notably excellent name and I always liked that about him."

Kate smiled at Mr. Barnum. Her dad and Mr. Barnum were both named Phineas.

"And he was the finest horse trainer Turner ever hired. And your mother? An angel on horseback. The world is a smaller place without the two of them."

"Oh, Mr. Barnum. Thank you so much. I've been out of the circus for some time now and no one I know now has ever met my parents. To hear you talk is like having them back, if only for a moment."

Phineas Taylor Barnum took Kate back to his office where they spent an hour having a lovely gossip about all the circus people they knew.

After a while, when she could not put it off any longer, Kate changed the subject. "Mr. Barnum, I would not for the world have you think I came to see you for any reason other than affection, but in truth, I need a favor." She smiled hopefully at the older man.

He looked at her and grinned. "Why Katie dear, it surely took you long enough to get 'round to it. I could tell you had

272

something on your mind the moment I saw you in the lobby. You have but to ask."

So she did. And he said yes.

Afterwards he gave her a tour of his museum.

"I figured out how to make circus money, without all the trouble of moving tents, animals and people from place to place. That infernal loading and unloading 'bout killed me and I was a young man back then."

"It is pretty smart," Kate agreed. "Put it all in one building and make people come to you."

For the rest of the morning they looked at Mr. Barnum's collection of oddities, both inanimate and alive. Kate saw a miniature replica of the Niagara Falls and detailed models of New York, Boston and Philadelphia. Some rooms featured magicians and jugglers, while others exhibited freaks, including a sickly looking albino man, a scantily clad tattooed lady and an exceedingly large man billed as a giant. Kate knew that Madame Clofullia used to work as a bearded lady at the museum in winters, when most of the circuses were in winter quarters, though these days she wintered at Kate's house in Chicago. Mr. Barnum was the best of men, but Kate was glad the Madame was at home with Mrs. Barrow in Chicago. The freak exhibits made Kate sad though she knew they did the work of their own free will. Still, what did free will count for in a world that counted some people as freaks in the first place.

Finally she had to tell Mr. Barnum her time was up. "I've a meeting at two o'clock," she said, "and then I have to leave town. You can guess why. "

"Before you go, I'd like you to see one more thing." He guided her in the direction of his office. He opened the door next to his office and as grandly as possible said, "Behold, the Feejee Mermaid!"

Kate nearly doubled over laughing. Years ago Barnum perpetrated one of the most famous hoaxes in circus lore—the Original Feejee Mermaid. Hundreds of thousands of people paid to see it, though it turned out to be no more than the head and torso of a monkey, sewn to the back end of a large fish and pickled in a huge jar. Uncounted circuses and sideshows reproduced Barnum's hoax, though generally they used a dried carcass that they passed off as a mermaid mummy. The Feejee Mermaid made Barnum a legend in the circus community because even after the 'mermaid' was exposed as a hoax people were still willing to pay to see it.

Kate stopped laughing and wiped her eyes. "It occurs to me Mr. Barnum, that national politics are not unlike your mermaid here—one thing, masquerading as another, and everyone pretending it's real."

"I thought you might take a lesson from her," the showman said. "Who's to say what is real anyway? A thing is real because people decide its real. And once people decide, they stick to their beliefs. You need to do some deciding of your own, don't you?" He paused and gave Kate a piercing look. "But beware of adherence to one belief—you are not a fool to be taken in by mermaids. A daughter of the circus must be flexible in all things."

Before she left the museum Kate turned toward Barnum and asked him the question she'd been wanting to ask all morning. "Mr. Barnum, what do you think of Mr. Lincoln? Is he a mermaid or is he the real thing?"

"Well, like I said, I'm not sure what the difference between the two really is. But think I know what you're asking. I'm proud to say I voted for him. This country shouldn't have slavery of any kind. Not for colored people, or women, or immigrants, not even the Catholic ones. I figure Mr. Lincoln's the right man for the job, which is exactly why I invited him to my museum for a visit. You can count on me. I'll do what I can."

"Thanks for the help Mr. B. And the fine afternoon."

He nodded at her, his face a study in gravity. Then he ruined the effect by winking.

Kate checked her little watch. Two o'clock on the dot. She knocked on the door to Mr. Lincoln's suite. Mr. Judd opened the door and welcomed her in. The suite's sitting room was every bit as large and ornate as her rooms at the Barnum. It was nice to know the president-elect had accommodations as fine as a senator's mistress. Mr. Sandford stood and nodded at her. He did not smile. Hazzard, on the other hand, stepped toward her, face lit in pleasure and warmly pressed her hand with his.

A man in a resplendent military frock coat introduced himself as Colonel Sumner. "I've met your Mr. Pinkerton, Madame. He seemed a sensible man to me. I hear we are to call you Mrs. Barley?"

"We've included Mr. Lamon in this meeting, as well as Colonel Sumner," Hazzard said. He gestured at the large man standing near the room's far corner. He was a bear of a man, large, unkempt and scruffy in his appearance.

Ignoring Kate, he stepped forward and said, "I don't know why we're supposed to trust some woman who won't give her name and whose only credential is a letter that could have been written by anyone." Having spoken he stuck his hands into his pockets like a petulant child.

Hazzard stepped in. "Now, Mr. Lamon, you know we've discussed your objections and plan to address them, should the lady agree."

They all sat and Hazzard explained. "We're all inclined to believe your letter, even Mr. Lamon, despite his protestations to the contrary."

Lamon snorted. "No one here wants to keep Mr. Lincoln safe more than myself."

Hazzard waved his hand at Lamon. "I know that Mr. Lamon. *Everyone* knows that." Hazzard turned toward Kate again. "We five have spoken at length and decided that if we're to take action we need to speak to Mr. Pinkerton."

Kate sighed. She hadn't wanted to come, but now that she was here she'd be damned if she'd be treated like an errand girl. *Perhaps a short lesson is in order.*

"Gentlemen, it would be helpful if you understood that right now the Pinkerton's are not detecting. The Pinkerton's are spying. We cannot abandon the task at hand just to meet with you, particularly in the crucial days before Mr. Lincoln comes to Baltimore. Our situation is dangerous beyond your comprehension. A number of Pinkertons are in the confidence of the plotters, including myself. Excuses were made for my absence, but mine alone. Additional absences will be noted and the operation blown if the plotters suspect that they have been infiltrated. Moreover, operatives' lives will be placed in danger. "

"Then why are you here? If you're so all fired important? Won't they miss you?" Lamon asked, belligerence showing in every line of his face.

Kate snapped. "I told you Mr. Lamon. Excuses were made for my absence. The excuses were believable because men do not take women seriously. I collect an astounding amount of intelligence because of that fact. Like you, they dismiss me as an empty headed fool." She stood and picked up her shawl. "Either you gentlemen accept me as your envoy or I am leaving. I have no desire to add insult to my day."

Hazzard leapt to his feat. "Please stay." He wheeled and faced Mr. Lamon. "Mr. Lamon! This lady is trying to keep Mr. Lincoln alive. She deserves respect."

Lamon thrust out his lower lip. "Well I'm sorry, but I don't trust her and I don't trust Pinkertons I've never spoken to."

Hazzard turned toward Kate and motioned for her to sit back down.

She hesitated for a moment, but the naked, pleading look on his face convinced her. She settled back into her chair and tried to look more in control than she felt.

Hazzard took his own seat again and turned to Mr. Lamon. "Sir, you well know you cannot meet everyone in a spy circle. These things are not decided with everyone at the table."

Kate spoke up. "What if, hypothetically, you had a man imbedded deep within the new Confederate government. Could that man waltz into a Richmond hotel and meet with half a dozen Unionists?"

Lamon's eyebrows rose in surprise. "Well, I guess not, Ma'am."

She opened her reticule and took out that morning's telegram. She held it out to Lamon, who took it from her. "Mr. Pinkerton says that Baltimore bookmakers are laying odds on

Mr. Lincoln's chances of safely making it through the city. What does he say the odds are Mr. Lamon?"

Lamon studied the telegram, but did not speak.

"They're making book on this?" Colonel Sumner asked, shock in his every syllable.

"Yes, they are Colonel. That tells you something about the city right there."

"And the odds?"

"Mr. Lamon?" Kate was going to make him say it, even if his head exploded from it.

"Ten to one," he said dolorously. "Not in Mr. Lincoln's favor."

After a colorful discussion of the impropriety of betting on a future president's life, Hazzard redirected the conversation. "Mrs. Barley, do the Pinkerton's have a plan to subvert this plot?"

"We do, but I am not at liberty to discuss it. May I assume then that you all accept the facts as they are laid out in the letter?"

Colonel Sumner stood and assumed a kind of military parade rest. "We agree that the facts of the investigation appear solid and that the Pinkertons' conclusions about our man's safety, or lack thereof, are valid."

Kate smiled around the room. "We're making progress then."

The Colonel took an envelope from an inside pocket of his tunic. "Here are your tickets to Philadelphia. We're not leaving New York until late tonight. We have the tour of Barnum's museum and then dinner here at the Astor. I saw no reason you shouldn't travel at a more amenable time. Your train is in," he checked the clock, "an hour and a half. I've taken the liberty of telegraphing the hotel we'll be using in Philadelphia and reserving a room for Mrs. Barley."

"I see you counted on my cooperation," Kate said wryly.

Lamon snorted.

Mr. Judd stood. "Madame, Captain Hazzard assured us that we could rely absolutely on you. Having met you, I was inclined to agree with his assessment. Mr. Lamon thought we should offer you this little test." He turned towards Lamon. "Do we agree that she passed her examination?"

Lamon stood as well, nodding in Kate's direction. "Ma'am, I'm sorry for the offense I've offered you. I'm not used to getting help with this Lincoln protection business."

"Mr. Lamon, we want the same thing. I understand your investment in Mr. Lincoln's safety is a good deal more personal than mine. I would expect you to be correspondingly more demonstrative." She smiled gently at him, causing Lamon to thrust his hands deep into his pockets and shuffle his feet before sheepishly smiling back at her.

Kate glanced over at Hazzard, catching that odd look on his face again. If it hadn't been Hazzard and they hadn't been standing in Lincoln's sitting room trying to prevent an assassination she would have thought the look was naked longing. Lust even. She gave her head a minute shake.

Hazzard walked her out to the hall, where he took one of her hands. "I have to be with him. You understand?"

She nodded. "Of course. I'll see you tomorrow."

He bent and pressed a kiss to her hand.

"Whatever you do, Hazzard, promise me this."

"Anything," he said earnestly.

She looked him straight in the eyes and as seriously as she could manage, said, "Don't miss the fabulous Feejee Mermaid. You've never seen anything like her."

Chapter 27

Kate strode down the Philadelphia depot platform, eager to find Allan. They spotted each other about the same time. She hugged him and then held him at arm's length. "I thought you couldn't leave Baltimore."

"This is a half day trip. I needed to see Felton to finalize some of the details of my plan and his office is right down there." Allan waved down the platform to the large depot building. "I'll be back before dinner. Luckett thinks I'm sick in bed. At dinner last night I consumed a prodigious number of oysters. I sent him a note saying I had a bad oyster. Anyone who knows how the body reacts to bad oysters will stay away from my room."

"Men are gross," Kate said, then she laughed and let him go. "I forgive you for sending me to New York. It went about as well as can be expected. What next?"

"Here's the plan." He handed her yet another thick sheaf of papers. "Needless to say, don't let it out of your sight."

While she tucked the papers into her bag he patted at his jacket pockets. "Where did I put it? Oh, yes, here it is." He pulled a single piece of note paper out of his pants pocket and held that out to Kate. "This is also for the Lincoln contingent. Hand it around the room before you let them see the plan."

Kate looked at the note. It was thrice-folded and sealed with wax, stamped with a stylized P. "Do I get to know what's in it?"

He smiled a wicked smile. "Let them see it's sealed before they read it. You may look at it after they do."

"You're up to something, aren't you?"

"Always, my dear," his Scottish burr thicker than usual. He looked down the tracks. "Here's my train." He busked her on the cheek and walked away, whistling as he went.

A few hours later Kate found herself in yet another hotel room in yet another meeting with Mr. Lincoln's gang of five. After shaking the gentlemen's hands Kate found a chair between the two Army officers and sat.

"Gentlemen," she announced briskly. "You know the gravity of the situation. I met Allan Pinkerton at the train station this morning. He had to get back to Baltimore so he handed me his plan and reboarded the train. He asked me to deliver this sealed note to you before I shared the plans." Kate held out the note.

Colonel Sumner took it, broke the seal, read it and smiled. He handed it off to Mr. Sanford, who had much the same reaction, as did the other men, even Mr. Lamon. Hazzard threw back his head and laughed when he read it. He handed the note to her.

Gentlemen:

Quit acting like ninnies. Listen to my Operative and follow her advice.

Most Sincerely,

Allan J. Pinkerton

Pinkerton Detective Agency (We Never Sleep)

Kate fought the urge to scamper around the room squealing, nah, nah, nah, nah, nah. Instead she pasted on her 'mature face,' and began. "Gentlemen, we are in agreement. The plot to disrupt the Lincoln Special's passage to Washington City and assassinate the president-elect is dangerously real. It is time to discuss solutions. I assume it is clear to everyone in this room that Mr. Lincoln needs to abandon his special train schedule?"

"Can't we just put him in a different car?" Lamon asked. "And limit his appearances in Baltimore?"

"No, we can't Mr. Lamon. Any special train, traveling through Baltimore at any time, may trigger the riot." Kate paused for a moment and then pressed on. "And we must prevent a riot at all costs. I've been in Baltimore. I've seen the people that live there. Innocent men, women and children will suffer terribly if this riot goes forward."

"We can't all stay with Mr. Lincoln either," Judd pointed out. "The damned reporters would be on to us in a heart beat and once again our schedule would be in the newspapers."

"Perceptive Mr. Judd. You've hit on one of the chief problems of the Lincoln Special. How many people are in this party?" Kate turned and looked at Colonel Sumner.

"Including the Vice President, his wife, Mrs. Lincoln, the children, servants and all of us? Thirty-five," Sumner replied.

"Ah, well, about that." Kate looked around the room and prepared to confess. "This afternoon, on Mr. Pinkerton's behalf, I put Mr. Hamlin and his wife on a train to Washington. A pair of our most trusted operatives will meet them in Havre de Grace, just north of Baltimore and accompany the Hamlins to the capitol. As of this moment, we are the only people in America, besides the Hamlins and two Pinkerton operatives, who know the future vice president's whereabouts."

Kate privately thought Mr. Hamlin showed a great deal more good sense than Mr. Lincoln. She'd met with him and his wife for about twenty minutes and they'd both agreed to a change in plans with no fuss whatsoever. Having met the Hamlins, Kate also thought Hattie and Timothy would have their hands full. He was a feisty old guy who said exactly what he thought and his wife Ellen only encouraged him. Still, it would be nice if Mr. Lincoln were half so accommodating.

At the news of the Hamlin's defection a round of general complaining and dissatisfaction commenced.

Kate let it go on for a few minutes and then put up her hand and said loudly, "Gentlemen. Mr. Hamlin asked me not to confer with you. He made this decision, not me. He does not think the future vice president should travel with the president any further. Which, in my view, is a most sensible way to think. It's done and we need to move on. Does anyone in this room know the name of the man running the Lincoln Special? The actual train?"

No one spoke.

"That's a bit of a security problem, don't you think?"

"Yes it is Ma'am," Hazzard chimed in, mostly so Kate would know how much he was enjoying himself.

Kate continued. "You have no idea who's in charge of your train or any other part of your journey." Kate reminded herself that these men knew so little about security that they had no idea how little they knew. All the Pinkertons could do now was fix the problem before disaster struck.

"This is what we need." Kate held up one finger. "First, Mr. Lincoln needs to ride a regular train, but in secret. Secrecy means only a small group of people may accompany him, not three dozen. Second, he needs to travel in disguise. He's distinctive so he'll be hard to hide, but hide him we will. Third, he needs to be in and out of Baltimore under the cover of darkness and arrive in Washington well ahead of schedule, preferably before dawn. No fan fare whatsoever must announce his arrival in the capitol. Fourth, and most obviously, Mr. Lincoln *has* to be told. Tonight." She took another sheaf of papers from her reticule and held it out to Colonel Sumner. "Here. Mr. Pinkerton has written it all down."

Kate stood, wiping her sweaty palms surreptitiously on her skirt. "I'm going to dinner. I urge you gentlemen to speak frankly with Mr. Lincoln. No more molly-coddling. No more allowing him to pretend he'll be fine. It's irresponsible. While you sit here time is running out."

Kate turned and sailed out of the room. No stage role ever afforded her an exit quite so dramatic or satisfying.

Chapter 28

Someone knocked on Kate's door so early the next morning it was essentially still night. She was up anyway, sleep having become optional at this point in their operations. They really were running out of time. *What if Mr. Lincoln ignored the Pinkertons advice? If he does people will die. And it will be my fault for not being convincing enough.* The very thought made Kate's stomach churn.

When she opened her door she though Hazzard looked as exhausted as she felt. "You look tired," she said. *Why do I keep saying stupid things to this man? I'm an idiot.*

"You too," he replied. He shook is head, as if he realized he too was an idiot. "I've got someone with me who wants to talk to you."

Hazzard stepped out of the doorway. An extremely tall, dark haired man hove into view.

"Mrs. Barley?" he asked, in a gruff, yet gentle voice. "I need a few moments of your time. Could I come in?"

"No, I mean yes. I mean, please come in Mr. Lincoln." She ceased her sputtering, stood back and gestured him into the room. She looked back at Hazzard. He made a shooing motion and shut the door, leaving himself out in the hall.

"I've been told to call you Mrs. Barley. I assume that is not your real name?"

She fought the impulse to tell him her real name. Certainly Mr. Lincoln could be trusted, but she didn't know if she could trust all the men he might talk to later. "Mrs. Barley will do for now, sir."

He nodded one slow nod. "Could we?" He gestured towards the chairs.

All the pictures and all the words didn't do him justice. He was wearing a beard, which was new, at least to Kate. Everyone talked about how tall he is, but until you stood in front of him his height was just a theory. He walked over to one of the chairs and waited by it. He had a peculiar, shuffling gate, as if his feet were too big for his legs.

Oh, he's waiting for me to sit down. Kate sat. Rather abruptly. Mr. Lincoln joined her.

The two of them examined each other. People often said he was ugly, but he wasn't. True, his features were large and rough, as if the artist who sculpted him hadn't finished the work, but his large brown eyes were entirely kind. His drooping eyelids added more than a touch of sadness to his countenance. And while he didn't seem to have full control over his long limbs, his awkwardness seemed endearing, rather than foolish.

Kate mentally shook herself. "How can I help you Mr. Lincoln?"

He contemplated her for a moment longer. When he spoke his voice was deep and deliberate. "I hear you and Mr. Pinkerton believe I am in grave danger. My advisors seem both

288

alarmed at the facts you convey and dismayed that you are a woman. And then Mr. Barnum had a word with me yesterday. He took me aside in the middle of his museum tour and told me to listen to you. It seems that you have been most thorough."

"Mr. Lincoln, I heard you admire the way Mr. Barnum's made something big out of his life, though he started out poor. Like you did, sir. I thought you might listen to him." Kate paused, steeling herself to be brutally clear. "Your life is in very real danger Mr. Lincoln."

"Is it?" he said, in a low tone that conveyed doubt more effectively than his words.

"Yes sir, it is. Which, if I may speak frankly sir, may or may not be the point. I'm a citizen sir, and your life is not my main concern. I'm not your wife, nor your daughter."

"No, my dear, you most certainly are not. The Lincolns have never had that particular shade of red in their hair." He smiled a slow smile at her.

"Well, yes." Did she look as foolish as she felt right now? "My point Mr. Lincoln, is that my mission is not only to preserve your life. If you'll forgive me for saying so sir, but your importance is national and both real and symbolic. You are a sum greater than your parts and you need to quit pretending you're just another man."

He shook his head, a chuckle rumbling through his narrow chest. "Women? Will they never cease to remind me of how little I matter?"

"You weren't listening sir. That's not what I said." Kate said earnestly.

He smiled at her and crossed his legs.

For the second time that morning Kate thought, *I'm an idi-ot.*

"Mr. Lincoln. If I could I would have voted for you. My best friend and pretty much the only family I have in this world is a free black man and he would have voted for you too. If he could, I mean." She didn't think she should mention that Juba was also currently acting as his body servant. That was a secret best kept for a little while longer. "I love this country, but slavery will kill our democracy if it's not eradicated. Slavery is about hate. Any kind of thinking that makes one group better than the other is about hate. Hate makes fear and fear kills democracy. Fear leads to violence."

He nodded slowly. "But some would say that violence, or the threat of it, is an essential part of self defense. And certainly you would agree that all people, have a right to self defense."

Kate shrugged. "Maybe. But violence is repugnant when it is used to protect the ability of some Americans to stomp all over the rest of us. It offends me sir, but more importantly, it's an offense against American democracy. Either we're all Americans or none of us are because there's no America. Not really."

Lincoln sighed and leaned forward. "It offends me as well Mrs. Barley. I'm about to take an oath to preserve this country and everything it stands for. I take these matters seriously. I assure you, I believe there is a plot to kill me. I suspect there's quite a few such plots. General Scott tells me he set a brace of New York policemen investigating, first in New York and then in Baltimore. Apparently they found the threat of mob violence quite real, thus corroborating the Pinkerton investigation. So I believe you. But I must be the president, not only of the states that voted for me, but of the states that did not. I must bind up this nation's wounds and I can see no way to do that while cowering in fear."

Kate sighed and shook her head.

"What?" he asked.

"Men," she answered with another sigh. "Always with the high flying philosophy and the grandiose words to justify what they do or do not want to do anyway. Mr. Lincoln, life is not grand philosophy and high toned words. It's grubby and mean and brutal. Real life will crush philosophy every time. Your intention to do good will not erase the fear and hate of the men who would destroy this country to protect white male supremacy. Keep giving speeches about binding and see if that makes you any less dead when the assassin's bullet finds you."

Lincoln unfolded his legs and leaned forward, bringing his face only inches from hers. "What do you suggest I do Mrs. Barley?"

She took yet another chance. "Quit being a coward."

In a tone so mild it could only be interpreted as dangerous he asked, "A coward?"

"Yes Sir. You want to ignore the very real threats against you. You think if you don't acknowledge them they'll go away and you won't have to face the awful task before you."

"Which is?" His tone remained mild, but his expression made it clear she'd stepped over the line.

Kate almost laughed. "I know. I'm being impertinent. You don't need me to remind you of the horror facing the nation."

They looked at each other. The silence stretched into discomfort, at least for Kate.

Desperately, she said, "Mr. Lincoln, it takes a brave man to admit he needs help. I'm asking you, as a citizen of this country, to take the hand the Pinkertons extend to you. Let us help you."

He held out his huge hand to her. "I believe I'll take your hand. Whatever your name."

She grabbed his over-sized hand with both of hers and pulled them both to their feet, giving out a great whoop as she did.

Mr. Lincoln looked at her in stunned amazement and then began to laugh.

She thought the future president had a laugh almost as beautiful as Juba's. *I've known this man for a sum total of five minutes and I'll cry for the rest of my life if something terrible happens to him.*

Hazzard opened the door and poked his head in. "Everything all right?"

Lincoln turned with a deliberation that looked both stately and clownish. "I believe I just made this lady exceedingly happy."

Kate threw back her head and laughed again. "You have no idea, sir."

"I have one condition," Lincoln said. "Maybe two."

"Anything," she said. At that moment she meant it too. He could have anything he wanted.

"I will give my speech in Harrisburg this afternoon. I shall turn myself over to you after that, not before. That is condition number one."

"And the second?" She glanced at Hazzard, and then back at Lincoln.

"Today is George Washington's birthday. I'm raising the flag at Independence Hall at dawn." He pulled out his pocket

292

watch and clicked it open. "In about a half an hour. I'd like you to come with me."

Kate found herself standing in the grey, pre-dawn, winter light on a platform built for the occasion. They were in front of the red brick building where the founders signed the Declaration of Independence. She shivered against the chill air and the excitement of the moment.

Mr. Lincoln stepped to the front of the platform. Seeing him, the crowd cheered. They sounded more polite than enthusiastic. Lincoln looked out over the crowd until they quieted down. As if on cue the sun broke over the horizon. He stepped forward and raised the flag. More polite clapping followed.

Hazzard stepped over to Kate's side. "I think he's got something up his sleeve," he whispered in her ear.

She shivered again, this time not from cold.

He reached down, took her cold hand in his and tucked it in his pocket.

Something in her belly, or lower, turned over.

Mr. Lincoln stepped forward to the railing at the front of the platform. He looked out at the multitude and then his voice rang out, impossibly clear and strong.

I am filled with deep emotion at finding myself standing here in the place where were collected together the wisdom, the patriotism, the devotion, the principle, from which sprang the institution under which we live. It was not the mere matter of the separation of the colonies from the mother land; but something in that Declaration giving liberty, not alone to the people of this country, but hope to the world in a future time.

He paused as the crowd expressed mannered approval.

It was that which gave promise that in due time all should have an equal chance. Now my friends, can this country be saved on that basis? If it can, I will consider myself one of the happiest men in the world. If it can't be saved on that principle, it will be truly awful. But, if this country cannot be saved without giving up that principle—I was about to say I would rather be assassinated on this spot than surrender to the forces that would deny all people liberty.

Lincoln paused again.

Kate mouth gaped in disbelief. She thought she'd never admired anyone quite so much as she admired the awkward and eloquent man before her.

He spoke again. When he did his voice was louder. Firmer.

My friends. I did not expect to be called upon to say a word when I came here. I was supposed to only do something towards raising a flag. I may therefore have been indiscreet. I have said nothing but what I am willing to live by, and, in the pleasure of Almighty God, die by.

The crowd's cheering escalated. They were no longer just being polite.

Mr. Lincoln bowed and stepped away from the podium. He walked towards Kate and lowered his head to hers. Forehead to forehead he said, "I'd rather be killed than surrender to the fear mongers, but if you could help me do neither, I'd be mighty happy." Then the crowd of men on the stage enveloped him and moved him away from her.

Hazzard squeezed Kate's hand, reminding her that he was standing right there with her. He pulled her inside the building, out of the cold and noise. "He's something else, isn't he?"

Kate turned and looked straight into Hazzard's dark eyes. "I've got so much to do and I'm running out of time. Would you like to help?"

He offered her his elbow. With a smile, she took it.

Chapter 29

K ate and Hazzard were sitting in her room pretending they weren't alone and in close proximity to a bed. They'd returned to the Continental Hotel well ahead of Lincoln and his entourage and had little to do but wait.

"When's the train for Harrisburg?" She knew, but she wanted to hear him say it.

Hazzard took a piece of paper out of his pocket and unfolded it. "We leave the hotel at 8:30 AM," he paused and pulled his watch from his pocket. "It's 7:45 right now. We're at the train station by 9 and leaving at 9:30.

"And what's the Harrisburg schedule?"

Hazzard consulted his paper schedule again. "It's four hours to Harrisburg, but they're making a short stop in Lancaster."

"Lancaster? Why? Isn't that Buchanan's home town?"

"It's also Thaddeus Stevens' country and Mr. Lincoln owes the old reprobate for helping him win the state. Lancaster will be fine. He's not even getting off the train. He'll meet some city functionaries, give a short speech from the rear carriage and we'll be gone."

Kate's mind whirled. "After Lancaster?"

"Once he's in Harrisburg he's got a speech in the afternoon and an early dinner event afterwards. We're scheduled to spend the night at the Jones Hotel."

Kate opened her mouth, but Hazzard anticipated her question.

"His schedule says he'll arrive in Baltimore tomorrow at 1 o'clock in the afternoon and then do the hand shaking, reception and public speaking thing all afternoon."

Kate's door opened and Allan stuck his head inside. "Need some help?" he asked cheerily.

Kate leaped up, grabbed her boss and pulled him into the room before soundly hugging him. "I thought you'd gone back to Baltimore. I was about to send you a telegraph— I was going to advise murdering Mr. Hutchinson and meeting us in Philadelphia." She held him at arms length and beamed at him. "And here you are!"

Allan smoothed his jacket in a vain attempt to regain his dignity. "It remains to be seen if poor Mr. Hutchinson will survive his confrontation with oysters or not. I sent Bangly to Hutchinson's office to pack up a bunch of worthless papers. Bangly will suggest Mr. Hutchinson has gross bodily complications of the sort that should keep Luckett away."

"Mr. Bangly? You didn't tell me he was coming."

"Lately arrived my dear. On the principle of 'all hands on deck' I emptied the Chicago office."

Allan turned towards Hazzard. The two men shook hands. "Good to see you Captain. I've been formulating some variations on the plan. Juba gave me some advice—he wanted to

296

be here, but he's helping Mrs. Lincoln with the boys." Allan turned to Kate. " We have about an hour to solidify details and make a time table."

Hazzard snapped to attention. "Whatever the final plan, Kate should take it to Mr. Lincoln. He's taken a shine to her."

Allan smiled wickedly at Kate. "Yet another victim of your charms my dear." Before she could protest he took a sheaf of papers from his pocket and gestured the two of them over to the little corner table. "I've made some modifications to my original plan. Tell me what you think." The three of them got to work.

The Lincoln Special pulled out of the Philadelphia train station right on schedule. Before it did Mr. Judd handed out fresh copies of Lincoln's official schedule to the gaggle of reporters traveling with the train.

"Gather 'round gentlemen," Judd called out, sounding a lot like a man with no troubles. "This is the last schedule you'll get. As you can see it covers today and tomorrow."

The men each took a sheet of paper. The official schedule put the Lincoln Special in Harrisburg by afternoon and leaving the next morning for Baltimore. They would arrive in Baltimore Saturday afternoon, after which the president would attend a reception at Eutaw House. At 6 o'clock the Special would depart Baltimore for Washington City, arriving late that evening.

Not one whit of it turned out to be true.

Juba hated this part of attending to Mr. Lincoln— listening to Mrs. Lincoln's loud recriminations, which were sometimes aimed at her husband or, more often, at some member of their traveling party. To be fair, Mrs. Lincoln had every right to be anxious. Her husband was in near constant danger, which in turn put herself and her sons in danger. The way Juba understood it, Mrs. Lincoln hadn't been a fan of the Lincoln Special in the first place, and again, Juba didn't blame her. And to give the lady credit, she could have stayed in Springfield and followed her husband on a later train, thereby avoiding the danger inherent in being in her husband's proximity. But, no, she got on the train and stood next to her husband in public every chance she could. She had gumption, all right, but she could be down right exhausting.

Earlier in the afternoon, just after they arrived in Harrisburg, Kate and Captain Hazzard came to Mr. Lincoln's dressing room. With Juba standing by in his capacity as the president-elect's body man, Kate explained the new traveling plans to Lincoln. Watching his Katie politely but ever so firmly give the next president his marching orders tickled Juba to no end.

After Kate and Hazzard left Lincoln turned to Juba and pinned him with his hound dog eyes. "I'm going to have to tell my wife about the change of plans. She hates change." He heaved a sigh and sat heavily in a chair much too small for him.

"Sir, we need to get you dressed for dinner. The missus going to be mad enough at you. You stand before her in your rumpled up, second best traveling suit and she'll have your guts for garters on general principle."

Wearily Lincoln stood and shrugged off his coat and then his shirt. Juba wanted to put his hand on the big man's shoulder, so down-hearted he looked, but instead he handed the poor man a fresh shirt.

"It's just that she'll want to come with me. I know everyone thinks Mrs. Lincoln is a difficult woman." Lincoln held up his hand to forestall Juba and stepped into his best pants. "No use denying it. Maybe she is. But she loves me and my sons and her fear for us has just about undone her." He buttoned his pants and then his white vest and shrugged into his newest frock coat, a double-breasted affair that made him look slightly less cadaverously thin.

Juba silently nodded and held out a pair of freshly shined black boots.

"The thing is I need her to not yell at me. Not this time. This plan of Pinkerton's depends upon absolute secrecy and if she gets going they'll hear her in Baltimore." Lincoln smiled weakly, and then looked up at Juba. "I thought if you were in the room . . . ." His voice trailed off.

Juba never wanted to yell "Hell No" so badly in his life, but he found he couldn't. So he didn't.

Which is how he found himself standing in Mrs. Lincoln's hotel room watching a quiet but fierce marital spat.

Finally he intervened. "Mrs. Lincoln, excuse me for interrupting."

"How dare you!" She hissed at him.

Juba didn't react. He knew she grew up in a slaveholding family and she probably hadn't ever brooked any interference from someone who looked like him."

Lincoln reached his hand out to his wife. "Now Mother, none of this is Mr. Johnson's fault. In fact, he's been one of the many people working to keep us all safe."

She froze where she stood, considering. "Have you?" she asked Juba. "Have you really?" She was a tiny thing, and well formed for a lady who'd had several babies. Juba could see why Mr. Lincoln adored her. When she wasn't being a "hell-cat," as some of the fellows called her, she had a quality about her that made men want to please her.

"Yes Ma'am." Using language a woman from a slave holding family might understand he said, "I would die before I let anyone harm any of you." The statement had the double benefit of aligning with slaveholders' desire to believe in loyal slaves and being true. "And if I might," Juba bobbed his head in an unspoken apology, "Your husband will be a sight safer if you stay here. And Ma'am, your boys will be safer. A man as tall as your husband, traveling with, if you'll forgive me for saying so, a good looking woman and two handsome boys, will be easy to spot."

"Then why not leave from here?" She stepped towards Juba. "If it's so important to get him to Washington as soon as possible, why go back to Philadelphia?

"Because Mother, smart men and women worked on this plan. I have to trust them and follow it."

Mary Lincoln shot her husband an exasperated look and turned towards Juba. "Well?"

"Ma'am if there was a train leaving Harrisburg tonight for anywhere but Philadelphia, we'd be on it. But there's not."

She looked steadily at Juba, then she squared her shoulders and asked, "All right. What can I do to help?"

Juba smiled to himself. "We need help with a disguise. He needs to look like an old man."

Mrs. Lincoln thought for a second or two and turned towards her husband. "I've got your old coat with me, the one you didn't want to pack because you said it wouldn't be cold enough. I'll get it." She turned to go, then turned back. "Mr. Johnson, could we borrow your hat? We can't have him wearing one of his stove pipes."

"Well, Mrs. Lincoln, that's a fine idea, but I 'spect my head's a mite smaller than your husband's. I'll run ask Mr. Lamon for his hat."

Mrs. Lincoln's face brightened. "And I've got a dark plaid shawl. You'll look like a sick old man."

Mr. Lincoln stepped over to his wife and kissed her firmly on the forehead. "That's the spirit my dear. And I need my black grip bag. It shall suffice as my only baggage."

She stood and thought for a moment. "You gave it to Robert when you got off the train." She opened the door to the adjoining room and called out. "Robert, we need Father's black bag. Could you bring it please."

A handsome young man stepped into the room. Juba thought it was a mercy that Robert Lincoln looked more like his mother than his father. At seventeen he was tall, but not near so tall or awkward as his father. He had the soft clear skin of the young, complicated by the meager beginnings of a mustache. The blood drained from his face at his mother's question.

He looked down at his feet, and then back up again. "I gave it to a hotel clerk and haven't seen it since."

Lincoln frowned and scratched at his forehead. "Bob, I gave you my bag with strict instructions to bring it safely to our rooms. I thought you would understand the importance."

For the first time in their brief acquaintance, Juba heard Mr. Lincoln sound angry. "Tarnation, son!"

The boy just stood there, hands hanging limply at his side. His expression indicated this was not the first time he'd disappointed his father.

Lincoln turned toward Juba. "Come with me. We *must* find that bag."

That day Juba found out just how fast Mr. Lincoln could move when motivated to do so. In seconds they were down the stairs and striding through the lobby. Lincoln didn't pause as he approached the front desk. He put a hand on the counter and vaulted over it. Juba took the slower route around the end of the counter.

"Your baggage room!" Lincoln barked at the astounded clerk, who could do no more than point at a small room behind him. Lincoln entered the room and rifled through the pile of hand luggage on the floor, throwing bags willy-nilly. He yanked a black carpet bag from the pile and produced a small key from his pocket. When the key fit the lock Lincoln visibly relaxed. He opened the bag and began to laugh.

Juba stepped closer and looked over Lincoln's shoulder. The bag contained three paper shirt collars and a large bottle of whiskey.

"Serves me right," Lincoln said, still laughing at himself. "I guess I lost my certificate of moral character, written by myself and this here is my comeuppance. Mother will have much to say to me."

Juba spotted another bag, much like the open one before Lincoln. He pulled it from the pile. "How about this one sir?"

But that bag wasn't Mr. Lincoln's either. They opened two more black leather bags, each with the same key, before they found the right one.

Lincoln pulled out a pile of papers with a great sigh. "It's my inaugural address. The only copy. I've been working on it for weeks."

"I understand sir. That's a lot of work to lose."

"It is Mr. Johnson, but that wasn't my chief concern." He tapped the pile of papers with his left hand. "I've been conciliatory and meek in every speech I've given on this trip. This one," he tapped again, "is not near so humble."

"Sir?"

"You'll see soon enough Mr. Johnson." He stood and turned toward the door. "Let's go. In my panic I spoke harshly to my son and my wife shall have words with me if I don't rectify my mistake."

While they'd been rifling through the bags like a pair of incompetent burglars a small crowd of hotel employees gathered behind the desk. They'd been watching in amazement as the next president of the United States broke into luggage.

Juba could only laugh. "I'll take care of this mess sir," he said, pushing Lincoln out the door. "You better go upstairs and get it over with."

That evening the president-elect attended a public dinner in the Jones House dining room. Most of the men in his entourage were there, as was Andrew Curtin, the governor of

Pennsylvania. As his body man Juba stood near the dining room door, his hands clasped loosely behind his back.

At 5:45 Mr. Lincoln rose, rubbing his head as he did. His hair stood up on end in little spikes, as if he'd just risen from his bed. From across the room Juba heard him say, "Gentlemen, please excuse me. I need to freshen up before I visit the Governor's mansion with Mr. Curtin. I'll be back down in a few minutes." Ward Hill Lamon rose to go with him, as did Colonel Sumner and Captain Hazzard.

Juba took that as his cue and stepped out of the dining room. Once out of sight of the diners he dashed down the hall for the back stairs. There he found the bundle he'd left earlier in the evening. He snatched it up and looked up the stairs, his heart in his throat. Moments later Mr. Lincoln, followed by Lamon, Sumner and Hazzard, came down the hotel's narrow back stairway.

Juba pulled a folded jacket from the pile and held it out to Lincoln, who shed his good black frock coat and shrugged on the worn and misshapen dark blue wool jacket. He next handed his new black beaver top hat to Sumner and donned a soft cap Juba held out to him. He tugged it over his head and pulled the brim down low over his eyes.

Hazzard gamely offered Lincoln the shawl, trying not to laugh as he did. Lincoln whirled it about his shoulders as gallantly as if it were a black velvet opera cloak. The men shared a nervous laugh.

While they'd been re-dressing Mr. Lincoln Mr. Lamon removed a tub of boot black from his pocket and rubbed it into Colonel Sumner's silver beard. Juba motioned to the area under Sumner's chin. Lamon applied more boot black. The Colonel summoned the authority and dignity of a lifetime of

304

military service in an effort to keep the beard darkening proceedings from degenerating into what they were, a farce. Lamon screwed the cap back on the polish, stepped back and surveyed his efforts. He spared a glance toward Juba, who nodded. He too mustered a lifetime's training in his effort to not laugh. This all felt too much like the last minute rush of back stage, just before the curtain went up.

The colonel snapped to attention and spoke. "Sir, it's not too late. I can still take you straight through Baltimore with a regiment of infantry for good luck. We'll cut our way through the secesh rascals, making them regret the day they were born."

Lincoln clapped Sumner on the shoulder. "Colonel, I admire your bravery, but no one should die on this journey. I fear there will be dying aplenty soon enough. Besides, I'd hate to waste your disguise." Lincoln pointed at Sumner's darkened beard and grinned.

Sumner swung Mr. Lincoln's good hat up onto his head and saluted this next commander-in-chief. The men shared a grim smile. With that Lincoln, Lamon, Hazzard and Juba went out the door and climbed into a plain black, enclosed carriage waiting in the hotel's side alley. Only Colonel Sumner stayed behind.

Minutes later Governor Curtin walked out of the Jones House front door accompanied by a tall, darkly bearded man in a black top hat. The crowd roared at the brief glimpse of the two men before they entered another closed carriage, this one considerably more ornate than the carriage that had just left the hotel's alley. It was a good day for Pennsylvania.

Chapter 30

February 22-23, 1861
Philadelphia & Baltimore

Two miles outside of the Harrisburg city limits a man climbed a telegraph pole in the dark, assisted only by the small lantern on his helmet. He pulled out his pocket knife and sawed through the telegraph wires. Over the years Andrew Wynne's boss had given him a number of orders, but he'd never been told to cut a line. But if Mr. Sanford wanted the lines cut Wynne thought he probably had good reason. In fact, he had his own suspicions, but he kept his mouth shut just the same. On poles outside of Philadelphia and Baltimore other men clipped more telegraph lines. In the span of a few minutes rapid communication between the two cities became impossible.

A plain black steam engine sped past Mr. Wynne, leaving him to the dark that followed the train. Andrew stared after the train, certain he'd just had his suspicions confirmed. He climbed down the pole, mounted his horse and rode for home. On his way home he saw few people and spoke to no one.

Kate stood in her Philadelphia hotel room and looked around. Had she forgotten anything. Her eyes strayed to wheel chair standing in the corner of the room. Her small traveling bag lay on its seat. She briefly checked the mirror. She'd hidden her hair under a dowdy bonnet and used a grease pencil to subtly line her face. And she was wearing her gray dress again. If this night ever ended she was going to consign the much abused dress to the trash bin. Nonetheless, it did serve to reinforce her transformation into a spinster woman of uncertain age.

A knock came at the door. Before she could answer it Allan opened it and poked his head in. In his right hand he had, his own carpetbag. "I came to say goodbye."

"You're *really* not going with us?" Kate knew the plan, but a small part of her hoped that Allan would change his mind.

"I am not." Allan looked at his pocket watch. "I'll be back in Baltimore in time to make a miraculous recovery and join Mr. Luckett for dinner."

"I don't understand." Kate still couldn't grasp that Allan Pinkerton was going to put the entire mission in her hands.

"Because if the conspirators suspect anything Luckett will tell me. And they will suspect something if I'm conspicuous by my absence. This way I can be your Baltimore alarm. Watch out the window as the train pulls into the Baltimore station. If you see me on the platform, stay on the train and we'll call in the Colonel's troops."

"And fight our way out of Baltimore?" She shook her head. "It would be a blood bath." She held out her hand and they shook. "Here's hoping I don't see you in the near future."

From Philadelphia they planned to put Mr. Lincoln on a regularly scheduled passenger train on the principle that any unscheduled or special train would be noticed. Timothy and Hattie's intelligence made it clear that the National Volunteers had men watching the tracks between Philadelphia and Baltimore.

The weakness of the plan was that a regular passenger might recognize Mr. Lincoln, either in the Philadelphia station or on the train. Kate's job was to make sure that didn't happen.

Kate arrived at the Philadelphia station a little over an hour early. She tried to reserve four double berths together in the sleeping car on the 10:50 train, but found to her dismay that the tickets were general sleeping car tickets, allowing each passenger to chose their own berth on a first come, first served basis. She stood at the ticket counter for a second, stymied. This was the problem with hastily constructed plans. How many other things had they missed?

She decided to buy tickets for eight berths, effectively reserving a whole car.

Kate boarded the train and found there was actually two sleeping cars. Yet another flaw in their plan. One of the porters entered the car.

She pinned on her 'helpless maiden' face and turned to the porter. "Excuse me sir. I wonder if I might ask you for a favor." She batted her eyelashes at him a tiny bit and added a tremolo to her voice. "You see, my father is very sick and he'll be taking this train with his doctor and two attendants. I'm to meet them. Daddy told me to reserve a whole car. He was most particular." She threw in a helpless little sob. "I bought eight tickets, but there are two cars so I'm in a bit of a pickle."

"We don't ticket that way. I'm sorry miss."

Kate dug in her reticule and pulled out a half dollar. "I wonder if you could hold this car for Daddy. You know, make sure the other passengers use the second car. So he's not angry with me." More eyelash fluttering followed.

He snatched the coin from her hand with dignified haste. "I'd be glad to help Miss. Night trains are quiet like, so I'll just stand here and warn people off." He stationed himself at the door of her chosen sleeping car. "You go find your daddy now." He shooed her off, as solicitous as a mother hen.

Kate had about thirty seconds to feel relieved before another problem presented itself. A train with one car pulled into the station. Kate looked at the timepiece she kept pinned to her dress bodice.

They were thirty minutes early. She hustled back to the ticket counter where she'd left a wheel chair. Earlier in the day she'd visited a hospital and paid an orderly far too much money to turn over a cumbersome old chair to her. It had large metal wheels and a banged up wooden frame. She'd had to pay a hansom cabbie extra to transport the monstrosity to the train depot.

Kate pushed the chair across the station lobby and met three white men and one small black man entering from the outside platform. A fellow in a plaid shawl leaned heavily against one of the white men and the small black man.

"I'm here Daddy," she called out and pushed the chair forward.

Mr. Lincoln shuffled over to the chair. He turned ponderously and dropped himself into the seat with a thump.

"There, there Daddy. Let me get you tucked in." She leaned down and tucked a lap blanket she had with her

310

around Lincoln's legs. Her bonnet brim and his hat brim met and under their combined shelter Kate and Lincoln smiled wickedly at each other. "Nice acting," she whispered.

Kate turned toward Hazzard. "Dr. Smith, I can't thank you enough for assisting Daddy with this trip." There, now everyone's bonafides were established. One sick old man, one Doctor, two attendants, one burly for heavy lifting, one black for the undignified stuff, and one anxious daughter. Slumped in the chair Mr. Lincoln looked not one whit like the next president of the United States.

She leaned down again. "If this president thing doesn't work out," she whispered, "you could always try the stage." She heard him chuckle as she straitened up.

With much sound and confusion the party boarded the waiting passenger train. Once onboard Juba and Mr. Lamon made a great show of transferring their infirm charge to a sleeping birth. Kate pulled the window shades down, leaving the four of them in relative privacy.

Hazzard pulled Kate aside. "Could I speak to you for a moment?"

She nodded and they stepped back onto the platform.

"How are you?" He looked intently at her.

Kate fervently wished she were wearing something besides her wilted grey dress and the kind of bonnet only an old maid would wear. "I'll be fine come morning," she said firmly.

He smiled at her and squeezed her hand.

"I was thinking," Hazzard said, "Instead of all of us in the one car, you stay with the president-elect and we gentlemen will be in the fore car. We can keep wandering passengers away from you." Hazzard gestured up the line at the rest of the train. A first class passenger car lie immediately in front of their sleeper, with the second sleeper in front of that, effectively sandwiching the first class car between the two sleepers. "You guard Mr. Lincoln and we watch the entrance. How does that sound to you?"

Kate tried not to look taken aback at the fact that an Army captain was asking her approval. Her surprise must have shown on her face.

"Mr. Pinkerton made it abundantly clear that he expected you to be in charge of this midnight run. I'm also supposed to keep Mr. Lamon out of your hair. Mr. Pinkerton doesn't much care for the man—called him a fool."

"That sounds like Allan," Kate conceded. She glanced at her watch again. "The train leaves in four minutes. I agree to your plan."

"Kate, I hate to ask, but, are you armed?"

She pulled a tiny gun from her harmless looking rabbit fur muff, which hung around her neck by a cord. She held it out to Hazzard, for his inspection.

"It's an Allan and Thurber four barrel pepperbox revolving pistol. It's .34 caliber and it works like a charm in close quarters." She smiled at the captain. "And it fits in my muff so it's close at hand."

"In other words, perfect for what you're up against and I should mind my own business." Hazzard handed the gun back to her.

Kate felt an awkward blush of pleasure at his approval. Still, it was nice to know she could surprise him.

Kate re-boarded the sleeping car and sat on the berth opposite Mr. Lincoln. He lay bent at the knees and neck to fit a bed not meant for men of prodigious height.

"Change of plans sir," she said quietly, and explained. The train started rolling as she spoke.

"So it's just you and me to Baltimore?" he asked. "And will I be calling you Mrs. Barley the whole time?" His eyes twinkled merrily as he spoke.

The question gave Kate pause. *If I can't trust this man, then why am I guarding him?*

She held her hand out, across the aisle. "My name is Katherine Warne sir, but everyone pretty much calls me Kate."

"It's nice to meet you Miss Warne," Lincoln said gravely. "I apologize for not standing. I've been told I'm much too infirm."

"Oh, yes," she said, matching his tone. "You're exceedingly aged and weak." They shared a smile. "And far too long for your berth, I see."

"Miss Warne, I've been too long for every bed I've slept in since I was fourteen years old. And it's not just beds. I'll tell you, the best thing about getting myself elected president— someone made me shoes that fit my monumental feet." He waggled his sock clad toes at her and looked pointedly at the boots sitting in the aisle next to his bed.

"Why, Mr. Lincoln," Kate said in mock excitement, "I do believe if this train falls into a river we could row ashore in your boots. One for you and one for me." They snickered at each other, though her jest wasn't all that funny. Kate couldn't believe that the man could laugh at a time like this.

"Miss Warne, was your childhood pleasant? Were you happy?"

He startled her with his abrupt change of topic. She thought about it for a second and said, "I guess I was happy.

My parents died when I was fifteen, so I try not to think about that time. But before they died we were happy. Exceedingly so, I think."

"I wonder then, if I could impose on you. I'm sure you've had a day and week and even month as hard as any you've ever had—true?"

She nodded.

"Myself as well Miss Warne," he said. The heaviest, deepest, most melancholy sigh she'd ever heard from anyone issued from his body. "And there's more to come—for both of us no doubt."

She nodded again, feeling much less merry than she had a minute ago.

"Still, and all, I wonder if you could tell some stories from your youth. Happy stories that take the two of us away from this terrible night, if just for awhile. Could you?"

She smiled at the man who lay curled in a berth to small for him, like he was the largest lost child in the history of the United States. "I could. But I must warn you sir," she stood, swayed with the train and bowed with a flourish. "I am a daughter of the circus. I can walk a high wire, balance on a galloping horse and tell people's fortunes. I know clowns and con men, jugglers and jesters, ladies of dubious reputation and women of immense talent. And that's just to start."

"Then lay on Macduff, and damned be him who cries 'Hold!'"

"Ah, Shakespeare. A learned man, in spite of his canoe sized shoes."

She started with a story about Juba, thinking he'd like to hear about his valet. She told how Juba danced so fast and so fine that no one could best him and how he'd had to die be-

314

fore his dancing killed him. That story led her to a story about Hattie, a runaway slave girl who taught Kate to read fortunes, or at least how to pretend to read fortunes.

Mr. Lincoln interrupted her in the middle of her Hattie story.

"I hate slavery for just those reasons. Because it takes away people's choices when it takes their freedom. People think that because I refuse to say I'm going to abolish slavery that means I like it. I don't. Not one whit." He tried to sit up to emphasize his point and bumped his head for his efforts. "Tarnation!" he muttered, rubbing his head and lying back down.

"Then why not abolish it?" Kate asked, surprised at Mr. Lincoln's vehemence.

"The question itself suggests that you, like so many other Americans, do not understand the job of president. I will be President, not King or God. My job, when I take that oath of office two weeks from now, will be to uphold the Constitution and the law. No law, no article of the Constitution, gives me power to abolish slavery. Moreover, the president's job does not include the imposition of his personal feelings upon the American people. Presidents are not above the law. But make no mistake, Miss Warne, I *will* uphold the Constitution." His face became grave and grim as he spoke.

She stared at him for a couple of long seconds. In their silence the trains wheels clacked and rumbled beneath them.

He smiled gently at her. "Mrs. Lincoln says I have a habit of sermonizing." He dug his watch out of his waistcoat pocket and clicked it open. "You've been talking for almost an hour. Do you need a rest?"

She shook her head. She could talk as long as this man needed to listen.

315

He smiled gratefully. "Then I could use another story. You said your parents died when you were young? Do you mind telling me about it?"

She looked at him and considered. She never told this story. For a long time it had been too painful. But maybe now it was time. Time to remember and accept. If this man could face all the hate and division in the nation she could face her parent's death.

"My parents were circus people. Which means I was too."

"Was?" His eyes crinkled in concern.

She nodded and began.

Chapter 31

Eleven Years Ago
Glen Falls, New York

When Momma and Poppa practiced, Kate's job was to circle the ring picking up dropped balls and scooping the occasional horse dropping. Momma had this act where she juggled balls Poppa threw at her while she balanced on the back of a cantering horse. Juggling the balls was easy. Momma taught Kate how to juggle three and then four balls back when Kate was just a wee thing. The hard part was catching Poppa's throws. Kate circled the 40-foot ring, plucking balls from the sawdust, being careful to stay out of Excelsior's path.

She loved the way the big top smelled in the evenings after the crowds left, like horse poop and sweat and popped corn and damp canvas. The patter of rain on the canvas and the sound of the night wind swirling and trying to get in, made it all the more cozy inside.

As her mother circled the ring under yellow lantern light, Kate thought about how fun it would be to ride an elephant, if only their circus had one. But not in front of people. Performing gave Kate what Momma called 'the butterfly tummy.'

Much better to stay in the background. Poppa said she'd grow to enjoy the spotlight, but Kate doubted it.

"Katie, we need to practice flip-flaps," her dad called across the ring. His basso voice carried easily across the lantern lit center ring. "Your mother wants to land three in a row. We could be here till dawn." He smiled at his wife to show he was joking. In a flip-flap the rider stood on the horse's back, flipped forward into a hand stand and then back to her feet. The trick, done once, impressed the crowds, who loved the equestrian acts best of all the circus acts. Momma was trying to do three flip-flops in quick succession. She'd be the darling of the ring if she could pull off the trick.

Excelsior was already a crowd favorite. Mr. Rice trained Excelsior to do math and answer yes and no questions. Or at least that's what the rubes thought. Excelsior was really responding to clicks of Mr. Rice's fingers, hidden in his spacious coat pockets. Mr. Rice loaned Excelsior to her parents, thinking if the horse could also work a rosin back act he'd be all the more valuable. Kate suspected that increasing Excelsior's value and the plan to acquire an elephant were related. An elephant would be all well and good, but Kate loved Excelsior almost as much as Momma and Poppa.

Kate didn't mind how long practice took. She could watch Momma all night, specially when she was working Excelsior. They seemed to float around the ring, a blur of white in the yellow-grey of the lamplight.

"Off ye go now," Poppa insisted. "You have your own practice in the morning and you'll be a disappointment to Mr. Blondin if you're tired."

Kate heaved herself off the bench. Poppa was right. Mr. Blondin was teaching her to walk the high wire and she couldn't do that with tired legs. Momma and Poppa thought if Kate could both wire walk and perform in equestrian acts she'd always have a job. Kate couldn't convince them she had no desire to perform. She wasn't like Momma that way.

"G'night," she called, waving to them both. She stepped outside the big top and bent her head against the rising wind. It was the last time she saw them alive.

Poppa always parked their wagon on the far side of the back yard, away from the worst of the circus noise. Although performances were usually in the late afternoon, to take best advantage of the light, circus people tended to stay up late, practicing and socializing. Much to Momma's disapproval, socializing often involved intoxicating spirits, which led to further noise. Kate had long ago learned to sleep through the constant background noise of circus life, but not Momma.

"Hey Katie, git yourself over here!"

Kate peered through the dark and found a circle of clown performers off to her left. She walked over, a smile stretching her face. "Hey Pete."

"I heard Juba was back. You seen him?"

Kate shook her head. "Nope. I bet I see him at breakfast. You know how he is about Big Ella's cooking."

Pete nodded and gestured toward a three geese, a sheepish smile sneaking onto his saggy face. "We're trying to get these beasts to walk this here teeter-totter," he gestured toward a plank they'd laid against a short sawhorse, "but they act like they're afraid of us."

The other clowns nodded in agreement.

Kate looked at the clown's set-up, then took a handful of grain from a nearby bag and laid it in a trail, down the center of the board. One of the geese approached the board and pecked at what it could reach. Kate gently nudged it. The goose-stepped up the board, gobbling grain as it walked. Once the goose passed the middle of the board it slowly tipped. The goose was too busy eating to notice.

Kate looked up at Pete and his fellow clowns. "Tadaa!" she half whispered, so as to not upset the performing poultry. She spread her skirts and took a deep bow.

Walking away she thought, that thing with the goose was exactly the kind of stuff she liked to do. Figuring out problems was fun. So was helping people. And when the clowns premiered their teeter-tottering goose act she'd be happy to watch from the side-lines while someone else got the applause.

The sound of screaming woke Kate up from her dream. She'd been standing atop Excelsior as he galloped around the ring faster and faster.

"Blow down," echoed through night, carried across the circus backyard by the wind. Kate rolled over and listened. Blow downs scared circus folk more than fire. With fire a person could, if they were lucky and fast, get out of the tent. Blow downs were another matter entirely. The tons of collapsed canvas, usually made heavier by rain, maimed and killed anyone unlucky enough to be inside.

More yelling. The wind had become a howling gale while she slept. *Momma? Poppa?* She leaned over the edge of her narrow bunk, no more than twenty inches from the wagon's roof and looked towards her parent's bed. *Were they in there?* She couldn't tell. *Too dark.* She tried to listen for their breathing. *No good—too much wind.* She dropped down to the floor. She patted her parents' bed. *Empty. Cold and empty.* Maybe they were in the cook tent. It was wicked outside. They must have quit when the wind kicked up. They could have stopped for a hot drink before coming to bed. Kate opened the door at the back of the wagon, looked for the big tent and didn't see it. She charged out of the wagon, heedless of her bare feet and ran pell mell across the yard. Mud splashed the back of her legs as she ran.

A crowd milled around the fallen big top, the light gray canvas hard to see in the dark. The center pole had collapsed, pulled down by the weight of pools of water in the canvas and the push of the wind. Tent pegs with slack ropes attached to them circled the fallen canvas. Roustabouts, big armed, dark skinned men, struggled to lift the canvas. Kate watched them, her heart thumping wildly.

The wind came in sideways, pushing her night shirt up against her legs. The rain, driving in at an angle, must have washed out the tent stakes. She knew the dark men who did the circus's hard labor. They'd feel responsible, even if they weren't.

Somewhere in the middle of the fallen tent, something moved under the canvas. "Cut 'er open!" The cry carried on the wind to Kate's ears. Dark forms crawled over the lumpy mess that had once been a big top.

It had to be her parents. She gripped her upper arms, suddenly cold in the wind and stepped toward the tent. Strong hands grabbed her.

"No, you don't Miss Kate. It's too dangerous."

Kate recognized Uncle Juba's voice. She turned and threw herself at him. She looked up at him, but not by much. She was only a little shorter than him these days, seeing how he wasn't much over five foot tall. His eyes and teeth gleamed in the dark. "Have you seen Momma and Poppa?" she asked him, her mouth tight against the question.

"No baby," he said, looking away at the fallen tent, "I have not."

"They were practicing. I left them there and went to bed. I just went to bed and left them there." Kate's voice rose to a hysterical pitch.

"Now you just hush child," he told her, holding her at arms length and giving an infinitesimal shake. "If they're in that mess there's nothin' you could have done. They'd want you safe out here."

"It's the horse," one of the roustabouts yelled, his voice carrying on the wind.

Kate's heart rose and fell. They'd found Excelsior, but not her parents.

Mr. Rice, who stood next to Uncle Juba, started for the canvas sea, then stopped. He called out, "Phineas and Emmeline? Are they there?" The big horse screamed and struggled to his feet. His pale equine body glowed yellow-white in the lantern light. Kate could hear voices, but no words.

Mr. Blondin appeared on Kate's left and wrapped a blanket around her shoulders. She gripped it tightly in her fists. "I'll go see about Excelsior," Mr. Rice said over his shoulder and marched off into the dark.

As the night moved on everyone with a strong back pitched in cutting sections of the tent and rolling them back.

Others held lanterns for the searchers. Uncle Juba stood by her side. He didn't say much. He just stood there with her.

Not long after he left them Mr. Rice came back leading Excelsior. The white horse bobbed his neck up and down as he limped along. Blood dripped off the side of his head in a thin rivulet. He didn't even look at Kate as he went by.

At dawn there was a flurry of activity out on the canvas. One of the roustabouts called Mr. Rice and Mr. Mabie over. Kate watched the two men traverse the fallen tent. Juba held her fast.

Mr. Rice reached the circle of men, looked down at the crumpled ground for fifty years, or so it felt to Kate, and then turned and looked right at her.

"Noooo," she whimpered. She wanted to scream at the top of her lungs, but Poppa always said Warnes were circus people and circus people didn't scream. They didn't cry. At least not in front of anyone. Circus life was hard, and sometimes dangerous. People died. They learned to move on, literally and metaphorically.

Juba tightened his hold on her shoulders. Mr. Rice trudged toward her, walking as if his boots were made of cast iron. She straightened her spine and lifted her chin. He stopped in front of her. The look on his face told her all she needed to know.

The muffled sounds of the circus's efforts to get the big tent sorted out reached Kate through the thin walls of her parents' wagon. Except it wasn't their wagon anymore. She supposed it was hers now.

A soft knock came to the rhythm of "shave and a haircut." Uncle Juba always knocked that way, and her father always knocked back "two-bits" before opening the door. It seemed to delight them every time they did it, though Kate had no idea why. Once she'd asked Mama, but Mama only shook her head and said, "Katie, men are the oddest mixture of child and adult, or at least the good men. You meet a man who doesn't have any child left in him, you run the other way." Kate still didn't precisely know what Mama meant, but the smile on her face when she said it told Kate that Mama loved both Papa and Juba.

"Go away," she called. Instead Juba added the double answering knock himself and opened the door the tiniest bit.

"You decent Kate? If so I'm coming in, like it or not."

Kate didn't say anything. She felt like she was mired in sticky mud, like that Georgia mud they'd had to drive through last spring.

"Well, then, I'm coming in." Juba stepped up into the cramped space of their enclosed wagon. Kate, in her bed above the table, found herself eye-to-eye with her father's best friend, a man she called Uncle, though he was a free black man and no relation to either her Papa or Mama. Papa once told Kate that Uncle Juba was a famous dancer and minstrel performer. Juba made a lot of money winning dance contests, or so Papa said, but he always came back to the circus because circus people didn't much care about the color of a man's skin.

Juba put his hand on the edge of Kate's bunk. "What you thinkin,' baby girl?" he asked softly.

Kate liked that he didn't ask her how she felt. Juba never talked about his family, ever. She'd asked him once and he'd only said that it was too sad to tell.

"I can't go out there." Kate paused, tightened her jaw and said the one thing she could say to no one else. "I hate this circus."

"Oh, you poor baby girl," Uncle Juba crooned into the space between them. He reached out his hand and smoothed back her tumbled hair. "I 'spect you do and that's fair enough. But the circus is your family too, and you're going to need these people."

"I'm not," she said, pressing her lips together. In her deepest, darkest heart, Kate also felt a tiny bit relieved that she never had to tell her parents she didn't want to follow in their footsteps. That relief cut through her heart like a rusty knife.

"You sure?" He looked steadily at the young woman in the bunk. "This is all you've ever known."

"Yes," she said with such finality that Juba thought it best to believe her. Her eyes never wavered from his. "I have to get out of here before the circus kills more people I love."

Juba sighed. "I've got an idea. Give me a day or two." He patted her hand and was gone, leaving behind him the smell of fresh air and rain. Kate decided the sky was right, so she began to cry again.

They buried her parents two days later. Glen Falls let them have a lot at the edge of the South Side Cemetery. It was a lovely cemetery, full of trees and birds. Kate thought it was as good a place as any to leave her parents. The circus couldn't wait any longer— it had to move on. Towns ahead expected a big top circus, not a mud show exposed to the sky, which was what they were going to get. The show had to go on anyway.

325

After the burial Big Ella served a funeral lunch in the dining tent. When everyone had eaten Kate pushed back her plate and stepped up on a bench. "Excuse me," she hollered. When she had everyone's attention she spoke again. "I appreciate what you all have done for me and what you're willing to do for me now, offering to keeping me on and all. But we all know circuses don't stay together forever and life on the road is hard even for the most successful among us." The crowd nodded and murmured their assent. "No one here needs the extra burden I'd be." The crowd murmured amongst itself again, this time in disagreement. Kate held up her hand. "Thank you. All of you. But my mind is made up. I need to leave the circus and find a new life. Can you understand that?" She stood there, before them, her heart breaking for the truth she told.

And because they all loved her they let her go.

Kate and Uncle Juba left the circus that afternoon for Miss Haines School for Girls. It was a long time before she saw her circus family again.

Kate's voice trailed off when she heard a soft snore. She watched Mr. Lincoln sleep for a few minutes, thinking he looked like an old hound dog. The poor man, already so care worn and not yet the president. It wouldn't get easier after he was inaugurated. And he would make it to his inauguration if she had anything to do with it. And she did.

Kate settled back in her seat. She'd refused to think about the circus and her childhood for years. But that was ridiculous, wasn't it? Visiting Mr. Rice in Baltimore had been wonderful. *I've been spectacularly stupid. I insisted on thinking of myself as an orphan when I had a family all along.*

She took her pistol out of her muff and laid it in her lap. While she watched the door and the sleeping president-elect, she thought about old times and happiness.

Chapter 32

February 23, 1861
Baltimore & Washington City

A screech of breaks warned Kate that they'd arrived at Baltimore's President Street Station. Remembering Allan's admonition she raised one of the window shades and peered out. The train slowed to a stop. *No Allan.* That was good. Kate checked her watch once more. It was 3:30 in the morning.

A knock startled her. She pulled her pistol and pointed it at the door. "Yes?"

"Shake a leg, Mrs. Barley," came the answer.

It was Juba. Kate breathed a sigh of relief.

"Baltimore?" Mr. Lincoln's voice was bright though he'd been soundly asleep only moments before.

"Yes. The coast appears to be clear." Kate waited while Mr. Lincoln pulled his boots on and settled himself in the wheelchair. She opened the train's door to find Hazzard and Juba waiting. Predictably, Mr. Lamon loomed in the background.

"Your carriage awaits," Hazzard said, sweeping his arm back towards the depot doors with a grin.

Juba pushed Mr. Lincoln's wheel chair across the platform and through the depot lobby. Kate walked slightly ahead of them, her derringer clutched tightly in her hand, which lay hidden inside her muff. Hazzard took the rear of their little procession. Though she could see no weapon on him, she assumed he had one secreted somewhere about his person.

She pushed through the depot's double doors into the cold night air. Though she'd been expecting it, she stared in open-mouthed delight at the sight before her. A half dozen circus wagons sat outside the train depot, each one more outlandish than the last.

Dan Rice vaulted down from the front wagon. It was a Chinese red, lemon yellow and gilded confection tiered like a wedding cake, it's paint so glossy it merrily reflected the light from the gas street lights. It had a roomy central box with oval doors adorned in gleaming brass hardware. A dark skinned driver sat in a seat high up on the third tier dressed in a bright red suit. Harnessed to the glitzy passenger car were four bay horses, each bedecked with red ribbons. Right behind it was the calliope wagon, painted in the same gaudy paint scheme. Thankfully, the organ wasn't pumping steam. Calliope organs in full steam could wake the long dead. Kate peered down the street. A third wagon, pulled by eight horses, held Old Put, the only trained rhino in the world, at least as far as anyone knew.

Mr. Rice stepped from between the first two circus wagons and toward Kate, Lincoln, Juba and Hazzard. He swept his hat off and bowed a deep, ringmaster's bow.

From his wheel chair, Mr. Lincoln started a deep, rumbling laugh that threatened to ring through the night air. Realizing his mistake, put his hand to his mouth. Still, a low chuckle rumbled out of him as he abandoned his wheeled chair. Kate stood next to Mr. Rice, her derringer held discretely down at her side and motioned Mr. Lincoln inside the first circus wagon. Understanding she wanted to be last in and first out he temporarily abandoned his manners and took his seat inside, bending sharply at the waist to fold himself into the seat.

Just then Mr. Lamon stepped through the depot doors. He froze, whipped off his hat, smacked it against the side of his leg and barked, "What the hell?"

Just then the rhinoceros pawed at his straw and snorted, somehow managing to sound eerily like Mr. Lamon. From inside the scarlet circus carriage Lincoln chortled with undisguised glee.

Unwilling to let Put have the last word, Lamon snorted back at the rhino and then glared at Kate and Mr. Rice. "It's a damned circus parade."

Mr. Rice nodded in agreement. "Right you are, sir. Step inside please."

Lamon harrumphed his way past Kate and Rice. Kate waited while the two men climbed inside the circus wagon.

Mr. Lincoln leaned forward towards Kate, who was still outside the carriage. "Miss Warne, if you'd told me we were running off to join the circus I'd have agreed to your plans a lot sooner." He held out his hand and pulled her inside.

Juba, who'd contained himself thus far, let ring his marvelous, deep laugh.

Lincoln looked at him in wonder. "Mr. Johnson, you should laugh more often."

Juba eyed the president-elect. "I'll make you a deal Mr. Lincoln. I'll laugh for you every day if you can convince people to quit trying to kill you."

Lamon harrumphed from his red velvet corner. "I demand to know the meaning of this, this . . . travesty."

Mr. Rice looked at Kate for permission and then said, "It's like this Mr. Lamon. Kate here came to me about ten days ago. Seeing the Baltimore writing on the wall, as it were, she figured the most dangerous part of this whole endeavor would be getting your friend here across the city. So we're hiding in plain sight."

Kate shifted in her seat, jostling against Mr. Rice as the carriage began to roll. "Mr. Lamon, if you've seen any of the Baltimore newspapers you know that Mr. Rice recently began making pro-Southern speeches at performances, which have played exceedingly well with Baltimore audiences. At my request he also announced that his circus would stage a parade to compete with Mr. Lincoln's day in Baltimore."

Juba laughed again. "Don't tell me. The circus is scheduled to parade from the Camden Street Station, where we're going, to the President Street Station, which we just left. About mid-day."

Kate beamed at her friend. "Exactly."

Juba continued. "So if anyone's awake at this hour all they see is circus wagons getting into place for a parade."

"And not just any circus. One publicly at odds with Mr. Lincoln and his ilk," Mr. Rice gestured out the glass door. "Classic misdirection. It's the key to any con."

"Right," Kate said as the carriage rolled down the gas lit cobble stone street. "I'd been worrying myself sleepless, trying to come up with a plan that moved Mr. Lincoln through this city unseen. Then I remembered that magicians don't really disappear objects, they deceive people by shifting the audience's focus from one object to another."

"So you've disappeared me inside a secessionist circus, is that right young lady?" Mr. Lincoln asked, his eyes crinkled at their corners.

When all of this was over, Kate would think about the look on Mr. Lincoln's face as he rode inside the histrionically theatrical circus wagon. It wasn't a look she or anyone else saw much in the four years that followed that wagon ride.

"Damned fool idea, if you ask me," Lamon grumped, peevishness tightening his posture. "And not befitting the dignity of the President-elect."

"How about I worry about my dignity Hill and you worry about keeping me alive," Mr. Lincoln intoned in his deepest voice.

Behind them, loudly enough to be heard over the rumbling of the wheels, the rhinoceros issued a squealing, trumpety roar, seemingly in agreement with the president-elect.

When they arrived at the Camden Street station Mr. Rice bounded out of the circus wagon and took a look around. He popped his head into the carriage. "Train's not here. Hold tight till it arrives."

"I'll go buy tickets." Hazzard climbed over Kate, giving her knee a discrete squeeze as he did. Kate watched anxiously out the window as Hazzard approached the depot building, gripping her pepper box pistol inside her muff. She checked her watch. Four o'clock in the morning. The train to Washington was due in at 4:15, but the station seemed deserted. Where was everyone? She handed her tiny pistol to Juba and climbed out of the circus wagon.

333

By the time she'd caught up with Hazzard he'd found the night watchman. Hazzard asked the man where the ticket agent might be found.

"Oh, he's asleep this time 'o the mornin' for sure." The night watchman was a large, red-face, Irish man who seemed entirely unsurprised by the missing agent. He walked over to a closed office door and pounded on it with his club, calling "Captain, it's four o'clock." This bringing no reply, the watchman repeated his pounding and calling every minute or so, each time saying "Captain, it's four o'clock."

Kate stood by the office coming quietly unglued. *Was the man killed by the conspirators? Are we about to be ambushed after all?*

Unable to stand still, she walked back to the circus wagon.

Mr. Lincoln reached through the open door and tugged on her arm. "I wish I could have this fellow in the president's house with me—it appears to me he can stop time."

"What?" Kate asked. She stared blankly at Mr. Lincoln.

"Well, didn't you notice. It's been four o'clock for coming on ten minutes now. If I had this fellow in my employ I could stop time and avert the disaster that's coming."

Kate crooked an eyebrow at the president. "If you don't mind me saying so sir, you'd make a fine clown."

He crooked an eyebrow at her. "Oh, I don't mind. There's those that say I'm one already."

Kate stood outside the wagon on high alert, pepper pot pistol held down at her side, hidden by her skirts. What if it all went bad now? No one was getting at Mr. Lincoln unless they first killed her. The thought didn't make her feel all that much better.

Kate heard the distinct chug and clang of an approaching engine. When the Washington train pulled into the station it's clatter seemed to finally awoken the ticket agent. The ticket window popped open and everyone shifted into motion. Hazzard stepped up to the window, Mr. Rice opened the circus wagon door. Mr. Lincoln unfolded himself, stepped out and gravely shook Rice's hand. In a formal voice he said, "Sir, I thank you for the part you played tonight. If I'm ever bored I may call upon your services again."

"That would be grand Mr. Lincoln," Mr. Rice enthused.

Juba hustled up just then with the wheel chair, which had crossed Baltimore aboard the calliope. Mr. Lincoln took his seat.

The circus master turned toward Kate. He was about to hug her when he caught sight of her gun. Instead he kissed her cheek. "Your parents would be very proud of you," he whispered into her hair. Then he turned, leapt up into the wagon seat and thwacked the reins. The small procession moved down the block, where it would wait to make an entirely meaningless spectacle later that day.

The small party boarded the train with no surprises or unforeseen problems. Hazzard held the door, stopping Kate after Juba pushed Mr. Lincoln's chair through the door.

He waited until it was just the two of them on the platform and then took up Kate's hand and pressed a kiss into her palm.

She took an unintended deep breath. Who knew mustache bristles could be so tantalizing?

"Fair warning Kate—when we are safely in Washington I'm going to kiss a good deal more than your hand."

"I should hope so." Kate pulled her hand from his, looked the Captain in the eye and gave him a firm pat on the cheek. Then she stepped into the train carriage. A glance over her shoulder confirmed her suspicions. Hazzard was standing where she'd left him, open mouthed and flat footed.

On this last and shortest leg of their middle-of-the-night expedition, everyone sat up, anxiously watching out the windows. Everyone that is, except Mr. Lincoln who managed another nap. Juba took his post by the forward carriage door again, looking as grim and determined as any man ever had, while Hazzard and Lamon up guard on the rear door. Kate sat next to Mr. Lincoln, putting herself between him and the aisle. She admired his ability to sleep in moments like this. Either he had nerves of steel or utter faith in his guards.

The train rattled and clacked down the line, on through the dark as it had done a thousand times before. Kate's hand cramped from holding her pistol too tightly. Though the trip from Baltimore to Washington took only an hour and a half, the ride seemed nightmarishly endless. She wished she had a story to tell and someone to tell it to.

The train slowed as the entered Washington City. They passed blocks of half-built houses. The breaks screeched, steam whistled. The night was losing its grip on the sky when they pulled into the Washington station. Kate gently shook Mr. Lincoln's arm before standing to give him a some stretching room. She heaved a huge sigh of relief.

He rose and once more offered her his hand. "Miss Warne, I commend you for being a delightful traveling companion. Should my life ever be in danger again I will call upon your services."

"Thank you Mr. Lincoln," Kate replied, blushing to her hairline. "But nothing happened and here you are, safe and sound, with no help from me."

"Miss Warne, others will make that mistake, but you should not. Nothing happened because the Pinkerton intelligence and plan turned out to be flawless. Nothing happened because you made sure nothing would happen. And if something had happened, why, I saw clearly enough that you planned on putting yourself between me and an assassin's bullet. For your both your planning and intent, I owe you a great deal." He bowed to her, his eyes twinkling as he did.

Then he turned to Juba. "And you Mr. Johnson, or whoever you are. I watched you all night, as you've watched me for days. I owe you a debt of gratitude every bit as large as the one I owe Miss Warne."

Juba's eyes glittered wetly. He looked down at his boots. When he looked up again he said, "We expect great things from you Mr. President."

Hazzard stuck his head through the compartment door. "Hey, you all want to make a Mormon marriage and stay on this car, or do you want to get off? Mr. Lamon's scouted the depot and declares it clear. He's going to have kittens if we don't get a move on."

Mr. Lincoln rumbled a laugh. "I 'spect we should get moving. A polygamous marriage wouldn't increase my popularity, dubious as it already is."

The three of them talked among each other as they stepped out onto the platform. The men paused to let Kate go first, but she gestured them on ahead. She'd forgotten her bag. She turned back, found it on her seat and wearily picked it up. She was going to have a long hot bath when she got back to the hotel.

She followed the men out the door. Hazzard turned and said something to Mr. Lamon.

Kate gazed across the platform and saw something unspeakable.

Their carriage door was just opposite the first of six columns on the station's platform. A man wearing something dark on his head stepped out from behind the sixth column. *What is that on his head?* He advanced toward their small party. No one saw him but Kate.

Before she could say anything the man's arm came up.

In perfectly enunciated English the hooded creature roared, "I thought as much! Perfidy!" He continued to advance as he yelled. Kate saw it all as if it were in slow motion. He was slightly built. His boots were shined. *He has a gun.* She felt no more anxiety about it than if he'd pulled a bouquet of flowers. *Can I pull my pistol and fire in time?*

He howled three words more. She couldn't hear him because she'd made a decision. He was too far away to trust her gun and if she yelled a warning to the men he'd shoot. She threw herself at Mr. Lincoln, putting everything she had into it. Both her hands slammed into the small of his back. She noticed the warm wool of his coat against her palms. The impact reverberated through her wrists and up her arms.

Mr. Lincoln went down in three acts. First he stumbled, then he dropped to his knees and finally he tipped over like a felled tree. Something slammed into Kate's left shoulder, hurling her back. She saw a puff of smoke rise from the hooded man's revolver. He turned to flee.

A sharp pain screamed in her shoulder. She looked down. A crimson flower bloomed on her bodice. She looked at it, entirely surprised. Then her knees gave out. She fell hard, banging the side of her face on the cold marble of the depot floor. She rolled onto her side, stretching out her right arm as she did. She felt her pistol, still in her hand. She lifted her head and sited down the derringer's blunt nose. When had her tiny gun become so heavy? Her sight blurred. She squinted and fired at the fleeing man's back. The man didn't fall or change his course. She'd missed.

She dropped her head back to the floor, resting her cheek against its cool surface. She saw Hazzard look over at her. She watched his head turn away. She saw him decide. She smiled, or tried to, meaning to encourage him. He ran after the man. She sighed out a breath she hadn't known she was holding.

Kate found herself contemplating the depot's floor. *Why did I lie down?* Someone rolled her over. Her shoulder screamed again, which made her mind waver. Juba's face appeared above hers. *Why does he always look so worried?*

Juba took a huge gulping breath. "You just hold on."

Hold on to what? Had she dropped something? Someone pressed hard on her shoulder. Pain ripped through her. The world whirled around her in a swirl of black and grey.

"The president?" she asked. It came out like a whisper.

Mr. Lincoln's homely face appeared just beyond Juba's shoulder.

"I skinned my knee Miss Warne, but otherwise I'm fine." He smiled his kindly smile at her.

And then she was gone, into the darkness she'd been staring at all night.

Chapter 33

March 4, 1861
Washington City

Louis T. Wigfall wanted to strangle someone. Anyone really, but most of all one of those damned abolitionist varmints. First his Baltimore plan failed. And then his back-up plan to kill Lincoln came to nothing. And now? To be personally and publicly embarrassed like this?

This morning he walked from his office to the Senate Chamber to take his seat for the last meeting of this Congress. Once Mr. Lincoln was inaugurated, later this morning, congress would adjourn. Before the doors to the chamber stood Solomon Foot, newly elected senator from Vermont. Wigfall knew him from a reception in Senator Wilson's chambers the day before. Foot had a mane of white hair, a nose that looked like it could cut through a steak and a self-satisfied smile. He was buttressed by the senate secretary, a man of exceptional age who called the roll and kept order. The secretary had with him two burly senate clerks.

As Wigfall strode up to the door Foot spoke. "I'll ask you to stop there Senator." With a little flourish Foot handed Wigfall a piece of paper. "Sir, you are formally expelled from the United States Senate."

Louis took the proffered paper and examined it. *How dare they!* "You can't do this," he asserted and tried to step past Foot.

Foot blocked Wigfall with his shoulder and said mildly, as if amused by Wigfall's affront, "Of course we can expel you Senator. You represent the state of Texas. Texas seceded from the union on the first day of February. You have been illegally attending this body since that day."

"The secretary here continued to call my name—that proves I have a right to be here."

Foot gestured to the gray, stooped man standing next to him. "Mr. Dickens has come to see the error of his ways. He regrets his mistake and is here to correct that wrong." Foot paused and looked sternly at Asbury Dickens, who only nodded his assent. Wigfall stared at Dickens. The secretary was an Alabama Democrat and, before today had been sympathetic to pro-slavery men like Wigfall. "I can't believe you're going along with this Mr. Dickens."

Dickens looked rebelliously at Foot. "I don't have much choice Senator. I'm sorry." He stepped in close to Wigfall and grasped his hand. "Be gone before the new president is in place," he hissed.

"Now Mr. Dickens, none of that," Foot said forcefully, pulling Dickens away from Wigfall. "You are enforcing an order, as is your duty." Foot turned toward Wigfall. "Be reasonable Senator. When Texas seceded your senatorial post ceased to exist. All the other senators from seceded states withdrew weeks, even months ago. I'm sorry Texas did not chose loyalty to the nation, but there is nothing I can do to change the facts."

A small crowd gathered behind Wigfall, mostly senators from northern states wishing entry into the Senate chamber. Mild mannered Massachusetts Senator Henry Wilson stepped forward and extended his hand. "Senator Wigfall, I thank you for your service."

Wigfall slapped Wilson's hand aside. "I don't need thanking from a pup like you. Damn you all. And damn your abolitionist Senate." He turned and fled down the hall.

An hour later, mostly because he couldn't help himself, Wigfall found himself outside, in front of the east portico of the Capitol building, amidst the crowds awaiting the inauguration ceremony. The area closest to the portico bristled with armed soldiers, while mounted cavalry officers patrolled the crowd's perimeter looking for troublemakers. Louis found small solace in the fact that the crowds were sufficiently thick that no senator sitting on the portico's dais could spot him in this sea of humanity. How humiliating to be standing about in the drizzle, water running down the back of his shirt collar, being jostled by the hoi polloi. Among damned nigrahs too. What an abomination! The jubilant crowd was full of them.

Mr. Lincoln, accompanied by Chief Justice Taney, stepped to the front of the portico just as the sun broke through the clouds. The crowd roared. Wigfall thrust himself forward, heedless of the people he pushed aside. He would listen now and report later.

Lincoln's voice rang out over the crowd, deep and loud.

Apprehension seems to exist among the people of the Southern States that by the accession of a Republican Administration their property and their peace and personal security are to be endangered. There has never been any reasonable cause for such apprehension.

Wigfall snorted loud enough to cause the man next to him to turn his head and stare.

I have no purpose, directly or indirectly, to interfere with the institution of slavery in the States where it exists. I believe I have no lawful right to do so, and I have no inclination to do so.

He'd never heard such nefarious prevarication in his whole life. Everyone knew the wretched man intended to destroy slavery.

. . . no State upon its own mere motion can lawfully get out of the Union; that resolves and ordinances to that effect are legally void, and that acts of violence within any State or States against the authority of the United States are insurrectionary or revolutionary, according to circumstances . . . . I trust this will not be regarded as a menace, but only as the declared purpose of the Union that it will constitutionally defend and maintain itself.

Secession unlawful? Poppycock! Wigfall couldn't believe his ears. All these damned free nigrahs roaming the streets ought to be unlawful, not the secessionists. As if the weather agreed with him, it began to rain.

In your hands, my dissatisfied fellow-countrymen, and not in mine, is the momentous issue of civil war. The Government will not assail you. You can have no conflict without being yourselves the aggressors.

Wigfall could barely contain his astonishment. If the man wanted aggression, why he'd get all that he could handle and more.

I am loath to close. We are not enemies, but friends. We must not be enemies. Though passion may have strained it must not break our bonds of affection. The mystic chords of memory, stretching from every battlefield and patriot grave to every living heart and hearthstone all over this broad

344

land, will yet swell the chorus of the Union, when again touched, as surely they will be, by the better angels of our nature.

Lincoln looked out at the crowd for a few seconds and then sat down. The crowd roared again. Hats flew into the air. Wigfall thrust his fists into his pockets and made his way out of the crowd. They didn't seem to notice they'd made a devil into a president. Instead they stood about gabbling happily like a flock of turkeys that didn't have the sense to come in out of the rain.

On the walk back to his office Wigfall decided to cede the field of battle. There was no purpose in staying in a government run by that abomination he'd just heard speak. Yet, he'd found it blasted convenient to continue to sit in the Senate. He'd been recording everything the senators said and sending on important information to President Jeff Davis down in Montgomery. They were thinking of moving the Confederate government from Alabama to Virginia. It was a damned good idea. It would make communicating Washington intelligence to the Confederate government that much easier.

He sat down to write his last letter from the United States capitol.

President Davis:

I have just witnessed Lincoln's inaugural speech. No one can now doubt that he intends war. Our delay is to his advantage. Let us take Fort Sumter, before we have to fight the fleet and the Fort. Policy and Prudence recommend war at once. Let me urge the order to attack most seriously upon you.

L. T. Wigfall

He sanded the fresh ink, then folded his letter and sealed it. He walked down the hall, hailed a congressional page and directed the young man to mail the letter immediately. He returned to his office and surveyed the room, considering what he should take with him. While he'd been out someone had placed several wooden boxes inside his door, undoubtedly to encourage his departure.

As he packed his books and whiskey bottles Louis congratulated himself on the important work he'd accomplished for the Confederacy, both in Washington and Baltimore. After Lincoln's election, when they'd first begun to take secession seriously, Wigfall and several other senators checked the last census count. The free states contained almost four million white men, while the deep south had only half a million. To be sure, one southerner was worth at least four northern varmints. Nonetheless, the Confederacy's best chance of survival lie in striking at the northern states before Lincoln became president. The plots to kidnap Buchanan and kill Lincoln had been good ones, though somehow both failed. Louis suspected they had a mole in their operation. He grimaced as he considered that reality. If he ever found the man he'd make the traitor wish he'd never been born.

He stopped his packing and smiled grimly to himself. Leaving Fanny and Luckett in charge had been a stroke of pure genius. When he'd taken Fanny to the bank to set up the account he'd been careful to have her sign all the papers. The delightful dimwit hadn't even noticed. No trace of Louis T. Wigfall appeared on any of that lovely, ill-gotten money. And the clerk who'd set up the account in the first place was found-dead in an alley the next night.

What made the whole plan all the more delicious was how eager Fanny had been to go along with it. That crazy man who attacked Fanny in the theater, the one he himself stopped, why he'd been a gift from the heavens. Louis only wished he'd thought of the attack himself. That one incident was proof that God smiled on the Confederate cause.

A small part of Louis's conscious wriggled at leaving Fanny holding the bag, but if truth be told, no one would hold the young woman responsible for any crime. One interrogation would reveal she was no criminal mastermind. Fingers would undoubtedly next point at James Luckett, which bothered Louis even less. Men like Luckett existed, whether they knew it or not, to sacrifice themselves so that great men could accomplish the crucial tasks set before them.

Come what may, Fanny would surely forgive him. Unlike his wife, Fanny understood how lucky she was to be a member of his intimate circle. Why, it wouldn't be going too far to say the poor girl worshipped him.

A knock came at the door as Wigfall tucked his favorite whisky decanter in the box, bolstering it with dusty books he'd never read. Before he could respond the door opened.

"I say Sir. Who the hell do you think you are."

Before he could continue the intruder, an unassuming man of middle age and middle size, held up a hand. In it was a formal document. His exuberantly bushy mustache twitched as he spoke. "I am Major Webb, newly appointed superintendent of the Metropolitan Police. I am here to place you under arrest."

Wigfall froze. His mind raced. Suddenly he remembered the Senate secretary's warning. *Get out before the new president took office.* He'd been so angry he'd forgotten. Stalling for time he thrust his hands into his pockets and asked, "Under whose authority?"

"President Lincoln's sir." The man had a self-assured air about him that set off warning bells deep in Wigfall's skull.

"You're lying. The baboon hasn't been president for more than two hours."

The mustachioed man stepped forward and placed a single sheet of paper on Wigfall's desk. Wigfall picked it up and examined it.

"One of the president's first official acts was to sign a order placing myself in charge of the city's police force. I'm to round up all the treasonous scum and you're my first job. The president himself signed that warrant." Webb pointed at the piece of paper in Wigfall's hand. "It orders your arrest for high crimes and misdemeanors, including abuse of authority, bribery, embezzlement. Oh, and let's not forget plotting to kidnap one president and assassinate another, both of which are high treason."

At this announcement Webb stepped behind Wigfall's desk. Before he could react Webb grabbed Wigfall's right arm and twisted it up behind his back. The man shoved him so hard his head made a thick thumping sound as it hit the wooden desk top.

Stunned at this turn of events, Wigfall offered little resistance, even as his cheek began to throb. "Goddammit. I'm a senator. You can't do this to me," he sputtered. A spray of spittle decorated the desk top.

"But I can." Webb's tone revealed a man deeply satisfied with his work.

From the corner of his eye Wigfall saw the new police superintendent take a pair of wrist shackles off his belt. The two horse shoe shaped pieces of iron, held together with three iron links looked an awful lot like a pair he used on recalcitrant slaves. The senator saw them briefly before he felt them click around first one wrist and then the other.

Webb abruptly pulled his prisoner up off the desk and shoved him toward the door. Louis shuffled his feet, trying not to trip and fall. Webb stopped him at the door with a rough tug. "If it were up to me I'd march you out through the main hall so everyone could see you and know what you are."

Webb's voice was ripe with scorn. "But the President asked me to be discrete. So here's what we're going to do. You behave and I'll take you down the side stairs and out the back of the building to a closed carriage, which will transport you to the Capitol prison. No one will know you've been arrested. But I'm warning you, any trouble, any at all, and I turn you around and march you right through the Senate Chamber shouting the charges against you as I go. Got that?" Webb shoved Wigfall's bound wrists into the small of his back for emphasis.

Wigfall nodded dumbly. His mind whirled pell-mell. Clearly he'd been betrayed. *But how? Who knew of his involvement in plots against both presidents? And the money? Who knew all that and would tell? Most everyone knew one side of the plots or the other, but not both. Who dammit?*

As Webb pushed him down the hall and through the door leading to the back stairs Wigfall reviewed the men he'd worked with. None of the Baltimore men knew about the

349

Washington plot. He was sure of it. And that crew working out of Surratt's boarding house, they'd only known about the Washington plot. Only one man knew details about both plots. Vice President Breckinridge. *Impossible! There's no more committed slavery man in the nation than Breckinridge.*

Webb pushed him through one of the capitol's ground floor doors toward a waiting carriage. As he took his seat an epiphany struck Wigfall like a hammer blow. It was true that the only men who knew details from each plot were himself and Breckinridge, but Fanny was no man. *Hell, I told her everything.*

Webb took the seat opposite him in the carriage. He removed his Colt revolver from his inside jacket pocket and trained it on Wigfall.

Wigfall barely registered the man and his gun. He was busy running through his association with Fanny. Realizations flooded through him, almost too fast to process. He'd never checked her identity, never once questioned her motivation. And no wonder he couldn't remember her so-called attacker. There'd never been one. And he'd given her access to the money and account books. Egad. He'd been thoroughly and entirely hoodwinked. By a woman, no less. He'd been blinded by her youth and beauty, by her admiration for him and by his needs. She hadn't worshipped him at all. She'd used him. Wigfall shifted on his bench seat, far more uncomfortable with his realization than with his physical situation. *If word gets out, I'll never live it down. Never. I'll be a laughing stock for the rest of my life. Louis Trevant Wigfall, foolish philanderer, hoisted on my own petard by a mere slip of a girl.* Despair filled him. It was bad enough that he was on his way to jail. But to have been taken in by a woman. He was a damned fool.

The ex-Senator put his chin down on his chest and fought the urge to weep. He lost that battle just as the carriage stopped in front of the Old Capitol Prison.

Chapter 34

Confusion reigned for a time. Sounds and sensation entered the cave her mind had become, but no light. At one point, fourteen years or fourteen minutes after she went dark, someone pushed a spike into her shoulder. At least that's what if felt like. She felt herself lifted into someone's arms, the rough texture of wool against her cheek. Then there was jostling, a rolling bumping she recognized as a carriage. *Where they taking her for a ride? Now? Couldn't they see she was trying to sleep?*

She kept hearing voices. She recognized only one. Juba. And a jacket again, rough against her cheek. Why did he keep carrying her around? She tried to open her eyes to tell him to quit hurting her. Instead she drifted away.

Time went on like that for awhile. Sometimes she woke up, but only for brief periods of time. Once she awoke in the night to find Juba sleeping in a chair next to her bed, which was odd. *Did he lose his dancing job?* Another time she swam up into bright light, like sunshine. She must have said something, or moved, because Hazzard's face loomed into view.

"You're awake," he whispered at her. "We've been so worried."

Why is he whispering? Kate was about to ask him when his face disappeared and the great black and white wimple of a nun hove into view, her pale face wreathed in a gentle smile. *A nun? What in heaven's name?* Her silent joke made her smile.

The sister held a cup of water to Kate's lips. "Drink."

Kate did. She thought she'd never tasted anything quite so delicious. *Do nuns have special water?*

"Lie still now. I'll notify doctor and then maybe we'll try some broth."

Hazzard's face reappeared above her. "Juba's been here night and day. He'll be furious that you woke up when he wasn't here."

"Where?" she croaked at Hazzard, embarrassed to find her voice sounded as rusty as an old horseshoe.

"You're at St. Elizabeth's Hospital."

Kate's face must have told Hazzard all he needed to know about his response to this information.

"On, no, don't worry. You're not insane. You're recovering from a gun shot wound and blood poisoning."

The nurse reappeared and sent Hazzard away. She spooned tiny sips of broth into Kate's mouth. The broth tasted even better than the water had. *Do nuns have secret powers?* A strange man appeared after the broth, and fussed with her shoulder. Kate fell back into darkness.

The next time she surfaced Juba was in his bedside chair.

"Hey," she croaked again.

Juba bolted up from his chair. "Hey yourself baby girl." He stopped abruptly and wiped some errant moisture from the corner of his eyes. "Let me call the nurse."

Kate reached out and grabbed his hand before he could turn and go. A dagger of pain shot through her left shoulder, though she'd used her right arm.

"No. Explain." She didn't have the energy for a bunch of extra words. Her fingers tightened on his wrist.

"All right. That seems fair. What do you remember?"

Kate just shook her head, feeling panicked at the notion that she had no idea why she was in the hospital.

"Don't worry. The doctor said that might happen. You remember the train station? Getting Mr. Lincoln through Baltimore?"

She nodded.

"Well, that's good baby girl, real good."

She frowned at him.

"It is! Don't look at me that way. You don't know how badly you scared us all."

Kate let go of Juba's wrist and waved her hand, as if to say, 'get on with it.'

"There was a man at the station. Hazzard can tell you more about that when he gets here, but suffice it to say this fellow tried to shoot Mr. Lincoln. You saw him before any of us did and pushed the president out of harms way. And took the bullet yourself."

Kate nodded again. That seemed familiar.

"It was something awful, I'll tell you that. The shooter took off running, with this black cape billowing behind him like he were the devil himself. Hazzard went after him. Mr. Lamon grabbed Mr. Lincoln, who was trying to help you. Mr. Lamon wanted to get the president away from the station, but Mr. Lincoln made him hold the carriage—I scooped you up and we three took you to the hospital—the one across from City

355

Hall and right next to the jail. You kept bleeding. Mr. Lincoln gave me all his handkerchiefs; apparently his Missus makes him keep several on him at all times. Then we used my jacket. You just kept bleeding."

"Sorry." Kate smiled, trying to make Juba feel better.

"As you ought to be, you wretched thing. You bled all over my best jacket." They looked at each other for a few seconds, each acknowledging they were all the family the other had.

"The doctor said you were lucky."

Kate tried to push herself upright a little. Juba helped her resettle before continuing. "Lucky? Someone shot me. Ferrandini?"

Juba shook his head. No one knows for sure, but the Italian seems an unlikely suspect. I don't if you remember, but the would-be-assassin didn't have an accent. Hazzard thought he sounded English."

Kate frowned. "Ferrandini sounds distinctly Italian."

"Right," Juba said briskly. "It turns out Mr. Scully has had the Italian under watch since he disappeared. He couldn't get away to telegraph us, but Scully swears Ferrandini never left the rooming house he holed up in. Also, apparently the would-be assassin didn't know spit about guns. Hazzard saw the slug they pulled out of you— he called it a .22 short, which is a kind of pre-made cartridge made for revolvers. Hazzard says its only good for small game, squirrels and birds and such. Also, Hazzard said a .22 short is commonly used in the Smith and Wesson Model 1 revolver. He brought one in and showed it to me one afternoon when we were sitting here waiting for you to wake up."

Kate crooked her eyebrow at Juba.

"I'm telling this story, so settle down Missy." Juba pretended to glare at Kate. "As I was saying before I was so rudely interrupted. Hazzard says a Smith and Wesson Model 1 was exactly the wrong weapon to use in that sort of situation, which tells us something about the shooter. According to your own intelligence the National Volunteers up in Baltimore were fairly organized. I don't think they'd have set their man up with a single action revolver. It has to be cocked every time it's fired, which makes it inaccurate if time is of the essence. And, as I said, it's not powerful enough to kill a man, particularly if the shooter has imperfect aim."

"So not Ferrandini. Someone else. Someone we never saw, never suspected." What had it all been for anyway?

"Probably. But you stopped him. And you're alive. You seeing him like you did, he had time to get off only one well aimed shot. And he missed Mr. Lincoln because you pushed him out of the way. The assassin hit you by accident. You probably would have been fine in a couple of days, but your wound festered and you came down with the blood fever. "

"How long?" Kate began to get the idea that she'd been out of commission for quite awhile.

"Well, let me think darlin'." Juba scratched at his short hair and said, "Today's the fifth of March, the second day of Mr. Lincoln's presidency."

"I missed his inauguration?" Kate sighed.

"I missed it too. So did Hazzard. There's a copy of his speech in the *Evening Star*." Juba picked up a folded newspaper from a pile on the table next to Kate's bed. "I saved if for you. Thought I could read it to you when you woke up."

"Later. I want to finish *this* story first." "Well, where was I? You were shot on Saturday and we took you to the old hospital. Mr. Lincoln came to see you on Sunday. By then you were feverish and by Monday morning you were burning up. Mrs. Lincoln came that day. She didn't like that hospital one bit and to tell the truth, she was right. The place was dark, cold and none too clean. Mrs. Lincoln said you caught the infection from the damp miasmas in the hospital. She had her husband order you moved."

"Mrs. Lincoln?" The thought astounded Kate. *If I was her, I'd be furious with me.*

"Oh, yes. You saved her husband's life."

Kate stared at Juba.

"So, like I was saying, St. Elizabeth's is only eight years old and it's got modern gas lights and running water and an infirmary for when their patients are sick—which is where you are. The nursing sisters kept you alive. Dribbling water and broth into you with a teaspoon and bathing you with cold water till I thought they'd plum wear off your skin. Sister Mary Katherine, she's the one that takes care of you mostly, she regards something called 'Miss Nightingale's Treatise' mighty highly. Miss Nightingale commands cleanliness in all things to keep patients alive. At least that's what Sister Mary Katherine says."

Kate had to smile. Juba quoted the nursing sister like she'd come down from the mount with the ten hospital commandments.

As if on command, a nun in a voluminous black habit hove into view, like a frigate coming over the horizon. "Right now Sister Mary Katherine says her patient needs to rest." She gently pushed Juba away from the bed and pulled Kate's blanket up around her chin. "You sleep now," she commanded. She turned toward Juba. "You too. I don't want to see you back here until tomorrow morning. And if you haven't gotten a full night's sleep I'll know and send you straight away."

"Yes, Ma'am," Juba said, throwing a little salute and heel click at the nun before he turned and sauntered away.

"Yes, Sister," she called after him, but smiled as she did. Kate fell back into sleep knowing all was right in the world. Even nuns were not immune to Uncle Juba's charm.

The next time Kate woke up the sun was no longer shining. A small kerosene lamp on her bedside table gave off a soft yellow glow against the night. This time Hazzard was sleeping in the chair and her shoulder felt better, it's throb distant like thunder past the horizon.

She watched him for a time. He really was lovely to look at. She shouldn't hold that against him. Yes, Henry had been a beautiful specimen of manhood, but spoiled more by his father's wealth than his good looks. In contrast to Henry, Hazzard all but gave up his commission to protect Mr. Lincoln, even when few people thought he needed protecting. Unlike Henry, Hazzard tried to do the right thing and more often than not succeeded. Kate found she could remember the events on the platform and she remembered most clearly Hazzard's helpless expression before he'd run after the black clad shooter. He wanted to stay with Kate, but his sense of duty wouldn't let him. He left her in good hands and ran into danger, not away from it.

Kate pushed herself up into a semi-reclining position, scrunching the pillows behind her as she did. As she suspected, her squirming woke Hazzard.

Like Mr. Lincoln, he went from asleep to entirely awake in an instant. "*What* are you doing?" He stood and fussed at her pillows. "You are an entirely infuriating woman, you know that?"

"I am?" He was leaning over her, perilously close.

"Yes, you are." And he kissed her. Just a little bit, but enough for it to be quite satisfying.

After a time she pushed him back, towards his chair. "Juba's told me his story. I suspect you have one to tell me as well. Did you catch him?"

Hazzard caught himself. He'd been about to sit down again, but her question brought him up to attention.

"No. I did not. To my everlasting shame, he got away. And now he's out there. Somewhere."

He looked as if the idea was eating away at him. She didn't like the idea much either.

Hazzard paced the room. "He had a horse outside. He got to it before I got to him."

Kate thought about that morning at the depot. "He had something on his head, didn't he? Like a black bag with eye holes cut in it?"

"He did. But he tore it off his head after his shot went awry, I think so he could see where he was running. I found it on the station floor when I came back for you. They'd already put you in the carriage and were driving away. There was this big puddle of blood where you'd been. I thought you were dead." He stood still, his arms hanging at his side, his shoulders slumped at the memory.

Kate patted her bed. "Until the good sister comes in and throws you out of the hospital for indecent behavior, come sit with me."

360

He remembered himself, straightened up and smiled his pirate smile at her, all dark mustaches and shining white teeth. *All he needs is a gold earring and a cutlass between his teeth.* When he was perched next to her on the bed's edge she asked, "Do I remember him yelling something before he fired?"

"Yes, a line from Shakespeare's *Julius Cesar*. 'Sic Semper Tyranus.' It means,"

Kate interrupted him. "Thus always to tyrants." She smiled. "Miss Haines School for Girls in Grammercy Park," she said by way of explanation.

"It's an odd line to yell. I mean, I understand the reference, but most men wouldn't yell a line of Latin from Shakespeare, even if Julius Cesar is one of the popular plays."

"I see your point," Kate mused. "It's like the cape and the hood—overly dramatic. Which sounds exactly like Ferrandini."

Hazzard leapt to his feet. "Exactly. Except the gun man didn't sound like Ferrandini. And Juba told you about Mr. Scully and explained the gun, didn't he?"

Kate nodded. "Ferrandini was in Baltimore. And the gun was the exact wrong weapon."

"Like you I think Ferrandini is a fool, but he's a well connected fool."

"Right," Kate affirmed. She liked that he'd gone right into debrief mode with her instead of treating her like a delicate invalid.

"It stands to reason then that they'd have known enough about firearms to know that the pistol and ammunition were absolutely wrong for the job. Didn't you say they had Army officers drilling their volunteers?"

Kate nodded. "Timothy Webster saw it in Perryville."

"Absolutely. So, if there were military men in the operation, why arm their assassin with a Model 1 Smith and Wesson, loaded with short cartridges?" While he talked Hazzard leaned toward her a little.

"I don't think they would have." Kate took a deep breath in and pushed it out in relief. "So our assassin wasn't one of the Baltimore plotters. We didn't miss anything?"

Hazzard nodded in assent. "No, we didn't. Apparently there was another investigation up in New York."

Kate bit her lip, deep in thought. "I think Mr. Lincoln said something about that to me. I'm not sure. I'm a little hazy."

"You remember it right. Our guy could be from anywhere. I think he mistrusted the newspapers that said the Special would arrive that afternoon, which was why he yelled that first thing . . ."

"Perfidy," Kate supplied.

"Yes, that. I think he yelled that because he really was surprised we arrived so early. He was prepared for us to be early, but wasn't sure when we would arrive. So he essentially yells 'treachery' at us, because he expected us to be on a later train. I'd bet my commission he planned to spend the day watching the trains and that he arrived just before we did, because we were on the first train of the day."

Kate stared at Hazzard. "So in focusing on Baltimore we missed an entirely separate plot."

"Maybe, but that way lies madness. There are undoubtedly hundreds of plots to kill Mr. Lincoln afoot right now. The Pinkertons identified the most well funded and dangerous plot. Mr. Pinkerton says they're fit to be tied in Baltimore."

Kate grinned at Hazzard. "I bet Allan's laughing up his sleeves at them." She thought of something and stopped smiling. "What about the senator?"

Hazzard rocked back on his heels and laughed. "I'm sorry to tell you your swain has quit the field of battle. The papers say the Senate threw him out on inauguration day. I checked and he's not in his rooms. It's a good bet he's gone to Montgomery, where the rebel government sits."

Kate laughed. "So Fanny can die a dignified death. I'm glad. I was quite tired of her."

"Truth be told, I might be a wee bit jealous of the Wigfall, what with the way Fanny spent so much time with him." Hazzard gave Kate a teasing look, which she rewarded with a swat to his arm.

Hazzard wasn't done with Wigfall. "He made a speech in the Senate the day before they tossed him out, full of the usual puffery and slave rights nonsense." He rifled through the pile of folded newspapers on Kate's side table. "Where it is? Ah, here. 'I wish to live in no country where the man who blacks my boots and curries my horse is my equal.'"

Kate snorted. "He'd have to be twice the man he is right now to aspire to a boot black's level. And to think I felt sorry for him."

Hazzard eyed Kate. "You know, my Daddy used to say that every man is the hero of his own story. Wigfall's like that. The whole lot of them are. Because they think they're right. Which is honorable in its own way."

"Honor," Kate said dismissively. "Honor makes me tired. Men forget all the really important things in life—"

"Do they?" Hazzard asked with a speculative gleam in his eye.

Kate opened her eyes as wide as they would go and nodded gravely.

Sister Mary Katherine swept into Kate's room a few minutes later and pretended to be scandalized to find kissing taking place. She was not so scandalized as to prevent the dashing Captain from claiming an additional good night kiss before she shooed him out of the room.

Two days later the good sisters decreed that Kate was well enough to sit outside in the weak spring sunshine for an hour or two. St. Elizabeth's Asylum had beautiful grounds, populated in the afternoons by the least disturbed patients. Kate found most of them not only harmless, but charming conversationalists. She even made friends, of a sort, with an older woman who said she was the Queen of England. After months of pretending to be someone other than who she really was, Kate didn't think she had much room to judge an imaginary queen.

On her third afternoon outside Sister Mary Katherine sailed up alongside Kate's bench. "You've got a visitor, dear," the sister said, sounding more than a little flustered. Sister Mary Katherine was not the kind of woman who flustered. Kate turned to see who ruffled the generally commanding nun.

There stood Mr. Lincoln, looking seven feet tall in his new top hat. He smiled sheepishly at her and doffed his hat. The sister tipped Kate a wink and sailed away, dried leaves whirling in her habit's wake.

"Mr. Lincoln, I mean, Mr. President, what are you doing here?" Sister Mary Katherine wasn't the only flustered lady on the hospital grounds this afternoon. "I mean, Sir, is it safe for you here?"

Mr. Lincoln stepped towards Kate's bench. "May I?" he asked, sweeping his hand toward the empty half of the seat.

Kate swallowed and nodded. "Of course Mr. President, I'd be honored."

"Now, Miss Warne," he said to Kate, "We'll have none of that between us. It is I who am honored. I am sensible to the fact that you saved my life and however disappointing your act may have been to a great many citizens, I thank you. So too does my wife, who near bursts into tears every time your name is mentioned."

Kate didn't know what to say to that so she wisely said nothing.

Mr. Lincoln helped her out. "Of course, everyone says my wife is just a touch high strung, so you pay her no mind."

"She's not high strung Mr. Lincoln," Kate said fiercely. She looked him in the eye. "She's passionate. And she's afraid. She's found herself in a situation where the people she loves most, her husband and her sons, are in danger and there's nothing she can do about it. It would upset any feeling person and Mrs. Lincoln is a lady who feels things deeply."

Mr. Lincoln turned and smiled gently at Kate. "You've nailed her in one go. So few people understand Mother. I know they wonder why I saddled myself with her. They don't understand that I never have to wonder if Mrs. Lincoln loves me. That's a quality I much admire in her. I'm an odd duck and I know it. People admire me or hate me, but love me?"

Kate patted Mr. Lincoln's black clad leg as if he were a forlorn child. "Oh, I think you underestimate yourself Mr. President. If you'll forgive me for saying so, I think a good many people love you and a good many people would die for you, which is something beyond love, wouldn't you say?"

The president stared off into the distance, as if discomfited by the question.

Kate patted his leg one more time. "Like me. And Captain Hazzard. And Colonel Sumner, and Mr. Lamont and Mr. Lane and Mr. Pinkerton and probably a dozen more whose names I don't know."

"Ah, there you have it. You bring me to the reason for my visit." Mr. Lincoln stood up and faced Kate on her bench. "I spoke to Mr. Pinkerton and Mr. Lane and they've agreed with my plan. They've assured me you will agree as well, but I wanted to ask you in person."

He paused and examined his exceedingly large boots. "The rebels are trapped in a corner and see no way out but war. The nation is in need of a spy network and one loyal to the Union. I want the Pinkertons to begin the job. I want you, Miss Warne and I can free up some War Department money to make it happen."

Kate gazed up at the man before her. His offer meant she wouldn't be going home to Chicago anytime soon. The job wasn't done. It had only begun. Maybe it was time she committed herself to something long term. "Mr. President. Whatever the country needs." What she really meant to say was "What ever you need," but he'd prefer it if she pledged herself to the nation. Nation's were too abstract for Kate. People weren't. She'd do it for Juba and Hattie, for Hazzard and Mr. Rice and for the man standing before her. Kate realized she'd do it again and every time she was called upon— she'd throw herself in front of a bullet meant for this man.

And she was right about one thing. She wouldn't be alone. The idea scared her a good deal less than it used to.

Chapter 35

March 12, 186
Washington City

The day Sister Mary Katherine decreed as Kate's last in the St. Elizabeth's infirmary dawned clear and sunny. Washington reveled in a glorious, early spring, though the *Evening Star* said a snow storm was on the way.

Juba brought Kate's favorite navy blue skirt and Garibaldi shirt to wear. Her poor, abused grey dress had not survived the shooting. The red Garibaldi covered up the mass of scar tissue that marred the left side of her chest, up toward her shoulder. She thought mournfully of her cream and gold dress. She wouldn't be wearing it ever again, or anything cut like it. So much for her femme fatale personae.

Which was fine, Kate thought. She'd never had to sustain a performance as for long as she had Fanny. It was an odd thing. After four years as a female detective, she'd thought she was used to the job and the lies she had to tell to break a case. But the last few months had been different from anything she'd ever done. Lying about the hospital recovering had come as an almost welcome relief. Two weeks with no responsibility, no life or death circumstances. Still, Kate surprised herself with her eagerness to leave the hospital and get back to her life, no matter how complicated.

"Ready to go?" Juba walked over, picked up Kate's carpet bag and offered her his elbow, as he'd done so many times before. It was all Kate could do to not to burst into tears. Sister Mary Katherine stood by the front door, waiting to say goodbye.

"I'll be back," Kate said to her.

"I most fervently hope not," the nun replied.

Kate laughed. "To visit, I mean. You and the Queen."

Excelsior waited outside, harnessed to the little two-wheeled shay, his white head turned toward the hospital front steps. He whinnied vigorously as Kate came out the door. She scrambled down the steps and threw her arms around her horse's neck.

Like he'd done four years before in Chicago, Juba stepped back and gave the two some time.

When Kate had kissed Excelsior's nose for the seventeenth or seventieth time, Juba interrupted. "Hows about we get going? You're horse needs his dinner."

"Sounds fair to me." It suddenly occurred to Kate that she had no place to go. "I can't go back to the Surratt's, can I?"

"No, the Surratt house is boarded up and locked tight. Mrs. Surratt and her boys decamped weeks ago. We think they're at their farm in Virginia, but we're none too sure."

Kate thought about that for a second. "Seems like someone ought to get a bead on that, doesn't it?" Her brain perked up a little bit.

Juba through back his head and laughed. "Mr. Pinkerton's put Timothy on the job, so you no never mind."

"Well, with the southerners gone the Willard would be safe. Oh, but what about Miss Stephens?"

Juba looked reproachfully at Kate. "You were supposed to read all those newspapers I left for you."

"Oh Juba, I needed a break. Just tell me what I missed."

"Well, ole Mr. Alexander Stephens is the Vice President of the Confederate States of America. Don't know what they're thinking, him being so sickly and all— they're calling him 'The Little Pale Star from Georgia.' Don't that just beat the band?"

"So yes to the Willard?" Kate asked hopefully.

"Nope." Juba looked fit to explode with self-gratification. "You just wait. Watch your horse and enjoy the day."

St. Elizabeth's Hospital lie on the far side of the Anacostia River from Washington City proper, almost directly across from the U. S. Navy Yard. They traveled over the small toll bridge to East Eleventh, up to Pennsylvania Avenue, where they turned left, following a gaily painted horse drawn omnibus up the wide avenue. Nine or ten blocks later, Kate lost count, they skirted the Capitol grounds and turned up New Jersey Avenue.

"The Kirkwood Hotel?" Kate guessed, thinking Juba was taking her back where she'd begun her Washington sojourn.

"Nope."

"Am I going to stay with you at Columbus's feed store?"

"Nope." Each time he said it Juba looked more pleased with himself.

Kate gave up guessing.

They turned left, down F Street and stopped in the middle of the third block. Juba looked over at the four story brick house on his right.

Exasperated, Kate said, "This is the home of the F Street Mess. Allan can't possibly want me to start another job right now, could he? I want a cup of tea first."

"You're forgetting something baby girl— the southerners all done left town. And in a hurry too. Senators Hunter and Mason were both expelled from the senate the day of inauguration, along with your Wigfall fellow. Hunter's found a new job as the Confederate Secretary of State and Mason's their ambassador to England and France, or some such thing. And that nasty old Atchison has scarpered back to Missouri, where they say he's running the Border Ruffians as his own private army."

"Reeeaaally," Kate drawled, looking at the house that had once been the headquarters for a contingent of radical slavery men.

Juba could contain himself no longer. He hopped out of the gig and swept his arms toward the house. "Would you like to come in?"

Kate looked at the house. Like so many Washington houses, it was a row house, sharing common walls with its neighbors. It had a dignified federal style front door, but otherwise looked a lot like their Chicago house, with the half submerged basement, elevated first floor and a fourth floor under a steep roof. "What about Excelsior?" she asked, thinking about the small stable and back yard at the Chicago house.

"No stable, not yet, but there's a back yard and room to build. Columbus knows some fellows who can do it for a fair wage." He handed her a small key. "I had the door locks replaced, just in case some of those southern rascals try to come back. There's a nice room for you on the second floor and I've taken the basement again."

Kate felt a little over whelmed. "What about the Chicago house?"

"Well, there's a tale, for sure, but suffice it to say that Madame Clofullia bought out my half of the house. She and Mrs. Barrow are going to have a boarding house for retired circus folk and pay you rent. I used my money to buy this house." He looked anxiously at Kate, not sure how his surprise was going. "I got it for almost nothing. People think the new Confederacy will attack soon, what with Washington surrounded by Maryland and Virginia. Once the nation's capitol is under secessionist control the Union will crumble—at least that's the theory. People figure when that happens houses in this town won't be worth spit. I think differently."

"So it's a bit of a gamble, isn't it?" Kate heard herself. "I know, I know . . . you're going to say it's a gamble worth taking and you're right."

"Come see the inside. I think you're going to like it." They left Excelsior standing in the street and walked up the front stairs. Juba opened the glossy black door and they stepped into a front parlor with scruffy carpet. "We'll have to spruce this room up, but it'll do for now," he said and gently pushed Kate toward a door at the back of the room. "There's something I want you to see in the kitchen."

Kate pushed through the tall swinging door.

A crowd of people yelled "Surprise!"

She stopped, mid-doorway.

Juba put his hands on her shoulders and steered her into the kitchen. Timothy was there, his pale blue eyes twinkling merrily, alongside his wife Charlotte, who was wearing a flour covered apron. Hattie grinned from her perch atop a kitchen counter and waved a hand with a cookie in it. Hazzard hastily stood up from his seat at the table, upsetting the small mountain of cookies before him. He waved half a cookie at Kate. Allan sat at the table with Hazzard.

Her boss took one look at Kate's face and through back his head in merriment, sprinkling ash from his cigar about the room as he did. "The gang's all here," he said through his laughter. "Juba, you fair to killed her with shock."

Kate broke her pose and moved around the room, hugging and crying as she went. Even with visitors, the hospital had been a lonely place.

Juba jumped up on a wooden kitchen chair and cleared his throat. "Here's the plan. Allan's going back to Chicago for the time being, but he'll be back and forth as need be. Same with Hazzard, except he's going back to the Army. Charlotte is going to run this here house and we're all going to live here: you, me, the Websters and Hattie over there. You and Hattie can have the second floor and the Websters the third. We'll be the East Coast Division of the Pinkerton Detectives Bureau and headquarters for Lincoln's new secret service." Juba threw a little heel, toe shuffle onto the chair and asked, "How's that sound?"

Kate looked around the kitchen at these people who had become her family. Was she changing her life yet again? And why not?

She smiled. "It sounds like home."

The End

The Real and Not So Real Stuff

I have attempted, insofar as it was convenient to the story, to be historically accurate, but this is a novel and novels are fiction. Fiction requires a flexible approach to historical reality (not unlike many "real" history books).

A note on words. Some of my characters are pro-slavery southerners. They would have used words to describe persons of color that are now considered racially offensive, for good reason. It's their language, not mine.

The reality of the Baltimore Plot is so freakishly complicated that any attempt on my part to reproduce it in full would have resulted in a manuscript as unwieldy and difficult to read as *War and Peace*. Thus, this story leaves a lot of details out.

Alan Pinkerton really did hire Kate Warne as the first female Pinkerton operative. He really was an anti-slavery man and he really did meet John Brown. William Henry Lane, or Juba Brush, invented tap-dance and was considered the greatest dancer in the country in the late 1840s. He died in 1850 or 52, but I resurrected him for my own purposes. The word "tap" was not used as a category of dance until 1903.

Senator Wigfall is real, as is his complicity in the plot to kidnap Buchanan. The stories of his duels are real, though he was not arrested on inaugurationdayl, nor was he ever jailed. Obviously Buchanan, Breckinridge and Lincoln are real though I invented their conversations. Colonel Sumner, Ward Hill Lamont and the other guys were with Lincoln before his inauguration. Captain George Washington Hazzard did take a leave from the army to protect Lincoln. He was on the Lincoln Special and he was an artillery specialist. I don't know what he looked like, but it seemed to me that a guy named 'Hazzard' would be smoking hot.

Dan Rice was a famous nineteenth century circus man. Excelsior was quite famous in his day. Phineas T. Barnum did own a huge museum in New York that was crowded with oddities. Mr. Lincoln did visit it. The Feejee Mermaid was one of Barnum's most famous hoaxes. The Mabie Brothers Circus was real, as was Blondin and Madame Clofullia (and her son).

Dan Rice's *Great Show* played Baltimore's Front Street Theater in April 1860, not 1861, while Blondin appeared a few months earlier with the *Great American Consolidated Circus*. The *Floating Palace* existed, but it was built in 1852, a few years after I suggested.

Timothy Webster, Hattie Lawson Harry Davies, John Scully and George Bangs were all Pinkertons, though I changed Mr. Bang's name to Bangly to avoid confusion with a Mary Poppins character. I also entirely invented Hattie's past because she's even more of a mystery than Kate Warne. Timothy's wife really was Charlotte and Alan's wife was really Joan.

The threatening letters to Lincoln are real. The excerpts from the letters and speeches are accurate. The National Theater in Washington DC burned down in 1857. I moved it's rebuilding forward one year.

Alexander Stephens was a sickly congressman from Georgia who became the Vice President of the Confederate States of America, but he was not in office in 1860, having been replaced by John Jones in 1859. Nor did he have a loquacious sister who went with him to Washington.

Columbus Scribner and his feed store are real, as is the John Howard Livery Stable. The Surratts did keep horses at the Howard stable. Isaac and Mary Surratt are real, as is the Surratt boarding house in Washington DC, though Mary probably wasn't at the house in 1860, but at the family farm and inn outside of Washington.

Laura Keene did own a theater in New York, did appear in *The Seven Sisters*, which really was a naughty musical extravaganza. Mr. Lincoln was watching Keene on stage the night he was killed. Joseph Jefferson was one of the era's most famous actors and comedians. He did not have a niece named Fanny.

Both the Baltimore & Ohio and the Baltimore, Wilmington and Philadelphia Railroads existed. The B& O was pro-southern. Railroad magnate Samuel Felton funded the Pinkerton's investigation in Baltimore. Luckett was one of the Baltimore Conspirators, as were Hillard and Ferrandini. Ferrandini and Hillard did testify before the Select Committee of Five, but they did not do so until on Feb. 5 and 6 respectively. Allan Pinkerton really did set up offices as a fake stockbroker in Baltimore and befriend Mr. Luckett. Kate is absent from the historical record at this time, but she was employed by the Pinkertons so she might have been in Baltimore. And she might not have been.

Though the characters in this book refer to Ferrandini as Italian, he was actually Corsican. I didn't think most Antebellum Americans would make the distinction. He was a barber at the Barnum in Baltimore and he probably did plot to kill Mr. Lincoln.

Anna Travis ran a well-respected house of ill repute in Baltimore. According to sources it looked much as I've described, though my father pointed out that my description bears a striking resemblance to the Victorian mansion in Helena Montana that was for a long time the Lamphier family home. That resemblance is entirely accidental. Sorry Mom and Dad.

Governor Hicks did write a letter soliciting Lincoln's assassination, though he wrote it in November, days after Lincoln's election. I moved up the Maryland secession convention three days, so it would take place before Kate traveled to New York. The Barnum Hotel and Astor house were both upscale hotels.

The episode with the lost bag, with the only copy of the inaugural address inside it, really did happen. The plans to get Lincoln from Harrisburg to Washington City, both the public plan and the secret plan, are fairly accurately described here. Kate Warne did meet the Lincoln party in New York and attempt to explain to them how much danger the president was in. In reality, Kate took Lincoln as far as Baltimore, but no further, leaving the train unharmed. Alan Pinkerton was on the train for it's last leg, but Hazzard was not. Lamon and Pinkerton really did not like each other. At all.

Wigfall's letter to Jeff Davis was written on April 10. I modified it and changed the date to suit my purposes, fully aware that the senator is probably rolling in his grave at my insolence.

Lincoln did appoint William B. Webb the first superintendent of the District's Metropolitan Police, but not until after Congress authorized the centralized police force in August, 1861. As Wigfall was never arrested, Webb never arrested him.

St. Elizabeth's exists today, though it is no longer an asylum for the insane. The F Street Mess, so called because pro-southern senators lived together in a house on F Street, did include Atchison, Hunter and Mason.

As to the rest, maybe it's real, maybe it's not.

Questions for Book Clubs

1. Describe the Kate and Juba's personality traits, motivation and inner qualities. How has their pasts shaped their lives? Do they remind you of people you know?

2. Discuss the novel's structure and plot. *The Lincoln Special* is based on real events and we all know Lincoln wasn't killed on his way to Washington. Did that make the plot predictable?

3. Why does the author shift Points of View (the person in a chapter or section who's view point the novel uses). What difference do these shifts make in story structure?

4. One of the main themes of the novel is the constraints women and people of color operated under in mid-nineteenth century America. How do Kate and other female characters resist nineteenth century ideas about womanhood? How does she conform? What about other characters? And Juba?

5. Was there any passage or section that struck as particularly insightful? One that encapsulated a character or nailed down *The Lincoln Special's* themes?

6. Was the ending satisfying? If not, how would you have changed it?

7. If you could ask the author a question, what would it be? (Note: If you like you can email Peg and she'll try to answer your question: pegalamphier@gmail.com).

Drum Roll Please . . .

Thanks for reading this book. You are so fabulous!

I'd greatly appreciate it if you left a review on Amazon or Good Reads. I know you're busy so thank you in advance. You can also follow me at either of those sites or at my Facebook author page. You can sign up for my newsletter by going to www.peglamphier.com. You can also email me at pegalamphier@gmail.com.

If you liked reading about Kate, I've got 3 more novels in various stages of readiness and am currently writing the 5th. The second book will be out August, 2017 (There's a blurb and cover photo at the end of this book!).

I work hard to make my books as error free as possible. If you find a typo I would appreciate it if you emailed me so I could fix it.

Writers write alone but they do not work alone. Special thanks to Stephanie McKinney. She proposed we quit talking about novel writing and actually do it during our summer break, using each other as support. It worked for both of us.

Thanks to my beta readers Anna Sorum, Marlene Burke, Adrienne Harwell and my dad Paul Lamphier. If you liked the chapter where Wigfall gets arrested thank Dad. He also restored Wigfall's penis when I shot it off. Men everywhere thank you Dad.

Rosanne Welch content edited this manuscript and had some good ideas for a vexing problem I didn't know how to fix. She's a great editor and friend. Her congenial husband Douglas Welch helped me with my web page and some other technical stuff.

Thanks to all the strong women in my life who model Kate-like strength. Biggest thanks go to my mom, Jackie Lamphier. She's my model for self-reinvention. And to all my lady friends, Anna, Marvelle, Rosanne, Stephanie and Andy (just seeing if you were paying attention) for the comic relief. And to Emma Burke, the best daughter a woman could ever have. She listened to about 3000 story ideas and always had good feed back.

Thanks to the tenured and administrative faculty at Cal Poly Pomona. Their commitment to mediocrity and a fundamentally unfair two-tiered professorial system pushed me to reinvent myself.

Daniel Aley designed the front and back cover for this book (and the next one too) and I think he's swell. Marvelle Thompson took my author photo and in the process showed me the coolest tree ever.

Thanks to the good people at Baby Elephant Thai Restaurant in Walnut who provided a welcoming oasis in the midst of a long work day.

Lastly, thanks Leo Burke. He believed in me, but let's be honest, moral support isn't nearly as important as a guy who'll fold the laundry and mop up dog pee when you're trying to finish a chapter. Thanks Dude.

Selected Bibliography

Cuthbert, Norma B. *Lincoln and the Baltimore Plot, 1861, From Pinkerton Records and Related Records.* 1949. Cuthburt worked as a librarian at the Huntington Library in the 1940s and gathered together all the Pinkerton records pertaining to the Baltimore Plot.

Kline, Michael. *The Baltimore Plot: The First Conspiracy to Assassinate Abraham Lincoln.* 2008. This guy is a lawyer and he built an air-tight case for the many permutations of the assassination plot.

Knowles, Mark. *Tap Roots: The Early History of Tap Dancing.* 2002. For William Henry Lane, also known as Master Juba, and the African roots of 'dancing juba.'

Renoff, Gregory J. *The Big Tent: The Traveling Circus in Georgia, 1820-1930.* 2012. Renoff explores a wealth of material on such matters as tent sizes and circus show structure and other delightful circus details. It was an immense help in understanding Kate.

Coming in August, 2017
The Great Show
Book 2
Kate Warne, Civil War Spy Series

Before Kate can settle into her new life as a spy for Mr. Lincoln the world turns upside down. The Confederates fire on Fort Sumter to begin the Civil War and Uncle Juba disappears from Washington. Kate doesn't know the worst of it. Though he's a free man, Juba's been kidnapped and sold into slavery to fund a network of pro-Confederate spies. He faces a terrifying ordeal, sold to slave traders, transported south by ship, whipped for trying to escape and sold again in New Orleans.

Kate and the Pinkertons must figure out where Juba is and mount a rescue into the heart of enemy territory. Kate gathers her Pinkerton allies, and enlists Dan Rice to take his circus, *The Great Show*, on a southern tour, hiding their rescue mission behind elephants an clowns. Mr. Lincoln sends Captain Hazzard to help, giving him time to teach Kate a thing or two about fighting and love.

When they arrive in New Orleans they discover that rescuing Juba isn't enough. Juba's friend Columbus was sold to an up-river plantation, a little girl has to be saved from child prostitution and her mother has fallen into the clutches of the Countess, a masochistic brothel owner. The Countess may be a psychopathic serial murder, but she's a white woman in a state that says she has a right to do whatever she wants with her slaves. Deep in the heart of the Confederacy Kate and her people face death or re-enslavement if they fail. Kate must face the worst sort of evil to free her friends. And live with the consequences when she does.

About the Author

Peg A. Lamphier lives in the mountains of Southern California with five dogs, eight tortoises, a huge cat, two canaries, one husband, one daughter and a collection of vintage ukuleles. When she's not writing fiction or otherwise fooling around she's a professor at California State Polytechnic, Pomona and Mount San Antonio Community College. For more information see www.peglamphier.com.

Peg A. Lamphier

Made in the USA
Las Vegas, NV
10 December 2020

12671961R00236